Guilty as charged . . .

He came into her jail cell and stopped near enough for her to divine the dark gold hue of his hair, the sun-burnished strands that brushed his shoulders, the tawny stubble shading his jaw. But his eyes continued their maddening shift between gray and green. He was taller than she'd realized, lean and lanky without an ounce of wasted fat on his broad-shouldered frame.

She held her breath as he reached out his hand. But instead of throttling her as she'd feared, he caressed a fallen curl from her cheek. His calloused thumb lingered against her smooth skin.

"Holler," he said.

"Pardon?" she whispered, believing she'd misunderstood him.

"The sheriff promised to come running if you hollered. I think it might be a good idea."

She drew in a shaky breath. "I may have swooned beneath the weight of extreme duress, sir, but surely you haven't mistaken me for the hysterical sort of female who screams at the slightest provocation."

His lashes swept down to mask his eyes as he lowered his lips toward hers.

Esmerelda screamed.

Also by Teresa Medeiros

NOBODY'S DARLING

TERESA MEDEIROS

BANTAM

New York Toronto London
Sydney Auckland

Nobody's Darling
A Bantam Book / April 1998

All rights reserved.

ISBN 0-553-57501-5

Published simultaneously in the United States and Canada

Bantam Books are published by Bantam Books, a division of Bantam
Doubleday Dell Publishing Group, Inc. Its trademark, consisting of the
words "Bantam Books" and the portrayal of a rooster, is Registered in
U.S. Patent and Trademark Office and in other countries. Marca Reg-
istrada. Bantam Books, 1540 Broadway, New York, New York 10036.

PRINTED IN THE UNITED STATES OF AMERICA

OPM 10 9 8 7 6 5 4 3 2 1

For my grandfathers, John Hatcher and Clarence Dame, who always appreciated a good western yarn. Wish you were still around to read this one.

For Zerelda James and all the other outlaw mothers who loved their boys.

And for Michael, whom I will always adore for making me watch *McLintock!* seven thousand times.

NOBODY'S DARLING

PROLOGUE

London, 1878

The duke of Wyndham's outraged bellow echoed through the cavernous halls of Wyndham Manor, throwing his household into utter chaos. Two underfootmen came rushing through opposite doors in a blind panic, colliding with a painful thud. In the basement kitchen, a startled cook threw a tray straight up in the air, raining fresh biscuits down upon her head. One of the parlor maids dusted a priceless Ming vase right off of its terra-cotta pedestal while old Brigit, who had served the lords of Wyndham longer than anyone still alive could remember, crossed herself as if she'd just heard the wail of a banshee arising from an open grave.

In truth, none of them had ever heard their master's voice raised above a scathing murmur. Which only made its current volume more alarming.

The duke's servants came scurrying from all corners of

the massive estate. Half running, half stumbling, they skidded to a halt in the marble-tiled foyer outside the smoking room's towering teak doors and congregated in a nervous huddle, transfixed by the unintelligible howls coming from inside the room.

Not a single one of them dared to intrude upon His Grace's private domain until his normally imperturbable sister, Anne, came flying down the curving staircase, her trembling hands struggling to fasten a brocaded wrapper at the waist. Having never seen her hair in anything but a tidy chignon, most of the servants gaped to realize the iron-gray mass tumbled nearly to her rump.

"Dear God, Potter," she gasped, yanking a knot in the wrapper's tasseled sash. "What happened?"

The butler sniffed, as if Lady Anne's frantic question somehow implied that he was to blame for this debacle. "I can't possibly say, my lady. I brought the duke his buttered scones and his *Morning Post*, which I had just finished ironing because he does so love the pages to be nice and crisp. I folded his napkin and salted his porridge for him, then I—"

"I'm well aware of my brother's daily habits," Anne snapped. "He hasn't varied them since Victoria came to the throne."

"Oh, and there was a letter," Potter added, wrinkling his patrician nose with visible distaste. "From America."

Anne paled. An inexplicable silence fell within the room, somehow louder and more disturbing than the cacophony that had preceded it. Dragging her apprehensive gaze away from Potter's, Anne closed her icy hands around the crystal knobs and threw open both doors at once.

The servants cowered behind her, plainly expecting to find their master sprawled facedown on the Persian rug, felled by a fatal bout of apoplexy.

Anne peered through a jungle of potted palm fronds, thinking rather uncharitably that if Reginald were dead, her first act as mistress of the house would be to turn this Turkish-decorated monstrosity with its leering Oriental masks and grim leather furniture into a nice sunny sewing room. Stale pipe smoke assailed her nostrils, making her eyes water. Potter rushed over to the window and threw open the velvet drapes.

Morning sunlight flooded the funereal gloom. Anne and the servants recoiled as one at the shocking sight that greeted them.

Contrary to their fears, their master did not lie prone on the carpet, a final sigh seeping from his lungs. Instead, the duke of Wyndham, whose dignity had been unimpeachable for nearly three-quarters of a century, appeared to be having a full-blown slipper-stomping, cane-banging tantrum. This was no minor bout of pique or flare of annoyance that might result in a withering rebuke or a stinging lash of his acidic tongue, but a genuine temper fit. His square face ruddy with rage, he sputtered and coughed like an overgrown toddler, literally choking on his fury.

Anne clapped a hand over her mouth to smother a horrified laugh. She'd never seen her brother in such a snit. As a child he had only to hint at his vaguest wish to have his every desire granted. Their parents had found it far easier to give extravagant gifts than affection. Except to Anne, to whom they'd given neither.

Finding himself the object of fascination for a gaping audience did little to improve the duke's disposition. He leaned forward in his wheelchair and brandished his cane, his face darkening to a striking shade of purple.

Alarm banished Anne's amusement. Guilt and panic assailed her as she realized her brother might actually work himself into a stroke.

Scandalized by her lapse of Christian compassion, she swung toward the servants. "Stop gawking like a flock of dim-witted sheep and return to your posts immediately. If any one of you breathes a word about what you've seen here this day, you'll be dismissed without so much as a farthing."

"Aye, mum."

"As you wish."

The servants dutifully filed out, the bolder ones casting curious glances over their shoulders.

"Brandy, Potter," Anne commanded, sweeping the doors shut before rushing to drop to her knees at her brother's side.

While the butler fetched a snifter of brandy from a satinwood cupboard, she gently pried the cane from Reginald's grip and laid it aside. His hand immediately fisted in the lap rug, kneading the thick wool into a ball.

"What is it, Reggie?" she whispered urgently, addressing him by a nickname she hadn't dared use since they'd shared a nursery. "What terrible thing has vexed you so?"

Before he could answer, Potter returned to press a brimming glass to his master's whitened lips. The duke gulped the brandy instead of sipping it, causing a fresh coughing fit. Potter pounded him vigorously on the back.

"Hell and damnation, man," he wheezed, shooting the butler a murderous glare. "Are you trying to kill me?"

Potter wisely withdrew to a far corner of the room. Smiling wryly, Anne settled back on her heels, reassured that her brother would make a full recovery.

He turned his black scowl on her. "What in the bloody hell are you staring at, woman? Haven't you ever seen an old man lose his senses?"

"Not without good reason," she retorted, refusing to be shocked by his profanity. "Now suppose you share it with me?"

Reginald flung a finger toward the fireplace where a piece of paper lay crumpled on the hearth. He had apparently hurled it at the flames only to have it fall short, worsening his rage. It was then that Anne noticed the rosewood box overturned at his feet, the yellowing letters spilled across the rug, the locket chain tangled around his fingers.

"It's that lunatic granddaughter of mine," he bit off. "Impossible chit will be the death of me yet. She's just like her bloody mother."

Anne sighed, knowing that no more contemptuous slur could have been cast. Reginald's iron will had been thwarted once and only once, by his cherished daughter Lisbeth, who had left her father's handpicked suitor, the earl of St. Cyr, languishing at the altar while she eloped with that most despised of all creatures—an American. Not even a wealthy American, but a painfully earnest writer whose modest aspiration had been to become a reporter for the *Boston Gazette*. Bartholomew Fine had stolen Lisbeth's heart and what was left of Reginald's as well, leaving nothing but a charred hollow in its place.

Lisbeth had been an accomplished musician. Before she ran away, the house had rung with music and laughter. After, it echoed only with silence.

Although she'd written faithfully every month, reassuring her father of her happiness and pleading for his pardon, Reginald had never forgiven her betrayal. He refused to acknowledge her letters in any way, although he kept them carefully preserved within the satin-lined confines of a rosewood box.

On a chill autumn eve thirteen years ago, another letter had arrived, this one penned not in Lisbeth's sophisticated script, but in a hand that was girlish, yet painfully precise. Reginald had read the letter, his craggy face expressionless, before handing it to Anne.

It had been written by Lisbeth's twelve-year-old daughter to inform Reginald that both Lisbeth and her precious Bartholomew were dead, struck down by an outbreak of cholera. Although the child's account of her parents' death betrayed no trace of self-pity, the smudged ink whispered of fallen tears, hastily blotted. Oddly enough, the girl was not writing to beg charity for herself or her six-year-old brother, but to inform her grandfather that she would honor her mother's dying wish that he continue to receive a monthly letter apprising him of their circumstances.

In terse parentheses, she had scrawled, *Why Mama should have continued to love such a cold and unforgiving ogre is beyond my comprehension. However, it is not mine to question her final wish, but to see that it is granted.* The child's bold rebuke had made Anne smile through her tears.

The letter had been signed *Miss Esmerelda Fine* and had been accompanied by the silver locket the duke had given Lisbeth on her sixteenth birthday.

Reginald had never acknowledged his daughter's death, publicly or privately, but from that day forward, he had not risen from his wheelchair.

Esmerelda's letters had followed every month without fail. Although Reginald gruffly "harrumphed" and "pshawed" at their arrival, he would eagerly clutch at them, tearing them open when he thought no one was looking. Sometimes Anne would slip into the smoking room to find him chuckling over some witty anecdote or gleefully savoring one of the thinly veiled insults the girl managed to sneak into nearly every letter. Although he would have denied it with his dying breath, his admiration for his resourceful granddaughter was growing. He silently applauded her successes and fretted over her failures.

His admiration, however, did not extend to his grandson. "A scribbler like his father," he would mutter, scowling over some lengthy passage detailing little Bartholomew's accomplishments. "Worthless boy won't amount to anything."

After reading and rereading each letter, Reginald would gently tuck it into the tiny rosewood coffin he had chosen to preserve his daughter's memory.

Stricken by a sudden nameless dread, Anne gazed at the forlorn scrap of paper on the hearth. "Oh, my God, Esmerelda's not—"

"Dead? No, but she soon will be if she pursues this daft scheme of hers."

Shooting her brother a baffled glance, Anne dove for the hearth, rescuing her niece's letter with shaking hands. She scanned it, the rapid movement of her lips betraying her agitation.

As she reached the end, her knees gave way. She sank down on a brocaded ottoman before the fire, gazing blindly into the dancing flames. "Dear God. What must she be thinking? To travel across an entire continent, alone and unchaperoned, in pursuit of this . . . this"—she reread the last paragraph of the letter, shuddering violently— "desperado."

Reginald stomped his slippered foot. "She's not thinking at all! The chit's just like her mother. Weak, willful, and at the mercy of every ridiculous feminine whim that drifts through her empty little head."

Anne felt compelled to defend the niece she'd never met. "Esmerelda has always struck me as such a practical little creature. She survived her parents' death. She established a music school in her own home and tended her brother when she was little more than a child herself."

Reginald shook a finger at her. "It's that wretched boy

who's to blame. The father cost me my Lisbeth and now the son is imperiling Esmerelda." He faltered as they both realized it was the first time he'd ever spoken his granddaughter's name aloud.

"This letter is dated over two months ago," Anne noted softly. "She might already be . . ."

Their eyes met. This time, neither of them was able to complete the grim thought. Reginald's gaze strayed back to his lap. With a gentleness utterly foreign to his nature, he pried open the silver locket.

Anne knew what he would find there. A faded daguerreotype of a young girl with a plump toddler cradled in her arms. The little boy with the dimpled cheeks and nest of dark curls had been unable to resist smiling at the photographer, but the girl, striking despite her severe braids and starched pinafore, stared dutifully ahead, her solemn eyes betraying the faintest hint of wistfulness.

The duke studied the locket for several minutes before snapping it shut. "Potter, my cane."

"Yes, sir." The butler emerged from his corner to retrieve his master's cane.

Anne fully expected her brother to resume brandishing it like a rapier, but to her surprise, he planted its brass tip firmly on the rug. Her surprise deepened to shock when he staggered to his feet. An alarmed Potter rushed at him, but Reginald waved him away, growling a warning.

Anne backed away from him as well, clutching her throat. "What in God's name are you doing?"

She held her breath without realizing it as her brother straightened his hunched back with an almost audible creak. Beneath their gray-fringed brows, his dark eyes glowed with determination.

Standing fully erect for the first time in thirteen years, he pounded his cane on the floor once for emphasis and said, "I, my dear sister, am going to America to rescue my granddaughter from that . . . that . . ."

"Outlaw?" Anne whispered. "Renegade?"

Reginald's upper lip curled in a regal sneer, warning that only the vilest of epithets was to follow.

"Cowboy."

PART ONE

She took me to the parlor,
She cooled me with her fan,
She swore I was the prettiest thing
In the shape of mortal man.

She told me that she loved me,
She called me sugar plum.
She throwed her arms around me,
I thought my time had come.

"CINDY"
American Folk Song

CHAPTER ONE

Calamity, New Mexico

Esmerelda Fine eyed the Wanted poster nailed to the porch post of the stagecoach station with a jaded eye. "Billy Darling," she murmured. "A rather harmless name for such a wicked man, isn't it?"

"Beggin' your pardon, ma'am, but Billy ain't wicked. He's just a man that does what needs to be done. If someone needs killin', he kills 'em." The grizzled cowhand who had overheard her musing spat a fat wad of tobacco on the plank sidewalk, barely missing the pleated hem of her skirt. "You cain't fault a man who enjoys his job. Why, Billy's the only Darlin' since the war to turn his hand to good honest work."

Drawing her skirts close to her legs, Esmerelda cast the man a withering glance. "Which means he kills for profit instead of amusement?"

She turned her attention back to the image of the hired

killer glowering down at her from the Wanted poster. The handbill was a weathered twin of the one she'd kept neatly folded in her silk reticule during the long, arduous train and stagecoach journey from Boston. Seeing his ignoble image displayed before all the world gave her some small measure of comfort, reassured her that he wasn't some imaginary devil woven from the fabric of her darkest fears and fantasies.

A thick growth of whiskers obscured the outlaw's features, but the menace in his eyes was palpable. How many men had gazed into those steely eyes over the barrel of a pistol and known them to be the last sight they would see on this earth? An invisible cloud shadowed the sun as Esmerelda remembered that her brother had been one of them.

Bitterness tightened her lips as she shifted her gaze from the poster to the cowhand. "So how did such a paragon of industry end up with a price on his own head?"

"Aw, them U.S. marshals got all riled up when Billy brought one in dead that was wanted alive. Seems they needed the feller to testify against a band o' bootleggers that'd been sellin' whiskey to the Comanche."

"But your Mr. Darling saw fit to administer justice himself. How terribly noble of him."

Her sarcasm did not escape the old man. "From what I heard tell, miss, Billy had every right to be riled. The feller shot him in the back. If he hadn't been so all-fired contrary, Billy wouldn't have had to blow his damn fool head off."

Esmerelda felt herself blanch. Alarmed by her fading color, the cowhand jerked off her bonnet and began to fan her with it. "Now, miss, you ain't goin' to swoon on me, are you?" He reached for her reticule. "You got any smelling salts in that there fancy bag?"

Shocked by the stranger's familiarity, Esmerelda clutched

the reticule to her bosom, comforted by its solid weight. "I should say not, sir. It's simply the heat. I'm not accustomed to such a brutal climate."

That much was true. The brave little bonnet that had elicited such a pang of yearning when she'd seen it displayed in the window of Miss Adelaide's Millinery Shoppe had done little to deflect the ruthless rays of the sun. The saucy pair of bluebirds affixed to its brim had wilted just west of St. Louis. Esmerelda breathed a sigh of relief at being freed from the bonnet's sweltering confines. A whisper of a breeze, arid yet sweet, teased the damp tendrils of hair at her temples.

But a lady did not march bareheaded into adversity. Snatching the bonnet from the old man's hands, Esmerelda slapped it back into place and secured it with a fastidious bow. "If you would be so kind as to direct me to the livery stable, sir . . . ? I am in need of a mount and a dependable guide. If I'm to locate this outlaw before he reaches the Mexican border—"

"Well, hell, miss," the cowpoke drawled, "there's no need to go to all that trouble just to have a set-down with Billy." He winked at her. "There weren't never a Darlin' born that weren't willin' and eager to oblige a purty lady."

Esmerelda cringed at both his offhand profanity and his leering implication. Her dealings with the male sex had been limited to the wealthy Boston merchants who hired her to teach music to their pampered daughters, but she could still summon a disturbing, if fuzzy, image of the methods a ruffian like Billy Darling might use to *oblige* a woman.

Dashing a trickle of sweat from her cheek with a gloved hand, she scooped up her violin case and hefted the battered leather trunk that contained the few meager belongings she hadn't sold to finance her journey. "I can assure you that your honorable Mr. Darling won't be quite so eager to have a *set-down* with me."

"Why don't you ask him yourself?"

Esmerelda's gaze flew to the old man's smirking face. The trunk slid out of her grip and thumped to the sidewalk. She barely managed to catch her precious violin case before it followed suit. "You've seen him? Where? When? Was he alone? Was he armed? Which direction did he take?"

The cowpoke pointed across the dusty street.

Esmerelda shaded her eyes against the sun, struggling desperately to gauge its position. "West? South? How long ago did he depart? Hours? Days? What color horse was he riding?"

"He weren't ridin' no horse, miss. He just walked out o' Miss Mellie's whorehouse a little after noon and moseyed right on over to the saloon."

The plank sidewalk seemed to buckle beneath her feet, giving Esmerelda cause to regret that she hadn't packed a vial of smelling salts. Her stunned gaze drifted to the weathered facade of the saloon across the street. The tinny notes of a poorly tuned piano spilled out of its swinging doors, barely penetrating the roaring in her ears.

He was there. Now that she knew he was there, she could almost feel him. Coiled. Deadly. Waiting for her.

She swallowed in a vain attempt to stifle the flutter of raw excitement in her throat. She had never dreamed her quest for justice would be fulfilled with such ease. Shock made her voice sound distant and quavery, even to her own ears. "You must fetch the sheriff immediately, sir. I shall insist he march over to the saloon and take the renegade into custody."

The cowpoke scratched his balding head, his expression

oddly reticent. "Uh, miss, the sheriff is already at the saloon. Been there since this mornin'."

Esmerelda blinked in confusion. "And what, pray tell, is he doing there?"

"Playin' poker, most likely. He and Billy've had a runnin' game for almost three months now. Ever since Billy got shot up and moved into the whorehouse."

Her eyes widened in disbelief. Nearly choking on her outrage, she glanced frantically around, earning nothing but a polite tip of a passing gentleman's hat for her trouble. "What manner of place is this Calamity? Surely the townsfolk aren't content to stand idly by while their sheriff consorts with outlaws!"

"Aw, don't be so hard on Sheriff McGuire. He'd arrest Billy if he thought it'd do any good. But our jail cain't hold him. Before the marshal could come to take him to Santa Fe for trial, his brothers would just bring a bunch o' dynamite and blast him out. You see, miss, Billy's brothers is outlaws to the last man. They come from Missoura after the war and there's some that says they even rode with Quantrill's Raiders and Bloody Bill Anderson, just like them James and Younger boys."

Esmerelda shivered. The exploits of those Confederate desperados who had refused to accept that their cause was lost had reached as far north as Boston. The wild-eyed boys and their ruthless leaders had struck terror in the heart of a nation already ravaged by four years of war.

The cowpoke shook his head. "You don't want to mess with them Darlin' boys. They set a high store by Billy, him bein' the baby o' the family and all."

Esmerelda clenched her teeth against a frisson of rage. How could a cold-blooded killer like Billy Darling be anybody's baby? Her brother's face drifted through her memory as it had so many times in the months since his disappearance—his plump, rosy cheeks pale and sunken, his sable hair dulled by blood, the spark of mischief in his eyes doused by the icy, black waters of death.

Beset by a strange and dangerous calm, Esmerelda gently placed her violin case on top of her trunk and dipped a hand into her reticule to caress its sleek contents.

As she stepped off the sidewalk into the dusty street, the cowhand called after her. "Miss! Oh, miss, you forgot your fiddle and trunk."

"Watch them for me, won't you?" she replied, studying the beckoning doors of the saloon through narrowed eyes. "I won't be long."

Esmerelda Fine's arrival in Calamity on that lazy Wednesday afternoon had garnered more attention than she realized. While the townsfolk had grown accustomed to having the stagecoach pass through, they were not accustomed to seeing anyone actually disembark from it. Especially not a slender wren of a lady garbed in a bustle and bonnet the provincial folk of Calamity assumed was the very pinnacle of city fashion.

When Esmerelda plunged into the dusty street without a visible care for her high-heeled kid leather boots, curtains twitched and children came creeping out of alleyways. When it appeared her destination was to be none other than the Tumbleweed Saloon, shopkeepers emerged from their deserted stores to sweep the sidewalks, trading curious and wary looks.

They breathed a collective sigh of relief when Esmerelda paused just outside the saloon, obviously realizing her error. No true lady would ever darken the doorstep of such an establishment. The townsfolk nodded and smiled at one another, their faith in the innate nobility of woman-kind restored.

Until the young woman squared her slender shoulders, thrust open the swinging doors, and disappeared inside.

The sudden shift from sunlight to gloom nearly blinded Esmerelda. Long shadows cut a swath through the interior of the saloon. The isinglass windowpanes admitted only enough light to gild the dust motes drifting through the air.

A garishly painted woman straddled a chair in front of the piano, banging out a rollicking dance-hall tune with her crimson fingernails. A bartender stood behind a long counter, polishing glasses in front of a row of amber-tinted bottles. A handful of stragglers slumped at the bar, but most of the chatter and merriment in the room seemed to be coming from a table situated just below the upstairs balcony.

Two bleary-eyed cowboys flanked a broad-shouldered man whose mouth was dwarfed by a drooping mustache. His silver hair flowed past his shoulders like lustrous waves of corn silk. A tin star was pinned to his satin waistcoat.

The esteemed sheriff McGuire, Esmerelda deduced, fortified by a fresh surge of contempt.

The trail of bills and silver scattered across the table's pitted surface led directly to a fourth man. A man who sat with his back to the wall and his face shadowed by his hat brim. A thin cigar was clamped between his lips. A dimpled whore perched on one knee.

He was watching her, Esmerelda realized, repressing a shiver. His regard might be nothing more than a wary gleam penetrating the shadows, but it was powerful enough to draw every other eye in the saloon to her frozen form. It was almost as if she hadn't existed until the moment he had chosen to take notice of her.

The piano fell mute. The bartender's cloth ceased its circular motions. Curious faces appeared in the saloon windows, struggling to peer through the gloom. Avid eyes peeped over the top of the saloon door, abandoning all pretense of discretion.

Chin up and one foot in front of the other, girl, Esmerelda heard someone say in her head. *If you keep putting one foot in front of the other, you'll eventually get where you're going.* Although she had never heard her grandfather speak, Esmerelda knew exactly who that clipped British voice belonged to. She might loathe the man for turning his back on her mother, but it was his pitiless scolding that had prodded her to get up off the bed and stop feeling sorry for herself after her parents had died, that had goaded her into drying little Bartholomew's tears when she was still blinded by her own.

Despite her hatred of her grandfather, or perhaps because of it, his gruff, no-nonsense tones never failed to calm her fears.

Until now.

She marched to the table, stopping directly across from the man she had traveled over two thousand miles to find. The woman on his lap wrapped a possessive hand around his nape, surveying her with sloe-eyed amusement.

"Mr. William Darling?" Esmerelda winced when her voice cracked in the unnatural silence.

His only acknowledgment of her presence was the faint twitch of a muscle in his jaw. Smoke wafted from his cigar, curling toward her like tendrils of brimstone.

"I am," he finally drawled, stubbing out the cigar and tipping back his hat with one finger.

Esmerelda had braced herself to confront a bewhiskered fiend. She nearly dropped her reticule when the shadows retreated to reveal lean cheeks shaded by the barest hint of stubble and a pair of dark-lashed, gray-green eyes that failed to betray even a glimmer of shiftiness. Those eyes assessed her, taking her measure with disturbing bluntness.

Praying that she had practiced in front of the mirror often enough to do it without shooting herself in the foot, Esmerelda fished the derringer from the satin-lined depths of her reticule and leveled it at his heart.

"You're under arrest, Mr. Darling. I'm taking you in."

CHAPTER TWO

♥
_____

Billy Darling was a jovial drunk.

Which explained the dangerous edge to his temper as he surveyed the haughty young miss who had presumed to interrupt his poker game. His first whiskey of the day sat untouched on the table just inches from his fingertips. The way his day was going, he doubted it would be his last.

The woman disagreed. Noting the direction of his glance, she gave the brimming glass an imperious nod. "You'd best finish your whiskey, sir. It may be the last you taste for a very long while."

Billy barely resisted the urge to bust out laughing. Instead, he curled his fingers around the glass and lifted it in a salute to her audacity. She really ought to be flattered by the stir her announcement had caused. Noreen had gone tumbling off his lap in a flurry of scarlet petticoats while Dauber and Seal went diving under a nearby table, scattering bills and coins.

Only Drew had remained upright, but even he had scooted his chair back a good two feet and thrown his hands into the air. The waxed tips of his mustache quivered with alarm. Billy suspected he would have joined the cowboys under the table if he hadn't feared rumpling the new paisley waistcoat he'd had shipped all the way from Philadelphia. You could almost always count on Drew's vanity overruling his cowardice.

It wasn't the first time Billy had faced a woman across the barrel of a gun, and it probably wouldn't be the last. Hell, he'd even been shot once by a jealous whore in Abilene. But she'd cried so prettily and tended the wound and the rest of him with such gratifying remorse, he'd forgiven her before the bleeding stopped.

It wasn't even that he particularly minded being shot by a woman. He just wanted to do something to deserve it first.

He sipped the whiskey, narrowing his eyes to study the woman over the rim of the glass. Her hands were steady, but an unnatural flush heightened her color. Any woman with a gun was dangerous, but he suspected this one might be more dangerous than most. Her delicate nostrils flared like a high-strung mare's each time she exhaled.

He searched his memory for any transgression he might have committed against her. She didn't look the sort to thrust some squalling brat into his face, claiming it was his. He swallowed a shudder of distaste along with a mouthful of whiskey at the thought of inflicting another Darling on the hapless West.

His gaze roamed briefly over her trim form. She was as slender as a reed—downright underfed by his standards.

She most definitely didn't favor the busty whores who bore the brunt of his romantic attentions.

Billy frowned. He'd woken up on more than one occasion with women whose faces and names he could barely remember, but it troubled him to think such an encounter could have escaped him completely. He studied the pristine curve of the woman's cheek, wishing he could see the hue of the hair hidden by that ridiculous bird's nest of a bonnet. As his gaze lingered on her mouth, he decided he had never known her, biblically or otherwise. If he'd have ever persuaded those prim lips to part for him or made those snowy cheeks flush with pleasure instead of indignation, he damn well would have remembered it.

He drained the rest of the whiskey in a single searing swallow and thumped the glass to the table, making her flinch. "Why don't you put the gun down? You really don't want to get powder burns on your pretty white gloves, do you, Miss . . . ?"

"Fine. Miss Esmerelda Fine."

She flung her name at him like a challenge, but it failed to trigger even an echo of recognition. "Esmerelda? Now that's a rather lofty name for such a little bit of a lady. Suppose I just call you Esme?"

He would have thought it impossible, but her mouth grew even more pinched. "I'd rather you didn't. My brother was the only one who called me Esme." Then that same mouth surprised him by curving into a sweetly mocking smile. "Unless, of course, you'd rather I call you *Darling*?"

Billy scowled at her. "The last man who cast aspersions on my family name got a belly full of lead." In reality, he'd gotten only a bloody nose, but since Billy didn't plan to give either to this persistent young lady, he didn't see any harm in embellishing.

"It wouldn't have been my brother, by any chance,

would it? Is that why you gunned down a defenseless boy? For hurting your poor, delicate feelings?"

"Ah." Billy's good humor returned as he folded his arms over his chest and tilted his chair back on two legs. "Now we're getting somewhere. Do refresh my memory, Miss Fine. You can't expect me to remember every man I'm supposed to have killed."

He felt a surprising flicker of remorse when his jibe drew blood. The gloved hand wrapped around the derringer trembled ever so slightly. Dauber and Seal cowered deeper beneath their table, all but hugging each other.

"I should have expected no less than such callous disregard from an animal like you, Mr. Darling. A cold-blooded assassin masquerading as a legitimate bounty hunter." Her contemptuous gaze flicked to Drew. "Sheriff, I demand that you arrest this man immediately for the murder of Bartholomew Fine III."

"What happened to the first two Bartholomews?" Dauber whispered. "Billy kill them, too?"

Seal elbowed him in the ribs, earning a sharp grunt.

Drew twirled one tip of his mustache, a habit he indulged only in moments of great duress. "Now, lass," he purred in that lilting mixture of Scottish burr and western drawl that was so exclusively his. "There's no reason to get your wee feathers all in a ruffle. I remain confident that this private quarrel between you and Mr. Darling can be settled in a civilized manner without the discharge of firearms."

"Private quarrel?" The woman's voice rose to a near shriek. "According to that Wanted poster out there, this man is a public menace with a price on his head. I insist that you take him in!"

Drew sputtered an ineffectual retort, but Billy's melted-butter-and-molasses drawl cut right through it. "And just where do you propose he take me?"

Miss Fine blinked, her face going blank for a gratifying moment. "Why, the jail, I suppose."

Billy slanted Drew a woeful look. Avoiding Miss Fine's eyes, Drew polished his badge with his ruffled shirt sleeve. "Sorry, lass, but our jail's not equipped to hold Mr. Darling. You'll have to take your complaint to the U.S. marshal in Santa Fe."

Righting his chair, Billy favored her with a rueful grin, briefly entertaining the notion that she and her sad little bonnet just might admit defeat and creep away to let him finish his poker game in peace. After all, any fellow hapless enough to be stuck with the name of Bartholomew was probably better off dead.

She dashed his hopes by swaying forward, her voice husky with menace. "If this miserable excuse for a law-man—"

"Now wait just one minute there, lass!" Drew cried, his Scottish accent deepening along with his agitation. If she got him any more riled, there would be *g*'s dropping and *r*'s rolling all over the saloon. "There's no need to insult my—"

She turned the gun on him; his defense subsided to a sulky pout. She returned it to Billy, aiming it square at his heart.

"If this miserable excuse for a lawman won't take you in," she repeated firmly, "then I will. I'll take you to Santa Fe and turn you over to the U.S. marshal myself. Why, I'll hog-tie you to the back of a stagecoach and drag you all the way to Boston if I have to, Mr. Darling."

Rubbing the back of his neck, Billy sighed wearily. She'd left him with no choice but to call her bluff. As the smile faded from his eyes, the bartender vanished behind the bar, Drew inched his chair backward, and Dauber and Seal plugged their ears with their fingertips.

Billy rested his hands palms-down on the table, flexing his fingers with deceptive indolence. "Oh, yeah?" he drawled. "Who says?"

Little Miss Fine-and-Mighty cocked the derringer, her face going white with strain. "I've got one shot in this chamber that says you're coming with me."

The Colt .45 appeared in Billy's hand as if by magic, accompanied by a personable grin. "And I've got six shots in this here Colt that say I'm not."

Esmerelda stared dumbly at the gun in Darling's hand. His movements hadn't betrayed even a hint of a blur. One second his hand had been empty. The next it had been cradling an enormous black pistol. The imposing barrel dwarfed the stunted mouth of her derringer, making it look like a toy. Darling's smile was unflinching, but all traces of green had disappeared from his eyes, leaving them ruthless chips of flint.

Esmerelda sucked in a steadying breath, cringing when it caught in a squeak. She'd spent so many sleepless nights in the past few months dreaming of the moment when she would confront her brother's murderer. But none of the possible scenarios had included engaging him in a standoff. Billy Darling was rumored to be a crack shot, lethally accurate at thirty yards, much less four feet. What was the proper etiquette in these situations? Should she suggest they choose seconds? Step outside and draw at twenty paces? She flexed her numb fingers, choking back a hysterical giggle.

Almost as if he'd read her mind, he said, "It has occurred to me, Miss Fine, that this may very well be your first gunfight. We have both drawn our weapons so all that remains is to determine which one of us has the guts to pull the trigger. If you'd rather not find out, then I suggest you lay your gun on the table and back out of here. Nice and slow."

"Now, William," the sheriff whined. "You know you've never shot a woman before."

Darling's affable smile did not waver. "Nor has one ever given me cause to."

"Drop your weapon, sir," Esmerelda commanded, praying the derringer wouldn't slip out of her sweat-dampened glove. She waited a respectable interval before adding a timid, "P-p-please."

"I asked you first."

Her hands were starting to shake in earnest, and there seemed to be little she could do to still them. The sight infused her with frustration and bone-deep weariness. She had sold everything she'd worked for since she was twelve years old—her beloved music school, her tidy little house with its red shutters and gardenia-filled window boxes, the precious books and sheets of music she'd bought with pennies hoarded from her own food money.

She'd forfeited all she held dear just to come to this godforsaken town and bring her brother's killer to justice. And there he sat, smirking at her with cool aplomb, all the while knowing that he had crushed her brother's life beneath his bootheel with no more concern than for a discarded cigar butt.

He had robbed her of everything that made her life worth living, and now he dared to threaten that life itself.

Esmerelda suddenly realized that she no longer wanted justice. She wanted vengeance. Her finger tightened on the trigger. A scalding tear trickled down her cheek, then another. She dashed them away with one hand, but fresh ones sprang into their place to blur her vision.

She did not see the sheriff rock back in his chair, grinning with relief. Billy Darling might be able to stand down

the meanest desperado in five territories or gun down a
fleeing outlaw without blinking an eye, but he never could
abide a woman's tears.

"Aw, hell, honey, don't cry. I didn't mean to scare you. . . ."

Billy was out of his seat and halfway around the table,
hand outstretched, when Esmerelda Fine, who had never
so much as swatted a fly without a pang of regret, closed
her eyes and squeezed the trigger.

CHAPTER THREE

When a lone man emerged from Miss Mellie's Boardinghouse for Young Ladies of Good Reputation and sauntered across the dirt road later that afternoon, the crowd gathered outside the sheriff's office fell silent. Not one of them dared to protest. Not even when he strolled right past them and into the office just as pretty as you please, although the sheriff had threatened to blow off the head of the first man fool enough to stick it in the door.

The man found Sheriff Andrew McGuire reclining in an oak spindle chair, his feet propped on his desk. Both his boots and the tin star pinned to his satin vest had been buffed to a near-blinding shine. He had his nose buried in a book and was paying no more heed to the rumbling purr of the yellow cat napping on his chest than to the loaded shotgun laid across his lap. The cat had been a gift from Billy Darling, the shotgun a retirement present from the governor of Texas for surviving twenty-five years as a Texas Ranger—a survival ensured by his blatant distaste for danger.

"Afternoon, Drew," the man drawled.

The sheriff leveled a glance over the top of the book. "Afternoon."

His visitor jerked a thumb toward the door. "Quite a mob you have out there. You expecting a lynching?"

Drew rolled his eyes. "A cotillion, more likely."

The man propped his hip on the edge of the desk and nodded toward the cat. "If Miss Kitty there is accounted for, then what might be the source of that godawful cater-wauling?"

Although Drew appeared to be making a valiant effort, the sound was almost impossible to ignore. It wafted out from the corridor behind him where the back cell was located, not so much off-key as woefully shrill and set at just the right pitch to make even a long-suffering man grit his teeth in pain.

The wailing rose to a crescendo, making Drew wince. "It's *her*. The lass has been praying and singing church hymns ever since she woke up from her swoon. She claims to be a music teacher." When his companion's eyebrows shot skyward in disbelief, he leaned forward and confided, "'The Battle Hymn of the Republic' seems to be a partic-ular favorite of hers."

The man's jaw tightened. Drew knew damn well that every man who'd fought on the losing side in the War of Secession, or lost someone who had, despised that song above all others.

Drew chuckled. "The lass even had the audacity to ask

if I had a copy of the Good Book on hand. I offered her this volume, but she declined."

The man plucked the book from Drew's hands and examined the cover, cocking a skeptical eyebrow. "*The Amorous Adventures of Buxom Belle?*"

Drew snatched it back. "Well, it's a damn good book, if you ask me."

His friend's eyes were strangely thoughtful. "Has she shown any signs of remorse?"

The sheriff stroked the slinky curve of the cat's back. Despite his grave tone, his own feline smirk revealed that he was enjoying himself more than was strictly proper. "She claims she's resigned to suffering the earthly consequences for taking a man's life, but insists the good Lord in his infinite mercy will surely pardon her for ridding the world of a heartless vermin like Billy Darling."

The man's eyes narrowed. "The good Lord probably would. But I sure as hell won't."

A particularly grating note floated out from the corridor. Throwing a black scowl over his shoulder, Drew caressed the hammer of the shotgun. "One more chorus of 'Nearer, My God, to Thee' and I'm going to have to shoot her. Or myself."

The man reached across the desk to pluck a ring of iron keys from a hook on the wall. "Why don't I spare you the trouble?"

Drew sprang to his feet, earning a sulky look from the displaced cat. He'd seen that wicked sparkle in his friend's eyes before and knew it boded nothing but trouble. "Now, you wait just a minute there, lad. The woman might be prepared to meet her Maker, but she sure as hell isn't prepared to meet you."

The man neatly sidestepped him, the keys setting up a merry jingle as he headed for the shadowy corridor. "She should have thought of that before she came to Calamity. I intend to find out exactly why such a prissy little peahen would come gunning for the likes of Billy Darling."

"If the lass screams," Drew called after him, "I'm going to come a-running."

The man tossed a grin over his shoulder. "And if I scream?"

Drew settled back into his chair, propping his boots on the desk and raising the book to shield his smile. "You, my friend, are on your own."

As the final note of "Onward, Christian Soldiers" faded from her lips, Esmerelda clasped her hands and turned her eyes heavenward. She had hoped for some visible sign of God's approval—a light streaming down from heaven, perhaps, or a chorus of celestial harping. But the plaster ceiling remained, its chipped and water-stained surface making her wonder how many other condemned murderers had sat on this very bunk, gazing wistfully toward a heaven they might never reach.

Rising from her aching knees to plop down on the bunk, she chafed her arms through the thin silk faille of her basque. Although the air was warm and dry, the short jacket that flared into graceful flounces over her bustle did little to protect her from the chill that had clung to her skin since she'd first awakened in this windowless cell. An awakening made all the more cruel in contrast to the dream she'd been having. A dream where she'd been cradled against the broad chest of a man who smelled of tobacco and leather. She'd wrapped her arms around his neck and nuzzled his throat, feeling safe for the first time since her parents had died.

Swallowing around the lump in her throat, she warbled the first few notes of "Amazing Grace." But she got no further than the chorus before the melody died on a hoarse croak. It was just as she'd feared all along. She'd been singing less out of pious conviction than to drown out the voice of her conscience telling her she had done a terrible thing. A voice growing louder and more strident by the moment.

His eyes haunted her.

She couldn't remember now if they'd been gray or green, which only made her feel worse. If you were going to take a man's life, then you ought to at least be brave enough to look him in the eye while you did it. But she'd been the lowest sort of coward, closing her own eyes to blot out the dreadful finality of what she was doing. She supposed it wasn't much better than shooting a man in the back.

She couldn't remember the color of his eyes, but oddly enough, she could remember the exact texture of his eyelashes. They'd fringed his eyes like threads of gold silk, giving the dangerous planes of his face the disturbing illusion of vulnerability.

But it hadn't been an illusion. Billy Darling had been as vulnerable as any mortal man to a woman with a gun in her hand. Now those extravagant lashes would forever rest on his pale, still cheeks.

Pressing a hand to her mouth to stifle a moan of shame, Esmerelda rose from the bunk and began to pace the cell. She'd already compounded her sin of murder by lying to the sheriff about her prospects for eternity. She wasn't nearly as afraid of being hanged as she was of going to hell. The tin kerosene lamp suspended from a peg in the corridor outside the cell cast writhing shadows on the wall. From the corner of her eye, they looked like the flames of perdition licking at the bars of her cell.

The devil himself was probably chortling with delight at

her predicament. Since her parents had died, she'd striven to be a paragon of Christian virtue her younger brother could emulate. And aside from the occasional uncharitable thought about her grandfather, she'd succeeded. Every naughty impulse and selfish desire had been ruthlessly squelched beneath the iron fist of duty.

A hysterical laugh welled from her throat, sounding more like a sob. Her steadfast devotion to virtue had all been in vain. Each time she'd bitten back a blasphemy when she'd scorched the biscuits. Each time she'd forced herself to hasten past a store window without pausing to covet the pearl-inlaid combs and pleated rosettes. Each time she'd given Bartholomew the last slice of bacon in the house when her own stomach was cramping with hunger.

Despite her years of unflinching self-denial, Satan was going to get his bony claws into her after all. And all because of some born sinner who'd probably spent every waking moment of his abbreviated life indulging his selfish desires.

Bitter regret flooded her, for all the delicious sins gone uncommitted and all the guilty pleasures she would never know.

"Damn you," she whispered fiercely, clenching the cold iron bars of her cell. "Damn you straight to hell, Billy Darling."

"Now that's not a very charitable sentiment, ma'am, even for a woman who's already done everything in her power to send me there herself."

CHAPTER FOUR

The laconic drawl came out of the darkness, a thousand times more damning than the voice of her conscience.

Esmerelda backed away from the bars as Lucifer himself emerged from the shadows wearing a butternut shirt, black vest, scuffed boots, and a pair of sinfully tight copper-riveted Levi's. There didn't appear to be so much as a scratch on him, proving that he was indeed Satan incarnate. Unless Old Nick, not content to wait for her arrival, had sent one of his most devoted emissaries to escort her to his unholy kingdom.

The wicked sparkle in his eyes made a mockery of his sympathetic frown. "Perhaps you should sit down, Miss Fine. You look like you just saw a ghost."

Esmerelda had no choice but to obey. In her attempt to put as much distance between them as possible, she'd backed all the way to the bunk. Her knees buckled and she plopped down on the lumpy mattress.

"I shot you," she blurted out, unable to come up with anything more coherent. "You're supposed to be dead."

"Am I?" He drew off his hat to reveal a devilish grin. "Ma always said I was never any good at doing what I was supposed to."

With the reddish glow of the lantern haloing his disheveled hair, he looked less like a demon than an avenging angel come to claim her soul. In that feverish halflight, she could no more determine the color of his hair than the color of his eyes.

Esmerelda rose from the bunk, drawn toward the apparition by a dangerous combination of fascination and fear. He curled his hands around the bars and cocked one knee through them, all but daring her to approach.

When she reached the bars, she stretched one trembling hand toward his chest. If he'd have grabbed her hand or whispered "Boo" at that instant, she would have crumbled into hysteria. But he simply watched her without blinking, his expression almost as wary as her own.

Her fingertips slowly came to rest against his chest. Beneath the faded fabric of his shirt lay a solid wall of muscle and bone. His heart throbbed beneath her touch, proving beyond the shadow of a doubt that her visitor was no demon or phantom, but Mr. William Darling in the flesh.

She recoiled from the bars with a soft cry. She could not have said herself if it was one of relief or dismay.

Darling smoothed back his tousled hair with one hand. "Sorry I couldn't oblige you by being dead, Miss Fine. I'm afraid that little jaunt to hell you had planned for me will have to be canceled. Or at least postponed."

His quip made Esmerelda wonder just how long he'd been standing in the shadows watching her anguished pacing. He looked so earnest, it was impossible to tell if he was teasing her. "How?" she croaked.

He shrugged, his rueful smirk giving her the eerie sensation that he really could read her mind. "Luck of the devil, maybe? I really can't fault your aim. You put one hell of a hole in my chair, right where my heart would have been."

"If you had one?" she mumbled, still battling shock.

He gave her a reproachful look. "*If* I'd still been sitting there. But I was halfway around the table when you fired. You really should learn how to shoot a firearm without closing your eyes first. It's a dangerous habit. If I'd have been a different sort of fellow, I might have shot you dead instead of catching you when you swooned."

"You?" she whispered, horrified anew. "*You* caught me?"

He nodded. "I couldn't very well let you bang your pretty head now, could I?"

Esmerelda had no reason to doubt his claim. She remembered only too well how the pistol had materialized in his hand. He had the grace and reflexes of a cougar. But if Darling had been the man who caught her, he'd also been the man who had carried her to the jail. The man who'd smelled so utterly delicious—like the leather of book bindings mingled with the aroma of tobacco. The man she'd clung to as if she were a frightened child and he her only salvation.

She began to sputter, mortified beyond speech.

He held up a hand. "There's no need to thank me, ma'am. It was my pleasure."

This time there was no mistaking the mocking quirk of his lips. Esmerelda blushed to the roots of her hair. Dear Lord, what liberties had the scoundrel been allowed to take while she lay defenseless in his arms? Her reticule, gloves, and bonnet had all been missing when she awoke. She touched a hand to her disheveled topknot, then to her throat to find the modest lace collar of her basque still buttoned to her chin. She licked her lips, breathing a sigh of relief when she tasted no whiskey upon them.

Esmerelda returned her attention to Mr. Darling to find him staring at her mouth, his expression impossible to interpret. But when he raised his eyes to meet hers, they were darkened by scorn. "If I'd have compromised you, honey, I'd have made damn sure you remembered it. It may even surprise you to learn we Darling men prefer our women conscious."

Esmerelda couldn't help but notice that he hadn't mentioned willing. Refusing to be further intimidated by the ruffian, she stiffened her spine and lifted her chin. "If I didn't kill you, Mr. Darling, and more's the pity, then why am I being held here? Against my will?"

"I believe the charge would be assault with attempt to kill." All traces of good humor had vanished from his eyes, leaving them icy and flat.

She took an instinctive step backward, thankful for the sturdy iron bars that separated them. Until she saw the ring of keys dangling from his finger.

As he inserted one into the lock, their cheerful jingle seemed to toll her doom.

She backed toward the farthest corner of the cell, chilled to the marrow. She was completely at the outlaw's mercy. No one even knew that she'd come to this place to seek her brother's murderer. No one except her grandfather.

And he didn't care.

"Now, Mr. Darling," she said, her words tumbling out in a nervous rush. "I can certainly understand why you might be just a little angry—"

"Furious."

She swallowed, but only succeeded in wedging the lump of fear deeper in her throat. "*Furious* with me for—"

"Trying to shoot me down in cold blood," he provided with an agreeable smile.

"Firing my derringer in your general direction," she

gently corrected. As he swung open the cell door, her gaze flicked to the gunbelt slung low on his lean hips. "But you left me little choice. Had you surrendered yourself to the sheriff as I requested—"

"Demanded."

"Insisted," she conceded. "Then the entire unpleasant incident might have very well been averted."

"And it would be me behind those bars instead of you."

She smiled brightly. "That would be the logical conclusion. You, after all, are the criminal."

"Accused, judged, and condemned by one lone woman."

He sauntered toward her, but she was forced to stand her ground. There was nowhere left to retreat. "On that charge, I stand convicted. I had no right to take the law into my own hands." She elevated her chin another notch, which barely brought it to the level of his breastbone. "But no one else seemed willing or able to do it."

He shook his head. "I never heard of your brother, Miss Fine. And I sure as hell never killed him."

His words rang with just enough conviction to give Esmerelda the first pang of doubt she'd suffered since leaving Boston. A doubt compounded by the bewildering flutter of her pulse at his approach.

He stopped near enough for her to divine the dark gold hue of his hair, the sun-burnished strands that brushed his shoulders, the tawny stubble shading his jaw. But his eyes continued their maddening shift between gray and green. He was taller than she'd realized, lean and lanky without an ounce of wasted fat on his broad-shouldered frame.

She held her breath as he reached out his hand. But instead of throttling her as she'd feared, he caressed a fallen curl from her cheek. His calloused thumb lingered against her smooth skin.

"Holler," he said.

"Pardon?" she whispered, believing she'd misunderstood him.

"The sheriff promised to come running if you hollered. I think it might be a good idea."

She drew in a shaky breath. "I may have swooned beneath the weight of extreme duress, sir, but surely you haven't mistaken me for the hysterical sort of female who screams at the slightest provocation. . . ."

His lashes swept down to mask his eyes as he lowered his lips toward hers.

Esmerelda screamed.

When Drew came skidding around the corner, he found Billy and Esmerelda on opposite sides of the cell. His prisoner stood rigidly in the corner, the knuckles of her demurely clasped hands white with tension, while her visitor lounged against the wall, hat in hand. Oddly enough, she was the one who looked flushed and guilty, while Billy was the very picture of wide-eyed innocence. Molasses probably wouldn't melt in his mouth.

Drew scowled, instantly suspicious. "You look quite natural behind bars, William. Have you done something to make me leave you there?"

Billy shrugged. "Ask the lady."

Drew deliberately gentled his voice as he addressed his prisoner. "I heard you scream, lass. Did Mr. Darling give you a fright?"

"I wasn't screaming," she replied, shooting Billy a defiant glance. "I was . . . singing."

Puzzled, the sheriff rocked back on his heels. But having heard the lady sing, he had no choice but to believe her.

"I'm glad you happened by, sheriff," Billy said. "Miss Fine and I were just discussing the penalty for assault with attempt to kill should I choose to press charges."

Esmerelda gaped at him, amazed at the ease with which the scoundrel lied. Although he appeared to be giving all of his attention to shaping his hat brim between his long, sun-bronzed fingers, his eyes reflected a calculating glint that only deepened her apprehension.

The sheriff rubbed his clean-shaven jaw. "Well, all I can do is hold her until a U.S. marshal passes through town. Which could be weeks from now. Or months."

"And if I don't press charges?"

"Now, William, you know I can't have some hotheaded female running around town shooting people every time the whim strikes her. I am sworn to provide law and order for Calamity." Ignoring Esmerelda's derisive snort, McGuire gave the waxed tip of his mustache a thoughtful tug. "However, I might just be persuaded—pending the receipt of the appropriate amount of bail money, of course—to release the lass into the custody of a responsible party."

"How much?" Darling asked without a beat of hesitation.

"Fifteen dollars," replied the sheriff. When Darling drew a wad of bills from his pocket, McGuire grinned and added, "In gold."

Although his glare could have crumbled the remaining plaster from the ceiling, Darling drew a pouch from the opposite pocket and tossed it to the sheriff. "That should stake you for tonight's game."

McGuire caught it with one hand. "Much obliged, William. She's all yours."

Darling slapped his hat on his head. "Shall we go, Miss Fine? A jail is no place for a lady."

Esmerelda had watched the entire exchange in dumb horror. When she finally recovered enough of her wits to do more than sputter in outrage, she marched out of the corner, her very petticoats rustling with indignation. "How dare you! I'm not a cask of whiskey or a sack of sugar to be bartered between the two of you."

Billy raked a speculative glance from the tip of her kid boots to her unraveling topknot. "That's one mighty tart sack of sugar."

She whirled on McGuire. "And you dare to call this man a 'responsible party'? He may or may not have killed my brother, but he's still wanted for murder. He has a price on his head."

McGuire waved off her concern. "Only until the U.S. marshals need him to hunt down another rifle runner or stage robber. Billy's the best tracker in the Territory and they know it. As soon as they require his services, they'll come crawling back on their knees with a sack of gold and a promise of amnesty."

Esmerelda swept a disbelieving stare between the two men. There was obviously to be no reasoning with either of them. So she simply wheeled around and marched back to the bunk, sinking down on the yellowing mattress as if she intended to spend the remainder of eternity there. "I'd rather rot in jail than give myself over into the hands of that miscreant."

"There's no need for name-calling, ma'am," Darling said. "If you're not careful, you might bruise my tender feelings."

She turned the full force of her scorn on him. "I sincerely doubt that a man of your character has any feelings."

"You might just be surprised." He spoke the words softly, but his gaze trapped and held hers in a velvety vise broken only by the sheriff's heartfelt sigh.

"I have to respect the lady's wishes, William. It wouldn't look good to the townsfolk if I let you drag her out of here against her will."

Darling shook his head ruefully as he turned to go. "I

understand, sheriff. Let's just hope that marshal gets here before my brothers do."

Esmerelda bounded to her feet. "Your brothers? Why would your brothers come here?"

Billy turned back, but it was McGuire who replied. "Gossip spreads like prairie fire on the range, miss. The Darling boys probably won't take very kindly to hearing about their brother's narrow escape from death. They might just want to pay the lass responsible a wee social call."

She shuddered, remembering the wizened cowhand's warning. *You don't want to mess with them Darlin' boys. They set a high store by Billy, him bein' the baby o' the family and all.*

"Just how many brothers does he have?"

"Four," the sheriff replied. "William here is the runt of the litter."

Esmerelda swallowed hard before slanting Darling a wary look. He probably stood all of six feet two inches— without his boots. As their eyes met, an emotion that might have been remorse flickered across his face. Surely he must realize he was asking her to choose between the gallows and the firing squad.

She could not have said what made her even consider entrusting herself to his hands. He didn't try to coax her into coming or offer her his arm, but simply stood there, awaiting her verdict.

When he'd denied killing her brother, the conviction in his voice had been unmistakable. But he could be a liar as well as a murderer. Or he could be innocent. If she let him walk out on her without so much as a backward glance, she might never learn the truth.

She jerked on the hem of her basque and smoothed her overskirt to hide the trembling of her hands. "Very well, sheriff. If you'll be kind enough to fetch my bonnet and reticule, I shall accompany Mr. Darling from the jail."

CHAPTER FIVE

Billy had to admire the lady's nerve.

Once she decided to accept his offer, she sailed from the cell as if it had been her idea all along, her delicate nose tilted to an imperious angle. He and Drew exchanged a wry look before trailing after her like a pair of mismatched footmen.

She tapped her foot impatiently while Drew retrieved her personal belongings from the bottom drawer of his desk. Her composure didn't waver until she saw her bonnet. The homely little hat had been knocked from her head and thoroughly stomped on during the chaos in the saloon. Billy's own boot print scarred the battered crown.

Her lips puckered in dismay as she tried to coax some life back into the bonnet's bedraggled feathers. Billy scowled, both touched and annoyed by the pathetic gesture. How could the woman mourn a bonnet when the undertaker might be measuring her for a coffin at this very moment? His scowl darkened as he swept his gaze down her slender form. A very small coffin.

He leaned down and whispered, "The next time you swoon after trying to murder me, Miss Fine, I'll leave you to be trampled and save your hat."

Drew chose that inopportune moment to place her derringer on the desk. She snatched at it, but Billy swept it neatly out of her reach.

She smiled at him through gritted teeth. "Why, Mr. Darling, surely you can't object to the sheriff returning my gun. After all, it's not even loaded anymore."

His answering grin was equally tender. "That can be easily enough rectified." He slid the miniature gun into his pocket. "If I turn up dead, Drew, check my back for hat pins."

Exchanging her smile for an open glare, Miss Fine slapped on the bonnet. It sat askew on her head, the bird that hadn't flown the coop bobbing over one of her narrowed eyes like a broken spring. Billy swallowed a sigh of regret. Her hair was a warm chestnut tinted with honey and cinnamon and he rather enjoyed the sight of it hanging all cockeyed like that. It made her look like she'd just rolled out of some man's bed.

Before he could follow that dangerous thought to its inevitable conclusion, he thrust her reticule into her hand and herded her toward the door.

Her brash courage didn't falter until they reached it.

She clutched his arm and gazed up at him, her brown eyes the precise shade of candied maple sugar. "I can't go out there. Can't you hear the mob? They're howling for my blood."

Billy cocked his head to the side. He did indeed hear an ominous rumbling, punctuated by the occasional masculine bellow. Tucking a grin into the corner of his mouth where she wasn't likely to see it, he dipped his head close to her ear and murmured, "You'd best stay close to me, ma'am. They're bound to be a bloodthirsty lot."

Although he knew it must have galled her, she shrank into his side as he eased open the door. He'd expected her to be all angles and sharp edges, but she was much softer than she looked.

As they appeared on the stoop, the shouts and cursing dwindled to an expectant silence. It seemed the entire male population of Calamity had turned out to gawk at his companion. Billy even spotted Dauber and Seal in the crowd, their eager faces scrubbed free of trail dust and their hair slicked back with enough bear grease to fry an elephant.

As he ushered Esmerelda onto the sidewalk, the men retreated to a respectful distance. A shoving match between two grizzled sodbusters broke out on the fringes of the crowd.

"Git back! I done seen her first!"

"Shit, Elmer, ye're nearsighted as a prairie dog. You ain't seen nothin' in nigh on twenty years."

"I see good enough to know ye're nothin' but a yellow-bellied, two-timin' old sonofa—"

"Gentlemen!" boomed Horace Stumpelmeyer, the recently widowed town banker. "I urge you to remember that there is a lady present."

Both men immediately snatched off their dusty hats and clutched them to their hearts. A stripling cowboy, still young enough to have a chin furred with peach fuzz, lifted his hand. Esmerelda ducked as if she expected to be pelted with a rotten tomato. But he only smiled shyly, revealing a mouthful of crooked yellow teeth, and thrust a bouquet of wilted ragweed beneath her nose.

She gave Billy a puzzled look before accepting the offering. Capturing her elbow, he guided her firmly through the throng. A mounting chorus of mutters and whines marked their progress. Some of the bolder men began to declare themselves.

"I got me ten acres and a mule, miss."

"My Effie birthed me nine younguns afore she died at the tender age o' twenty-four, God rest her sweet soul, and they sure do need a ma."

They were halfway across the street when a cowboy tore off his hat and tossed it on the ground. "Hellfire, Billy! You git all the purty ones. It jest ain't fair."

Esmerelda waited until they were safely out of earshot before casting a baffled glance over her shoulder. "Who were those men?"

"Your suitors," he replied shortly, tightening his grip on her elbow.

"I don't understand. I never had any suitors."

He shot her a skeptical look. If that were true, the men in Boston must all be more nearsighted than old Elmer. Her finely chiseled features were only enhanced by a straight, narrow nose with just the faintest hint of a cleft at its tip.

"You do now," he said. When she continued to look doubtful, he sighed. "You see, Miss Fine, the male population in Calamity outnumbers the unmarried female population by at least twenty to one. And that's even counting the whores and old Granny Shively."

Esmerelda's ripple of laughter caught him off guard. "Surely they must realize that I'm far too old to marry."

Billy shot her an even more skeptical look. Although many men chose to raise their brides from teenagers, he had always preferred women to little girls. Esmerelda talked like she was doddering toward the sunset of her dotage, but her dewy skin was still tinted with the first blush of dawn. She might be slender and small-breasted, but those curvy hips of hers were ripe enough to turn any man's mind toward breeding.

Even his.

He jerked his gaze back to her face, gruffly clearing his throat. "Granny Shively's rumored to be over one hundred and seven years old, and she received a dozen proposals in the last year alone. She's broken many a heart by claiming she's still waiting for the right fellow to come along."

"I suppose you can't fault the woman for being choosy." Esmerelda stole another dubious look over her shoulder.

Billy knew exactly what she'd see. A horde of eager male faces—some hopeful, some earnest, some crestfallen—their tongues all but lolling from their mouths. They'd have torn out their hearts and offered them to Esmerelda for nothing more than an encouraging smile. Billy both pitied and scorned them, even as he hoped like hell their lovesickness wasn't catching. He still couldn't figure out why he'd been tempted to steal a kiss from the prickly Miss Fine. Under the guise of adjusting his hat, he brushed his brow with his fingertips. Was it his imagination, or did he feel a touch feverish?

All this talk of matrimony must be making him sick.

He felt suddenly compelled to blurt out, "Drew and I are the only men in town above seventeen and under eighty who aren't looking for a wife."

If the news disappointed her, she hid it well. "The rest of them were even willing to court a woman accused of attempted murder?"

"Unless you'd been convicted of poisoning your last five husbands, they'd court you. And a few of them might overlook even that minor transgression."

She studied the droopy little bouquet for a moment before murmuring, "How sweet."

Aw, hell, Billy thought, slanting her a disgusted look. The last thing he needed was a romantic on his hands. Sugar melted too easily in the blazing New Mexico sun, but vinegar kept its tart tang even under the most brutal circumstances.

He deliberately hardened both his voice and his face. "It's always sweet when a man can get a poke he doesn't have to pay for."

She shot him a shocked look, blushed, then stiffened. For a brief moment, Billy regretted disillusioning her. It had been too easy. Like swiping a peppermint stick from a baby.

She was too incensed to notice that they'd reached their destination. "Perhaps those gentlemen possess purer motives than your own, Mr. Darling."

He just barely resisted the urge to snort. "I'm sure you're right, ma'am. That would explain why they hoard their earnings all week so they can donate them to this charitable establishment every Saturday night."

That said, he pushed open the door of the two-story clapboard house that sat on the most prominent corner of Calamity's only street and ushered her inside. Shafts of sunlight filtered through the stained-glass windowpanes Miss Mellie had imported from San Francisco to prevent potential customers from peeking without paying.

Billy glanced down at his companion, gratified to discover the loquacious Miss Fine had finally been struck dumb.

Everything about the parlor, from its plush Oriental carpets to its brass-studded leather furniture, had been chosen to please a man. But the women sprawled about the room in graduating states of undress were savoring the precious afternoon hours in which they were allowed to please only themselves. Although their faces still bore traces of the rouge they'd worn the night before, their smiles were sincere and their giggles almost girlish.

Maude napped on a high-backed divan, her dimpled knees in a shameless sprawl. Caroline, clad only in a scanty wrapper, dabbed scarlet paint on Esther's toenails. Eliza, Bea, and Dorothea clustered around an occasional table, trading last night's earnings back and forth in a riotous poker game. All three of the women puffed gamely on cigars pilfered from their clients.

Miss Fine's delicate nostrils twitched. The cigar smoke mingled with the fragrance of cheap lilac water and the stale musk of sex, creating a cloying aroma Billy had never noticed before. As overpowering as it was, the tantalizing fragrance of fresh peaches wafted to his nose, making it twitch with curiosity.

It was only then that he realized Esmerelda had inched even closer to him. He swept his gaze across the parlor, seeing the women through her widened eyes—the spill of pale flesh over half-unlaced corsets, black lace garters peeping out from gaping wrappers, mussed sausage curls, ruby lips still swollen from the kisses of strangers.

Esmerelda's affronted innocence should have amused him, but it made him feel something he hadn't felt in a long time—shame. Although he enjoyed needling the prim Miss Fine, he should never have brought a lady to this place.

Since it was too late to rectify his mistake, he grabbed her hand and drew her toward the back stairwell. The abrupt movement had the opposite effect of what he'd intended. Every eye in the parlor turned to stare at them.

Billy scowled fiercely, hoping to discourage comment. When it came to teasing, the girls could be more merciless than a bevy of older sisters. But his murderous expression was to no avail.

A sultry giggle sounded behind them, warning him that Maude had awakened from her nap. "She the gal that tried to shoot you, Billy? I do hope your aim is better than hers."

Esther shook a finger at him. "Now, Billy, you know Miss Mellie said no more bringing home strays unless they sleep in the barn."

Caroline gave one of Esther's newly painted toenails a suggestive blow. "Oh, I dare say he'll find a place for this one to sleep."

The girls erupted into gales of laughter. Almost wishing he were the sort of man who *could* shoot a woman, Billy quickened his steps.

Dorothea winked at Esmerelda over her hand of cards. "Don't worry, sweetheart. He may be in a rush now, but our Billy *always* takes his time when it counts the most."

Foreign prickles of heat surged up the back of his neck. Fortunately, they'd already ducked into the shadows of the stairwell. When they reached the first landing, Esmerelda began to drag her feet. By the time they arrived at the top of the stairs, she was practically dead weight.

He drew her into the largest of the two attic rooms and slammed the door behind them as if they were being pursued by a cloud of harpies. Before he turned around, he braced himself to receive another well-deserved lecture on his morals. Or lack of them.

But when he faced his guest, he discovered that she'd backed halfway across the room. All the color had bled from her cheeks, revealing a faint sprinkling of freckles across the bridge of her nose.

"Please . . ." she whispered. She backed into the bedpost, then flinched as if a monster had grabbed her from behind.

I sure hope your aim is better than hers.

Our Billy always takes his time when it counts the most.

As he gazed into her tear-glazed eyes, he realized exactly who she thought that monster was.

She actually believed he'd brought her to this place to ... that he intended to punish her for nearly shooting him by ...

He rested his hands on his hips, incredulous. "Just what kind of man do you think I am?"

Her convulsive swallow was answer enough.

Billy couldn't have said why her reaction stung so deeply. People had believed the worst of him most of his life. Everyone knew bad blood ran in his veins. Darling blood. The same blood that was even now pooling hot and heavy in his groin and making him wish he was every bit as bad as she thought he was.

He had no defense except to do what he'd always done—try not to disappoint. Folding his arms over his chest, he drawled, "I realize you're mine, Miss Fine, bought and paid for. But I don't intend to take a pound of your pretty flesh as penance for your crime. There's more flesh in this whorehouse than even a man of my voracious appetites requires. You must have a pretty inflated opinion of yourself if you think I'd spend fifteen dollars on you when I could have any one of those girls downstairs for a dollar."

Esmerelda didn't bluster or bristle as he'd hoped. She simply dragged off her bonnet, the tremble in her hands more pronounced than before. Her rapid blinking warned him that she was still dangerously near tears. Seeing her try so valiantly not to cry was almost worse than seeing her cry.

"Forgive me, Mr. Darling. It's been a rather trying day. I thought—"

Billy had no use for her apologies. "When's the last time you ate, Miss Fine?"

"This morning," she replied, just a shade too hastily.

"Give me your reticule," he said gruffly. When she only clutched it tighter, he sighed. "I'm not going to rob you. I try to confine myself to stealing family heirlooms from little old ladies and candy from babies."

She gave him a sullen glance along with the reticule, but allowed him to dump its contents on the bed. It yielded a pair of rumpled gloves and a single coin—a two-cent piece with *In God We Trust* inscribed on its bronze face.

She averted her eyes before confessing softly, "My money ran out in North Fork."

North Fork. Three stagecoach stops before Calamity. A two-day journey.

Billy didn't say a word. He simply spun on his heel and slammed his way from the room.

CHAPTER SIX

The slam of the door was still echoing in Esmerelda's ears when she rushed across the room and twisted the brass knob. The door swung open easily beneath her touch. A husky ripple of feminine laughter drifted up the stairs from the parlor below.

She eased the door shut and sagged against the wall, feeling oddly defeated. If the door had been locked, she would have done everything in her power to escape from this room. But being granted her freedom only reminded her that she had nowhere left to go. She didn't think she could bear to creep past those women again, with their sly eyes and mocking smiles. Billy was probably down there with them at that very moment, laughing at her pathetic assumption that a man like him would want to take *her* to his bed when he had all of those willing, and vastly more experienced, women at his disposal.

Groaning, she buried her face in her hands. What had possessed her to make such an utter fool of herself?

She shuffled over and plopped down on the edge of the bed, truly seeing the room for the first time. It was sparsely furnished with a cedar bedstead, a wardrobe, a small table, and a battered bookcase. The exposed beams of the sloping ceiling gave the room an undeniable aura of coziness, as did the long-haired calico cat napping in the rocking chair by the recessed window.

Esmerelda frowned, baffled by the absence of mirrors on the ceiling, red velvet bed hangings, or any of the other sordid trappings her limited imagination had expected. The sheets weren't woven of black satin, but plain cotton, worn and slightly scratchy to the touch. Seized by an odd impulse, she brought a handful of fabric to her nose, expecting it to be scented with the musky perfume of Billy's most recent lover.

Instead, the sheet smelled of leather, soap, and an indefinable spice that was so distinctly masculine she could not resist drawing in a deeper whiff. A jarring realization struck her. This room wasn't just a trysting place for anonymous strangers. It was Billy Darling's home.

The sheet slipped from her limp fingers. Disturbed by the intimacy of sitting in a man's unmade bed, she bounded to her feet.

Utterly baffled, she wandered the room, pausing only to give the wary cat a distracted stroke. What manner of man would live in a brothel?

The room bore little evidence of a woman's touch. She drew her fingertip through the thick layer of dust furring the top of the wardrobe before realizing she was being ridiculous. When Billy Darling invited a woman to his room, it probably wasn't to dust his wardrobe or wax his hardwood floor. The women residing in this establishment were more likely to rumple his sheets than wash and starch them.

A curious pang in her midsection almost spoiled her righteous indignation. She must be hungrier than she'd realized.

She was also wasting the perfect opportunity to search for clues regarding her brother's murder. She doubted an accomplished rogue like Darling would be foolish enough to leave a trail of evidence, but she certainly wasn't above a bit of snooping to make sure.

She dropped to her knees to peek beneath the bed, but found nothing more incriminating than a chubby basset hound who eyed her mournfully before returning to its nap. The bookcase, however, contained something she'd never thought to find—books. Unable to resist the lure of the printed word, Esmerelda drew one of the thin volumes from its cubbyhole, noting that it was free of the mantle of dust that had descended over the rest of the room.

A wistful ache tightened her throat when she realized it was a dime novel, cheaply bound in orange paperboard. The lurid cover showed a sketch of a man standing with his boot propped on the chest of a fallen outlaw, an over-sized tin star pinned to his lapel. The lawman managed to look both noble and smug as he pursed his lips to blow on his smoking pistol.

"Eldon Nesbith, Fearless Texas Ranger," she murmured. She drew out another book. *"Micah Delancey, Scourge of the Outlaw Gangs."* Then another. *"Haversham Deveraux, Pride of the Canadian Mounties?"*

She was growing more puzzled by the moment. Why would Darling collect books about lawmen when he could be reading sensationalized epics glorifying the bloody exploits of gunslingers like himself? She flipped to the novel's frontpiece only to find his name etched there in a painstaking script utterly unlike the loose and lazy scrawl she would have expected. She traced the signature with her fingertip, so engrossed in the discovery that she didn't hear the door swing open.

Her host stood in the doorway, a plate of beefsteak and potatoes in one hand. Accusation darkened his smoky eyes. Esmerelda felt herself blush as if she'd been caught rifling through his pants pockets after a torrid assignation.

He set the plate on the table, then strode over to her. She barely resisted the childish urge to hide the book behind her back. But he simply took it from her hand and tossed it back on the shelf.

"They belonged to the fellow that had the room before me." His blunt gaze dared her to contradict him.

Esmerelda simply arched her eyebrows. Darling wasn't nearly as good a liar as she'd expected him to be, but that didn't make his conduct any less confusing. During her years teaching music, she'd encountered several children and a few parents who were deeply ashamed because they could not read. But she'd never met a man ashamed because he could.

Deliberately risking his wrath, she plucked the book back off the shelf. "These are precisely the sort of books my brother Bartholomew always wanted to write." She thumbed through the flimsy pages, caught off guard by a crushing wave of heartache. "Even as a boy, he used to beg me to read him tales of the Wild West and the men who sought to tame it."

Billy snorted. "Suicidal fools like George Armstrong Custer, no doubt."

Sighing, she let the book fall shut. "I'm afraid my brother was more enamored of the seamier inhabitants of pioneer life—the gamblers, the outlaw gangs . . ."

"The gunslingers," he provided, flashing her another of those devilish grins.

She chose to ignore his barb. Gently returning the book to the shelf, she said, "My parents died of cholera when I was twelve and Bartholomew was only six, but it was always their dream that my brother attend university. I managed to save up enough money for a full year's tuition at Boston College." Her halting explanation didn't even begin to encompass the years of sacrifice, of doing without all but the barest necessities. Of surrendering her own dreams so Bartholomew might pursue his.

Darling backed up to lean against the bedpost. "So why isn't this upstanding young man in college right now?"

She inclined her head. "We had a terrible quarrel. He promised that he would attend university, but only after he spent a year out west researching his first novel. I, of course, forbade him."

Billy folded his arms over his chest, secretly amused to imagine this little slip of a girl forbidding him anything.

"When I awoke the next morning, the tuition money was gone and so was he." She lifted her eyes to his. Their crystalline brown depths reflected both guilt and despair.

Fighting a treacherous urge to comfort her, he forced an indifferent shrug. "Maybe he just got tired of clinging to your skirts. Most men would rather get under a woman's skirts than hide behind them."

Her delicate jaw stiffened. "My brother wasn't like most men."

Noting her use of the past tense, he said, "So this would be the same brother I'm supposed to have killed."

"It would."

"You're an enlightened woman from Boston, Miss Fine. I would think you wouldn't be so hasty to convict a man without any evidence."

"Oh, I have evidence, Mr. Darling. Irrefutable evidence."

Billy narrowed his eyes. She probably thought he didn't know what *irrefutable* meant.

She surprised him by unbuttoning her high collar and reaching into her ruched basque to draw forth a weathered envelope. Billy was tempted to stand on tiptoe to see just what else she might be hiding down there. Their hands brushed as he took the envelope from her, sending a shock of awareness through him and a shudder through her. A shudder of distaste, no doubt, he thought grimly. Her hands were cold, but the warmth of her bare skin still clung to the envelope.

While she refastened her collar, he opened the envelope without ceremony, turning it upside down over the table. Out slid a gold pocket watch, a mourning brooch woven of silky hair the same honey-and-cinnamon shade as Esmerelda's, a silver fountain pen, a folded piece of paper, and a recent daguerreotype of a grinning young man wearing that very same pocket watch on a handsome fob. Billy could well imagine the photographer's consternation when the cocksure young fellow couldn't resist smiling for his invisible audience.

He reached for the watch, but Esmerelda's hand got there first. It was almost as if she couldn't bear the thought of his touch sullying the precious objects. Her pale fingers played over them with wrenching tenderness, sending a strange shiver through his soul. It seemed like a lifetime since anyone had touched him with such care.

"The watch and pen were our father's," she said softly. "The hair our mother's." She boldly met his gaze. "My brother's things, Mr. Darling. All he owned in the world before he died."

Billy squinted at the daguerreotype. No matter which angle he came at it, he couldn't find any resemblance between the black-haired man with the plump cheeks and the mischievous twinkle in his dark eyes and his prim, stiffnecked sister.

"How old was your brother?"

"Nineteen." Esmerelda traced a finger across the image, as if to caress her brother's dimpled cheek. "Just a boy. . . ."

She missed the incredulous look Billy slanted her. At thirteen he was already riding with Quantrill's successor, Bloody Bill Anderson. At fourteen, he'd killed his first man and tasted his first woman—both on the same night, when his elated brothers had taken him to a whorehouse to celebrate the kill. Billy couldn't remember what the whore looked like, but he could still remember the haunted look in the Yankee's eyes as he'd stretched out a bloodstained hand to him in the heartbeat before he died.

Billy swept the daguerreotype out from under her hand and studied it through narrowed eyes before tossing it back down. "I've never seen this man before."

"Oh, no? Then explain this." Esmerelda whipped the paper from the table and presented it to him with a regal flourish.

Billy cocked one eyebrow at her before cautiously unfolding it. He hadn't even reached the third paragraph before his lips began to twitch. The handwritten report related a tale more melodramatic than anything he'd ever found between the pages of a dime novel. A tragic account of a botched stage robbery, a virginal girl journeying to a Mexican convent to take her vows, a noble and naive young man who took a bullet in the heart rather than allow his traveling companion to be ravished by a gang of bloodthirsty outlaws. As he read the final paragraph, written in a prose so purple as to be nearly black, he turned away so Esmerelda wouldn't see the tears that had began to fill his eyes.

To his keen shock, he felt the slight weight of her hand descend on his quivering shoulder. "There now, Mr. Darling. Perhaps your soul isn't quite as jaded as you feared." Her voice deepened to a smoky murmur, making him wonder what she would sound like at night with the lamps extinguished and nothing between them but skin and darkness. "Even for a villain such as yourself, God always offers a chance for repentance and redemption."

Billy could no longer contain himself. A strangled whoop of laughter escaped him. As Esmerelda circled around to peer into his face, he swiped his streaming eyes, unable to hide the guffaws shaking his body. He had to wait until they subsided to chuckles before he could muster the strength to rattle the paper at her.

"Whoever wrote this piece of"—he cleared his throat before continuing—"*tripe* failed to do their research. I don't rob stages for a living, ma'am. I apprehend stage robbers. Perhaps the subtlety eludes you, being from Boston and all, but there is a distinct difference."

Esmerelda snatched the paper from his hand, a frown betraying her first trace of doubt. "I don't understand. Mr. Snorton swore that—"

"Mr. Snorton?" Billy repeated. "You wouldn't be referring to a Mr. Flavil Snorton, would you?" When she only pressed her lips together in mute defiance, he held a hand up to his breastbone. "Little man, about yea high with ears bigger than he is and a voice like a gelded grasshopper."

Esmerelda's lips slowly parted until her jaw hung slack. Billy gently nudged it back up with one finger, enabling her to whisper, "He told me he was the very best detective the Pinkertons could provide."

Billy drew his hand back from the silky skin beneath her jaw, thinking he'd do well to keep it to himself. "He's not a Pinkerton. Never was. He's a card sharp, a confidence artist. Hell, Flavil Snorton is wanted in more states and territories than I am. I ran him in myself in Kansas City only last summer, which might explain why my name sprang so smoothly to his lips when he was looking for someone to blame for killing your brother."

Esmerelda began to back away from him, her eyes growing wilder than an unbroken filly's. "Why should I believe you? You claim Mr. Snorton is a confidence artist, but you're nothing more than a man who'll sell his gun to the highest bidder."

"Did you go to the Pinkertons, or did Snorton come to you?"

Her brow furrowed. "I went to the Pinkertons when Bartholomew first disappeared. But they turned me away because I didn't have enough money to hire them. Two months later Mr. Snorton showed up on my doorstep. He informed me that the Pinkertons had been secretly working on the case all along and if I could just raise enough cash to finance his journey west . . ." She blinked up at him as if emerging from a blinding fog. "I closed my school and collected all my accounts. I sold my mother's pianoforte. I gave him everything except the pittance I believed I would need to fetch Bartholomew home when he was finally found."

"And in return he mailed you your brother's belongings in a nice tidy package all tied up with brown paper and string. Case closed."

As Esmerelda sank down on the bed, clutching her stomach, Billy almost regretted his ruthlessness. He could remember only too well how it felt to be sickened by your own naïveté.

Her chin began to quiver, giving him a brief moment

of panic. But instead of bursting into tears, she clenched her teeth against a spasm of rage. "Why that wretched little man. That miserable, pathetic . . ."

Billy's ears perked up. Was there a chance the saintly Miss Fine might actually resort to swearing?

". . . jug-eared dwarf!" she finished, leaving him vaguely disappointed. "Oh, dear God," she whispered, gazing up at him with dawning horror. "I almost shot and killed an innocent man."

Billy propped one boot on the bedstead, practicing his most lascivious grin. "I may be many things, Miss Fine, but innocent isn't one of them." Gratified by the return of color to her cheeks, he shrugged. "If you'd have killed me, you could have just marched into the U.S. marshal's office in Santa Fe, collected your reward, and been back on your merry way to Boston, believing your brother's death avenged."

"My brother's death . . . ?" she echoed hoarsely.

She bounded to her feet, forcing him to stumble backward or be trampled beneath her dainty kid boots. As she paced the length of the room, he winced in anticipation. But she whipped around a scant inch before her head could slam into the sloping ceiling. Her eyes sparkled with elation. "Don't you see? My brother may not be dead after all!"

Billy hated himself for dousing her hopes, but knew it would be crueler to kindle them. "You shouldn't set your heart on that, ma'am. You do still have his belongings."

Esmerelda carelessly swept the trinkets back into the envelope. "But what do they really prove? That he was robbed by one of Snorton's accomplices? That he might have run out of money and sold his valuables to buy food or supplies? What if he's out there somewhere? Lost and alone?" Her expansive gesture seemed to imply that every inch of territory west of St. Louis was nothing but a vast wasteland. She cocked her head to the side, giving him a speculative look that made the hair on his nape tingle with apprehension, just as it did before an Indian attack or a particularly ill turn in the weather. "Sheriff McGuire said you were the best tracker in the Territory. If anyone can help me find him, you can."

Billy couldn't have been any more flabbergasted had she proposed marriage. He splayed an open hand on his chest. "Me? You want to *hire* me? Just a couple of hours ago you wanted to kill me."

Her cheek dimpled in a coaxing smile. "Ah, but that was nothing more than a regrettable misunderstanding, Mr. Darling."

For the first time, his name sounded like an endearment falling from her lips instead of an epithet. He didn't much care for its effect on him.

He shoved the plate of beefsteak across the table at her. "I think you'd best eat something, ma'am. Hunger must be making you loco."

She shoved it right back at him. "I've lost my appetite. And my brother. You have brothers, Mr. Darling. How would you feel if one of them disappeared without a trace?"

"Lucky," he replied shortly. Whenever one of *his* brothers went missing, he never had to look any farther than the nearest jail, whorehouse, or saloon.

A door slammed in the next room. Esmerelda shot the wall a nervous glance, but Billy ignored it. Dorothea must have an early customer, probably one of those strapping Zimmerman boys from the lumber mill. They'd been known to indulge more than just their appetite for bratwurst and strudel during their afternoon break.

"Didn't you just tell me you were destitute?" he asked. "How do you intend to pay me for my services?"

"How much do you cost?"

"More than you've got."

A deep-throated groan interrupted them, followed by a feminine squeal of delight and the rhythmic squeak of a rusty iron bedframe.

Esmerelda slowly turned to gape at the faded cabbage roses on the wallpaper, as if she couldn't quite believe what she was hearing. A haze of pink crept up the delicate curve of her jaw.

She suddenly seemed to be having great difficulty meeting his eyes. And breathing. Her hand fluttered at the air. "Would it be possible for us to go somewhere else to negotiate our transaction? This hardly seems to be the appropriate place."

Billy grinned, afraid he was going to bust out laughing all over again if she started fanning herself. "On the contrary, Miss Fine. Transactions are negotiated nearly every hour of the day and night in this establishment. But if it'll make you more comfortable . . ." He marched over to the wall and banged on it with his fist. "Hey! Keep it down over there! I've got a lady in here."

His request was greeted by muffled laughter, both male and female, and a resumption of the moans and squeaking at a more leisurely pace. As he sauntered back over to the table, Esmerelda gave him a look of withering disdain.

He knew she was done trying to charm him. He just didn't know if the hollow feeling in his belly was regret or relief.

The woman was clearly a hazard, both to herself and to his peace of mind. He could just imagine her marching into seedy saloons all over the Territory, seeking a tracker to find her greenhorn of a brother. The image sent an invisible shudder through him. He'd seen too many innocent young girls come west to seek their fortunes only to end up flat on their backs like Dorothea in the next room, servicing immigrant mill hands and grateful cowboys for silver dollars. He doubted the genteel Miss Fine would survive such a fate. His only hope was to send her scurrying to catch the next stagecoach out of Calamity.

"I may not have cash on hand, Mr. Darling," she said, "but I can assure you that I have other resources."

He looked her up and down, deliberately insinuating the worst. "Oh, I never doubted that."

Their gazes locked as the sounds next door escalated to a wild crescendo. Billy's room suddenly seemed too small and close for them to stand without touching, even though neither of them had moved.

A guttural roar nearly drowned out a woman's sobbing moan. After a brief silence, the clink of coins was followed by the thud of a door gently closing. Zimmerman probably hadn't even bothered to unhook his suspenders, Billy thought wryly.

Esmerelda tore her gaze away from his with visible difficulty and took a shuddering gulp of air. "I'll have you know, sir, that my grandfather is a peer of the realm."

He rocked back on his heels, feigning ignorance. "Is that a treatable condition?"

"He's a duke," she bit off. "An extremely wealthy man." When he failed to drop to one knee or doff his hat, she hastily added, "And he dotes on my brother. He always has. Once my letter informing him that Bartholomew is missing reaches London, I'm sure he'll be more than eager to offer a handsome reward for his nephew's return."

Billy squinted at her. "Dead or alive?"

If looks could kill, she'd have no further need of her derringer. Her jaw was still clenched when she lowered her lethal gaze and began to pace around the table. "Bartholomew is Grandfather's sole heir, you see, and there's always been a deep and abiding affection between the two of them. I mailed my letter over four months ago when I first began to prepare for my journey west. Why, Grandpapa may have already received it! And if so, he probably caught the first steamer departing for America. He could arrive at any moment! That's why it's even more imperative that you agree to help me, Mr. Darling. You'll get every penny I owe you. You have my word on it."

She stopped near enough to touch him, those maple candy eyes of hers melting to an imploring amber.

Billy tipped back his hat, pretending to ponder her offer. He had played his first hand of poker at four years old. He could recognize a bluff when he saw one. The virtuous Miss Fine was lying through her pretty white teeth. Her deceit intrigued him, but not enough to dissuade him from trying to chase her back to Boston where she belonged.

It seemed that task was going to require more drastic measures than he'd anticipated. Which was precisely why he decided to call her bluff for the second time in that day.

"I'll accept your offer, Duchess, but only on my terms. If your grandfather hasn't arrived with gold in hand by the time I locate this brother of yours, then I'll require payment in full." He cupped her cheek in his hand and captured her gaze with his own, determined to leave no doubt whatsoever about the nature of his demand. "From you."

As he awaited her response, he allowed his thumb to roam freely over the inviting softness of her lower lip. Her eyes widened. Her lips trembled, parting slightly beneath the pressure of his thumb. Her breath quickened, causing her small, plump breasts to rise and fall in an uneven cadence.

Billy had anticipated the effect his touch would have on her, but he was not prepared for its effect on him. Desire squeezed his groin in a ruthless vise, making him wish for a brief but piercing moment that he was exactly the sort of man he was pretending to be.

Emotions flickered across her face. Fear. Outrage. Desperation. And something more elusive. Something that made him wonder just what she would do if he slid his hand through the disheveled skein of her hair, tipped her head back, and caressed her lips with his mouth instead of his thumb.

But before he could succumb to that dangerous temptation, her expression hardened to contempt.

Billy braced himself for the slap he knew was coming. The slap he deserved for daring to make a lady such a scandalous proposition.

Her face was as pale as milk, but her eyes glittered with scorn. "Very well, Mr. Darling. Consider yourself hired."

"What?" Billy nearly shouted the word. His hand fell numbly to his side. He'd expected her to run shrieking from the room in maidenly horror, not accept his crude proposal.

But it seemed he had underestimated both her determination and her devotion to her brother. A mistake he dared not make again.

While he stood there, still reeling with shock, she bustled around the room with businesslike efficiency, tying on her battered bonnet and gathering up her belongings. "I shall be at the hotel, assuming this provincial village has one. I'll meet you at the restaurant promptly at seven tomorrow morning so we can discuss our plans."

Billy's eyes widened further. He hadn't risen before ten since he'd retired to the whorehouse to recover from his gunshot wound.

She snapped on her gloves, then hesitated, frowning in dismay. "I hate to trouble you, sir, but might I borrow enough money to pay for a night's lodging?"

He reached into his pocket and handed her a fat wad of his poker winnings. She could have taken the whole thing and he would have been too dazed to protest.

She peeled off one of the smaller bills and handed back the rest. "Just add it to my tab," she suggested, her smile sharp enough to raise welts.

"My pleasure, ma'am." He suspected his cocky grin was only a wan shadow of its former self.

She started for the door, then returned to sweep up the plate of beefsteak and potatoes. "No point in letting a perfectly good supper go to waste."

When she had departed, the plate cradled tenderly in the crook of her arm, Billy sank down on the bed and dragged off his hat, not knowing whether to laugh or cry. Miss Patches surveyed him from the rocker, her feline hauteur unruffled, while Sadie waddled out from under the bed to lean against his knee.

He gave the hound a distracted scratch before raking a hand through his own hair. "Well, I'll be damned," he breathed. "I will be damned."

But for the first time in more years than he could remember, he didn't feel like it.

CHAPTER SEVEN

My dearest Grandfather, Esmerelda wrote in her neat script. She nibbled on the end of the fountain pen for a thoughtful moment before going back and marking out the *My* and the *est.*

"Dear Grandfather," she read aloud.

Scowling, she slashed through the *Dear,* leaving only *Grandfather.* She had thought to pen an earnest plea for deliverance, but even that stark salutation rang false to her ears. She crumpled the stationery in her fist before dragging a fresh sheet across the desk. It was well past midnight, but restlessness plucked at her nerves, making sleep impossible. If Sheriff McGuire hadn't been kind enough to retrieve her trunk and violin case from the old cowpoke and have it sent to the hotel, she would have been penning her letter on the back of Billy Darling's Wanted poster.

Lord Wyndham, she scribbled, forsaking her flawless penmanship for an impassioned scrawl, *It is with great trepidation and no little regret that I am writing to inform you that due to your enduring neglect and indifference, I have been forced to barter my virtue to a ruthless desperado.*

She pressed a hand to her cheek, distracted by the memory of Billy Darling's possessive touch. He had sought to bully her, yet his touch had been as tender as a lover's caress. The realization provoked a curious shiver that she prayed was fear. She'd nearly killed a man today, then lied shamelessly to his face. She didn't think she could bear to add wantonness to her growing list of sins.

Curling her bare toes beneath the hem of her gown, she resumed her brisk scribbling. *I trust you will suffer no distress on my behalf, since you never have before. Ever your devoted granddaughter . . . Esmerelda Fine.*

She dotted the final *i* with savage violence. The pen spat an ugly blob of ink onto the page.

Groaning, Esmerelda lowered her head to the desk, tempted to bang it in frustration. She could post this letter at dawn and it still wouldn't reach England for weeks. And even if it were to miraculously wing its way there on the morrow, she knew that it would meet with nothing but her grandfather's apathy and scorn. She'd lingered in Boston for nearly three months after posting that first letter to him, hoping for a reply that she'd known in her heart would never come.

She tossed the letter on the growing pile, wondering what had possessed her to weave such an absurd fable. To boast that her grandfather would cross an ocean to come to her rescue when he wouldn't cross a London street to toss a farthing in her cup if she were begging barefoot in the snow.

Once she'd started lying, she couldn't seem to stop. Her desperation had only kindled the fantasies she'd never dared admit, even to Bartholomew. Fantasies of a man she might call "Grandpapa"—a man with snowy white hair and a bristling mustache that would tickle her cheek when he folded her into his strong, loving arms. A man who would stroke her hair and murmur, "There, there, girl. You've done well, but there's nothing more for you to do. It's time to come home now."

Although the dream was sweet, it left a bitter taste in her mouth. Because she knew when it was over, she would be left, as always, with nothing to rely on but her own wits.

And a dangerous stranger.

Since her parents' death, she'd refused to let herself need anyone. But she needed Billy Darling. Without him, she might never find Bartholomew.

Her brother might actually be alive! She savored a thrill of joy at the thought. She'd found it difficult enough to carry on when he'd ran away, but believing him dead had been nearly intolerable.

She closed her eyes, overcome by memories of the first time she had almost lost him. They'd been at the cemetery placing flowers on their parents' freshly turned graves when he had put his little hand in hers and tugged, complaining that his tummy hurt. Despite the oppressive heat of the July day, she had glanced down to find him shivering violently.

Stricken with absolute terror, she had nursed him day and night, pouring every ounce of her energy into holding the shadow of death at bay. When the doctor had paid his final visit, shaking his head sadly as he snapped his black bag shut, she had cradled Bartholomew's bloated little body against her chest and begged God to let him live. Guilt had torn at her even then because she didn't know if she was more afraid of losing him or of being left all alone. Tears had coursed down her cheeks as she vowed that she would take care of him, would raise him to be the man her parents had always wanted him to be. If only God would let him live . . .

Esmerelda opened her eyes, surprised to find them stinging but dry. Taking care of Bartholomew had been the sole focus of her life since that moment. She had thought only to hold him close and keep him safe, but she had squeezed too tightly and he had slipped right through her fingers. Losing him had been like losing herself, or at least the only person she still remembered how to be.

Hugging her shawl around her, she padded to the window and drew back the ruffled curtain. The town of Calamity slumbered in the moonlight, a tiny oasis of civilization in a vast sea of wilderness. Most of its lamps had been extinguished, but burning in the attic window of the clapboard house that sat catty-cornered across from the hotel was a single candle flame.

Mesmerized by its flickering glow, Esmerelda leaned her brow against the warped pane. Was Mr. Darling tucked beneath his faded quilt with a drowsing cat snuggled against his side? Had he drifted to sleep while reading one of those dime novels he denied owning but plainly cherished?

The front door of the establishment swung open, shattering the cozy image. A cowboy staggered onto the sidewalk, a woman tucked beneath his arm. She wiggled out of his drunken grip, but he snatched her back, grinding both his mouth and his hips against her in a crude rhythm impossible for even a spinster like Esmerelda to misinterpret.

She ducked behind the curtain, her cheeks burning. When she dared to peek back out, the woman was gone and the cowboy was lurching down the street toward the saloon. Her gaze flicked back to the candle. Whoever slept in that house, including the occupant of that attic room, doubtless did not sleep alone.

How Mr. Darling spent his nights didn't matter, she reminded herself sternly, as long as he spent his days searching for her brother. Once Bartholomew was found . . . well, she would just find a way to renegotiate their little bargain.

She'd always prided herself on her bartering skills. Her parents' bodies had still been laid out in the parlor in their Sunday best when the creditors had descended on their modest house like a flock of vultures, demanding payment of her papa's outstanding debts. Fearing they would call the constable and demand that she and Bartholomew be carted off to the Griswald Home for Orphans and Foundlings, where they might be forever separated, Esmerelda had managed to fend them off with a clever mix of promises and threats. She'd never begged or stolen, but neither had she ever paid a dime on Monday that could be put off until Friday. If she'd learned anything in the past thirteen years, it was how to handle creditors.

Her only fear was that a man like Billy Darling just might be more than she could handle.

"Sweet dreams, Mr. Darling," she murmured, letting the curtain fall.

Had she lingered at the window a moment longer, she would have seen the shadows come creeping across his room in the instant before the candle was abruptly snuffed.

Billy awoke to darkness and the cold barrel of a Colt revolver shoved against his temple. That didn't stop him from reaching for his gun, just as they'd known it wouldn't. The butt of the revolver slammed into his jaw. The coppery tang of blood exploded on his tongue. There were at least four of them. They should have brought five, he thought grimly, counting them lucky that the darkness blinded them to his icy grin.

He would have never survived being born the runt of the Darling litter if he hadn't learned how to fight dirty, how to kick and gouge and bite whatever appendage came closest to his teeth. His foot connected smartly with the nearest groin. A bit-off curse deepened into a tortured groan. The men swarmed over him like a horde of apes, all grunting and swearing and breathing heavier than he was. He knew Sadie would be cowering beneath the bed, but an offended screech warned him that one of them had stepped on Miss Patches's tail. The long, fluffy appendage was the calico's pride and joy.

Now he was really riled.

He got in a flurry of savage licks before they managed to bind his arms behind him and shove a feed sack over his head. They herded him down the back stairs none too gently, slamming his head against the wall when he tried to bolt. He fervently hoped none of the girls would hear the commotion and get scared.

The fecund smell of manure and fresh hay penetrated the musty feed sack, along with the whickers of agitated horses. Even before they shoved him to a sitting position against a wooden partition and jerked the sack from his head, Billy knew they'd taken him to the livery stable.

He took his own sweet time licking the blood from the corner of his mouth before lifting his head to meet the eyes of the man standing over him. "Winstead," he said without a trace of surprise.

The man offered him a curt nod, his smile remarkably pleasant. "Darling."

The man's gray-peppered hair was parted in the middle and slicked to either side. His eyes were like chips of coal, opaque and glittering all at the same time. His clothing was impeccably tasteful—his shoes polished, the creases in his wool trousers crisp, the stripes of his double-breasted vest perfectly matched. He held a leather satchel tucked under one arm.

Of all the U.S. marshals Billy had tangled with, Winstead was the only one truly worthy of his contempt. And his respect. He had served as a colonel in the Union Army during the war and Billy would go to his grave regretting that he'd been too young to face those glittering eyes across a battlefield.

Winstead's goons huddled behind him. One glowered at Billy through an eye swollen nearly shut. Another cradled an arm cocked at an awkward angle. Behind the four men stood a pale and silent sentinel.

"Et tu, Brute?" Billy murmured.

Even in the flickering lantern light, Drew's flush was evident.

"Don't be talkin' that French filth to Mr. Winstead," snarled one of the men. "You want me to smack him, sir?"

Winstead waved off the offer. "Don't be so hasty to brand your friend a traitor, Mr. Darling. Sheriff McGuire simply accepted our invitation with a bit more grace than you. I always like to keep the local law apprised of our endeavors." He drew a gold watch from his vest pocket and gave it a cursory glance. "I do hope you'll forgive me for rousing you so late in the evening, but I have a job for you."

"I suspected as much. Wouldn't it have been easier to just send a telegram?"

Again that implacable smile. "Easier, perhaps. But not nearly as discreet."

Never one to waste anyone's time, especially his own, the marshal flipped open the satchel and pulled out a rolled-up sheet of paper. With a snap of his wrist, he unfurled the poster in front of Billy's nose. "I want this man apprehended."

Billy squinted at the paper, then up at the marshal. "You'll have to forgive me, sir. I don't read so good with my hands tied. If you could just . . . ?" He shrugged to indicate his bound hands and was gratified to see every one of Winstead's men take a hasty step backward.

Billy blinked up at the marshal, giving him the same look he used to give his ma when she stormed out to the barn looking for the culprit who'd filched her freshly baked blueberry pie. She'd always said he could coax the devil into letting him out of hell with that look. She never could bring herself to whip him, not even after she'd spent an hour scrubbing the blueberry stains from beneath his fingernails.

Winstead wasn't quite as gullible.

"Sheriff, would you do the honor?" he called over his shoulder, earning an audible sigh of relief from his men.

They all but licked their bruised and swollen lips with anticipation as Drew squatted beside their captive to struggle with the crude knots. "I oughta break your nose," Billy muttered without moving his lips.

"I wish you wouldn't," Drew murmured, the exchange hidden by the silver waterfall of his hair. "It would ruin my profile."

The ropes unfurled. Drew slowly backed away, holding both hands in the air as if his friend held a loaded pistol on him instead of just a nasty glare.

Billy surprised them all by not bounding to his feet the instant he was free. He simply plucked the handbill from Winstead's hand and settled back against the stall to study it.

He read the caption at the bottom of the page before snorting up at Winstead. "'Black Bart?' What kind of self-respecting outlaw outside the pages of a dime novel would call himself Black Bart?"

"A very accomplished one, I'm afraid. The kind who robs banks, trains, and stagecoaches with equal flair. The kind who must be stopped."

Billy scowled down at the sketch. The artist had captured the outlaw's image in bold strokes. He'd never seen a dimple look quite so malicious or a boyish smirk so sinister. A dark beard shadowed the rogue's jaw, but did little to disguise the baby-faced cheeks underneath.

Cheeks that had only too recently borne the tender caress of Esmerelda Fine's hand.

Billy sent his stunned gaze traveling back up the sketch only to find himself staring into the twinkling black eyes of Mr. Bartholomew Fine III.

CHAPTER EIGHT

Meanness coursed through his veins. Billy could feel it slithering through him like rattlesnake venom, numbing first his limbs and then his heart. If Winstead and his men had known him better, they would have seen it, too. It was there in the set of his jaw, the faint thinning of his lips, the steely glint in his eye. He had called Esmerelda's bluff only to discover that she was holding a secret trump of her own.

As he came to his feet, only Drew was wise enough to back toward the stable door, plainly fearing they were all about to witness an eruption of that notorious Darling temper.

Disappointment and relief mingled in his expression when Billy simply shrugged and said, "Never seen the man before in my life."

"Oh, but I think you have," Winstead said. "I believe

you just recently made his acquaintance, perhaps this very afternoon when a certain charming young lady visited your room."

"How did you . . . ?" Billy's narrowed gaze swept the marshal's deputies, easily locating the one with the cockiest smirk. "So it wasn't one of the Zimmerman boys with Dorothea after all. Maybe you need to find a spy who's not so quick on the trigger, marshal. Your man couldn't have been in that room more than three minutes at the most."

Drew and the other deputies snickered. The man's smirk hardened to a snarl as he took a step toward Billy, growling beneath his breath.

Winstead waved him back. "He was there long enough to learn what I needed. That you were entertaining a woman who was attempting to hire you to find the man in this poster."

Billy nodded. "His sister, Esmerelda."

Winstead snorted. "Surely you didn't fall for that tired old ruse. An outlaw like Bart Fine probably has *sisters* in every cowtown and miner's camp from Kansas City to San Francisco."

There was something about Winstead's leer that made Billy want to smash him in the mouth. "She was pretty damn convincing when she tried to put a bullet through my heart because she thought I'd killed her baby brother."

"So I heard. An impressive and passionate display of her ardor, was it not? But was it the ardor of a devoted sister? Or a desperate lover?"

Billy could neither defend nor deny. To hide his troubled expression, he swung around, instinctively seeking the stall that housed Belle, his own mare.

Winstead followed him step for step, pressing his advantage. "I have it on good authority that Bart Fine is an only child. Fine doesn't know it, but I've even had the Pinkertons tracking this woman since she left the Boston residence she once shared with him. Until today, we didn't realize that she believed him dead. We thought she was coming west to rendezvous with the scoundrel. Since you were kind enough to persuade her that he might indeed be alive, we're hoping she'll do just that. When she does, I want you to be there to take him into custody."

Billy reached into the stall and stroked his mare's velvety nose. "You want me to use the girl for bait?"

"You can use the girl in any way you see fit, Mr. Darling." Winstead's callous words sent a primal shiver of anticipation through him. "I've arranged my own bait. I prefer to think of her as insurance."

"What's this fellow done to ruffle your feathers, marshal?" Billy asked, deliberately deepening his affable southern drawl. He'd learned through harsh experience that it was the most effective way to get someone to underestimate him.

"Made off with a shipment of treasury gold on its way to a prominent San Francisco bank. A shipment I was responsible for protecting."

"Made you look like a fool, eh? Well, no man should have to tolerate that. Not even a Yankee." He responded to Winstead's glare with a mocking grin. "Why do you need me? Why don't you just arrest him yourself? You do have an army of marshals and Pinkertons at your disposal, not to mention these fine upstanding young deputies."

He indicated the battered men with a sweep of his arm. They glared murder at him.

Winstead glanced over his shoulder at his men and snapped, "You're dismissed. Meet me back at the horses."

"But, sir, I don't think that would be a wise—"

"That's an order."

The deputies obeyed, skulking out of the barn like chastened schoolboys. Drew made a valiant effort to tiptoe after them.

"Stay," Billy commanded. "The marshal here might not want any witnesses, but I damn sure do."

Billy had always thought of Winstead as a straight shooter, but tonight a disarming aura of furtiveness clung to the man. "Why is this job different from any other?" He nodded down at his rumpled drawers. "Why'd you have to drag me out of my bed half-naked in the middle of the night to discuss it? We've done this a dozen times. You tell me who you want. I bring him in."

"Because this time I don't want him brought in."

Billy would have liked to blame the chill that shot down his spine to his shirtless state, but couldn't. "I'm a bounty hunter, marshal, not a killer for hire." It galled him that this was the second time in twenty-four hours he'd had to explain the distinction.

"You killed Estes, didn't you?"

"Only after he shot me in the back," he replied evenly.

Winstead sighed. "I'm not asking you to shoot this man down in cold blood. Just to arrange a little . . . mishap after he's taken into custody. He might take a tumble off his horse, slip beneath the water while crossing a river . . ."

"Choke on some stale jerky," Billy provided.

"Yes!" Winstead cried, oblivious to his sarcasm. "That's precisely the sort of subtlety I'm looking for."

Billy exchanged a dry look with Drew. "And if I accept the job, what's in it for me?"

"Your life, Mr. Darling. Your life for his."

The sparkle had disappeared from Winstead's eyes, leaving them utterly flat. The man was serious. Dead serious.

"If you reject this assignment, my deputies are prepared to take you back to Santa Fe tonight. You will stand trial for the murder of Juan Estes and most likely hang."

"I guess I can count on you to handpick the jury."

"I already have."

Silence hung in the air, thick with tension, until Billy chuckled softly. "Go to hell, Winstead. And take your deputies with you."

He started for the door.

"Wait!" Winstead cried. The raw desperation in his voice revealed that he had far less confidence in his men than he'd pretended to have. "What if I sweeten the deal? I might be able to offer you more than just amnesty this time."

Billy kept walking.

"What if I could promise you that badge you've always wanted?"

Billy froze, then slowly swung around. Winstead had extended his hand. Lying on his palm was a gleaming badge. The tin star seemed to twinkle in the lantern light, more out of Billy's reach than if it had been hanging in the night sky. He hated Winstead more in that moment than he ever had before.

"What good would a badge do me? We both know my first official act as deputy U.S. marshal would have to be arresting my own brothers and watching them hang."

"Not if I can guarantee amnesty not only for you, but for them as well. Provided, of course, that they agree to practice their . . . um . . . trade a bit farther south of the border in the future." Winstead held out the badge. "Go on. Take it. Try it on for size."

Painfully aware of Drew's troubled scrutiny, Billy reached for the badge. As he closed his fingers around the cool tin, the clasp's pin stabbed his thumb. A single drop of blood welled from its tender pad, the pain both sharp and sweet.

Winstead hooked his thumbs in his vest pockets, making a visible effort to salvage some of his genteel charm. "As you well know, I'm not a stingy man. If you cooperate, you can also expect the usual reward of five hundred dollars."

"One thousand," Billy replied without batting an eyelash. "Five hundred in advance."

Winstead hesitated only a heartbeat before offering his hand. When Billy didn't even deign to glance at it, the marshal drew a bloated canvas pouch from the satchel. "You'll receive a signed writ of amnesty for you and your brothers only *after* the job is done to my satisfaction."

Billy tossed the pouch to a stunned Drew.

The marshal fastened the satchel, his crisp motions betraying his eagerness to cleanse himself of the taint of his own dirty dealings. "Black Bart was last seen in the vicinity of Eulalie. One of my deputies has determined that his gang may have a hideout in the hills near there. I've taken the liberty of arranging to have another shipment of treasury gold pass through that area on Friday morning. The gold will make a fortuitous overnight stop at the Eulalie First National Bank. I've heard the accommodations in the vault there are quite lovely."

Drew paled, his plans for a peaceful retirement evaporating into thin air like the smoke from a Comanche peace pipe. "Hell, Winstead, if you've already leaked that information, you'll have every outlaw from Dodge City to San Francisco crawling over the Territory."

"Perhaps. But Mr. Darling here is only responsible for apprehending one of them." He turned his gaze on Billy. "I've made sure that both the bank employees and the local law will be expecting you. I would so hate for you to catch a bullet in the back for your trouble."

Billy frowned. "If you've already got the trap set, then why do you need the woman?"

"As I told you before—as insurance. I believe Mr. Fine will think twice about opening fire or making a run for it if he walks into that bank and comes face-to-face with his devoted mistress."

Mistress. Billy could hold four aces and the king of spades in his hand without betraying so much as a gleeful twitch of his lips, but there was something about that word that made him flinch.

A ghost of a smile flickered across the marshal's face. "I should warn you that our Black Bart has demonstrated quite a flair for the dramatic. No blowing up the safe in the dark of night for him. He prefers to thunder in at high noon with fire in his eyes and guns blazing." Winstead leaned closer, challenge glittering in his eyes. "So, Mr. Darling . . . will you be there when he does?"

Billy crumpled the sketch of Bartholomew Fine in his fist without realizing it. "Oh, I'll be there. You can count on it."

When Winstead had taken his precious satchel and gone, Drew blew out a low, shaky whistle. "Well, William, my lad, I guess I can go tear up that Wanted notice that bears such an unflattering likeness to you."

"I wouldn't be too hasty about that."

Drew frowned, more disturbed by his friend's acceptance of such an unsavory job than he cared to let on. "But didn't you just agree to—"

"Did I?" Billy blinked at him, his eyes as artless as a child's. "I never took Winstead's hand. I only took his money."

Drew cocked his head to the side, growing more confused by the second.

Billy shrugged. "I've been accused of selling myself to the highest bidder. Maybe it's time I started doing just that."

"But what could be worth more to you than your life, one thousand dollars, and a badge?"

Billy held the gleaming star up to the light, the expression in his narrowed eyes oddly unsettling. "That, sheriff, is just what I intend to find out."

CHAPTER NINE

The woman who called herself Esmerelda Fine slept in a puddle of buttery dawn sunlight. Billy gently eased the door of her hotel room shut behind him, her unexpected vulnerability softening the grim set of his lips. He had expected to find the uncompromising Miss Fine sleeping flat on her back, her hands folded neatly over her chest as if the undertaker had just arranged them.

Instead, she sprawled on her stomach, one leg half-cocked to her waist, her rump in the air. A checkered quilt lay in a defeated heap on the floor, vanquished in what appeared to be a violent battle of wills. The awkward angle of her leg caused her gown to ride high on her thighs and hug her bottom like a pair of loving hands.

Billy studied the alluring mound with the practiced eye of a man who'd spent the past three months of his life living in a brothel. Miss Fine might wear a corset and bustle because it was the current fashion, but she certainly had no need of the wire and horsehair contraptions to cinch in her waist or enhance the curves nature had given her.

She rolled to her back, flinging out one arm as if in supplication. Her hair spilled over the pillow like cinnamon sugar and an endearing little porcine snuffle escaped her delicate nostrils. Fascinated, Billy drifted toward the bed. Her lack of restraint in sleep was at direct odds with the stilted demeanor she wore like a starched veil when awake. Which only deepened his suspicion that it might be nothing more than a cunning disguise.

He scowled and fingered his swollen lip. Until his midnight encounter with Winstead, he'd had every intention of meeting her for breakfast in the hotel restaurant, pressing fifty dollars into her gloved hand, and putting her on the first stagecoach heading east. With or without her consent.

But Winstead's words had changed all that. He never could abide a mystery, and he had every intention of finding out just who wanted Bartholomew Fine the most and why.

Billy allowed his gaze to drift downward, lingering at the softness of her breasts and belly. He wondered what Winstead would have thought had his spy lingered long enough to learn of their shocking bargain. Esmerelda had agreed to his proposition with unsettling ease. Perhaps she made it a habit to offer that tender young body of hers to strangers in exchange for her brother's life.

Or her lover's life.

He searched her face, forcing himself to be ruthless. He still couldn't find any trace of the impish outlaw who called himself Black Bart. Sleep had heightened her color, reducing her freckles to a sprinkle of desert sand across the bridge of her nose. Her lashes curled against her cheeks like a whittler's mahogany shavings. Whatever her relationship to the outlaw, Billy couldn't afford to forget that her devotion to the man had nearly cost him his life.

As he leaned over her, his nerves sang to life as they always did at the approach of danger. His keenly honed instincts had kept him alive through many an encounter that should have proven deadly. They'd allowed him to dodge Yankee bullets and Comanche arrows and had prodded him to take a step to the right instead of the left in the instant before Juan Estes had pulled the trigger of his Remington revolver and shot him in the back. The bullet had grazed his ribs, leaving his heart untouched.

He was afraid he might not be so lucky this time.

He sank down on the bed, resting a hand on each side of the feather pillow. He couldn't remember the last time he'd woken up next to a woman without stale whiskey on her breath. Esmerelda smelled warm and sweet, like Miss Patches's fur on a chilly winter night. It was all he could do not to bury his face in the silken tangle of her hair. He'd assured her that the Darling men preferred their women conscious, but in her case, he just might be willing to make an exception.

When Esmerelda opened her eyes to find Billy Darling looming over her, her first thought was that she'd sold her soul to the devil and he'd wasted no time in coming to collect. Billy's thick golden lashes gave his eyes an angelic cast, but the cynical curl of his lips reminded her that he was not one of God's favored, but one of his fallen. She obliged him by letting out a shriek of the damned.

He winced and clapped a hand over her mouth. "Was that a scream, or were you of a mind to sing the Doxology?"

She glared at him.

He grinned at her. "Mornin', Duchess."

Desperate to dislodge the gentle but firm pressure of his palm against her lips, Esmerelda sank her teeth into the tender pad below his forefinger.

He jerked his hand back, then brought it to his lips to suck on the wound. Esmerelda felt a curious stirring in her belly at the sight of his mouth where hers had so recently been.

He lowered his hand, slanting her a reproachful look. "My mare used to nip like that. Until I taught her to trust me."

"You certainly didn't teach her to trust you by sneaking up on her while she was sleeping." Addled by his nearness, Esmerelda sat up and glanced wildly around the room. "How did you get in here?"

He held up a shiny brass key.

She blinked in dismay. "Do you have a key for every chamber in Calamity, Mr. Darling?"

"Only the ones I'm paying for." He dropped the key into the pocket of his buff-colored shirt. "It wasn't very hard to convince the hotel manager that the gentleman who pays for the lady's room should be allowed to come and go as he pleases."

She scooted as far away from him as the feather mattress would allow. "Why, he must think . . ."

"The very worst." Billy tipped back his hat with one finger, revealing an unrepentant dimple. "So if you want to go ahead with that scream, it might just increase my notoriety with the ladies."

If appearances were any indication, his notoriety didn't need any increasing. If anything, he looked even more debauched than he had yesterday. A day's growth of dark gold stubble shadowed his jaw, carving intriguing hollows in the clean planes of his face. A fresh bruise smudged his cheekbone. Esmerelda resisted a ridiculous urge to try and dab it away with the hem of the sheet, but she could not stop herself from touching a fingertip to the swollen split at the corner of his mouth.

"Who hurt you?" she murmured, thrown off balance by the depth of her dismay.

Billy caught her wrist, freezing her hand in its instinctive caress. Although he applied no pressure, she was achingly aware of his strength and the fragility of her own fine bones.

His aw-shucks affability vanished, making her realize it had been nothing but a facade all along. She would have almost sworn that something subtle had shifted in his attitude toward her. Something perilous.

"I had a bad dream," he drawled.

A bar brawl, more likely, Esmerelda thought. Probably over one of the buxom occupants of Miss Mellie's house.

She lowered her eyes, sliding her wrist out of his grip only because he allowed her to do so. "I've had my share of nightmares since Bartholomew disappeared." She decided now might not be the best time to confess that he'd figured prominently in most of them.

At the mention of her brother, he withdrew from the bed. He stood, drawing off his hat and turning it over in his hands. A worn leather duster draped his lanky form, the shoulder cape of the flowing coat emphasizing the breadth of his own shoulders. "That's why I'm here so early. I may have a lead on your brother's whereabouts. A man fitting his description has been spotted in a town south of here called Eulalie."

Before he could finish, Esmerelda had bounded out of the bed and began to paw through her trunk for a clean basque, skirt, and a set of fresh undergarments.

"If I hit the trail now," Billy continued, "I might just be able to catch up with him." The hardwood floor creaked beneath his boots as he started for the door.

Esmerelda spun around, hugging a pair of ruffled drawers to her breast. "Oh, no, you don't! You're not going anywhere without me. I learned my lesson from Mr. Flavil Snorton."

"I'm not Flavil Snorton, ma'am. I'll see to it that you get every penny of your money's worth."

He replaced his hat, tilting it low over his eyes, but Esmerelda could still feel the heat of his gaze branding her tingling skin through the worn muslin of her nightgown. He seemed to be taking a perverse delight in reminding her of their unholy alliance.

"And I'll see to it that you get every penny of your money," she forced herself to say crisply. "As soon as my beloved grandpapa arrives from England. But only if you agree to let me accompany you to this Eulalie to look for Bartholomew." She fought the temptation to plead, sensing somehow that this man would not be swayed by whining or cajoling.

His eyes narrowed as he looked her up and down, taking her measure. Esmerelda held herself straight and tall, refusing to betray how fearful she was that he would somehow find her wanting. Just as her grandfather always had.

He finally swept off his hat and made a mocking bow. "You're the boss, Duchess."

"I am not a duchess," she said stiffly. "I'm the granddaughter of a duke." She probably looked less like nobility than some wanton peasant with her hair unplaited and her naked toes peeping out from beneath the hem of her nightgown. "I need to dress and pack my belongings. If you'll excuse me . . . ?" Clutching her drawers even tighter, she nodded toward the door.

"Be my guest," he replied, nodding toward the dressing screen that partitioned off one corner of the room.

Refusing to be baited into further argument, Esmerelda took her armful of clothing and ducked behind the screen, glaring at him all the while. She quickly shed her nightgown, draping it over the screen so she could scramble into her drawers and chemise. She scowled down at the remaining undergarments, realizing for the first time how impractical the confines of corset and camisole, petticoat and bustle, would be in the blazing New Mexico heat. After a moment of contemplation, she discarded everything but the petticoat. Leaving off the bustle would make her skirt hang long, but she'd rather trip than swelter.

As she wrestled with the hooks of her basque, praying the thick merino would hide the absence of a corset, her nightgown began a sensual slither over the top of the screen. She was too mesmerized by its unexpected flight to reach for it until it was too late. She held her breath, oddly discomfited by a vision of Mr. Darling's calloused hands fondling the soft, skin-warmed muslin.

His voice, husky and far too near for comfort, further shattered her illusion of privacy. "So are you and this *brother* of yours very close?"

"Oh, very," Esmerelda replied, relieved that he'd chosen such an innocuous topic of conversation. "You'd have to travel long and far to find two people so passionately devoted to each other."

"How touching. I always did have a powerful hankering for a sister."

Esmerelda froze in the act of fastening the pearl buttons at her cuffs. Mr. Darling's sigh had been heartfelt, but she would have almost sworn she detected a lascivious note in his voice. She popped her head up over the top of the dressing screen to give him a suspicious look. He blinked at her, his long-lashed eyes as innocent as a lamb's. Her overwrought nerves must surely be affecting her imagination, she decided.

Shaking her head, she plopped down on the low-slung dressing stool to draw on her striped stockings and kid boots. The ominous sound of paper rustling sent her bolting out from behind the screen, one boot still half-unlaced. She just barely managed to hobble over to the desk and snatch the sheet of crumpled stationery from Billy's hand before he could read her unflattering description of him.

"I was writing Grandpapa," she said, tucking the incriminating note behind her back, "apprising him of the current situation."

Billy nodded. "That's very thoughtful of you. We wouldn't want to worry the old man, would we? Why don't you leave it at the hotel desk in case he arrives while we're gone."

Esmerelda hesitated, wondering if she was only imagining the sparkle of challenge in his eyes. Her own hastily scribbled words haunted her. *I have been forced to barter my virtue to a ruthless desperado.* Prodded by his expectant scrutiny, she retrieved an envelope from the desk, folded the note into a neat square, and tucked it inside. After all, it wasn't as if the spiteful old man would ever actually read it.

"I'll take it down for you," Billy offered, extending his hand.

"Oh, no," she said, clutching the envelope to her breast with even more desperation than she had clutched her drawers. "That won't be necessary. I'll just drop it off at the desk as we go."

He slowly withdrew his hand and nodded. "You do that, Miss Fine. You just do that."

A prickle of apprehension skated down her spine. Despite

his lazy grin, Esmerelda couldn't quite shake the odd sensation that Mr. Darling didn't trust her any more than she
trusted him.

"This horse seems rather tall. Do you have anything just
a tiny bit shorter?"

As Esmerelda turned away from the stall, rejecting its
velvety-eyed occupant just as she'd rejected the occupants
of all the other stalls lining the north wall of the livery stable, Billy blew out a snort of exasperation that would have
put his mare to shame. Although it was only late summer,
at this rate they wouldn't reach Eulalie until Christmas. Of
next year.

Esmerelda meandered over to the opposite wall, her
hands clasped behind her as if she were reviewing a line of
shaggy troops.

The stable's owner trotted at her heels, dabbing sweat
from his brow with a dingy red bandanna. The shrill pitch
of his voice revealed his growing desperation. "But, miss,
you said the last horse was too short. And the one before
that too broad. And the one before *that* too brown."

She peered into the next stall, making a nervous little
hop backward when the piebald gelding within nickered a
welcome. "He's a bit strident, don't you think? Do you
have anything quieter? More mannerly?"

The stable owner's bottom lip began to quiver as if he
was on the verge of bursting into tears. Taking pity on the
fellow, Billy stepped forward. "I'm sorry to disappoint you,
Miss Fine, but none of Mr. Ezell's horses were privileged
enough to attend finishing school. Why don't you just take
a look-see at this docile fellow over here?"

He caught her elbow in a less-than-docile grip and
dragged her to the next stall. The aged gray within lowered
his head and gave them a sleepy look. If he were any more

docile, he'd be dead. But this time Billy was standing near enough to feel Esmerelda's quiver of alarm.

"Miss Fine?" he murmured into her ear.

"Mm?"

"Have you ever ridden a horse before?"

She drew in a shaky breath. "I sat on a pony once at the county fair."

"Was the pony moving?"

She shot him a sheepish glance. "Only after I fell off."

"That's what I thought." He steered her toward the stable door. "Why don't you step outside while I choose your mount? I'm considered an excellent judge of horseflesh."

She cast him a skeptical glance. He gave her an encouraging wink before pushing her out of the stable and gently closing the door in her face.

"Excellent judge of horseflesh, my . . . my . . . jackass," Esmerelda muttered beneath her breath, eyeing the long-eared monster plodding in front of her with undisguised loathing.

She gave the reins a tentative flick. The hateful creature swiveled around to bare its long, yellow teeth at her and honked out a deafening bray. The basset hound perched on the bench of the wagon next to her threw back its head, jowls jiggling, and added a woeful howl to the chorus.

Esmerelda stuck her tongue out at the mule, only to end up biting it hard enough to draw blood when the rickety buckboard jolted through yet another rut. Her trunk and violin case were taking an awful beating in the bed of the wagon. If her bottom hadn't gone numb hours ago, she'd probably be howling in pain herself. She'd spent most of the morning silently bemoaning the absence of her bustle.

She shot the portly hound a menacing glance and hissed, "If you don't hush, I'll sit on you."

The dog subsided, giving her a doleful look that made her feel like the most heartless of bullies.

Her discomfort wouldn't have been so galling if Mr. Darling hadn't spent the entire journey loping ahead of the wagon on his chestnut mare as if he hadn't a care in the world. He rode with remarkable skill, his long-limbed grace serving him as well in the saddle as it did in a gun-fight. Esmerelda gritted her teeth when a cheerful whistle accompanied by the jingling music of his spurs drifted back to her sunburned ears.

Her misshapen bonnet was proving to be a poor pro-tection against the desert sun. The waves of shimmering heat had driven her to roll up the heavy sleeves of her basque. Her gloves shielded her hands, but she could almost hear the freckles popping out on her forearms. She sighed. There wouldn't be enough buttermilk in all of New England to fade them now.

She shaded her eyes against the sun, hoping for a glimpse of civilization, but saw nothing but more of the same—sweeping plains of grama and buffalo grass pep-pered with sparse patches of mesquite beneath a blazing swath of sky. As alien as the landscape was to her eyes, she had to admit it possessed a wild and stark beauty nearly as compelling as it was disturbing.

Much like her stoic guide.

Darling's cheery song had given way to the plaintive notes of "Johnny Has Gone for a Soldier." The mournful refrain sent a shiver of loneliness through Esmerelda's soul.

Desperate for human companionship, she flapped the reins on the mule's back. He lunged into a reluctant trot, nearly tumbling the hound paws over jowls into the bed of the buckboard. By the time the wagon caught up with the mare, Esmerelda was panting harder than the dog with the effort it took to control the cantankerous mule.

Mr. Darling slowed his own horse to a brisk walk.

"You whistle very nicely, sir," she said. "Shall we attempt a duet to pass the time?"

He immediately stopped whistling. "That might not be a good idea, ma'am. We wouldn't want to attract Indians. Or buzzards," he muttered beneath his breath.

She gave the sky a nervous glance. "I know the tune you were whistling. It's an old Irish folk song that was very popular in Boston during the war. My mother used to play it on the piano."

"Was your father a soldier?" he asked.

She shook her head. "Papa always felt he could best serve his country by wielding a pen instead of a sword. He was a staunch abolitionist. He wrote eloquent editorials for the *Gazette* denouncing the unfortunate tendency of the privileged to enslave their fellow man." The taut set of Mr. Darling's jaw beneath the shadow of his hat brim warned her that she might be at risk of offending him. Hoping to placate him, she hastily added, "Of course, some of Papa's friends insisted that the war was less about slaves than money."

Billy reined in the mare, swinging around to face her. His gray-green eyes had gone hard as flint, cutting straight to her heart. Esmerelda's hands involuntarily tightened on the reins. True to his contrary nature, the mule picked that moment to respond to her touch for the first time, bringing the buckboard to a lurching halt.

"My pa was a dirt farmer," Billy said, his voice oddly flat. "He didn't have any money or slaves. But when one of our neighbors accused him of being a Confederate sympathizer, that didn't stop the Union soldiers from hanging him from a tree in his own front yard while my ma watched. If it hadn't been for the war, Pa might still be alive. And Ma . . ." He trailed off to gaze at the distant horizon, a muscle in his jaw working savagely. "*That,* Miss Fine, is what the war was about for me and my kin."

Esmerelda remained frozen with shame while he wheeled his horse around and spurred it into a canter. For a moment, she thought he was just going to leave her there—an insignificant speck on that vast and windswept plain. But he reined in the mare at the top of a shallow rise and glanced over his shoulder, his lean form tense with impatience. It took her several agonizing minutes to bully the mule into motion. Only after she'd succeeded did Darling continue on, presenting his back to her with deliberate finality.

Esmerelda shivered as the fiery ball of the sun melted the horizon into a lake of gold. As breathtaking as the sight was, she knew night could not be far behind. Stars had already began to pierce the sky, tearing glittering holes in the lavender quilt of dusk. The steady rocking of the buckboard might have lured her aching body into a doze if she hadn't feared losing sight of the mute sentinel riding ahead of her.

Mr. Darling's unfailing vigilance reproached her nearly as much as his silence. He'd given her ample time to ponder her careless words. To her and her family, the war had been nothing but a battle of conflicting philosophies costing spilled ink instead of spilled blood. But it had cost Billy Darling both his father and his innocence. And what had become of his mother? she wondered. Had she been murdered by the Union soldiers as well? Or perished of a broken heart after being forced to watch her husband die in such a brutal manner?

Although Billy hadn't whistled a note since their earlier encounter, Esmerelda would have almost sworn she could catch snatches of "Johnny Has Gone for a Soldier" in the mournful wail of the wind. When the basset hound edged near enough to rest its chin on her knee, she scratched the dog behind its droopy ears instead of pushing it away.

As the light faded, the sloping walls of a canyon loomed out of the land to embrace them. Esmerelda found herself yearning for the bleak desert plain, the broad sweep of the sky, the absence of shadows cast by the towering rock formations that seemed to watch them from the gathering darkness.

Something howled in the distance, making her skin crawl. "Mr. Darling?" she called out, cringing at the note of near-panic in her voice.

He hesitated for a nearly imperceptible moment before guiding his horse in a wide circle and loping back to her side. Even he wasn't completely immune to their eerie surroundings. He rode with one hand resting lightly on the grip of the Winchester sheathed in the leather scabbard hanging from his saddle.

"Billy," he said curtly, capturing the reins from her hands with enough authority to draw the mule to a halt.

"How far to Eulalie . . ." Esmerelda cleared her throat. The use of such an intimate nickname seemed to imply a fondness they did not share. ". . . Billy?"

He squinted at the hint of horizon visible through the narrow mouth of the canyon. "About a six-hour ride, I'd wager. If we start out at dawn, we should make town before noon."

Esmerelda's mouth went drier than it already was while her stomach recoiled at the prospect of subsisting for another day on beans, jerky, and libations that tasted more like rusty tin than coffee or water.

"We won't reach Eulalie until tomorrow?" she asked faintly.

He nodded. "We'd best make camp now. After sundown, the desert can be a dangerous place. There's outlaws, scorpions, rattlers, varmints . . ." He hesitated long enough to warn her that he just might be enjoying himself. ". . . Indians."

Chewing on her lower lip, she cast him a dubious look. Sharing this man's bedroll could prove more hazardous than any of those perils.

He leaned down to capture a tendril of hair that had been jolted loose from her coronet of braids. He threaded his fingers through the silky strand, the unexpected tenderness of his touch sending a parade of gooseflesh across her skin. "Why, I've known Apache who would sell their grandfather's souls to get their hands on a scalp this pretty."

Esmerelda's first instinct was to flush with pleasure. Her second instinct was to snatch her hair out of his hand and berate him for deliberately trying to frighten her.

Before she could do either, a shot rang out.

Its echo hadn't even died when Billy launched himself off his mount, Winchester in hand, and rolled her over the side of the wagon to the ground.

"Down, Sadie!" he shouted.

Whimpering in alarm, the basset hound dove into the bed of the wagon. Billy's horse took off with a frantic whinny, galloping for the mouth of the canyon.

Esmerelda's breath hitched in her chest. She tried to rise, but Billy pressed her into the sand, using his body as a shield. She didn't comprehend why until a second shot struck the ground a few feet from the wagon wheel, sending up a blinding spray of grit. That was when she decided she just might be content to lie there all night, cradled beneath the shelter of his taut muscles.

With an ominous creak, the buckboard wheels turned half a revolution.

"Sonofabitch," Billy breathed into her hair.

Esmerelda didn't have the heart to chide him for his

profanity. She understood their dilemma only too well. If the mule spooked and galloped away with their only shelter, they were done for. She could see the reins from where she lay, dangling just out of arm's reach between the seat and the harness.

"Don't move, honey," he whispered. "Don't even breathe."

At first she thought his endearment was addressed to the mule. But that was before he inched forward on his elbows, dragging his hips across the softness of her bottom. Oddly undone by the contact, Esmerelda squeezed her eyes shut, once again mourning the absence of her bustle.

The chill night wind stung her skin as Billy rose to a crouch and peered over the bed of the wagon, Winchester in one hand, six-gun in the other. Esmerelda was surprised to learn that her curiosity was stronger than her terror. Ignoring his command, she wiggled to her knees and peered around the spokes of the wagon wheel.

The rising moon revealed a lone outcropping of rock sheltered by rubble on the far wall of the canyon—the perfect cover for an ambush. There was no way to determine how many attackers crouched on that makeshift platform. By squinting, Esmerelda could just make out the crown of one of their hats.

A shotgun blast thundered through the canyon. The mule bolted forward. Esmerelda made a panicked grab for the reins. She caught them just before they swung out of her reach, throwing her body's entire weight against the beast's forward momentum. Miraculously, he stumbled to a halt, his massive hindquarters still quivering with alarm.

"Nice mule," she murmured, closing her eyes against a dizzying surge of relief. "Good mule."

When she opened them, Billy was glaring at her. "I thought I told you to stay put," he hissed.

"You should have told the mule," she retorted, wrapping

the reins around her gloved hands. If the beast took off now, she was going to be dragged the rest of the way to Eulalie on her stomach.

Still shaking his head, Billy rose to one knee with fluid grace and sighted the outcropping of stone through the eye of the Colt. Esmerelda's blood froze. Had his arrogance blossomed into madness? she wondered. The pistol might have an advantage over the Winchester in accuracy, but not at such an impossible range.

The determination etched on his features made her breath come fast and short. If he hadn't been about to get them both killed, his concentration would have been a beautiful thing to behold.

He closed one eye.

His finger tightened on the trigger.

He fired.

The hat flew off, making one of their assailants yelp like a girl.

Esmerelda frowned in bewilderment as the yelp gave way to a confusing muddle of grunts and curses, followed by the sounds of a minor scuffle.

A timid voice wafted across the canyon. "That you, Billy?"

Billy collapsed against the wagon wheel, paling as if he'd been mortally wounded. Weakened by relief, Esmerelda crawled to his side and sagged against him. "Friends of yours, I gather."

"Worse." The grim set of his mouth banished her exhilaration. "Relations."

CHAPTER TEN

The Darling gang came charging down the embankment, whooping and hollering like schoolboys on the first day of summer. For a moment, Billy appeared to be nearly as paralyzed with shock as Esmerelda was.

Then he snatched her up by the shoulders, forcing her to meet his frantic gaze. "You've got to do whatever I say, gal. Swear you will." When she just gaped at him in dumb surprise, he gave her a slight shake. "Swear it, Esmerelda. Your life may depend on it."

It wasn't the strength of his grip that swayed her, but the desperation in his smoky green eyes. In that one elusive moment, Esmerelda would have promised him anything.

At her tremulous nod, he reached over into the bed of the wagon and snatched down a length of rope. Before Esmerelda could so much as murmur a protest, he had the thick length of hemp twined around her wrists. He jerked a knot in it, binding her hands in front of her.

"What in heaven's name do you think you're doing, sir? I never intended—"

"You promised," he reminded her sternly.

"I don't care what I promised! You have no right—"

"Shhhhh." He laid a finger across her lips, stilling them in midsputter. Their tense silence only emphasized the sound of his brothers stampeding across the canyon like a herd of drunken steers. Billy shook his head at her, his gaze softened by tender regret. "If you don't hush, sweetheart, I'm afraid I'll have to gag you."

"But I—"

As quick as that, Billy plucked the lace handkerchief from the breast pocket of her basque and stuffed it into her mouth. If she hadn't still been reeling from shock, she might have been able to spit out the wad of cloth before he secured it with the dusty bandanna he'd been wearing around his neck.

As he knotted the bandanna at her nape, his warm breath stirred her hair. "You'll thank me for this later," he whispered, causing her skin to tingle with an awareness that had as much to do with his absolute power over her as her sudden helplessness.

She was left with no recourse but to stamp her feet in outrage and emit a muffled shriek.

He circled back to the front of her, a crooked grin tugging at his lips. "That's perfect, angel. Pretend you hate me."

Even through the gag, it was possible to make out Esmerelda's mumbled "I do hachoo."

His brothers were nearly upon them now. Billy studied her through narrowed eyes. "Your color's sure high enough, but we might need to make a few minor adjustments."

She glared daggers at him as he dragged off her poor

beleaguered bonnet and carelessly tossed it aside. He plucked out her hairpins and raked his fingers through her coronet of braids, sending her hair spilling in a wanton tumble around her shoulders. As galling as that assault upon her person was, it was nothing compared to the shock of his lean fingers dancing down the high-necked collar of her basque. His deft skill with the tiny hooks only served to remind her that he'd probably had more experience undressing women than she had.

He didn't falter until the back of his hand brushed the naked swell of her breast, betraying the fact that she wasn't wearing a camisole, corset, or much of anything else, beneath the basque. His gaze flew to her face. Esmerelda felt a perverse flare of triumph at his stunned expression, his quick, indrawn breath.

His knuckles lingered against her skin in a motion too uncalculated to be called a caress. Yet it shivered Esmerelda to the bone. As their eyes met, the distant roaring in her ears drowned out everything but the harsh rasp of his breathing and the wild throb of her pulse.

"Where the hell you hidin', Billy? Ain't you glad to see us?"

The nearby shout startled both of them out of their reverie. A fierce scowl shadowed Billy's brow. His fingers flew back up her basque, hooking with even more haste than they'd unhooked only seconds before.

"We want you to look ravished, not ravishing," he muttered between clenched teeth, securing the hook beneath her chin with such enthusiasm she feared she might choke to death. "And try to look terrified," he commanded as the hoots and curses swelled to near deafening volume.

Esmerelda didn't have to fake it as he grabbed her by the elbow and shoved her ahead of him. But her worst fears were never realized. Before the scream building in her throat could escape the gag, Billy was snatched away from her and enveloped by a howling, back-thumping circle of men. One of them yodeled a rebel yell while another fired a volley of reckless shots into the air. They all reeked of whiskey, making it easy to understand why none of their shots had struck true.

Esmerelda stumbled to a halt, standing forgotten and invisible on the fringes of their reunion. The moon drifted over the lip of the canyon, giving her her first clear look at the notorious Darling gang.

The largest of the four men, a burly giant of at least six feet six, slapped Billy on the back hard enough to stagger him, then swept him up in a bear hug and swung him in a wide circle. "I knew that had to be you. Nobody but my baby brother could make a shot like that."

From the shocks of gray at the man's temples, Esmerelda deduced he must also be the oldest Darling. She might have been touched by the genuine affection in his embrace if Billy hadn't hung so stiffly in his arms.

He finally managed to struggle free, his nostrils flaring with distaste. "Hell, Virgil, with all the stagecoaches you've been knocking off, you could at least spare a nickel for a bath and a shave."

Virgil threw back his head and roared with laughter, his white teeth gleaming through his sandy beard in a wolfish grin. Even Esmerelda had to admit he was handsome, in a brutish sort of way. "Now, Billy, you know Jasper's always been the pretty boy in the family. Shaves twice a day. Splashes on so much lilac water he ends up smelling like a two-dollar whore."

"Better a whore than a hog," retorted the man Esmerelda assumed must be Jasper.

His jibe initiated a brief shoving match with Virgil.

Esmerelda cringed, fearing the two towering men were going to come to fisticuffs.

But Billy pushed his way between them without betraying an ounce of apprehension. "I wouldn't care to be downwind of either one of you."

Jasper knocked off Billy's hat and ruffled his tawny hair. "Where you been hidin', little brother? If I didn't know better, I'd swear you been avoidin' your own kin. Your very own flesh and blood."

A shudder rippled through Billy as he retrieved his hat and dusted it off, too faint to be noted by anyone but Esmerelda. He was spared from answering by Sadie, who bounded out of the wagon and began to sniff at Jasper's feet.

"Still got that mangy old mutt of mine, I see," Jasper said, nudging her away with the toe of his boot. "The bitch is too old to hunt or breed. I still don't know why you stopped me from shootin' her that time."

"Because I didn't want to have to kill you," Billy replied darkly.

As the two men stood glowering at each other, toe-to-toe and nose-to-nose, it was Virgil's turn to step in and avert a potential altercation. "Our little brother here has been one very busy feller," he said, turning to one of the two men lurking behind them. "Enos, where's that paper I gave you for safekeeping?"

Beneath his straggly hair and ragged yellow whiskers, Enos looked washed out, like a smeared charcoal draft of his older brothers. He blinked his red-rimmed eyes, shook his head, and jerked a thumb toward the nearly identical man who slumped next to him. "W-w-weren't mine to keep. No, s-siree. You give it to Sam."

Sam looked blank for a moment, then fished a folded

square of paper from his dusty chaps. He handed it to Enos who handed it to Jasper who handed it to Virgil.

Virgil shook it open with all the pomp of a governor making a formal declaration. Even from where she stood, Esmerelda recognized the sketch in his hand. She'd studied it with her eyes a thousand times, traced it with her finger until it haunted her every dream.

It was the poster branding Billy Darling a wanted man.

Virgil studied the poster, then scowled down at Billy. "I had hoped for better, son. I'm disappointed in you. What would Ma say?"

At the mention of their mother, all the brothers except Billy sighed in unison, then drew off their hats and pressed them over their hearts.

After a moment of respectful silence, Virgil slapped his hat back on and winked at Jasper. "Ah, who cares what Ma would say? I say it took him too dadburned long to get his picture in the family album."

"Amen!" the others chorused, surrounding their prodigal brother for yet another round of hugs and backslapping.

When Esmerelda realized they were congratulating Billy for being wanted for murder, she was appalled by their bloodthirstiness. But she was even more appalled by the cocky grin Billy wore as he accepted their gruff accolades. It chilled her to realize how much trust she had placed in a man who was little more than a stranger to her. As he basked in his brothers' fellowship, she recoiled without realizing it, taking several steps backward.

The motion caught Jasper's eye. As his gaze traveled from her scuffed kid boots to her bound hands to her tousled hair, a smile slowly spread across his handsome face. "What's this, Billy? You bring us a present?"

With his clean-shaven jaw and lanky grace, Jasper resembled Billy more than any of his brothers. His lips had been cut from the same sensual mold, but his crooked grin was a sinister shadow of Billy's smile.

Esmerelda took another step backward, alarmed by the sadistic glint in his eyes. As her gaze traveled between the two men—so alike, yet so different—she realized that what she'd mistaken for cruelty in Billy's eyes was nothing more than wariness. A wariness that deepened in their narrowed depths as he deliberately stepped in front of Jasper and swaggered over to her.

He snaked one arm around her waist and drew her against him. When she squirmed in protest, he snuggled the top of her head beneath his chin. "Sorry, boys, but this one's all mine. I thought I'd have a little fun with her, then sell her to the Comancheros for a profit."

An involuntary shudder coursed down Esmerelda's spine. Even she had heard of the Comancheros—renegade bands of Comanches, Mexicans, and outlaws who traded guns, liquor, and women up and down the Mexican border. An unspeakable fate awaited any woman who fell into their brutal hands.

Billy must have felt her quiver, because he gave her waist a hard squeeze. She might have been more comforted if she'd known whether it was intended to restrain or reassure. His own muscles were as taut as a rope stretched to the point of fraying.

"Aw, hell, Billy, don't be so selfish," Jasper whined. His greedy gaze dropped to her bosom. Although her basque was hooked all the way to her chin, Esmerelda felt even more exposed than she had when Billy's knuckles had grazed the swell of her naked breast. "She's a little mite, but there's more than enough to go around."

Virgil's tongue flicked out to wet his lips. "Jasper's right. I ain't had me a woman in nigh on a week."

"She shore is a p-purty little thing," Enos shyly added.

Sam nodded. "I bet she smells real nice."

Billy kept his voice soft and amiable. "If you're inclined to scrap over a woman, Samuel, then we will. But I'd have thought you'd have grown attached to that ear I left you with the last time we scrapped."

Ducking his head to hide a pout, Sam tugged his hat down over his ears. Or what was left of them. The gag smothered Esmerelda's horrified gasp.

Virgil and Jasper weren't so easily discouraged. They exchanged a sly glance, then began to ease away from each other, plainly intending to circle around and flank them.

Tension charged the air, making Esmerelda's nape tingle with apprehension. Her stomach churned with dread at the thought of their foul breath in her face and their filthy hands on her body. Billy no longer had to restrain her. She pressed herself against his lean, muscular body, instinctively seeking refuge.

"Don't pay him no mind, Sam," Jasper said, hooking his thumbs in the waistband of his chaps. "Billy's just bein' stingy. He always was a mama's boy."

Billy's good-natured laugh masked the sound of his pistol sliding out of its holster. When it appeared in his hand, all four of his brothers stumbled backward, their hands on the grips of their own pistols. But not one of them dared to draw.

A strange thrill of exhilaration shot through Esmerelda's veins as she realized that Billy wasn't afraid of his brothers. He never had been. He was only afraid for her.

Her discovery didn't lessen the shock of his pistol barrel grazing her temple. Her breath caught in her throat as Billy dragged the weapon down her cheek, then used the muzzle to tenderly tip her chin up so he could caress the vulnerable skin beneath her jaw. The cool, hard metal provided a stark contrast to the tensile heat of his hips pressed against her backside.

He slid the barrel down her throat and between her breasts, marking his territory, branding her as his own before his brothers and all the world.

He waited until he had every ounce of their slack-jawed attention before gently drawling, "You're right about one thing, Jasper. I never did like to share what was mine."

Esmerelda shivered. With the smoky rasp of his voice in her ear and the barrel of his pistol cradled between her breasts, it was nearly impossible to remember that he was only bluffing.

Wasn't he?

Virgil was the first one to raise his hands in surrender. Sam and Enos immediately followed suit. Only Jasper kept his hand hovering near his holster.

Billy ignored him. "If you gentlemen will be kind enough to excuse us, I believe the lady and I will retire to the grove of mesquite on top of that bluff for a spell. We would appreciate a little privacy." He accented his request by easing her hair aside and nuzzling her throat with his lips; the fresh shock of his warm, moist mouth against her skin made her knees buckle.

Taking advantage of her weakness, he began to waltz her backward, the pistol still gripped in his hand. "Oh, and Jasper, I'd be much obliged if you could fetch my mare. Your poor shooting gave her an awful fright."

Jasper's lips twitched in a feral snarl, but his hand remained frozen over his gun.

Virgil gave him a shove. "You heard the man, Jasper. Go fetch his horse."

Jasper shook off his brother's hand, then went plunging into the darkness, a vicious oath escaping his lips. Only then did Billy holster his gun. Enos and Sam slumped in relief.

As they passed the buckboard, Billy reached into the bed of the wagon with his free hand and snagged a bedroll.

Virgil rested his balled fists on his hips. "If you need a hand with her, just give a holler. We'd be more than obliged to help."

"That's a right kindly offer, but I do believe I can manage."

As he dragged her up the rise toward the mesquite grove on top of the bluff, Billy's grip was so implacable that Esmerelda couldn't help kicking her feet and choking out a whimper of protest. Had he rescued her or betrayed her? Was he the same man who had caught her when she swooned and tenderly cradled her in his arms, or a ruthless stranger who had every intention of carrying out his implied threat?

CHAPTER ELEVEN

♥
———————————

Before they could reach the tenuous privacy of the mesquites, Billy had a hellcat in his arms. Even with her hands bound, Esmerelda managed to twist around and club him in the chest. Her feet beat a savage tattoo against his shins. He cast a frantic glance backward to make sure they were out of his brothers' sight before hefting her over his shoulder where he hoped she could do less harm.

Her linked fists slammed into his kidney, making him bite off a heartfelt oath. He anchored her bottom with one hand, unfurled the bedroll with the other, then dumped her unceremoniously on top of the coarse woolen blanket.

Billy followed her down, thinking only to bury his laughter in the sweet-smelling spill of her hair. "That was quite a performance, honey. I doubt Sagebrush Sally down at the old Divine Theater in Santa Fe could have done any finer."

When her passionate squirming failed to subside, he lifted his head. His grin slowly faded as he realized her struggles were genuine—as genuine as the panic gleaming in her eyes.

"Aw, hell," he breathed. He'd spent too much of his life raging at his own helplessness not to recognize the signs in someone else.

"Hang on, sweetheart. Just hang on," he murmured as he reached around and began to tear at the knot binding Esmerelda's wrists.

As soon as she was free, she swung on him, her fist connecting soundly with his jaw. He took one or two of her clumsy blows, figuring she owed him that much, before recapturing her slender wrists in one of his hands and pinning them above her head.

He allowed her to buck and heave until she realized she wasn't going anywhere with six feet two inches of well-muscled male lying on top of her. Only then did her struggles subside. Only then did her eyes focus, glaring furiously at him over the gag.

Wisely keeping his fingers out of biting range, he loosened the bandanna and tugged the damp handkerchief from her mouth. Her breath escaped in a furious sob. Billy nearly smiled, pleased somehow that even now, she was more riled than afraid.

"How dare you take such frightful liberties with my person?" she hissed, bright enough even in a temper to realize that his brothers might very well be lurking just below the bluff, their ears pricked to hear their every word.

"I didn't have any choice," he hissed back. "I had to stake my claim on you before one of my brothers decided to."

"Why couldn't you simply explain to them that you were in my employ?"

He snorted. "Trust me. They wouldn't have been impressed. The very idea of one of their own working for a woman would have only made them itch to put her in her place."

"Which is?"

Billy briefly considered glossing over the truth, but decided it would do her far more harm to underestimate his brothers than to think the worst of him. He met her eyes squarely. "Flat on her back with her skirts up and her drawers down."

Esmerelda's mouth fell open, then snapped shut, as if she'd suddenly realized how perilously close she was to that exact posture. Her body quivered beneath his, but her whisper was steady. "Your brothers may be afraid of you, Mr. Darling, but I, most certainly, am not."

Sobered by her lie, Billy said, "I never wanted you to be. And I had no choice but to make my brothers afraid of me. From the moment I was born, they were bigger than me, stronger than me, and meaner than me. If I wanted to survive, I had to prove I was smarter, crazier, and a better shot."

"Is that why you shot off your own brother's ear?"

Billy frowned, baffled by her assumption. "I never shot off anybody's ear. I was only ten the last time Samuel and I scrapped." At her relieved sigh, his frown curled into a wicked grin. "I bit it off."

Esmerelda recoiled from his bared teeth, as if afraid he just might bite her, too. It wasn't as if he wouldn't like to, Billy thought, remembering the moment when he'd pressed his open mouth to her throat. By rights, she should have tasted like sweat and trail dust, but her flavor lingered on his lips, sweeter than anything he'd sampled for a very long time. Sweeter even than the ripe, juicy peaches she smelled like. It made him wonder what she might taste like in other places. Made him want to do something even more foolish than biting her, like stealing a taste of those tender lips trembling only a breath away from his own.

Stung by the raw power of the temptation, he released her wrists and rolled off of her.

He half expected her to strike out at him again, but she took advantage of her freedom to scramble to her feet. He caught her wrist before she could take a single step.

"Let me go!" she whispered between clenched teeth, attempting to twist out of his grasp.

"Not until I make sure you're not thinking about bolting out of here and tempting one of my brothers to put a bullet in your back."

Esmerelda sank down in a puddle of skirts, her sullen pout informing him that was precisely what she'd been thinking.

She made a great show of searching her wrists for bruises, frowning with disappointment when she didn't find any. "I hate to be rude, Mr. Darling, but I really don't care much for those brothers of yours."

He shrugged, hoping the casual gesture didn't reveal more than it hid. "They weren't always so bad. Prone to mischief as most boys are, I suppose. If it hadn't been for the war, they'd have probably raised a little hell, then settled down with the first farmer's daughter they got with child. Provided her pa wanted a wedding and a son-in-law more than a funeral and a bastard, that is." Esmerelda's shocked expression stopped him from telling her that would have probably been his fate as well. "But riding with Quantrill and Anderson changed them—cut a mean stripe in their hides that's been festering ever since."

She shivered and began to toy with the pleats of her skirt, avoiding his eyes. "What would you have done if they'd have called your bluff tonight when you drew your pistol? If Virgil had rushed you or Jasper had drawn his own gun?"

Billy's jaw tightened as he remembered how Jasper ogled her breasts, the greedy way Virgil's tongue had snaked out to wet his lips, as if she was nothing more than a cheap piece of horehound candy to be devoured in one brutal bite.

"I'd have pulled the trigger," he said flatly, surprised to realize he meant it.

Her head whipped up before he could wipe the murderous expression off his face. Her brown eyes shimmered with a curious mix of disbelief and wonder. "You'd have shot one of your own brothers. For me?"

Billy was as staggered as she was by the depth of his urge to protect her. He never could stand to see anyone bully a woman. Which was exactly why Miss Mellie and the girls had been so delighted to have him living in their attic. His presence alone discouraged most of their rougher customers. But what he felt as he gazed into Esmerelda's eyes was something more primitive. And far more dangerous. Especially for a man with his temper.

Although the shape no longer felt natural, Billy forced his mouth into a mocking smile. "I'd have done the same for any lady," he assured her, though he wasn't at all sure he would.

He would have almost sworn he glimpsed a hint of disappointment in her eyes, but before he could be sure, she bowed her head, hiding her face behind a curtain of hair. "How very gallant of you, Mr. Darling."

"Billy," he whispered, tipping her chin up so he could search her eyes.

"Hey, Billy!" Virgil's booming voice sent a violent start through Esmerelda. "It's awful quiet up there, son. You need me to come up and remind you how to make a woman squeal?"

Billy touched a warning finger to Esmerelda's lips before calling out, "Don't bother, Virg. I remember more about making a woman squeal than you ever learned."

A derisive hoot of laughter greeted his retort. Exchanging a wary glance, he and Esmerelda crawled forward on their stomachs and elbows to peer down into the canyon. The faint glow of a fire and the clink of a bottle being passed from hand to hand warned them that their worst fear had been realized. His brothers had camped in the small valley just below the bluff.

"Damn," he whispered. "I was afraid of this. They're not going to give us a moment's peace until we give them a taste of what they're hungry for."

"How about some arsenic?" Esmerelda muttered.

Billy bit back a grin. "A little noise should satisfy them for a while."

"Noise?" she echoed, turning her head to blink at him.

He cleared his throat, wondering why it had suddenly gotten so hard to swallow. "You know—a few whimpers, a couple of moans, maybe a grunt or two thrown in to make it convincing."

Even though they were both lying prone, Esmerelda still managed to look down her nose at him. "I do not grunt, Mr. Darling."

Although she seemed merely bemused by his request, Billy realized with horror that he was on the verge of blushing like a virgin. He rubbed the back of his neck and clenched his teeth. "If you could just make the sort of sound a woman makes when a man comes into her . . ."

Esmerelda looked so blank that Billy decided she was either utterly innocent or a much more cunning actress than he'd suspected. Then her cheeks burst into crimson flames. "Oh! You mean the sort of noises that woman was making back at the ... the ..."

"Whorehouse," he drawled, beginning to enjoy the game now that he was holding the winning hand. "Yeah, like maybe you don't like what I'm doing to you at first, but then I make you like it even if you don't want to."

He half expected her to slap him for his insolence, but she surprised him by rolling over on the blanket and pressing the back of her hand to her brow.

She remained in that dramatic posture for several minutes before lowering her hand and fixing him with a stern look. "Close your eyes, sir."

He pretended to comply, using the asinine eyelashes his brothers had always teased him so mercilessly about for the only thing they were good for.

"And no peeking!"

He swore beneath his breath, but obeyed in earnest this time. Until Esmerelda's first breathy whimper sent a prickle of awareness dancing across his flesh.

His eyes flew open. Esmerelda lay on her back in the moonlight with her eyes pressed shut. Longing and pain flickered across her features in a wistful duet. Her lips were no longer pressed together in prim disapproval, but parted to release throaty little gasps that soon had his own breath coming in feral pants.

Billy gaped in unabashed fascination as her whimpers deepened to a full-bodied moan, earthy and wildly stirring in its power. The dead silence drifting up from below warned him that his brothers must be similarly captivated. He could almost see them there in the firelight, their eyes glazed with lust, a forgotten mouthful of whisky dribbling down their chins.

Esmerelda arched her throat; her small, firm breasts strained against her bodice, a tantalizing reminder that there were no barriers of lace or linen between flesh and fabric. All he had to do was lean over and flick open one hook, then another . . .

He knocked off his hat and groped for his bandanna to mop away the beads of sweat forming on his brow. In the months that he'd slept in the attic at Miss Mellie's, the moans and grunts of pleasure being given and received had ceased to move him. Especially since he knew most of the girls were faking their cries of ecstasy in the hope that some gratified cowboy might flip an extra nickel on the bed before strutting from the room.

But his body throbbed in time to the irresistible rhythm of Esmerelda's song. As it reached a crescendo, the ache intensified, growing more bitter than sweet as he realized what its melody signified.

Winstead had been right. Either Bart Fine had taught her how to make those sounds or some other man had. The innocence shimmering in those big brown eyes of hers was an illusion. Just as much of a disguise as the mask an outlaw might wear to rob a bank. Only she wasn't using it to steal his money, but his heart.

Billy's keen disappointment did nothing to defuse his lust. He wanted to coax her out of his brothers' earshot and make her moan in earnest. He wanted her to watch everything he did to her until the sight of his face above her blotted out every memory of the man who had touched her first.

He wiggled forward on his elbows until he was looming directly over her. He didn't really want to know, but couldn't resist growling, "What in the hell were you thinking about?"

Esmerelda opened her luminous eyes and smiled up at him, her cheeks flushed with the rosy glow of a woman well satisfied. "A French cream puff."

Struck mute by her reply, Billy had no choice but to listen to her dreamy recital.

"After Mama and Papa died, I used to pass by this bakery on Beacon Street on the way to the market. Every morning, they'd put the tray of cream puffs in the window, fresh out of the oven. I desperately didn't want to want one because I knew we didn't have enough money to waste on such extravagances. But I wanted one anyway." She sighed wistfully. "I never succumbed to the temptation, but I used to stand there in the cold until my breath fogged the window, imagining what it would feel like to lick away the glaze of honey butter, to sink my teeth into the flaky pastry, to plunge my tongue into the cream-filled center . . ."

Billy held up a hand to silence her, his groin bound into a knot of sweet agony. If Esmerelda could get that worked up over some imagined indulgence, what might a taste of genuine pleasure do to her? He thought it a damn shame that she'd deprived herself of such a simple delight and spent the rest of her life regretting it. He'd never denied himself any pleasure he wanted.

Until now.

Esmerelda stretched and yawned, looking as drowsy and vulnerable as a woman who had actually experienced the release she'd so cleverly mimicked. "Do you think we fooled your brothers?"

Desperate to escape before she realized she'd made an even bigger fool of him, Billy threw the other half of the blanket over her and climbed to his feet. "I'll go find out," he said tersely. "You stay put. Get some rest."

"Yes, sir," she replied, touching her brow in a mocking salute.

He started to go, then hesitated and turned back. Esmerelda's eyes widened as he slipped her derringer out of his boot and tossed it on top of the blanket. "It's loaded.

Shoot the first man who lays a hand on you in a disrespectful manner."

"Even if it's you?"

He didn't return her wry smile. "Especially if it's me."

As Billy stumbled down the path wind and time had carved into the canyon wall, he ruffled his hair and unfastened the first two buttons of his Levi's. He was thankful both his brothers' wits and their vision had been addled by whiskey. If any one of them gave him more than half a glance, they would realize his hunger had been in no way satisfied by his tryst with Esmerelda. On the contrary, he was as hard and thick as a bundle of dynamite awaiting the kiss of flame to its fuse.

He swore, but the eloquent oath failed to give him its usual satisfaction.

As he approached the campfire, he shifted his walk into the deliberate swagger of a man who'd just proved his prowess to a woman for all the world to hear.

Virgil presided over the fire like a tribal king, puffing on a cigar Billy recognized as being stolen from his saddlebag. Jasper reclined on one elbow, nursing a fresh bottle of rotgut. His smoldering glare warned Billy that he was still sulking over their earlier confrontation. Sam was tearing at a ragged hunk of jerky with his yellowing teeth while Enos sat next to Sadie, absently fondling the basset hound's floppy ears. Her tail twitched a lazy welcome at the sight of her master. The aroma of canned beans wafted up from an iron pot dangling over the fire.

Virgil winked at Billy, his booming voice softened by mock concern. "I hope she was gentle with you, son. You did tell her she was your first, didn't you?"

Billy tucked his thumbs in his gunbelt and forced a grin,

hoping it didn't look as sick as it felt. "She must have been *your* first, Virg, because she swore I was the best she ever had."

Virgil's roar of laughter did nothing to lighten Jasper's black expression. He took another swig of the whiskey and cast the bluff above them a contemptuous look. "I bet I could give the little whore a ride she'd never forget."

A scarlet haze descended over Billy's eyes, blinding him with rage. He took a step forward, fully intending to launch himself across the fire and wipe the sneer off his brother's pretty face with his fists. But that was before he remembered that Jasper was only believing exactly what he'd wanted him to believe.

His amiable smile still couldn't completely buff the dangerous edge from his voice. "That might be true, Jasper, but it'd be the last ride you ever took. Last time I checked, horse thieving was a hanging offense."

Still spoiling for a fight, Jasper started to rise, but Virgil clapped a hand on his shoulder. "No need to scrap, son. I'm sure Billy only meant to say you were hung like a horse."

Enos and Sam stuttered out a nervous laugh while Virgil pried the whiskey bottle out of Jasper's clenched hand and offered it to Billy, along with one of Billy's own cigars. Jasper might be the brains of the gang, but Virgil had always been the muscle.

Billy accepted his brother's peace offering and sank down on the opposite side of the fire. Still acutely aware of Jasper's glare, he made a great show of wiping the mouth of the bottle on his sleeve before lifting it to his lips for a desperately needed swig. He had hoped the rotgut would sear Esmerelda's taste from his mouth, but it only intensified the yearning ache in his belly.

While he struck a match and lit the cigar, Sam finished off the jerky with an audible gulp and shot Sadie a predatory glance. "I shore is hungry. A fellow can grow mightily sick of canned beans and prairie dog."

Billy patted his thigh. Sadie ducked out from under Enos's hand and waddled to his side. He rewarded her for her obedience by gently stroking her grizzled muzzle. "I can assure you, Samuel, that my Sadie ain't near as tasty as those tender little ears of yours."

Sam sheepishly jerked down his hat and helped himself to a ladle of steaming beans.

Billy hid his smile behind a long draw on the cigar and another swig of whiskey. "Where you boys headed? I figured you'd be off somewhere raising hell instead of stuck out here in the middle of it."

Enos opened his mouth, but Virgil's booming voice drowned him out. "We been thinkin' about headin' south. To Mexico City."

Billy's spirits soared. Blood might make them brothers, but the badge tucked into his shirt pocket would make them mortal enemies. He'd love to see them well on their way to Mexico before he was forced to make use of it.

"A wise choice," he said. "I hear there are opportunities to be seized and fortunes to be made in Mexico City for enterprising young gentlemen such as yourself."

Virgil and Jasper exchanged a furtive glance, but it was Enos who piped up. "We ain't g-g-goin' to Mexico just yet. We're on our way to Eulalie first."

"Eulalie?" Billy echoed. He caught the smoldering cigar before it could tumble out of his slack mouth into his lap and disguised his blossoming dread with a bark of laughter. "Why Eulalie? I've always heard the only thing uglier than the town is the women who live there."

This time it was Virgil who opened his mouth and Enos's high-pitched giggle that drowned him out. "Why, we're g-goin' to Eulalie to rob us a b-b-bank!"

CHAPTER TWELVE

♥

———————————

When Esmerelda awoke, the heat had yet to tighten its relentless grip on the day. She sat up and pushed the blanket aside, indulging in a languid stretch. An arid morning breeze caressed her hair.

She smiled to find Sadie curled into a shapeless lump at her feet. If the dog hadn't wheezed out a melancholy sigh, Esmerelda would have been tempted to pry open one droopy eyelid and make sure she was still alive. Bemused, Esmerelda shook her head. Who would have thought she would sleep so soundly wrapped in a coarse blanket on a sandy rock next to a snoring hound with four incorrigible outlaws camped only a stone's throw away?

But as her gaze fell on the man sleeping across from her, she understood why.

Her guardian sat with his back against a rock and his hands curled around the stock of the Winchester laid across his knees. His position had to be painfully uncomfortable. He must have nodded off only after a long and harrowing battle with exhaustion.

Esmerelda found Billy's vigilance oddly irresistible. She'd forgotten what a luxury it was to sleep while someone else kept watch against the night.

Rising to her knees, she crept closer, eager to study him without the shield of his hat. Even in sleep, his was the wary face of a man who had known too little tenderness in his life, too many stolen kisses and bought caresses. His most recent wounds were already fading, but he still bore the scars of past battles, both won and lost.

A thin white knife scar bisected his right eyebrow, ebbing to insignificance dangerously near to his eye. A matching one marred his stubborn chin. His nose had been broken more than once. Esmerelda pondered it from all angles before deciding that she fancied it. It kept him from being too pretty, like Jasper. The harsh New Mexico sun had etched permanent creases around his mouth and eyes, but the tumble of his hair made him look younger than his years—boyish, yet every inch a man.

Caught off guard by a swell of tenderness, Esmerelda gave in to a temptation she had managed to resist ever since Bartholomew had grown old enough to roll his eyes, shove her hand away, and accuse her of mothering him. She reached over and gently brushed back the lock of hair that had fallen across Billy's brow.

He came awake at the first touch of her fingertips, swinging the rifle around to point the barrel at her breast.

Esmerelda slowly raised both hands in the air, just as she'd seen his brothers do the night before. "Don't shoot me. I surrender."

Although she uttered the words in innocent fun, the intensity of his smoky gaze seemed to imbue them with another meaning altogether, leaving her to breathlessly wonder what it might be like to surrender to a man like him. To lay down her own carefully chosen weapons and trust her lips, her will, her very heart into his keeping.

Sanity came rushing back with her next uneven breath. She nodded toward the gun. "I surrendered without a struggle. Isn't that your cue to put down the rifle?"

Billy lowered the gun and rubbed a hand over the thickening stubble on his jaw. "I ought to shoot you anyway. Didn't your mama teach you never to sneak up on a man with a loaded gun?"

Esmerelda managed a shaky laugh. "She probably didn't realize it was a social skill I would have need of. She was too intent on teaching me how to fold supper napkins, monogram handkerchiefs, and darn my father's socks."

Skills that had proved utterly useless once Esmerelda had been forced to accept that she would never have a husband or children of her own.

Discomfited at having revealed so much, she scowled at Billy. "Do you always wake up this grumpy?"

He swayed forward like a rattler poised to strike. "Wouldn't you like to find out?"

Stiffening, Esmerelda swayed backward. "Perhaps grumpy was too kind a description. Insufferable might be more appropriate."

He snorted. "You'd be insufferable, too, if you had to stay up half the night making sure my brothers didn't roast Sadie on the spit."

"You should have let them eat the mule."

He gave her a dark look before climbing to his feet. As he rolled back his shoulders to work the stiffness from them, his muscles strained against the worn fabric of his shirt. Raking a hand through his hair, he went to the edge of the bluff and stared out over the canyon with eyes that were red-rimmed from what Esmerelda suspected was too little sleep and too much strong drink. Desperation haunted his features, making him look even more dangerous and unpredictable than he had in the saloon where she had found him. A coarse oath and the aroma of brewing coffee drifted up from the canyon below, warning them that his brothers were already awake and stirring.

Esmerelda shuddered, chilled anew to remember the fate she had so narrowly escaped. Billy could growl and bluster all he wanted, but she knew very well that he hadn't forfeited his sleep to protect Sadie. She gazed up at his inscrutable profile, overcome by sudden shyness.

"Mr. Darling?" In the crisp, clear light of day, she couldn't quite bring herself to call him by his Christian name.

He swung around, reluctance plain in the stiff motion.

She forced herself to meet his eyes. "Thank you for looking after me last night."

"Just doing my job, Duchess." Although his voice was as mocking as ever, his eyes had lost their teasing sparkle. His level gaze made her skin prickle with a curious combination of apprehension and anticipation. "After all, that is what you're going to be paying me for."

Before she could break the strange spell his words had cast, a shrill wail shattered the tranquillity of the morning. Sadie bounded to her feet and threw back her head, her baying only adding to the dreadful racket.

Billy's eyes narrowed in bewilderment. "What the hell . . . ?"

Esmerelda clapped her hands over her ears in a vain attempt to dull the piercing screech. "Sweet God in heaven, it sounds like they're torturing a cat. . . ." Her eyes widened in horror as comprehension dawned. "A cat!"

Her dismay shifting to fury, she snatched up the derringer from the folds of the blanket and went scrambling down the slope, leaving Billy to gape after her in stunned disbelief.

By the time Billy managed to shake off his shock and race down the slope with Sadie loping along behind him, Esmerelda was already holding the entire Darling gang at gunpoint.

They stood in a frozen tableau, caught red-handed rifling through the belongings in her overturned trunk. Jasper held an unstoppered scent bottle beneath his nose while Virgil clutched a pair of ruffled pantalettes to his burly chest, his face rapidly purpling from the cigar smoke he was afraid to exhale. Billy narrowed his eyes at the sight of Virgil's meaty hands fondling Esmerelda's drawers. His reluctance to stain the delicate fabric was the only thing that stopped him from drawing his own pistol and shooting his brother down in cold blood.

Esmerelda's wrath was directed toward the man with her violin tucked beneath his quivering chin. He held the bow captive in his other hand, poised to assault the strings and evoke another of those piteous screeches for deliverance.

Esmerelda's voice rang like a mission bell in the morning stillness. "Take your filthy hands off my mother's violin." She drew back the hammer of the derringer. "I'm not bluffing, Samuel Darling. Unhand that instrument or I'll shoot you. I swear I will."

Her target gulped hard enough to make his Adam's apple bob in his skinny throat. "I ain't Sam, m-m-a'am. I'm Enos." He jabbed the bow toward the man buried up to his elbows in a pile of petticoats. "H-h-he's Sam."

Esmerelda's gaze darted between the two men as she considered that revelation. "Then I'll shoot the both of you." Her eyes narrowed to menacing slits. "Or maybe I'll just shoot off one of *your* ears, Enos, so no one else will be able to tell the two of you apart."

Enos's yellow teeth began to chatter. Billy could hardly blame his brothers for being cowed. With her cheeks flushed with rage and her hair whipping around her shoulders in a cinnamon froth, Esmerelda looked nothing like the meek captive he'd led them to believe she was. The regal sneer curling her lips was more suited to a queen than a duchess.

With an unexpected thrill of pride, Billy thought how pretty she was when she was riled. Nothing this side of Abilene rivaled the sight of Esmerelda Fine in a temper.

Virgil wheezed, puffing a stream of smoke out of his nostrils like a consumptive locomotive. Jasper's free hand inched toward his gunbelt.

"I wouldn't do that if I were you," Billy drawled, folding his arms over his chest. "The little gal's got a right twitchy trigger finger and a deadly aim. She almost shot me clean through the heart the first time we met, and us not even properly introduced."

Esmerelda tossed him a startled look, but he couldn't tell if she was surprised by his presence or his praise. He winked at her, rattling her composure enough to make the derringer waver.

Fortunately, Enos was already holding out the violin. "I didn't mean no h-h-harm, ma'am. I've just always been right partial to fiddle music."

Mollified by his polite surrender, Esmerelda laid the derringer in Billy's outstretched hand and rescued the violin. Oblivious to his brothers' hungry inspection of her shapely calves and trim ankles, she tenderly polished Enos's greasy fingerprints off the rich wood with the ruffled hem of her petticoat.

Targeting the brother with the nastiest leer, Billy snarled, "Give the lady her perfume, Jasper."

Jasper stole another whiff from the bottle. "Hell, this ain't no perfume. It's peach extract." His scowl curved into a grin as he elbowed Virgil in the ribs. "No wonder she smells good enough to eat."

Billy's trigger finger twitched again. What in the hell was wrong with him? He couldn't very well shoot a man for saying exactly what he'd been thinking.

Esmerelda surprised him by marching right over and plucking the bottle from his brother's hands. Even the arrogant Jasper looked chilled by the brittle insincerity of her smile. "Unlike you and your brothers, sir, I have to pay for what I want instead of simply taking it from those who are weaker than I. Why should I waste my money on lilac or lavender water when a dab of extract behind each ear will suffice?"

Billy frowned, pained as much by her dignity as her frugality. Hell, a woman like the Duchess deserved more than peach extract to scent her creamy skin. She deserved the most expensive perfume gold could buy, eau de cologne from Paris, frankincense and myrrh.

As Esmerelda snatched her drawers from Virgil's hands and moved to stuff them back in the trunk, Enos dogged her every step like a determined pup. "C-c-can you really play that there fiddle, ma'am?"

"I can."

His nasal voice rose to a wheedling tone Billy recognized only too well. "I do so love f-fiddle music. We all do. I don't suppose you'd do us the honor of p-p-playin' us a tune?"

Alarmed, Billy stepped forward. "I really don't think that would be a good idea." If Esmerelda played like she sang, the noise just might incite his brothers to murder.

He was too late. Esmerelda's cheek had already dimpled in a flattered smile. "Why, I'd be delighted, sir! I had no idea there were music lovers among you. What would you like to hear? 'Amazing Grace'? 'Onward, Christian Soldiers'? Or perhaps 'The Battle Hymn of the—' "

Billy clapped a hand over her mouth, then just as quickly withdrew it when her smoldering glare warned him that he was in imminent danger of drawing back five bloody stubs.

"Any old t-tune will do," Enos insisted.

Sam and Virgil shuffled closer, doing a poor job of hiding their eagerness. Jasper struck a match on the sole of his boot and touched the flame to a fresh cigar, but even his indifference seemed forced.

Billy shrugged his defeat. "You know what they say. Music soothes the savage beast."

"Breast," Esmerelda automatically corrected, tucking the violin beneath her determined little chin.

Billy squeezed his eyes shut, dreading the moment when that first hideous screech would echo through the canyon.

But when Esmerelda drew the bow across the strings, it was a thousand times worse than he'd anticipated. He'd never heard the like and never hoped to again.

The music flooded both the canyon and Billy's soul, utterly shattering in its beauty. There was no escaping it. He would hear it even if he clapped his hands over his ears, even if he shouted at her to stop or snatched the violin from her hands and dashed it to pieces against the rocks. The instrument sang with a purity and grace he'd only found before between the pages of a book. It made his throat tighten with a wistful ache—a keen longing for places he would never travel, the man he would never be, a woman he could never love.

Women, he corrected himself fiercely, opening his eyes to glare at Esmerelda. Her own eyes were closed in passionate concentration as she stroked the bow across the strings with the tender ferocity of a lover. Esmerelda Fine might sing like a harpy, but she played the violin like an angel.

The music ended on a plaintive note, leaving a raw scar where it had been.

Virgil and Enos exchanged a bewildered look while Sam scratched his head, obviously straining to be polite. "That there was real purty, ma'am, but it weren't like no fiddle music I ever heard before. Cain't you do 'Goober Peas' or 'Jim Crack Corn'?"

Esmerelda frowned, plainly dismayed to have disappointed him. "I should have known you wouldn't care for Mozart."

"I'm sure that Mo's a nice enough f-feller," Enos said, "but I did have a hankering to hear a few b-b-bars of 'Two Dead Varmints in the Cotton Patch'."

Esmerelda glanced at Billy. Despite his savage scowl, her own expression softened to a winsome smile. "Here's one you boys might know."

The very first notes sent a shiver of recognition down Billy's spine. It was "Dixie" as it was meant to be played— simple and sweet, not as a march or a dirge, but as a gentle tribute to innocence lost. One by one, his brothers drew off their hats and stiffened to attention, the ghosts of the boys they had been and the men they might have become transposed over their haggard faces.

As Billy met Esmerelda's gaze over the graceful dance of the bow, he realized the song wasn't for them, but for him. She was offering him an apology for any offense he might have taken when they'd discussed the war yesterday.

An apology he couldn't accept and didn't deserve. Not when she'd betrayed him by lying about her identity. And not when he had every intention of betraying her as soon as he came face-to-face with the man she had hired him to find.

He reached over and gently laid his fingers across the strings, silencing the song in midnote.

Sam slapped his hat on his knee in disgust. "Now what'd you have to go and do that for?"

Virgil shook his head sadly. "You'd best watch your step, little brother. We've killed men for less."

Deliberately avoiding Esmerelda's wounded gaze, Billy swung around to face his brothers. "However sweetly the lady plays, we don't have time to stand around in the sunshine all day listening to a concert. In case you've forgotten, we've got unfinished business to tend to in Eulalie."

CHAPTER THIRTEEN

"Are your brothers going to help us find Bartholomew?" Esmerelda shouted, tightening her grip on Billy's waist as he guided his mare through the bustling crowds clogging Eulalie's main thoroughfare.

"You could say that," he replied, forced to yell over the shrill jingle of harnesses, the deafening clamor of the crowd, and the constant hammering of new construction. "But it wouldn't make it true," he added beneath his breath.

Billy didn't know what disturbed him the most—the hopeful note in Esmerelda's voice, the sight of her white-gloved hands folded over his rigid belly, or the torturous softness of her breasts pressed against his back. When Enos had insisted on driving the wagon so she wouldn't blister her delicate palms tugging on the reins, Billy had had no choice but to invite her to ride with him. He sure as hell didn't want her bumping thighs with Enos or twining her arms around Jasper's waist. His brothers had taken care to ride behind them for most of the journey, reluctant to kick dust in Esmerelda's luminous eyes.

Billy shook his head in disgust. If Sherman had marched on Atlanta with Esmerelda playing "Dixie" on her violin, he could have conquered the city without striking a single match. He'd seen his brothers drink themselves silly on everything from moonshine to furniture varnish, but he never thought he'd see them drunk with adoration. For a fiddle-playing Yankee, no less. Even the jaded Jasper had drawn him aside and offered him a gold pocket watch and a pair of boots freshly pilfered from a dead man, hoping to convince Billy to sell Esmerelda to him instead of to the Comancheros.

As they trotted past the sheriff's office, Billy gave the bandanna knotted around his throat a nervous tug. It was beginning to feel more and more like a noose.

He'd already cursed Winstead to hell and back for spreading the rumor about the treasury gold spending the night in Eulalie, knowing all the while that he'd do just as well to curse himself. He never could resist a mystery or a pretty face, and it was precisely that failing that had sent him careening down the road from Calamity to disaster.

He swung the horse around a crippled wagon, narrowly missing a burly mule driver who swore and shook his fist at him.

Since his last visit over seven months ago, Eulalie had become a bustling metropolis. A recent silver strike in a nearby mine had brought miners and gamblers stampeding into the sleepy little town hoping to make their fortunes, followed by a stream of prostitutes hoping to earn theirs on their backs.

As they passed a saloon with whoops of drunken laughter and rollicking piano music pouring out of its swinging doors, a colorful flock of half-dressed women hung over the scrolled rail of the second-story balcony.

"Hey, cowboy, you new in town?" crooned a brassy blonde to the top of Billy's hat. "Why don't you come on up and let us show you the sights?"

"Why don't I come up instead?" Virgil bellowed. "They don't call me his *big* brother for nothin'."

The women trilled an aria of giggles and blew him and Jasper several inviting kisses. Virgil motioned to Enos and Sam, then winked at Billy. "At least this way you'll know where to find us tonight."

Billy nodded grimly. The whores stood a better chance of keeping his brothers out of jail for a few hours than he did. He'd managed to convince Virgil and Jasper that it would be best to dynamite the bank's safe after dark. He hoped to stall them until he'd had a chance to take Bart Fine into custody and clear out of town.

Billy scowled at a vision of Esmerelda wrapped in the scoundrel's arms. Arranging an untimely accident suddenly didn't seem like such a bad idea.

As Billy drew Esmerelda off the mare and deposited her on the bench of the buckboard next to Sadie, he discovered that she'd been mercifully deaf to the entire exchange between his brothers and the whores. She was too busy craning her slender neck this way and that, as if she expected the elusive Mr. Fine to come strolling right out of the crowd and into her adoring arms.

As Billy tethered his mare to the back of the wagon, she snapped out of her trance. "Where did your brothers go?"

"To start the search," he replied, climbing into the buckboard.

She nodded her approval. "We probably ought to check the missions and churches in the area first. If Bartholomew's been robbed or wounded, he might have sought refuge there."

Billy snapped the reins on the mule's back, turning his face away to hide the bitter twist of his lips. She knew as well as he did that his brothers stood a better chance of finding Bart Fine in a whorehouse than a church.

He drew the buckboard to a standstill in front of a handsome structure that still smelled of sawdust and fresh-cut pine. Its gleaming brass lanterns and diamond-paned windows clearly branded the Silver Lining Hotel the finest establishment in town. And why not? Billy thought grimly. The Duchess deserved the best. Especially when it was being paid for with Winstead's blood money. As cheery and imposing as the building was, Billy knew that it would be as lonely and forsaken as the rest of the town a few months from now when the silver strike played out.

As he untied the mare and unloaded Esmerelda's belongings, Sadie lumbered down from the wagon, her slack white belly brushing the plank sidewalk.

Esmerelda quickly joined the basset hound, giving the building a skeptical look. "This doesn't look like a church."

"That's because it's a hotel." Billy drew several bills from his pocket and pressed them into her hand. "Get us a room. Order yourself a hot meal and a bath. I have some business to tend to."

Without further explanation, he tipped his hat forward and ducked across the teeming street, leading the mare behind him. He glanced back only once to find Esmerelda and Sadie still standing on the sidewalk, staring forlornly after him.

Esmerelda paced the hotel room, utterly oblivious to its elegant brass appointments and cherrywood four-poster. She had eyes only for the gold-plated watch pinned to her bodice. According to the leisurely crawl of its gilded hands, a scant three minutes had passed since the last time she'd glanced at it. Billy had already been gone over two hours.

"He's probably halfway to the Mexican border with those outlaw brothers of his by now," she muttered, casting a rueful glance over her shoulder at Sadie.

The basset hound rested her chins on her paws, her drooping ears making her look even more dejected than Esmerelda felt.

Esmerelda made a nervous circuit around the copper tub that crouched on a braided rug in front of the hearth. As delicious as it had been to scrub the grit from her skin and hair, she hadn't been able to savor the steaming bath for fear Billy would come strolling in at any minute. When he hadn't, she'd been too disappointed to enjoy her meal. She could hardly be expected to eat with her stomach coiled into a miserable knot of apprehension. The veal cutlet had sat untouched on a silver tray until she'd thought to offer it to Sadie. The hound had wolfed it down, refusing to let despondency dull her appetite.

Esmerelda touched a hand to her damp chignon, wondering why she'd even bothered to don her finest Sunday-go-to-meeting walking dress and a full complement of underwear. The dress had been an extravagance she had convinced herself was a necessity, since she wanted to look presentable to her pupils' parents whenever she hosted a recital to show off the talents of their little darlings. The mellow peach hue of the wool flattered her complexion and wove shimmering strands of auburn through her mousy hair.

"I simply want to look my best when Bartholomew and I are reunited," she told her skeptical reflection in the cheval glass. It had nothing to do with igniting that lazy gleam of appreciation in Billy's eyes.

Disgusted with herself for lying, she marched to the window and shoved up the sash, hoping to catch a glimpse of a lanky, tawny-headed cowboy weaving his way through the crowds below.

Eulalie might lack the brick streets and ivied grace of Boston, but raw exhilaration perfumed the air. Esmerelda closed her eyes and drank in a deep breath, the mingled scents of sawdust and desert wind stirring her blood in a way the clouds of coal dust hanging over Boston never had.

She was so taken by the sensation that she might not have heard the soft rap on the door if Sadie hadn't pried open her droopy lids and let out a welcoming "Woof!"

Nearly tripping over the inert hound, Esmerelda tore across the room and eagerly flung open the door.

Her disappointment was so keen she collected only a scattering of impressions: a neatly knotted necktie where a dusty bandanna should have been; a dark suit and double-breasted waistcoat woven of the finest serge; a gleaming pocket watch on a gold fob. A tooled leather gunbelt peeked out from the parted folds of a handsome coat.

Realizing how imprudent she'd been to open the door to a stranger, she barely glanced at his face. "I'm terribly sorry, sir. You must have the wrong room."

She had already narrowed the opening between door and frame to a mere crack when one shiny black shoe protruded through it. "My deepest apologies, ma'am," he drawled. "They told me at the desk that this was where the crazy girl from Boston was staying."

Esmerelda stumbled backward in shock, leaving the door free to swing wide open. Her visitor leaned one brawny shoulder against the doorframe, his gray-green eyes sparkling with pure devilment.

"Mr. Darling?" she croaked.

"Billy," he gently corrected before sauntering past her.

Esmerelda had never dreamed that Billy's predatory grace would lend itself to such polished elegance. While he squatted to greet Sadie with a scratch behind the ears, she eased the door shut, struggling to steady both her hands and her rioting emotions.

When she turned to face him, he straightened and drew off his dapper bowler, revealing dark gold hair that had been cropped of some of its natural curl and smoothed close to his head. His face had also been shorn of its rugged stubble, baring the clean masculinity of his features. His jaw was more stern than she'd supposed, which only made his easy grin more beguiling.

Noting the direction of her gaze, he ruefully stroked his chin. "I decided to take the advice I gave Virgil and invest in a nickel bath and shave. It wouldn't do to roam around town like the spitting image of my Wanted poster. There are too many men out there looking to make an easy dollar."

"Men like you?" Esmerelda knotted her hands behind her to keep them from reaching up to explore the naked curve of his jaw.

He acknowledged her barb with a mocking nod. "Men like me."

"Where did you find the suit? I wouldn't think it would be possible for a tailor to so quickly fit a man of your, um . . ." Eloquence deserted her as she blinked up at him, feeling like a porcelain doll in his shadow. ". . . proportions."

Billy stroked his broad thumbs down the lapels of the coat. "I purchased it from the local undertaker." Esmerelda took a hasty step backward.

He caught her elbow to steady her. "Don't worry. The suit's fresh from a boiling at the Chinese laundry. And he promised me the fellow who owned it before me won't mind one lick. It's a trick I learned from Jasper. He buys all his finery there."

Esmerelda managed a breathless laugh. "Your brother probably gets a discount for providing them with so much business." Flustered by Billy's touch, she drew her arm away from his and started for the scarlet cord of the bellpull. "I've already eaten," she lied, "but I'd be delighted to order you some lunch."

"I can't stay. I've got a job to do."

Esmerelda changed course, heading for the wardrobe where she'd unpacked her scant belongings. "Then I'll be right with you." She dropped the room key into her reticule and hooked the tiny purse's braided cord over her arm. "Just let me find my bonnet and gloves and we can—"

"Not this time, Esmerelda." She swung around to discover the sparkle in Billy's eyes had sharpened to a grim glitter. "The streets of a town like this are no place for a woman like you."

Esmerelda took one step toward him, then another, sensing even as she did so that she was courting a far more devastating danger than any that could be found on the streets of Eulalie. "They are if I have a man like you to protect me."

Hanging his bowler on the doorknob, Billy took her by the shoulders, not to draw her nearer as she'd both hoped and feared, but to hold her at arm's length. The intensity of his grip revealed that his charm was nothing more than a thin veneer over some unspoken desperation. "There are some things even I can't protect you from."

Instead of shying away as he plainly hoped she would, Esmerelda gently cupped his forearms in her palms and tipped her head back to meet his fevered gaze. "If I believed that, Mr. Darling, I never would have hired you."

He drew her inexorably nearer, the rasp in his voice deepening to a smoky growl. "And would you still have hired me if I'd demanded payment in advance?"

Before she could catch her breath, Billy sought his answer from her parted lips. Esmerelda expected his kiss to be crude and punishing, but his lips simply grazed hers, as if to steal a taste of some forbidden sweet he desperately craved, yet feared he could never get enough of. Her lips melted beneath that delicious seduction.

Only then did he dip his tongue into the moist hollow of her mouth. Only then did he deepen his demand, urging her own tongue to respond in kind. Desire purled through her blood, thickening to warm nectar in the most scandalous of places.

Billy was no bounty hunter in that moment, but a ruthless outlaw, out to rob her of all she considered worthy and dear—her steadfast devotion to propriety and her stern self-denial. She might have been able to resist him had he sought only to take. But the ferocious tenderness of his kiss promised that he had much to give. More than she had ever dared hope for.

His mouth slanted over hers, one kiss melting inevitably into another. Her fingers crept up to shyly caress the fine hairs at his nape. He smelled nearly as delicious as he tasted—like leather and shaving soap mingled with a tantalizing hint of male musk.

He was the one who ended the kiss. Esmerelda could only cling helplessly to him, thankful for the possessive pressure of his arms around her. She couldn't have stood on her own had she wanted to. Although she'd never imbibed so much as a drop of cooking sherry, she felt drunk. Drunk from a single sip of pleasure that had only whetted her thirst instead of quenching it.

Billy rubbed his cheek against her hair, taking a ragged

breath. "I guess we'll just have to consider that a little bonus."

Exhaling just as shakily, Esmerelda rested her cheek against his chest. His heart was pounding just as madly as hers beneath the woven serge of his vest. Her trembling fingers plucked and kneaded the fabric, seized by a foreign longing to caress and explore the warm masculine expanse of skin and muscle underneath.

That was how she discovered the small flaw in the fabric. It lay directly over his heart, nearly invisible to the naked eye. As Esmerelda drew back to finger the neatly mended tear, a chill of foreboding cascaded down her spine.

"Don't go," she whispered, the plea coming from some elemental place deep within her. She tipped her head back to gaze into his eyes. Eyes that were heavy-lidded and glittering with desire for her. Esmerelda was shocked to discover in that moment just how far she would be willing to go to keep him safe in her arms. "If you walk out that door without me, I'm afraid you won't come back."

He cupped her elbows and gently set her away from him, his grin returning with its old heartbreaking ease. "I have to go. I wouldn't be much of a tracker if I let myself get distracted by every beautiful duchess who crossed my path."

Esmerelda realized with a start of alarm that he had taken advantage of her delicious languor to abscond with her reticule. Even as he bestowed that angelic smile upon her, he was fishing through it with methodical deliberation.

"Stay." Her voice cracked, then faded to a whisper. "If you do, I'll make it . . ."

His fingers froze in their task. His smile faded.

Esmerelda closed her eyes, unable to meet his wary gaze

while she bartered away the only thing of value left to her. ". . . worth your while."

She might have imagined his helpless chuckle, but she didn't imagine the tender brush of his lips against hers. "You already have, honey. You already have."

The door slammed. The key turned. Esmerelda opened her eyes to find both Billy and his bowler gone. She rushed to the door and frantically twisted the knob. Just as she feared, he had locked it from the outside, leaving her a helpless captive.

Esmerelda pounded on the door, shouting until she was hoarse. When no one came running to rescue her, she realized that Billy must have peeled some more bills off that fat wad of cash he always carried and paid the hotel manager to ignore her cries.

She collapsed against the door, dizzied by frustration and fear. Dear Lord, what had she done? She might finally find Bartholomew, but at what cost?

She opened her mouth to shout again, then abruptly closed it. Her mama had always taught her that her voice was a precious instrument, never to be strained without good cause. A determined smile slowly curved her lips. Outwitting Billy Darling just might be the best cause of all.

As Billy strode down Main Street, the crowds shied away from him. A well-dressed gentleman wearing wire-rimmed spectacles crossed the street to avoid him, while a mother snatched her tiny daughter out of his path, whispering frantically in the little girl's ear. Although he pretended indifference, Billy was only too aware of their desperate swerving and fearful glances.

He might be able to change his clothes, but he could do

nothing to disguise his gunslinger's gait—that lazy roll of the hips that made it possible to flip aside the hem of his coat, draw his Colt, and fire before his opponent had time to make his final peace with God.

Nor could he dim the predatory gleam in his eye, a gleam that always sharpened whenever he sensed his prey was nearby. As he passed the brothel where he'd left his brothers, he tipped the bowler forward to shadow his face, praying they were too busy spending both their money and their seed to spare a glance out the window.

His nape prickled as he crossed the street, making him wonder if Winstead had men out there somewhere, watching his every move. The notion made him itch to boolt. He might carry the badge of a deputy U.S. marshal in the breast pocket of his vest, but outlaw blood still pulsed through his heart, tarnishing everything shiny and beautiful that he dared to touch.

Everything but Esmerelda. He had gone to that hotel room determined to take her to the bank with him. He'd been fully prepared to drag her if necessary and force her to witness the havoc she had wreaked with her schemes and her lies.

But the minute she'd flung open that door, a welcoming smile softening her prim lips, he had realized that he could no more deliberately endanger her life than he could draw his own pistol and put a bullet through her heart.

Billy inhaled a ragged breath, trying desperately to clear his head. The musky sweet fragrance of peaches still haunted him. It clung to his clothes and his skin everywhere he had touched Esmerelda, tempting him to turn around and march right back to that hotel room. To throw open the door, lock it from the inside, and spend the rest of the day and night making hot, delicious love to her.

He could still see her as she'd stood before him—her eyes pressed shut, the cinnamon lace of her lashes resting against her cheeks. A convulsive swallow had rippled down her graceful, white throat when she'd begged him to stay. She'd looked less like some calculating temptress than a sacrificial virgin. In that moment he had known it no longer mattered whether Bart Fine was her brother or her lover. He didn't care if she'd had one man or a dozen. He didn't have to be the first man she took to her bed. He only wanted to be the last.

It was that shocking realization that had driven him from the room. Esmerelda would never know what it had cost him to spurn her offer. To steal one last bittersweet taste of her lips before turning away and leaving her there. Because she'd been right about one thing. He was never coming back.

Once he apprehended Fine, he had no intention of turning him over to Esmerelda. Given Winstead's desperation to be rid of the outlaw, he'd most likely hunt them both down before they could get out of New Mexico. Billy's jaw hardened along with his resolve, sending a grizzled miner scurrying out of his path. He'd decided to risk both Esmerelda's and Winstead's wrath by turning Fine over to Elliot Courtney, the U.S. marshal in Albuquerque. Countney still owed him for bringing in a notorious horse thief last fall and could at least be counted on to guarantee Fine a fair trial.

Which was more than Billy could expect. Winstead was not the sort to forgive or forget. As soon as he learned of Billy's betrayal, there would be a price on his head even higher than the one he carried now. Winstead was also likely to add those four words that were such sweet music to every bounty hunter's ears—*Wanted: Dead or Alive*. Billy would have no choice but to spend the rest of his life on the run or flee to Mexico with his brothers.

Like the specter of that grim future, the shadow of the Eulalie First National Bank fell across his path. Billy paused to purchase a newspaper from a freckled boy, studying the imposing two-story brick structure from the corner of his eye. The bank boasted two narrow side doors and one main door, through which a steady stream of newly prosperous customers passed.

He tucked the newspaper beneath his arm and entered the bank, holding the door open for a stooped, white-haired woman who shuffled past, leaning heavily on her cane. If Fine came in as Winstead had warned, with a belly full of sass and a blaze of gunfire, Billy was going to have to take him down fast or risk some innocent bystander getting shot.

He strolled over and sank down in a leather wing chair that offered him an unobstructed view of all three doors. One of the tellers perched behind the brass bars of his cage shot him a nervous glance, but a genteel smile and a reassuring wink seemed to set the young man at ease. If Winstead had done what he'd promised, the teller must suspect that Billy was the deputy sent to protect the shipment of treasury gold languishing in the bank's vault.

Opening the newspaper to hide his scrutiny of the doors, Billy waited.

He had learned quickly that a bounty hunter need possess only one virtue—patience. The patience to sit motionless on his mare with cold rain dripping from the brim of his slouch hat until a drunken horse thief came stumbling out of a saloon. The patience to keep smiling while he lost hand after hand of poker to a man suspected of bashing his wife to death with a frying pan and burying her poor, broken body in the vegetable garden. The patience to peruse a newspaper in a sunny bank lobby, knowing his presence there would cost him dreams he'd never even known he had until he had gazed into Esmerelda's sparkling maple eyes.

But this was one job that didn't require as much patience as he'd anticipated. The afternoon sun slanting through the bank's frosted glass windows had barely begun to shift angles when Billy's nape began to tingle. He stiffened. The newspaper slid from his lap to the floor.

That reliable indicator of danger was followed by the thunder of hoofbeats, cries of alarm, and a frantic commotion in the street outside the bank.

Billy eased aside his coat to rest his hand on the butt of his pistol. He slipped his other hand into his breast pocket to give the badge a brief caress. It would be the first and last time he would ever have the right to use it.

As the left side door burst open and four men with drawn pistols rushed into the bank, a woman screamed and Billy came to his feet.

"Everybody down!" he shouted. "On the floor!"

The customers obeyed, responding instinctively to the authority in his voice. Even the old woman's screams subsided to panicked sniffles.

Instead of rushing to the tellers' windows as everyone expected, the intruders stumbled to a halt a few feet from Billy.

The skinniest of the four, whose marked absence of a hat revealed that he only had one ear poking out from his tousled, straw-colored hair, pointed an accusing finger at Billy. "See! I ain't no dummy after all. I told you it was him that went strollin' by the whorehouse jest as purty as you please."

Billy rolled his eyes, wondering why he couldn't have been born into the James family or the Younger family or hell, even the Borgia family.

It didn't alarm him that Virgil's suspenders were unhooked and dangling over his massive barrel chest or that Enos's red drawers were peeking out of his half-unbuttoned pants. But the sight of the persnickety Jasper with his hair ruffled and rouge smudging his shirt did send a faint shiver of foreboding through him.

"You double-crossin' sonofabitch!" Virgil roared, the sheer volume of his voice enough to send the old woman cowering in the corner into a fresh fit of hysterics.

"Somebody slap her before she gets us all killed." The disembodied voice floated out from one of the teller's cages. The threat was enough to stifle the woman in mid-shriek.

"What'd you do this time, Billy?" Virgil bellowed. "Pay them whores to distract us? You too dadburned greedy to share all that treasury gold with your own flesh and blood?"

Billy raised one hand in a pacifying gesture, but kept the other fixed firmly on his gun. "Rein in those wild horses of yours, Virg. It's not what you think."

"I told you the bastard was selfish," Jasper purred, caressing the hammer of his pistol with his thumb. "That's what comes of bein' coddled by Ma all those years."

Virgil's ham-handed fist came swinging toward Billy. Billy's gun was half out of its holster when Virgil clapped him on the shoulder, a dazzling grin breaking over his broad face. "First you go and get yourself wanted for murder and now this. By God, son, I ain't never been so proud. You just might have Darlin' blood flowin' through those veins of yours after all!"

Billy choked out a strained laugh, but he was saved from replying by the fresh thunder of hoofbeats outside the bank. Four more men came rushing through the opposite side door, dusty bandannas tied across the bridges of their noses to mask their features.

They skidded to a halt, their whoops and hollers fading as they gaped in dumb surprise at the Darling gang. The Darling gang gaped back, their own jaws slack with shock.

Billy might have been tempted to duck out and let them shoot it out amongst themselves if the main door of the bank hadn't swung open at that precise moment to admit a petite brunette wearing pristine white gloves and a squashed bonnet.

Esmerelda stormed through the door, tugging a reluctant Sadie along behind her on a scarlet cord that had once been an elegant bellpull at the Silver Lining Hotel.

She marched right up to Billy, completely oblivious to the drama unfolding around them. He lunged forward, making a desperate but futile attempt to put his body between her heaving bosom and all eight pistols trained upon it.

She shook one white-gloved finger at him, as if he were some hapless piano student who had struck an off-key note during a recital. "There you are, you shameless deserter! I suppose you thought you were protecting me by locking me in my room like a child. Well, I'll have you know this is 1878, not 1778. Women are no longer content to languish in the parlor while you arrogant men march into battle on their behalf." She tilted her patrician nose in the air, looking even more smug than Jasper. "You're probably wondering how I escaped your clever little trap. As soon as I realized that you must have bribed the hotel manager to ignore my cries for assistance, I stopped screaming and started singing. All it took was twelve verses of 'Soldiers of Christ, Arise' and the poor man was begging me to leave his establishment before the rest of his guests did. Even after I quit singing, poor Sadie here wouldn't stop howling, so he evicted her, too."

The hound settled back on her haunches and cast Billy a reproachful look, as if to chide him for going off and leaving her in the care of a tone-deaf lunatic.

Standing on tiptoe, Esmerelda tried to peer around his shoulder. He feinted right, then left, frantically trying to block her vision.

She shot him a perplexed look. "What on earth are you doing? Have you had any luck finding . . . ?"

Her fingers uncurled. The leash slipped from her hand. Tears flooded her eyes, making them shine with a regard so hopelessly tender it made Billy ache to be the man she was looking at.

"Bartholomew?" she whispered.

Billy swung around to glare at the man behind him. There could be no mistaking the mischief sparkling in the black eyes above the scarlet bandanna.

"Esme?" the man croaked, those same eyes rapidly losing their sparkle and widening in horror.

Billy groaned aloud, knowing that he'd just lost his last chance of getting out of that bank without killing somebody.

CHAPTER FOURTEEN

"Bartholomew?" Esmerelda echoed, her vision blurred by tears. The shimmering haze surrounding her brother only deepened her conviction that she must be dreaming.

"Bartholomew?" the masked men chorused in disgust, swinging around to gawk at him.

"I believe he calls himself Bart now," Billy said quietly, his expression as grim as she'd ever seen it. "Black Bart."

"Black Bart?" Esmerelda wrinkled her nose. "What an abominable sobriquet."

"But it's one hell of an alias," Sam said, watching the proceedings with the sharp-eyed interest of a one-eared ferret. Virgil, Enos, and Jasper appeared equally captivated.

Bartholomew began to back away from her. He couldn't have looked any more alarmed had she waved a lit stick of dynamite under his nose. He clawed at the bandanna, jerking it up so high he nearly blinded himself.

His voice was muffled by the bubble of fabric he sucked into his mouth with each panicked breath. "You must have mistaken me for someone else, ma'am. I ain't never heard of this Bartholomew fellow. Now I suggest you step back before I'm forced to shoot you." He crashed into the bank's long counter, barely managing to steady himself with one hand.

Esmerelda tilted her head to study him. If memory served her, this wasn't the first time she'd come face-to-face with the dastardly Black Bart. As a precocious four-year-old, her brother had delighted in tying one of their mama's handkerchiefs over his pug nose in just such a manner. He would sneak up on Papa, poke him in the back with a wooden spoon, and demand all of his money. Pretending to quake with fear, Papa would empty his pockets of change, pouring the shiny coins into Bartholomew's greedy little hands.

Emboldened by his success as a robber, Bartholomew had even taken to jumping out of darkened corners at Esmerelda. At least until the morning she'd swung around and boxed his ears between two books. He'd bawled at the top of his lungs for over an hour, earning Esmerelda a stern lecture from their parents. But the satisfaction had been well worth it.

A flare of anger burned away the tears in Esmerelda's eyes, leaving them dry and aching. Suddenly she could see clearly. All too clearly.

Billy grabbed for her elbow, but she stalked forward, shaking off his grip. "Ain't?" she bit off, her voice pitched dangerously low. "*Ain't,* Bartholomew? Is that how I taught you to talk? Is that what you learned from studying thirteen years of grammar and elocution?"

"I knew a feller who was elocuted once," Sam remarked.

He shook his head, sighing sadly. "I told him not to stand under that tree durin' a lightnin' spell, but he jest wouldn't listen."

The other three masked men stood frozen, mesmerized by Esmerelda's fearless pursuit of their leader. Bartholomew flattened one hand on the counter, but the bars of the teller cages prevented him from vaulting over it. Before he could devise a new plan for escape, Esmerelda grabbed the bandanna by its triangular fold and snatched it down.

A flabbergasted silence swept the bank, broken only by the muffled whimper of the forgotten woman in the corner.

Bartholomew hung his head. If it hadn't been for the sinister beard shading his jaw, he would have looked exactly like the cherubic four-year-old whose ears she had boxed. She almost expected his plump lower lip to start quivering and tears to flood those big, dark eyes of his. It made her want to shake him and kiss him and smack him all at the same time.

She wagged a finger in his face instead. "Why, Bartholomew Ignatius Fine, I ought to turn you over my knee."

"Ignatius?" his men chorused again. This time, one of them even had the temerity to giggle.

Jasper elbowed Virgil. "She can turn me over her knee any day of the week."

One of the masked men eagerly raised his hand. "Or me!"

"How 'bout me!" volunteered another. "I've been a *very* bad boy."

Holstering his pistol, Bartholomew shook his hair out of his eyes and fixed her with a smoldering glare. The phony drawl disappeared from his voice, leaving it clipped and sullen. "See what you've gone and done now, Esme.

Those men respected me. At least they did until you came along and spoiled everything. You never did want me to have any fun."

"Fun?" Esmerelda choked out a disbelieving laugh, sweeping a hand toward the bank customers cowering in the floor. "Is this what you call fun? Terrorizing innocent citizens? Stealing the money they've worked for and sacrificed to save?"

He cocked his head back, as unrepentant as he'd been when she'd caught him gobbling lemon drops right out of the jar at the corner apothecary when he was nine. "I'm just doing research for my novel. A man's got to live life before he can write about it."

All the anger and hurt Esmerelda had hoarded in her heart over the past few months spilled into her eyes as fresh tears. "And I suppose it didn't bother you that while you were out here living life, I was back home thinking you were dead."

Genuine shame flickered across his face. "I'm truly sorry about that, Esme. I swear I am. I didn't hire Snorton to hurt you, but to protect you."

Esmerelda took a step backward, recoiling as if he'd slapped her. "*You* hired Snorton?" she whispered. "You hired that horrid little weasel?"

It was Bartholomew who stalked her now, stretching out his hands in supplication as she continued to back away from him. "You had to believe I was dead, Esme. It was the only way I could keep you safe. If you thought I was alive, I knew you'd take it into that obstinate head of yours to come out west and find me."

Esmerelda stopped, standing her ground. "So you had Snorton swindle me out of the pittance I had left and deliver that overwrought account of your death?"

Bartholomew's brow furrowed in a sulky frown. "Overwrought? That's not very generous of you. I found it to be a very moving piece of fiction. I had to stop and dab my eyes more than once while I was writing it."

Esmerelda heard a snort behind her that could have only come from Billy.

"You see, Esme," Bartholomew continued. "I made a man very angry—a dangerous and powerful man. I deliberately let him believe that I was an only child. I was afraid if he found out I had a sister, he might try to use you against me or hurt you out of spite."

"I doubt that he could have hurt me any more than you have," she said stiffly.

Bartholomew's words began to tumble out, propelled by his growing excitement. "Someday you'll understand that I did what I did for the both of us. As soon as the fuss died down, I had every intention of contacting you with the wonderful news." He clutched her shoulders, giving her the dimpled smile that had never failed to soften her heart when he was a little boy. "I'm a wealthy man now, sister. Wealthy enough to make sure that you never again have to scrimp or sacrifice or go hungry on my account. You won't have to listen to those spoiled rich brats pound on the piano all day. You'll be able to afford all the pretty gewgaws and ribbons you always deserved." He captured one of the curls that had escaped from her bonnet, tenderly coiling it around his finger. "You're not so old yet, Esme. If you fix yourself up with some powder and paint, you might even be able to snare some lonely widower and have some babies of your own to mother."

A wave of humiliation broke over Esmerelda, flooding her cheeks with heat. She might have been able to endure it with more grace if she hadn't known that Billy was back there somewhere, listening to the entire exchange. Did he find her as pathetic as her own brother did?

Before she even realized she was going to do it, her hand had crossed Bartholomew's face, wiping the self-satisfied smirk from his mouth with enough force to make every man in that bank wince in commiseration.

He staggered backward, rubbing his cheek. His dark eyes brimmed with reproach. "Esme, how could you? You haven't so much as swatted me on the bottom since Mama and Papa died."

"I know. And I'm beginning to think I made a very grave mistake."

They glowered at each other with simmering hostility. Esmerelda wasn't even aware that Billy was circling them, studying the unconscious mirroring of their stances, the pugnacious jut of their jaws—a trait their mother had sworn they'd inherited from their pigheaded grandfather.

"Well, I will be damned," Billy breathed. "You really are his sister, aren't you?"

Esmerelda whirled on him, fighting hysteria. "Of course I'm his sister. Who did you think I was?"

As their gazes collided, she realized exactly who, and what, he had thought she was. It was there in the wariness shadowing his eyes, the raw tension curling his fingers into fists. It had been there in every exchange they'd shared, but she'd been too much of a fool to see it.

The realization hurt more than it should have. Even more than her brother's betrayal. For a moment, Esmerelda didn't know if she was going to be able to breathe through the unbearable tightness in her chest.

"Who the hell is he?" Bartholomew demanded, jealous of her attention just as he'd been as a toddler. "And why is he looking at you like that?"

Esmerelda barely heard him. She had eyes only for Billy. "You knew all along, didn't you?" she asked softly. "You knew exactly what I would find in Eulalie."

Unlike Bartholomew, Billy didn't try to excuse his actions or charm her into forgiving him. He simply looked her straight in the eye and nodded, damning them both with his honesty.

Esmerelda's hoarse laugh sounded more like a sob, even to her own ears. "How utterly delicious! One of you thinks I'm a dried-up old spinster, the other some outlaw's whore."

Bartholomew stiffened to his full height, outrage glittering in his eyes. "Just who do you think you are, sir, calling my sister a whore?"

Billy gave her brother a look of pure contempt. "I'm William Darling, you ungrateful little whelp, the man you let Snorton accuse of killing you." Slipping his hand into his vest pocket, he pulled out something shiny. He shoved the object under Bartholomew's nose, distracting them all from the quicksilver grace of his other hand drawing his Colt. "I'm also the deputy U.S. marshal who's about to take your sorry ass to jail."

CHAPTER FIFTEEN

"Oh, son," Virgil wailed, squinting at the badge in Billy's hand. "Say it ain't so!"

Esmerelda stood transfixed by the sight of the shiny tin star while Bartholomew's gang went scattering in all directions. They shot through the three doors hard enough to leave them banging behind them. Only Sadie appeared unfazed by Billy's revelation. She reclined on her haunches and hiked one back paw for a lethargic scratch behind her left ear, yawning in satisfaction.

"Get the hell out of here, Virg," Billy ordered, never taking his eyes off of Bartholomew. "Take the boys and go before I have to haul you in, too."

Enos and Sam huddled together, looking even more sallow than usual. Jasper snorted in disgust while Virgil shook his head, genuine grief darkening his eyes. "I do believe my big ole heart is broken. I never thought I'd live to see the day a Darlin' crawled into bed with the law."

They silently filed out, Jasper pausing at the door just long enough to spit over his shoulder.

Ignoring the crude insult, Billy jerked his head toward the cowering bank patrons. "You're free to go," he called out. "And I wouldn't waste any time about it."

He didn't have to ask twice. They crawled, ducked, and scrambled their way to freedom, leaving Billy, Bartholomew, and Esmerelda alone in the deserted bank lobby.

Esmerelda was still reeling from shock when Bartholomew grabbed her wrist, bruising it in his desperate grip. "You can't let him take me, Esme. You don't understand. I'll never make it to trial alive. I'll never even make it to jail. *He'll* make sure of that."

"Step away from the lady," Billy said, his steely composure as unwavering as the pistol in his hand.

Bartholomew began to inch backward, freeing Esmerelda's wrist when he realized her feet were still rooted to the floor. "He paid you, didn't he?" he shouted at Billy. "Paid you to shoot me down in cold blood. Well, if I die, he'll never find out where that gold is hidden! And neither will you."

"What gold?" Esmerelda wailed. "Who are you talking about?"

Bartholomew stabbed a finger toward Billy. "Ask him. He knows who hired him to find me."

"Of course he does. I did."

That admission momentarily distracted her brother from his mounting hysteria. He squinted at her. "With what? You don't have any money."

Painfully conscious of Billy's heavy-lidded scrutiny, Esmerelda said, "Mr. Darling is well aware of my present impoverishment. A state, I hasten to remind you, that I owe solely to your selfish and callow pilgrimage west. However, he was kind enough to extend me credit. Especially after I explained to him how grateful our grandfather would be once you were found." She clenched her teeth in a frantic approximation of a smile. "We both know how generous dear Grandpapa is inclined to be when it comes to his beloved grandson."

"Grandpapa? *Grandpapa?*" Bartholomew parroted with a shrill squawk of laughter. "And you dare to call my fiction overwrought!"

"Step away from the lady and put your hands over your head, boy." Billy's lazy drawl warned them that he was running out of patience. Esmerelda had already deduced that the slower Billy talked, the faster he could move.

"Do what he says," she urged her brother. "We'll sort out all this confusion later."

"Why not sort it out now?" As Bartholomew shifted his attention from her to Billy, his eyes took on a calculating glint. "You and me, Mr. Darling, we could be partners. I'll even give you Winstead's share of the gold. Whatever he's paying you, it can't come close to what I've got stashed away only a few miles from here."

Although Esmerelda feared both men had lost their wits, her brother had left her no choice but to appeal to the least deranged of the two.

She ran to Billy, grabbed him by the lapels of his coat, and gave him a savage little shake. "What in heaven's name is he babbling about? Who is this Winstead and why is Bartholomew trying to bribe you?"

She might have thought she was invisible if Billy's arm hadn't clamped around her waist, drawing her hard against him. She barely managed to wiggle around enough to see her brother's face, which was now wreathed in a friendly smile.

"You're probably thinking you can't trust me," he said, taking a step backward each time he paused for breath. "But I swear I never would have double-crossed Winstead if I hadn't overheard him telling one of his hired guns to kill me after I returned with the gold."

Billy's exasperated sigh ruffled her hair. "I don't want your gold, son. I want you to put your hands over your head where I can see them."

A spasm of raw panic crossed Bartholomew's face. He began to scuttle backward in earnest, a strategy that might have been successful if he hadn't tripped over his own boots and gone sprawling on his backside. Even with the beard disguising his baby fat, in that moment he looked painfully young.

Esmerelda breathed a sigh of relief. Until she saw his hand fumble with the mouth of his holster.

"Don't do it!" Billy shouted.

"Bartholomew, no!" she screamed.

Billy drew back the hammer of his own pistol. The click rang in Esmerelda's ears, louder than a gunshot itself. Frantic with desperation, she wrenched herself out of his arms and stumbled across the lobby, flinging her body across her brother's.

Dead silence greeted her gesture. Bartholomew's chest heaved beneath her own, but his arm did not close around her as Billy's had. Raising herself up on one elbow, she twisted around until she could meet Billy's stricken eyes.

"Jesus Christ, sweetheart," he whispered hoarsely, his words more prayer than oath. "I could have killed you."

Billy lowered the gun, his hand unsteady for the first time in his memory. If he hadn't been gazing at Esmerelda in helpless horror, he might have heard Sadie's low-pitched growl, felt the hair at his nape prickle in warning.

As it was, he didn't see the black steel barrel emerge from beneath Esmerelda's arm until after the explosion. A fiery inferno erupted high in his chest.

His pistol clattered to the floor. He flattened his hand against his chest, then held it out in front of him, struggling to grasp why so much blood would be dripping from his fingers. As comprehension dawned, he shifted his disbelieving gaze to Esmerelda.

If she lived to be a hundred, Esmerelda didn't think she would ever forget the look of shock and betrayal on Billy's face. Her ears were ringing in earnest now. The caustic stench of gunpowder seared her nostrils, stung her eyes. Billy's knees seemed to buckle an inch at a time, sending his lanky frame crashing to the floor.

Esmerelda might have remained frozen in shock while his life seeped away if Sadie hadn't trundled over, still trailing the frayed cord behind her, and began to lick his face. Esmerelda couldn't tell if the frightened whimper she heard was the dog's or her own.

Easily disengaging herself from Bartholomew's limp body, she scrambled on hands and knees to Billy's side. The badge lay where it had fallen, only inches from his bloodstained fingers. His shirt was already soaked with blood, the ugly stain rapidly spreading to his vest. His chest hitched with each shallow breath.

Her fingers trembling, she gently brushed a lock of hair from his brow. With those thick lashes of his resting against his pallid cheeks, he looked terribly young, terribly vulnerable.

He groaned as Esmerelda gathered his head into her lap and pressed her gloved hands to the wound, instinctively trying to stanch the welling blood.

"Look what you've done," she spat at her brother over Billy's fallen form.

Bartholomew was gazing in mute horror at the gun dangling from his flaccid hand. It struck Esmerelda that it must be the first time he'd ever actually pulled the trigger and witnessed the destruction it could wreak. Once she might have felt pity for his predicament. Now she felt only scorn.

Blistering tears spilled down her cheeks. "Is this how you want to live life, Bartholomew? By taking another man's away from him? Have you something clever to write about now? Some profound new insight for your ludicrous melodramas?"

He slowly lifted his gaze to hers. She had hoped to find shame, or even repentance, in his eyes, but saw only panic. The instant they came back into focus, he shoved his gun into its holster and bounded to his feet.

He crossed the bank in two strides, grabbed her by the arm, and tried to jerk her to her feet. "We have to get out of here, Esme! It'll only be a matter of time before the law arrives."

She snatched her arm out of his grip, her voice surprisingly firm. "I'm not going anywhere with you."

Bartholomew shot the main door a frantic glance, plainly torn between argument and flight.

"Go with him." They both started at the rusty rasp of Billy's voice. Esmerelda looked down to find his eyes open and glaring fiercely at her. "Go," he gritted out between clenched teeth. "If you stay, I'll just arrest you," he swallowed hard, droplets of sweat bleeding from his clammy brow, "for giving aid and comfort to a known outlaw and obstructing justice."

Esmerelda summoned a teasing smile with an effort that nearly matched his own. "Then I'll just have to surrender myself into your custody and throw myself on the mercy of the court, won't I?"

"No mercy," he whispered, his eyes fluttering shut.

Although his words sent a faint shiver through her, she still bowed her head to tenderly graze his hair with her lips.

When Esmerelda lifted her head, her brother was gone. His disappearance only underscored the differences between the two men. She'd known Bartholomew since the day he was born. She'd known Billy only three days. Bartholomew had left her. Billy never would have.

Her brother's flight was marked by shouts from the street and fading hoofbeats. Esmerelda's alarm escalated to panic when Billy opened his eyes and began to struggle to his feet.

She tried to shove him back down, her gloves already slick with his blood. "Be still! We have to wait for a doctor."

He caught her by the frill of lace trimming the neck of her dress and hauled her roughly up against him. Near enough to see the pain furrowing his face, the savage desperation distorting his features.

"You're a clever girl, Esmerelda," he bit off. "I want you to listen very carefully. Winstead is the marshal your brother double-crossed. He promised to call off the local law while I apprehended your brother, but his men will soon find out it went bad. If Winstead gets wind that Bart told us he was in on that robbery before I'm back on my feet, I won't need a doctor. I'll need an undertaker. And so will you."

Esmerelda hesitated, torn by indecision. He couldn't take three steps on his own. He might die if she helped him flee. But if what he said was true, he would surely die if she didn't.

She finally nodded. "Then we'd better go. I'd hate for the undertaker to sell that cursed suit to another unsuspecting buyer."

"Back door," he rasped, hissing beneath a fresh onslaught of pain.

Esmerelda had to agree with his choice. Although the mule and wagon were tethered out front, the din coming from the street was growing louder and more strident by the second. Wrapping her arms around Billy's lean waist, she braced one shoulder beneath his, wishing desperately that she were taller. He refused to inflict the brunt of his weight on her slight form, choosing instead to brace himself against the counter until they reached the gate leading to the rear of the bank. As if their journey wasn't already torturous enough, Sadie kept insinuating her plump body between their legs, plainly terrified to let Billy out of her sight.

When their legs became tangled for the third time, Billy staggered to a halt and buried his face in the crook of her neck. "C-can't go on. You go. Alone."

Esmerelda struggled to keep from collapsing beneath his weight. She was surprised to find the thought of going on without him nearly as terrifying as leaving him there. When she opened her mouth, it was not her voice that emerged, but her grandfather's, in all of its astringent glory.

"I don't think so, Mr. Darling. When I hire a man to do a job, I expect him to see it through. Of course, if you decide to just lie down here and drown in a puddle of blood and self-pity, I won't have to worry about paying you for all your trouble, will I?"

He lifted his head to glower at her. His slumped posture brought them eye to eye, mouth to mouth. In that moment, she would have almost sworn he hated her.

"What difference would it make?" he growled. "You never planned to pay me anyway."

"That's where you're wrong, Mr. Darling. I always pay my debts."

Before she could lose her nerve, Esmerelda pressed her mouth to his, determined to kiss the snarl from his lips, no matter the cost to herself. At first his mouth was as stern and unforgiving as she feared. Then he yielded to her, taking her mouth with a primal ferocity that left her limp and trembling. She could taste the salty tang of sweat and desperation in his kiss, on his tongue. Her knees threatened to crumble. She dragged her lips away from his before she could swoon. One of them had to stay on their feet long enough to get them out of that bank alive.

This time when Billy buried his face in her hair, his groan was one of sweet agony. "Hell, woman, are you trying to kill me or give me a reason to live?"

"You'll just have to last long enough to find out, won't you?" she taunted, urging him into motion.

Billy had not exaggerated. His strength was nearly spent. By the time they reached the door left standing wide open by the fleeing tellers, Esmerelda was all but dragging him.

The narrow alleyway provided a welcome respite from the racket in the street. Her frantic gaze darted both ways. Billy's mare and a second horse were tethered to a nearby post. She blessed his foresight even as she realized that the second horse must have been intended for her brother. Her instincts had been right. Billy had never had any intention of returning to that hotel room for her.

Swallowing her bitterness, she steered him in the direction of the mare. He was weaving like a drunk now, barely maintaining his balance, even with her guidance.

"Dark," Billy muttered. "Didn't realize it was . . . so damn late."

Esmerelda glanced skyward. The sun still hung in the

afternoon sky, blazing like a merciless orb. Oh, dear God, she prayed, don't let it be too late.

Her despair only deepened when they finally reached the horse. The mare might as well have been twenty feet tall. Esmerelda had no choice but to try and heave Billy into the saddle using any means available.

She pleaded and ordered, cajoled and shouted. She even slipped in a few of the swear words he was so fond of, hoping the shock would prod him into motion. She almost had one of his long legs hooked over the pommel when the mare shied away, spooked by the coppery scent of his blood.

Billy fell heavily, sprawling to his back in the dust. His eyes struggled to focus, once, twice, then rolled back in his head and fluttered shut.

Sadie sank to her haunches, threw back her head, and began to bay as if her heart were broken. Esmerelda longed to do the same.

Instead, she dropped to her knees beside him. Tears spilled down her cheeks, dripping from her chin to his face. She gathered him into her arms and gave him a ferocious shake. "Don't you die on me, Billy Darling! Do you hear me? I won't stand for it!"

She pressed her mouth to his, hoping to force some of her own precious breath into his mouth, but even that desperate kiss failed to stir him.

She buried her brow against his, utterly defeated. She never heard the jingle of a harness, the clatter of wagon wheels, the dull thud of a massive pair of boots striking the dirt.

She didn't hear anything at all until a lumbering giant, his sandy hair haloed by the sun, reached down and took Billy from her arms as if he weighed no more than a child.

Tenderly cradling his brother's limp body against his formidable chest, Virgil winked at her, the twinkle in his eyes dimmed by concern. "We Darlins' might fight and scrap amongst ourselves, ma'am, but we're still bound by blood."

As he gently laid his brother in the back of the wagon, the beast in the harness swiveled around to honk at her and bare its yellow teeth. Esmerelda cupped a hand over her mouth to capture her grateful sob. She'd never seen such a welcome sight in her life as that cantankerous old mule.

PART TWO

*It matters not, I've oft been told
Where the body lies when the heart grows cold.
Yet grant, oh grant, this wish to me:
O, bury me not on the lone prairie.*

Traditional Cowboy Song

CHAPTER SIXTEEN

The moon dangled over the valley, a brittle cameo against the black velvet bodice of the sky. The shimmering pearl drained all the color from the sweeping plain of grama grass, leaving nothing but ash and silver in a skeletal tableau as beautiful as it was bleak. It also drained what little color was left from Billy's cheeks, leaving them pallid and gaunt.

Esmerelda leaned over him, relieved to hear the faint whisper of his breath against her cheek. He hadn't uttered a sound in several hours. She knew she should be thankful that he'd finally escaped the rough jostling of the buck-board by losing consciousness, but his unnatural stillness was somehow more frightening than all of his thrashing and groaning.

She pried the lid from the battered tin canteen and dribbled a few drops of water between his parched lips.

Although his eyelids never even fluttered, he roused enough to manage a half-hearted swallow. She dampened her handkerchief and dabbed at his brow, then splashed a handful of water on her own face, afraid the rocking of the wagon might lull her into a doze just as it had Sadie.

Last night Billy had watched over her. Tonight she would watch over him.

Reaching around to massage her aching neck, she tipped back her head to gaze at the stars. In all the years she'd spent in Boston, she'd never dreamed the sky could be so vast. Or so lonely.

But at least she wasn't alone in her vigil. Enos drove the wagon while Sam, Virgil, and Jasper rode ahead of it, slouched low in their saddles. Esmerelda shook her head, bemused by the irony. Only twenty-four hours ago, she would have been terrified to have been left alone with the Darling gang. Now they were her only hope.

Virgil had already used his pocketknife to dig the bullet out of Billy's chest. Only time would tell if it had pierced any of his essential organs. Muttering all the while about wasting perfectly good liquor, Jasper had poured a stream of rotgut whiskey into the angry wound. Billy's inert form had twitched in agony. Esmerelda had forced herself not to turn away, one hand cupped over her mouth to muffle her guilt-stricken sobs.

They'd escaped Eulalie without incident. No one had even bothered to stop them. After all, there had been no money stolen from the Eulalie First National Bank, no crime committed. Except for the one committed against Billy by her brother. But Esmerelda couldn't bear to think about Bartholomew right now.

The buckboard shimmied to a sudden halt.

"Enos, trot your bony ass over here!" bellowed Virgil from somewhere up ahead.

Enos swiveled around and shyly tipped his hat to her. "Pardon me, ma'am. I do believe my p-presence is required at yonder fork in the road."

He hopped nimbly to the ground and went loping off into the night. Esmerelda climbed to her knees to look over the wagon seat. The four men were indeed gathered at a fork in the dirt road. They appeared to be arguing. She caught snatches of profanity and glimpses of wildly gesticulating arms.

Of course, it was Virgil who lost the ability to whisper first. "We ain't got no choice, boys!" he roared. "He'll die if we don't!"

"But if we do, he'll wish he had," Jasper replied grimly.

Sam shot the wagon a furtive glance. Esmerelda tried to duck, but it was too late. She'd been spotted. Responding to Sam's nudge, Virgil stretched out his colossal arms and gathered his brothers into a secretive huddle.

A few minutes later, Enos came trotting back to the wagon. As he bounded into the seat, Esmerelda asked, "What is it? Is there a town nearby? Your brother still needs a doctor, you know."

Enos pulled his hat down low, shading his eyes from her probing gaze. "Don't you worry yore p-p-pretty little head about a thing, ma'am. We ain't g-gonna let him die."

Then he slapped the reins on the mule's back and tugged with all the strength in his wiry arms, turning the buckboard toward the left fork.

Despite her noble intentions, Esmerelda dozed off with Billy's head cushioned by her lap. Some time later she awoke with a start. The wagon's motion had frozen to eerie stillness. Billy's pallor had deepened to an unhealthy flush. She gave his brow a tender stroke before carefully wiggling out from under him.

Sadie whimpered as Esmerelda climbed to her knees, knuckling her bleary eyes. Clouds had smothered the moon while she slept. A violent gust of wind scattered them across the sky like giant tumbleweeds.

Moonlight streamed down, revealing that the wagon had come to a halt at the foot of a deeply rutted dirt track that wound up a shallow slope. Billy's brothers sat silent and motionless, gazing toward the top of that hill.

Unsettled by the dread in their expressions, Esmerelda followed suit. All she saw was a ramshackle barn and a rickety structure that looked more like a shack than a house silhouetted against the night sky. A crumbling stone chimney clung to one wall of the house like a withered vine. A sagging tin roof sheltered the narrow porch. A dead oak stood sentinel at the crest of the hill, its once-mighty trunk split into a jagged fork by some ruthless bolt of lightning. A melancholy air of abandonment hung over the entire place. If it had been a piece of music, Esmerelda thought with a faint shiver, it would have been played in D minor.

"Is this our destination?" she whispered to Enos's back.

Enos nodded grimly.

Esmerelda didn't know whether to be relieved or dismayed. But she did know she was growing impatient with their dawdling.

"Then let's proceed, shall we?" she said briskly. "Your brother is in desperate need of a clean, warm bed and some fresh bandages."

Virgil cleared his throat. Sam hemmed and hawed. Jasper fixed his hard-eyed gaze on the distant horizon, as if he'd like to be anywhere else in the world at that moment. Not one of them would meet her eyes.

Oddly enough, it was shy, timid Enos who finally worked up the courage to swivel around on the wagon bench and face her. He tugged off his hat, wringing its brim in his tense

hands. "We c-cain't go no farther, ma'am," he said with genuine regret.

"What do you mean you can't go any farther? Of
course, you can go farther." She pointed at the house. "All
you have to do is drive *this* wagon to the top of *that* hill."

Virgil clambered down from his horse. "Enos is right,
honey. You'll have to go on alone from here."

"Alone?" Esmerelda echoed. She cast the house a dubious look. It was beginning to look more haunted by the
second.

"Yeah, alone," Jasper drawled, the mocking curl of his lip
reminding her achingly of Billy. "We ain't welcome here."

That didn't exactly surprise Esmerelda. She couldn't
imagine many places where the Darling gang would
be welcome. "Just where exactly is *here*?" When they
exchanged furtive glances instead of answering, she sighed
with exasperation. "Surely you could at least accompany us
to the door. Help me explain what happened to whoever
lives here . . . ?"

Although she continued to press, her desperate pleas
fell on deaf ears. Virgil was already hefting Billy out of
the buckboard and draping him stomach-down over his
mare's saddle. After a moment of consideration, he drew
one of his own pistols and shoved it into Billy's empty
holster. Then, ignoring Esmerelda's continued protests, he
clamped his meaty hands around her waist and swung her
out of the wagon. Enos reached into the bed of the wagon
and tossed her trunk and violin case to the ground. Sadie
jumped down, landing on all four paws with an offended
"oomph."

Virgil pressed the mare's reins into Esmerelda's hand.
"Don't you worry none, honey. Our Billy has always been
lucky when it comes to cards, women, and gettin' shot up."

"That was before he met me," she said glumly. After all,

she'd interrupted his poker game, scared a woman off his lap, and nearly shot him through the heart at their very first meeting.

As Virgil mounted his horse, Enos ducked his head and said, "G-g-good luck, ma'am."

"She'll need it," Jasper added with a derisive snort.

Esmerelda studied the expectant expressions on their faces. She studied the reins in her hand. She studied the top of the hill. They plainly intended for her to climb that hill on her own, leading Billy's horse behind her.

Billy's ragged groan at that moment firmed Esmerelda's resolve. If there was help for Billy in that house, then, by God, she was going there, even if the devil himself stepped out on the porch to greet her, pitchfork in hand.

Straightening her shoulders to a regal angle she was certain her grandfather would approve of, she began to march up the hill, thankful for Sadie's stalwart presence at her side. She could feel Billy's brothers silently watching her.

She'd just topped the hill when the first shotgun blast shattered the night.

Acting on pure instinct, Esmerelda grabbed Billy by the seat of his trousers and dragged him off the horse. She landed on top of him in the tall grass, covering his body with her own. From Billy's brothers she heard a frantic jingling of harnesses and scattering hoofbeats that faded to distant echoes. So much for expecting any help from them. She lay with her eyes clenched shut, hardly daring to breathe. Even unconscious, the feel of Billy's hard, lean body beneath hers gave her a sense of security in a world turned topsy-turvy.

"Who the hell goes there?" shouted someone in a hoarse rasp that could have been either male or female.

Esmerelda opened her eyes and nearly yelped aloud to find Billy staring up at her. Oh, Lord, she thought, her clumsy handling must have killed him. Then he blinked and she realized the fall had simply jarred him to consciousness.

"Ma?" he whispered.

"Oh, you poor dear," Esmerelda muttered. "The fever must be making you delirious." This hardly seemed the time to remind him that his mother was dead. After all, what could be the harm in offering him such a simple comfort in moments that might very well be his last?

"That's right, darling," she murmured, stroking his sweat-dampened hair. "Mama's here."

She even dared to press a maternal kiss to his cheek. When she lifted her head, Billy's eyes were narrowed in a confounded squint. Esmerelda was taken aback. He was staring at her as if she'd lost her wits. She had almost convinced herself it was nothing more than a grimace of pain when he closed his hands around her waist and heaved her off of him with surprising strength.

Billy straightened to his knees in the tall grass, then staggered to his feet, weaving heavily. "Ma?" he called out. "It's Billy. I'm hurt, Ma. Real bad." He stumbled a few feet toward the house before dropping back to his knees. "I need your help." His voice faded to a mumble. "I need you."

Esmerelda's mind reeled. She would have sworn Billy had implied that his mother was dead, but she'd obviously been mistaken. She breathed a quick prayer, thankful to have found help for him.

The shotgun belched again, its fiery breath strong enough to ruffle Billy's hair. "Get the hell off my land, boy, before I pump your belly full of buckshot."

An eerie calm descended over Esmerelda. She scrambled to her feet and marched toward the house, jerking Billy's pistol from his holster without breaking her stride.

He grabbed for her, but got only empty air. "Don't

beg on my behalf, woman," he ground out between his clenched teeth. "I won't have it."

Esmerelda had no intention of begging. She marched right up to the porch steps, near enough to make out the amorphous figure standing in the shadow of one of the posts. She could also make out the flared muzzle pointed straight at her chest. But it was too late to do anything but pray that there was no such thing as a triple-barreled shotgun.

She jerked her head toward Billy. "Is William Darling your son?"

No answer. A curl of pipe smoke drifted into the night.

Esmerelda swung her arm up, aiming the pistol, and repeated her question.

The figure held its silence. Esmerelda's arm began to cramp. Then came the voice—unmistakably female, unmistakably sullen. "I ain't got no sons. They all died durin' the war."

"I believe you're mistaken, ma'am. Every single one of the Darling boys survived the war."

Esmerelda sensed rather than saw the apathetic shrug. "What difference does it make? They're dead to me."

Esmerelda pointed at Billy, her voice rising in frustration. "That man is going to be dead to everyone if he doesn't get a clean bed and some fresh bandages. Can you provide those, or would you rather help me dig his grave so I can bury him on your land?"

She sensed the woman's attention shifting to Billy. Although he still knelt in the grass, there wasn't an ounce of supplication in his posture. His hands were clenched into fists. His eyes glittered with a fierce pride that was nearly as dangerous as his fever. Moonlight made the bloodstains on his white shirt stand out in stark relief.

The woman shifted the pipe to the other side of her mouth. "Looks to me like he already dug his own grave."

Esmerelda sighed. "It has been a very long, very trying day, and you, madam, have just succeeded in exhausting my patience. Now are you going to step aside and let me bring him in the house or am I going to have to shoot you?"

A tense pause was followed by a gravelly chuckle. "Why, I almost believe you would."

In reply, Esmerelda drew back the hammer of the pistol.

Billy's mother waited a long time, long enough for Esmerelda's finger to tense on the trigger. But she finally lowered the shotgun, propping it up against one of the posts. When the woman stepped out of the shadows, Esmerelda stumbled backward.

Esmerelda had assumed the Darling boys had gotten their height from their father. She had been wrong. Billy's mother was a giantess, standing at least six feet tall in her bare feet. The massive arms she folded over her chest were roped with muscle, giving Esmerelda the impression that she was no less sturdy or immovable than the trunk of the dead oak in the yard. She half expected to see roots twining from the woman's scalp instead of an uncombed tangle of hair. Both her hair and the shapeless burlap dress she wore were faded to the same butternut hue as her sunbaked skin. Her face was nearly as broad as the rest of her, its blunt features carved by some clumsy whittler with a dull blade. It was impossible to imagine them having ever been wreathed in a smile or crumpled by grief.

"You can bring him in," she said. "But you'll have to tend to him yourself." The pipe flared orange, illuminating a stern jaw and a rueful mouth that was a shade too familiar for Esmerelda's comfort. "I ain't patchin' him up just so he can run off and get his fool self shot all to hell again."

A sudden rustling in the grass distracted them both.

Billy had vanished. A gurgling sound floated to their ears.

Esmerelda shot his mother a look of pure outrage. "Now see what you've done, you spiteful old hag! You waited too long and now he's dying!"

Gathering her skirts, she raced to where Billy had collapsed and flung herself to her knees in the grass. She couldn't bear to have come so far only to lose him now.

He lay on his back, one hand pressed to his bandage, the other clutching his side. His handsome features were contorted in agony.

Esmerelda cupped his face in her hands. "Breathe, Billy! Oh, please! You've got to try!"

He opened his eyes and sucked in a wheezing breath. That was when Esmerelda realized he wasn't dying. He was laughing. Laughing so hard that tears were coursing from the corners of his eyes and rolling into his ears. Laughing although every hitch and shudder of his battered body must have been pure torment.

Esmerelda snatched her hands away from his face, embarrassed by her zeal and furious at him for frightening her so badly.

As he gazed up at her, his eyes glowing silver in the moonlight, his laughter faded to a soft chuckle. "I was just thinking"—he lifted a hand to her cheek, his touch strangely tender—"that you're just the kind of girl I always wanted to bring home to meet my ma."

CHAPTER SEVENTEEN

Jaws dropped and eyes bulged as the private coach rolled into Calamity on a hazy Saturday afternoon.

Donley Ezell emerged from the cool shadows of his stable to gaze longingly at the six matched grays drawing the coach while old Granny Shively eyed the coachman in his scarlet livery and white powdered wig. Her wistful smile shaved ten years off her age, making her look a girlish ninety-seven.

"Why, he looks just like a beau who courted me when I was fifteen!" she exclaimed to her friend Maude.

"Look, Ma," shouted a little girl, tugging her mother's arm so hard she nearly dropped the bolt of calico she was carrying. The child pointed at the Wyndham coat of arms discreetly emblazoned in gold on the black lacquered door. "It must be the king of New Mexico!"

Inside the carriage, Anne let the curtain fall and slumped

back in her seat, unable to decide which was more oppressive—the dust, the gloom, or the heat. "I do hope you're satisfied, Reginald. We couldn't have attracted any more attention had we arrived in a giant pumpkin drawn by six white mice."

Her brother had long ago collapsed against the plush velvet squabs opposite her, his ivory linen shirt and fawn waistcoat wilted by the heat. Anne might have pitied him had he not been growing increasingly more petulant with every mile that separated him from the mist and meadows of his beloved England.

He mopped at his florid face and shiny pate with a monogrammed handkerchief, gasping for air like a beached cod. "It's intolerable enough that no one in this uncivilized wilderness serves afternoon tea. You can't expect me to sacrifice all of my creature comforts."

Anne snapped open her fan, selfishly hoarding the breeze it generated. "We've lost precious hours loading this infernal coach onto the steamer, then the train. Hours that could have been better spent searching for Esmerelda."

Reginald roused from his lethargy long enough to bang the brass tip of his cane on the floor of the coach. "I have no intention of transporting my only granddaughter back to England in some mule skinner's wagon."

Their gazes clashed, then they both looked away, neither of them willing to face the terrible fear that hung unspoken between them. What if they were too late? What if Esmerelda had already confronted the man she had described in her letter? The man who may very well have murdered her brother. Anne shuddered to imagine what such a cold-blooded villain might do to an innocent like her niece.

Unable to sit idle a moment longer, she wrestled Reginald's cane out of his grip and tapped on the ceiling of the coach. Before the vehicle could creak to a halt, she had gathered her reticule and parasol and flung open the door.

"Where the devil are you going?" Reginald demanded, clutching at her sleeve with all the querulous urgency of a frightened child.

Moved by the pity that had eluded her earlier, she gently patted his hand. "While you secure our accommodations, I shall make inquiries of the local constable. Perhaps he has news of our Esmerelda."

"Anne?" he called after her as the coachman appeared to help her down from the coach.

She turned, affecting an air of aristocratic hauteur to shield her from the impolite stares directed her way. "You'll find her, won't you?"

Anne simply touched two fingers to her lips, unwilling to make a promise she might not be able to keep.

Anne had been banging on the locked door of the sheriff's office for nearly five minutes when a grizzled old man sidled up next to her.

"Won't do you no good," he said. "The sheriff ain't there."

Anne wasn't sure whether she should be more appalled by the man's familiarity, his grammar, or the rank cloud of body odor surrounding him. She drew a scented handkerchief from her reticule and dabbed at her nose, hoping he wouldn't take offense at her own rudeness.

"Then where might I find him?"

He pointed across the dusty street. "Over yonder at the saloon."

The man was looking her up and down in a most curious manner. A manner that made her want to glance down and make sure the tiny row of mother-of-pearl buttons holding her camel-hair bodice closed over her breasts was still intact.

She started to brush past him, but he lurched directly into her path. "That there fancy stagecoach you climbed out of belong to you?"

Anne rolled her eyes, wondering just how long she was going to have to endure his abysmal manners. "It belongs to the duke of Wyndham."

"That Mr. Wyndham must be a mighty rich feller."

Anne's sigh was a breath of frost. "Wyndham is his title, not his name. The proper form of address for my brother would be 'Lord Wyndham' or 'His Grace'."

"You mean to say His Graciousness ain't yer husband?"

"I should say not. I'm unmarried."

A radiant smile brightened the man's dour face. Before Anne could question his odd behavior, he went scampering down the sidewalk, a definite hop in his step. "Elmer! Hey, Elmer! Ye're not gonna believe this, but we got us another one!"

Although she was somewhat dismayed to find herself the lone woman in a seedy tavern, Anne marched boldly up to the only occupied table. "Pardon me, sirs. I am seeking the town constable."

The two men dressed nearly identically in broad-brimmed hats, plaid shirts, and denim trousers, shot each other a nervous look over the dusty bandannas knotted around their necks.

"We ain't got no constable, ma'am," said one.

"But that there is Sheriff McGuire," said the other, pointing to the man opposite them.

The sheriff's gaze flicked briefly to her, then returned to his cards. "I'll be right with you, madam. After this hand."

Anne gaped at him, hardly able to believe that he'd dismissed her so coolly. Was Reginald right? Was everyone in this country an utter boor? She narrowed her eyes, studying the man more closely. If not for his sun- and wind-weathered face and fall of silver hair, she might have thought his broad-shouldered, lean-waisted form was in the full vigor of its youth. At least he didn't dress like a savage. His shirt was bleached a blinding white and his paisley waistcoat was crisp enough to meet even Reginald's exalted standards. A drooping mustache framed his full lips.

Anne looked away, oddly discomfited by the unbridled sensuality of that mouth. But after several more cards had been played, she decided she'd had just about enough of his indifference.

She pointedly cleared her throat. "I do so hate to interrupt your game, sheriff, but you must allow me to introduce myself. I am Anne Hastings, sister to the duke of Wyndham, and I'm looking for my niece—a young woman named Esmerelda Fine."

He glanced up, arching one silvery eyebrow. "You're not armed, are you?"

Taken aback by the peculiar query, she replied, "I should say not."

"Good." He grinned and winked at her. "Then I'll just finish my hand."

Growing more impatient by the second, Anne gritted her teeth and began to tap her foot on the plank floor.

Although he would have had her believe otherwise, Drew was keenly aware of the woman awaiting his pleasure. Aware of the *tap-tap-tap* of her dainty kid boot, the aristocratic flare of her delicate nostrils, the subtle floral scent of her perfume. He stole a look at her over his hand of cards. The soft gray hair peeping out from beneath her stylish bonnet was the exact color of a dove's breast. *Anne,* he mused. The name suited her. It was both elegant and no-nonsense. She might even be a handsome woman if her lips weren't puckered in such a haughty manner. They looked as if they were poised to suck a stick of sour candy.

Or be kissed.

Seal swore, jolting Drew out of his reverie. He dropped his gaze to the table to discover he'd just let Dauber best them both with a pair of fours. Ah, well, what did it matter? He had nothing of value in his own hand but a knave of hearts.

Feeling a bit like a knave himself, he tossed down the cards in disgust and retrieved his jacket from the back of the chair. As he came to his feet, Esmerelda Fine's aunt took a hasty step backward.

Twirling one waxed tip of his mustache to hide his smile, Drew bowed and made a courtly gesture toward the door. "After you, madam."

Anne lowered herself into the chair opposite the sheriff's desk, then bounced back up with a startled "Oh!"

"Sorry about that," he said, coming around the desk to rescue the yellow tabby she'd almost sat on. As he smoothed the cat's rumpled fur, the beast gave Anne a decidedly malevolent look. "There, there," he crooned. "My Miss Kitty is a wee bonny puss."

"You're Scottish," Anne remarked, glancing nervously behind her this time before she sat.

"No, I'm American." He set the cat on the floor; it went sauntering from the room, its tail still twitching with regal annoyance. "I had no choice but to flee the country of my birth as a lad when the king seized my father's lands and gave them to some fat English sot who'd never set foot off his London estate. Oh, I am sorry. I didn't mean to offend you." His pleasant smile deepened, warning her that he wasn't the least bit sorry and had every intention of offending her. "I can tell from your accent that you must be English."

Her smile was equally pleasant. "That's quite all right, sir. After all, it's not as if I personally drove you off your land." Her white-knuckled grip on the bone handle of her parasol warned him that she just might be capable of doing just that.

Drew settled himself behind his desk and rested his chin on his steepled fingers. "What can I do to assist you, Mrs. . . . ?" He stretched out the title to insulting lengths.

"Miss," Anne corrected briskly, refusing to shy away from the truth, however stark.

"Ah, *Miss* Hastings," he said, nodding smugly. "We have more in common than I realized. I, too, never chose to shackle myself with the chains from which there is no escape but death." When she only gazed blankly at him, he leaned forward and confessed, "I never married."

"Yes, well, I can certainly see why." Her acid tone wiped the smile from his face. Before he could recover his poise, she reached into her reticule, drew out a silver locket, and snapped it open beneath his nose. "Have you seen this girl?"

Still eyeing her warily, Drew took the locket and studied the yellowing daguerreotype nestled within.

"She wouldn't be a girl anymore, of course. She would be a young woman," Anne hastened to explain. "But I thought perhaps you might recognize a hint of something familiar in her features, some nuance of her expression that might jar your memory." She leaned forward in her chair, her icy veneer cracking to reveal the vulnerability beneath.

Drew recognized Esmerelda immediately. Her solemn eyes still held that poignant hint of wistfulness that gave her perfectly ordinary features the promise of extraordinary beauty.

He also recognized the plump, dark-eyed child in her arms. A child who had grown into a man who called himself Black Bart and, according to Thaddeus Winstead, U.S. Marshal, had traded playing with toy trains for robbing real ones. Drew leaned back in his chair to stroke his mustache. So Bartholomew Fine had a sister after all. What would Billy make of that? He stole a brief look at Anne Hastings. The one thing Billy never could tolerate, aside from a weeping woman, was a woman meddling in his business. And Winstead's offer had made both Bartholomew and Esmerelda Fine his business.

Until Drew lifted his gaze to Anne's hopeful eyes, he hadn't realized how much he would hate lying to her. He sensed that she was not a woman to forgive easily. Or ever. Snapping the locket shut, he shoved it back across the desk at her.

"I'm sorry," he said gently, and this time he meant it. "I've never seen your niece before."

"Oh." That single syllable was more a sigh than an exclamation. It took Anne Hastings a moment to gather both her composure and her belongings. She finally rose from the chair, giving him a rueful smile that was a weary echo of Esmerelda's. "I'm quite sorry to have troubled you, Sheriff McGuire. Thank you for your time."

Thinking only to be polite, Drew took the hand she offered. It was surprisingly soft, surprisingly white—a lady's hand. As their eyes met—his troubled, hers startled—he couldn't help but linger over it, tenderly caressing her knuckles with his thumb.

The door to his office flew open. Anne snatched her

hand back, flushing like a fifteen-year-old caught allowing an indiscreet suitor to steal a kiss.

Oblivious to her discomfiture, Reginald came storming in, his bald pate pink with excitement. He was waving a sealed envelope as if it were a battle flag.

"We're not too late, Anne. She was here! Our girl was here only three days ago!" He clutched the envelope to his chest. "Such a bold girl! Such a brave girl! It seems she fired a pistol at that dastardly outlaw and spent the afternoon confined in this very jail."

Anne slowly swiveled her head to give the man seated behind the desk a look that should have melted the set of iron keys hanging on a peg behind the desk. Drew suddenly took it into his head to examine his well-manicured fingernails.

Reginald was beaming like an idiot. "She left me a letter at the hotel desk. Can you imagine that? A letter for me! A cold and unforgiving ogre of a man if ever there was one!"

He tried to open the missive, but his hands were trembling with fear and eagerness, just as they always did at the arrival of one of his granddaughter's letters.

Growing impatient with his fumbling, Anne snapped, "For God's sake, Reggie, give it here."

He meekly obeyed, unaccustomed to being told what to do by his dutiful sister. Anne broke the seal with her fingernail and unfolded the letter.

" 'Lord Wyndham,' " she read, already alarmed by the untidy scrawl that was so out of character for her painstaking niece. " 'It is with great trepidation and no little regret that I am writing to inform you that due to your enduring neglect and indifference, I have been forced to barter my virtue to a ruthless desperado.' "

The sheriff made a noise that sounded suspiciously like

a laugh, but when Anne whipped her head around to give him another one of those basilisk's glares, he choked it into a cough.

She returned her attention to the letter. " 'I trust you will suffer no distress on my behalf since you never have before. Ever your devoted granddaughter . . . Esmerelda Fine.' "

Anne stood in stunned silence, trying to absorb her niece's message. Reginald gently took the letter from her hand and pressed it to his lips, closing his eyes.

Touched by the rare display of emotion, Anne squeezed his shoulder. "What is it, Reggie? Does she remind you of Lisbeth?"

"No." He drew a handkerchief from his pocket and sniffled into it with fastidious care. When he opened his eyes, they were bright with unshed tears and brimming with tender affection. "She reminds me of me."

CHAPTER EIGHTEEN

Zoe Darling was as good as her word. During the week that her son hovered in that misty netherworld between life and death, she never lifted a finger to nurse him.

Although she tended his mare without complaint, her only concession to Billy's presence in her house came the very first night. After Esmerelda had gotten him settled in the wooden bedstead in the back bedroom with an anxious Sadie draped across his feet, she went to drag her trunk and violin case back to the house. When she returned, she found a worn nightshirt neatly folded on the floor outside Billy's door. Esmerelda had fingered the faded cotton, wondering if it had once belonged to Billy's father.

While Billy battled the twin demons of blood loss and fever, the two women shared the small house, never speaking and rarely exchanging so much as a glance. Loath to ask for help, Esmerelda soon learned to pump her own water from the well so she could wash out Billy's sweat-soaked sheets and nightshirt. After only a few days of wringing them out with her bare hands before dragging them outside to dry, she began to understand how Zoe had developed the ropes of sinew in her mammoth arms.

Desperation made Esmerelda cunning. One afternoon she watched from the window of the timber-framed room that served as both kitchen and parlor while Zoe stalked a hapless chicken around the weed-choked yard. Several minutes later, the woman strode into the house and slapped the freshly plucked and dressed bird on the table.

While once she might have grimaced at such a spectacle, Esmerelda waited until Billy's mother had lumbered back out the door, then swiped the naked bird and plopped it into a pot of water she'd already set to boiling. When Zoe's shadow again darkened the stoop, Esmerelda was ladling steaming broth into a bowl for Billy and glibly humming beneath her breath. Snorting like an enraged bull, Zoe swung around and stomped back out to the yard to strangle another chicken for her own supper. Esmerelda suspected the woman would have rather crushed her own scrawny neck between those powerful fingers.

Twice, in the still, dark hours between midnight and dawn, while Esmerelda napped in the slat-backed rocker she'd drawn next to Billy's bed, she drifted out of a fitful sleep to glimpse a shadow at the bedroom door. From her place at Billy's feet, Sadie would lift her head to gaze solemnly at the door. Before Esmerelda could blink the fog of sleep from her eyes, the shadow was gone, convincing her that she must have been dreaming. Surely it would be impossible for a woman of Zoe's size to move so quietly.

After six days of unconsciousness, Billy took a turn for the worse.

As darkness fell on that humid August night, his fever

began to climb. Although the heat in the room was stifling, his teeth chattered as if he were buried in a snowdrift. He couldn't even unclench them long enough to swallow the drops of water Esmerelda struggled to spoon down his throat. As his shivering worsened, she piled all the quilts she could find on him, but his long limbs soon began to thrash and hurl them away.

He finally settled into an unnatural stillness more terrifying than anything that had gone before. Fighting despair, Esmerelda smoothed his damp hair from his brow. His skin was so hot it seemed to scorch her palm.

Esmerelda knew what death looked like. She knew the waxen cast of its skin and the arduous rhythm of its breath. She knew the bitter taste it left in your mouth when it had passed by, taking those you loved against their will and yours.

A fragile thread of hope wound through her despair. She had sent death begging once before when God had answered her tearful pleas by sparing Bartholomew's life. Perhaps she could do it again. Clutching Billy's limp hand in hers, she sank to her knees beside the bed and buried her brow against the bedclothes.

Prayers had always flowed easily from Esmerelda's lips, but this time eloquence deserted her. She would have gladly bargained with God, but wasn't sure she had anything of worth left to offer him. After several moments of agonizing silence, she could manage nothing more than a clumsy, whispered, "Please, God . . . oh, please . . ."

A hand fell on her shoulder. She slowly turned her head, believing for a dazed moment that her prayer had been answered. But the fingers curled around her collarbone weren't lean and tanned, but broad and spatulate, the nails cracked and seamed with dirt.

In Zoe Darling's other hand was a Bible, its black binding creased with age. "Go on and take it," the woman said, nodding toward the bed. "It's his."

Esmerelda reluctantly untangled her fingers from Billy's and took the book. To her surprise, his mother sank into the rocking chair. The floor creaked beneath her weight as she began to rock. Esmerelda gazed up at her through a blur of unshed tears.

"Billy was the first Darlin' who ever learnt himself to read." Although the woman's voice was matter-of-fact, Esmerelda would have almost sworn she glimpsed a trace of tenderness on those rough-hewn features. "When we lived in Missoura, he used to carve whistles and trade them to passing peddlers for books. But his brothers always laughed at him. They said readin' was for girls. They used to steal his books when he weren't around and burn 'em in the old cistern behind the house."

A bittersweet pang tightened Esmerelda's throat. She remembered Billy's peculiar behavior when she had discovered his stash of books back at the brothel, books painstakingly inscribed with his name. He had even gone so far as to deny owning them, as if a love of reading were something to be ashamed of.

Zoe nodded. "It was my idea to give him the family Bible. My Jasper was always mean as a baby cottonmouth, but even he knew better than to burn the Good Book."

Esmerelda opened the Bible and gently ruffled through the pages. They were so thin and fragile as to be almost transparent. She could see Billy as a boy, the burnished gold of his hair gleaming in the candlelight as he inclined his head and patiently sounded out the words on these pages. Stricken by the image, she let the book fall shut in her lap.

Zoe Darling rose from the rocking chair, towering over her. "I thought it might give him comfort to hear some of those old stories again. He was always partial to Daniel in the den of them mountain lions and that King David feller who shot that giant right betwixt the eyes."

As Zoe moved toward the bed, Esmerelda held her breath. The woman stretched out her hand, leaving it hovering over her son's cheek. Her fingers slowly unfurled like the petals of some homely wildflower that hadn't felt the touch of the sun for a very long time. But before her calloused fingertips could brush his burning skin, she closed them into a rigid fist.

"When he left here," she said softly, "I knew there was a grave out there somewhere with his name already on it." She swung around to give Esmerelda a probing look. "Do you know what they used to carve on the crosses durin' the war if a boy's face had been blown clean off by a cannonball or there just weren't no one left alive after a battle who knew his name?"

Esmerelda shook her head.

Zoe's eyes were dark and bitter. "'Somebody's Darlin'.'"

Somebody's Darling. Esmerelda shivered to imagine Billy lying there in one of those shallow graves—nameless and mourned only by those who would never know how, when, or where he fell.

"But he didn't end up in that grave," she said fiercely. "And he's not going to now."

Zoe gazed at her with blunt pity. "You his wife?"

Fighting an absurd longing to nod, Esmerelda whispered, "No. I'm . . ." *His friend? His employer? The bane of his existence?* Since only the latter seemed appropriate, Esmerelda simply trailed off into silence.

Zoe Darling shook a finger at her. "Then don't be lookin' on his nakedness, gal. It ain't fittin'."

An incredulous sob of laughter escaped Esmerelda. Then, moving as soundlessly as she'd come, the woman was gone, leaving Esmerelda alone with her son.

She sat there on the floor for a long time, hugging the tattered book to her breast and listening to the labored sighs of Billy's breathing. Despite her bold words, her pious and practical nature urged her to return to her knees and pray that God would forgive the sins of William Darling and give his restless soul a gentle passage into heaven.

Esmerelda rose to her knees. She hesitated for a moment, then crawled into the bed next to Billy, dislodging a disgruntled Sadie. Gingerly resting her head on his shoulder, she opened the Bible to the Book of Daniel and began to read.

When Esmerelda opened her eyes the next morning to find Billy gazing into them, it startled her so badly she shrieked and rolled right out of the bed, landing on an equally startled Sadie.

She was still lying on her back and clutching her pounding heart when Billy's head appeared over the side of the bed. A lock of hair dangled in his narrowed eyes. "Did you really call my ma a spiteful old hag?"

Esmerelda winced at the memory. "I'm afraid so," she croaked, hoarse from reading aloud to him until she'd fallen into an exhausted slumber near dawn. "I've always been afflicted with a sharp temper. That's precisely why I struggle to guard it with such care."

He sank back on the pillows, making a sound somewhere between a chuckle and a groan. "Damn lucky for us. Given your fondness for threatening to shoot anyone who doesn't give you your way."

Outraged, Esmerelda sat up. "I don't threaten to shoot just *anyone*. Only Darlings."

Her retort was answered by a gentle snore, leaving her to wonder if she'd dreamed the entire exchange.

Cocking her head to give Sadie a perplexed look,

she crept to her knees and peered over the side of the bed. Billy lay on his back, his mouth hanging open to reveal a line of endearingly uneven white teeth.

Esmerelda touched a trembling hand to his chest, taking care not to disturb his bandage. Beneath the crisp golden whorls of hair, his skin was cool, his breathing deep and even.

All the starch melted from Esmerelda's spine. She buried her face in her hands, breathing a thank-you just as fervent, but no more coherent, than her earlier pleas to God had been. Words just seemed to fail her where this man was concerned.

A hand brushed her hair. She lifted her head to find Billy gazing at her again, a pained expression in his gray-green eyes. "Don't cry, honey," he whispered, dusting a tear from her cheek with his thumb. His eyes slowly fluttered shut before he murmured, "I never meant to make you cry."

Billy slept through that day and half of the next. It was no longer the restless, fevered thrashing of a dying man, but the deep and natural slumber of a body seeking to recover from a grave insult. Even Sadie seemed to sense his improvement, for she left his side for the first time since the shooting, choosing instead to waddle after an indifferent Zoe.

When Esmerelda carried in the speckled tin basin to give him his bath the following afternoon, he was sprawled on his back with his head and shoulders propped on the pillows. His chest was exposed and one long leg dusted with wiry gold hair poked out from beneath the sheet. It wasn't until water sloshed on her feet that Esmerelda realized she was gawking.

Don't be lookin' on his nakedness, gal. It ain't fittin'.

Although she had deliberately waited for Zoe to stomp

from the house to do her afternoon chores, trailed by a newly infatuated Sadie, Esmerelda's cheeks still flushed hotly at the memory of his mother's admonishment. An unfair warning indeed, she thought with an offended sniff, when she'd taken such careful pains to guard both Billy's modesty and her own while she tended him. She'd kept her eyes closed and her face turned away for all but the most innocent of tasks.

Yet today as she approached his bed, she felt a curious stirring of trepidation. With the golden flush of health returning to his skin and the stubble along his jawline thickening to an outlaw's beard, he looked larger, somehow, and overwhelmingly masculine.

Esmerelda set the basin on the stool beside the bed and dipped her cloth in the soapy water. The warm water trickled between her fingers as she gently sponged off Billy's face and throat. She dipped the cloth again and ran it over his chest, taking care not to wet the clean bandage she'd wrapped around the broad expanse only that morning. The water beaded like morning dew in the crisp coils of chest hair below the bandage before trickling along the narrowing V to the taut plain of his belly.

As Esmerelda traced the trail with the cloth, sopping up the excess water, Billy shifted and moaned. She jerked back her hand, suffering a pang of contrition. The bath must be causing him more discomfort than she'd anticipated.

She gentled her touch to a mere caress, but he thrashed so violently she was forced to snatch at the sheet to keep it from sliding off of his lean hips.

Mopping her brow with her forearm, Esmerelda glanced toward the window and frowned. Although a fickle bevy of clouds flirted with the sun, the room seemed warmer than ever.

Growing more disgruntled by the second, she jerked

the sheet up over Billy's chest before peeling it from his legs. Although she tried to wash them quickly, they were so long it seemed to take forever. His feet were just as long-boned and well-sculpted as the rest of him.

When Esmerelda was done, she gently drew up the sheet, covering him from throat to toe.

She dipped the cloth in the water again, swallowing hard. This was the part she'd been dreading. When Billy had been caught in the grip of sickness and fever, bathing him as if he were a child had come naturally to her. After all, she had told herself sternly, it was no different from bathing her baby brother, which she'd been required to do quite often until he'd grown old enough to do it himself.

Esmerelda refused to be daunted by the task. Ignoring the treacherous quickening of her breath, she turned her face away, closed her eyes, and slid the cloth beneath the sheet.

Billy groaned. Esmerelda jerked her hand back and dared a glance at his face. It was still resting in angelic repose, his gilt-edged lashes betraying nary a flutter.

Battling a wretched fit of nerves that was making her heart pound and her ears buzz, she reached beneath the sheet again. As the cloth encountered the warmth of his flesh, she would have almost sworn there was something different about him today. Her hand continued its curious exploration. Her eyes widened in shock. Distinctly different.

Feeling utterly ridiculous and more than a little sinful, she lifted the sheet and stole a peek beneath.

"Find what you're looking for, Duchess?"

CHAPTER NINETEEN

Esmerelda froze at the sound of that unmistakable drawl. Her first instinct was to drop the sheet, spring away from the bed, and shove both hands behind her back as if she'd been caught sneaking them into the cookie jar.

Instead, she forced herself to calmly lower the sheet and meet Billy's gaze. "I was looking for the washrag."

Billy's eyebrow arched. "The one in your hand?"

Esmerelda glanced down at the dripping rag, beset by a desperate urge to fling it at his face and run. "Oh," she said, refusing to let her scalding blush spoil her dignity. "I could have sworn I'd dropped it."

"And I could have sworn I'd died and gone straight to heaven."

"As we've discussed in the past, Mr. Darling, I doubt that would be your final destination."

Esmerelda busied herself with returning the rag to the

basin, but was unable to resist stealing a furtive glance at Billy from beneath her lashes. His recent vulnerability had made her forget just how dangerous he really was.

While she'd been distracted, he had propped his hands behind his head. The casual motion had caused the sheet she'd so painstakingly arranged to spill back down his chest, baring him to the waist. The heated glimmer in his eyes as they followed her every motion warned her that he wasn't nearly as cool as he appeared. All he needed was his hat, a cigar clamped between his teeth, and a gun in his hand, and he would have looked just as forbidding as he had at their first meeting.

Since then she had learned there were emotions that could be more hazardous to a woman's heart than a bullet from a Colt .45. She gasped with shock when Billy's lean fingers shot out and closed around her wrist. At first she thought he meant to jerk her into the bed with him, but he simply turned her hand upward, using his thumb to probe her palm with a thoroughness that sent a wicked quiver of anticipation through her flesh.

"Nope. There's no doubt about it," he said. "Those weren't the claws of an imp bathing my mortal flesh, but the hands of an angel. I must surely be heaven-bound after all."

Their eyes met over her palm, hers wary and his knowing, as if he could discern her darkest secrets with nothing more than a mocking flicker of his lashes. She was so intent on denying what she learned of herself in those gray-green eyes that it took a minute for his words to sink in.

"You were awake?" she yelled, snatching her hand back.

He crossed his arms and shrugged, but his devilish smirk ruined the apologetic gesture. "Only since you washed behind my ears. And a mighty fine job you did of it, too."

Esmerelda blanched to remember the tender care she'd

lavished upon him, the way her hands had betrayed her by lingering against the muscled contours of his chest, the taut plane of his belly, the rangy length of his calves and thighs. She also remembered the tortured groan he'd uttered when she'd first reached beneath the sheet with the washrag. She could scarcely bear to imagine what he must have thought when he'd felt her caressing him with such familiarity. Mortified, she closed her eyes and bit back a groan of her own.

Esmerelda's blush made her look as fevered as Billy felt. His fever had nothing to do with his wound and everything to do with the delicious play of Esmerelda's hands over his skin. He couldn't remember the last time he'd been so vulnerable to a woman's touch.

When he'd first woken to feel her hands on him, he'd lain frozen, wanting her to stop, yet terrified she would. Then the fever began creeping through his veins like hot molasses, coursing downward with each stroke of the rag, each cool brush of her fingertips against his burning flesh, until it had crystallized in his groin, leaving behind an ache as hard as it was sweet.

An ache made practically intolerable by the curious stroke of her hand, the adorably naughty glance she'd stolen beneath the sheet.

He'd interrupted that shy peek not to embarrass her, but to keep from humiliating himself. Something he feared he still might do when his first clear look at her gave his heart a painful jolt.

"What happened to you, honey? You look like hell."

Esmerelda opened her eyes to discover that Billy's teasing grin had darkened to a scowl. She touched a hand to her bedraggled hair. She'd been too busy ogling him to give much thought to her own appearance. But beneath his probing scrutiny, she became painfully aware of the unflattering shadows beneath her eyes; the wrinkled dress she'd handwashed, wrung out, and donned while it was still damp; the sweaty tendrils of hair clinging to her temples.

Billy wasn't frowning at her face, but her body. He stretched out a hand, cradling her waist as if they were about to embark on a formal waltz. "Why, I can feel your ribs. You're nothing but skin and bones."

Esmerelda shrugged, touched by his dismay. "I suppose I've been too busy spooning broth down your throat to steal more than a few sips for myself."

His expression grew even more troubled. "How long?"

"Eight days."

He collapsed on the pillows, cutting her a sulky glance. "I haven't forgotten that it could have been you lying here in this bed with a bullet in your back. There was no call for you to go throwing yourself in front of that no-count brother of yours. I was only going to wing him."

"Where? In the heart?"

Billy's heavy-lidded glare darkened. "In the trigger finger."

Esmerelda arched an eyebrow skeptically, knowing even as she did so that he was probably capable of shooting a hangnail off Bartholomew's thumb without so much as skinning his knuckle. She felt compelled to defend her brother. "Despite your low opinion of him, my brother is not 'no-count.' He's simply callow, misguided—"

"Greedy, spoiled, dangerous."

"I raised him the best I could," Esmerelda cried, stung. "He lacked for nothing!"

"Maybe that's the problem," Billy replied softly.

Esmerelda turned her back on the bed, his compassion more damning than condemnation. Perhaps it was time to find out just how deep his own betrayal ran. Gazing at the wall without blinking, she asked him the question that had haunted her ever since Bartholomew had flung the accusation in his face. "Did that crooked marshal pay you to kill my brother?"

"No."

Esmerelda whirled around, prepared to forgive all. But the steely light in Billy's eyes stopped her.

"He paid me to kill your lover."

"How much?" she whispered when she could.

"One thousand dollars. Five hundred in advance. Five hundred when the job was done. He also promised amnesty for me and my brothers and a job as a deputy U.S. marshal."

Esmerelda was forced to sink down on the foot of the bed or risk falling down. A despairing little hiccup of a laugh escaped her. "At least no one can accuse you of selling yourself cheap. Given the marshal's generosity, you must have found my offer fairly pathetic."

Billy reached out and ran a finger down her arm in a slow, tantalizing motion that set the pulse in her throat fluttering. "Oh, there was nothing pathetic about what you offered me."

Esmerelda swallowed hard, hypnotized by the hungry glitter in his eyes. No man had ever looked at her that way before. She didn't know whether to be frightened or flattered. Or perhaps a little bit of both.

He'd left her with no choice but to deliberately misunderstand him. She stood, edging out of his reach. "You're absolutely right. I'm certain that my grandfather would consider Winstead's offer a paltry sum compared to the riches he'll be prepared to bestow upon the man who finds his grandson."

"Ah, yes. Your grandpappy. The duke." Although Billy's expression was bland, Esmerelda sensed he was mocking her.

It made her want to catch him in a few exaggerations of

his own. She narrowed her eyes at him. "According to your reputation, Mr. Darling, when you want somebody dead, they have a tendency to get that way. Yet you let my brother leave that bank alive. Even *after* he shot you."

Her aim struck true. Scowling, Billy pointed a finger at her. "Before you go thinking that I never intended to kill him at all, you might as well know that there was a moment there in that bank, before I realized Bart really was your brother, when I just might have done it."

"But you didn't," she replied softly. When he averted his eyes instead of answering, she shifted her gaze to the window. "Bartholomew's still out there somewhere. And so is that crooked marshal who wants him dead."

Billy nodded grimly. "As soon as I'm able, I intend to rectify that."

"Yes, but who will you be working for? Me?" She hesitated for a beat, knowing she might be risking more than just her brother's life. "Or Winstead?"

He gazed at her in stony silence for a moment before replying. "Your brother's dealings with Winstead convinced me the Yankee bastard can't be trusted. But as you were so kind to assure me back at that bank," his voice melted into a drawl, making her feel all hot and silky inside, "you always pay your debts."

Esmerelda saw reflected in his shuttered eyes the wanton kiss she'd pressed upon him in that desperate moment. So much for her hope that he'd been too delirious with shock and pain to remember her reckless promise. Irrationally furious at him for calling her bluff, she whirled around and started for the door.

"Duchess?"

"Yes?" She stiffly turned back, trying to decide whether to accept his apology or let him stew in his regrets for a while.

"You weren't quite done with my bath, were you, honey?" Blinking innocently, Billy fished the washrag out of the basin and held it out to her. "I was kind of hoping you could take up where you left off."

The frigid sweetness of Esmerelda's smile should have warned him, but Billy was too mesmerized by her eager approach to pay attention to his tingling nape. "Why, you're absolutely right, Mr. Darling. How thoughtless of me." She picked up the basin, cradling it tenderly in her hands. "I forgot to rinse you off."

Maidenly modesty be damned, Esmerelda whipped back the sheet and dumped the entire basin of cooling water in his lap. As she marched from the room, slamming the door behind her, Billy's roar of outrage mingled with his howls of laughter.

"Just you wait! I'll get you for that, gal! I swear I will!" he shouted after her.

Esmerelda sagged against the door, smothering a helpless sob of laughter with her hand. "That's just what I'm afraid of," she whispered.

To Esmerelda's relief, Billy seemed to have regained enough strength to bathe and feed himself. She peeked in on him later that afternoon to find his sheets draped over the windowsill to dry and Billy standing in front of a tarnished mirror, shaving himself with a bone-handled razor. Although he still had to flatten one hand against the wall to brace himself, the look he gave her in the mirror was potent enough to send her scurrying from the room.

That night Esmerelda slept wrapped in a quilt on the floor of the main room instead of in the rocker next to Billy's bed. She awoke the next morning to the tantalizing aroma of rising biscuits and sizzling bacon. Her stomach growled with delight, heralding the triumphant return of her appetite. With the tattered quilt still wrapped around her nightgown, she stumbled toward the table.

She knuckled her bleary eyes only to discover to her amazement that it was Billy presiding over the cast-iron stove and Zoe hunkered down over the table. Sadie crouched at the woman's feet, her big, brown eyes moist and hopeful.

Billy wore nothing but his trousers and a snowy-white bandage. The sight of the muscles rippling in his lean back as he flipped an egg with deft precision made Esmerelda's mouth go dry with a thirst she feared wouldn't be satisfied even if she drank the entire pitcher of frothy milk perched on the table.

As she watched, he slapped the egg on a plate, then slid the plate in front of his mother.

Zoe wrinkled her nose as if he'd spit in the biscuit batter and seasoned the bacon with a sprinkle of arsenic instead of pepper. She set the plate on the floor. Sadie shoved her nose into the feast, her tail thumping against the table leg in utter bliss.

Without missing a beat, Billy slid another plate in front of Esmerelda. Sunny yellow eggs, soft in the middle and perfectly browned around the edges, bacon fried into crispy curlicues, plump golden biscuits. She let out a blissful sigh. There had been mornings in her life when she would have sold her braid for such a feast. She flashed Billy a grateful smile, but he'd already turned back to the stove.

"Mornin', gal," Zoe boomed in a voice that would have made even Virgil cringe.

Caught off guard, Esmerelda nearly choked on her biscuit. "G-g-good morning, Mrs. Darling."

"Now, there's no need in us bein' so formal 'round here." Zoe reached across the table and gave her hand a maternal pat. "You can just call me Ma."

Esmerelda gaped down at the massive brown paw that had engulfed her hand. It took her a dazed moment to realize that the woman wasn't being kind to her because she'd been seized by a sudden fit of Christian charity, but to spite her son. From the wry twist of Billy's lips as he set his own plate on the table and straddled the chair across from her, Esmerelda knew that he realized it, too.

Zoe's smile was even more intimidating than her scowl. Before she could squeak out a reply, Esmerelda had to drain half a glass of milk to wash down the lump of biscuit still stuck in her throat. "That's very generous of you, ma'am. My own mother died when I was only a little girl."

Esmerelda tried not to cower as Zoe captured a corner of the quilt in her ham-handed fist and reached over to dab away Esmerelda's milk mustache. "I've often wished I had me a daughter instead of a passel o' no-count sons. A daughter might marry someday, but she'll always remain loyal to her ma." Zoe shook her head in wistful regret. "Every woman should have a daughter. At least when a daughter has younguns of her own, she can understand the grievous pain her ma suffered through to birth and raise her."

Thinking of Bartholomew, Esmerelda offered Billy's mother a sad little smile. "Perhaps your suffering isn't as unappreciated as you fear."

Zoe cast the top of Billy's head a black look. "My boys never 'preciated nothin' they couldn't eat, steal, or fu—"

Billy stopped shoveling in forkfuls of egg long enough to clear his throat and give his mother a level look.

She subsided with an audible "haarumph." Esmerelda picked up her fork, tucking a wayward strand of hair behind her ear with her other hand.

"Hell, gal, there's no need to eat with your hair all hangin' in your face that way."

Before she could protest, Zoe had shuffled over to retrieve a faded ribbon from her sewing box. Esmerelda tensed as Zoe gathered her hair, expecting to be yanked bald, but the woman's large hands were surprisingly gentle. As Zoe tied the ribbon in a clumsy bow at her nape, Esmerelda glanced up to see a flicker of something in Billy's eyes.

"There now. Ain't that nice?" Zoe said, stepping back to admire her handiwork.

"Why, thank you, ma'am, er, I mean Mrs. . . . um," Esmerelda had to clear her throat twice before managing to bleat, "Ma."

Billy grinned and leaned forward, resting his elbows on the table. "Since there's no need in us being so formal around here, Mrs. Darling, can I call you *Ma*, too?"

Zoe scowled. Grabbing an ax off the wall, she went stomping out the door like some sort of Norse berserker in search of some hapless livestock to slay. Sadie loped after her, her long ears flapping in the morning breeze.

Billy returned to his breakfast as if the entire incident had never happened.

"Doesn't it bother you?" Esmerelda asked. "To hear your mother speak so unkindly?"

"She's entitled," he said, biting off a chunk of biscuit and chewing with relish. "Besides, that's the most I've heard her say in fourteen years." He chased the biscuit with a gulp of milk. Esmerelda couldn't help but notice how his tongue snaked out to lick away the froth of cream on his upper lip. "When I told her I was heading back to Missouri to join up with Bloody Bill and the rest of the boys, she didn't say a word. Since I was the only one to come out to New Mexico with her to see her settled, I guess she'd taken it into her head that I'd be staying. When I walked out that door, she didn't pitch a fit or even ask me not to go." He shook his head ruefully. "I'd have felt better if she'd have hauled off and walloped me one. But I guess she'd done all the crying and begging she was going to do back in Missouri the night they hanged Pa." He ducked his head to snap off a bite of bacon, but not before Esmerelda saw the shadow move through his eyes. "I never could abide a woman's tears. I had to go after them. They made my ma cry."

"You were there," she breathed, stunned. "The night your father died."

He gave a curt nod. "I wasn't no more than a scrawny kid of thirteen, but I tried to stop them anyway. The soldiers held me back. By the time they left and I cut him down, it was too late."

Such simple words. Such a vivid scene. Even with her eyes squeezed shut, Esmerelda could still see it.

"I knew then that if I'd have had a gun in my hand, I could have stopped them. That's when I vowed never to be without one again."

Esmerelda could not let the icy glint in his eyes go unchallenged. "If you'd have had a gun in your hand, they'd have probably shot you dead and your mother would have spent the past fourteen years mourning you as well as your father."

"I reckon she did that anyway." After a moment, he went on. "I can't really blame her for taking my leaving so hard. I was her last hope. She always dreamed of us boys making something better of ourselves than dirt farmers or outlaws. Her favorite brother was a lawman back in Springfield."

The keen attention Billy suddenly devoted to his breakfast betrayed more than he intended.

"She must have loved you very much," Esmerelda said softly.

He flashed her a sheepish grin. "Jasper was right, you know. Ma always was partial to me. Hell, I'm lucky the boys didn't toss me down a well and sell me to some passing Midianites."

It was Esmerelda's turn to blink innocently at him. "Now, Mr. Darling, where would a self-professed heathen such as yourself learn such a story?"

"Must have stumbled on it somewhere," he mumbled, taking another hearty bite of biscuit.

Esmerelda knew exactly where he'd stumbled on it— between the cracked leather binding of that ancient family Bible. But if she pressed, she knew he would deny it. Just as he had denied owning all those books celebrating the courageous exploits of famous lawmen. Just as he would deny how natural that deputy U.S. marshal's badge had looked in his hand.

"Ma used to save me the choicest morsels of everything she cooked." He chuckled. "I used to plague her something fierce on baking day. She'd pretend to get all riled and shoo me out of the kitchen with her apron, but when I snuck back in, there'd be that bowl just sitting there unguarded on the table, waiting to be licked. Yeah," he said softly. "She loved me."

How could she not?

The thought rose unbidden to Esmerelda's mind, ringing so clear that for a moment she was terrified she'd spoken it aloud.

How could Zoe Darling not love a sunny-haired child with a hunger for learning so sharp he risked humiliation and physical torment to satisfy it? How could she not love a slender, handsome boy clever enough to use his wits to survive the brutish bullying of his brothers? How could she not love a boy who'd seen and done things no boy should ever have to see or do, yet had grown into a man so tenderhearted that he hadn't hesitated to champion a sad-eyed, flea-bitten basset hound whose hunting days were long over?

How could she not love him?

Time dwindled to nothing more significant than the dreamy waltz of dust motes around Billy's head as Esmerelda realized that she was no longer talking about Zoe.

She stood up abruptly, nearly overturning her chair.

Billy frowned at her. "What's wrong, honey? You're white as a bedsheet." He sniffed gingerly at his empty glass. "Was the milk curdled?"

Esmerelda shoved the chair aside, making a dreadful racket, and began to back out of the room. "Uh, no. The milk was just fine. Something else must have disagreed with me."

Something tall and lanky with a lazy grin and deceptively sleepy eyes that were even now narrowing to seek the thread of truth within her clumsily stitched quilt of lies.

Esmerelda turned to leave, but the blanket coiled around her ankles. Billy lurched around the table and caught her arm to steady her, his casual touch scorching her skin. She gazed up into his smoky green eyes with a helpless mixture of wonder and despair. He was too late. Not even his gunslinger's reflexes could stop her from falling. She'd already fallen.

Hard.

And it had knocked the breath clear out of her.

Wrenching her arm from Billy's grasp, Esmerelda fled the room as if Zoe Darling and a horde of ax-wielding giantesses were thundering at her heels.

CHAPTER TWENTY

Death was stalking Bartholomew Fine.

Dressed all in black, he camped outside the canyon cave where Bartholomew had been hiding since fleeing the bank in Eulalie. He was more handsome than Bart had imagined—a smooth-talker with a lazy drawl and a ready grin. A constant companion and a pleasant conversationalist. Although his manner was friendly, Bart would never have thought to address him by his first name, but respectfully referred to him as *Mister*.

Mr. Death wore his gunbelt low on his hips. A broad-brimmed slouch hat shadowed his face. Bartholomew lived in fear of the inevitable moment when he would reach up with one graceful finger and tip it back, revealing the hellfire in his eyes.

Whenever he could no longer bear the suspense, he would turn his face away from the mouth of the cave and take another long swig from the whiskey bottle. He'd never been much of a drinker, yet empty bottles littered the cavern floor around him. Although he would have died before admitting it to the men who had so briefly called him leader, the taste of alcohol made him a little sick. But not as sick as the prospect of facing the specter lurking outside that cave stone-cold sober.

He spent his days huddled against the cavern wall, paralyzed by his own fear. He'd shuffled into a dank corner of the cave to pee one morning only to come face-to-face with his own reflection in the fragment of mirror he'd used to trim his beard when the cave had been his gang's hideout. He'd recoiled with a high-pitched yelp, barely recognizing the feral creature gawking back at him with its wild, red-rimmed eyes and bushy beard. He'd buried that face in his hands and stumbled back to the wall, Mr. Death's laughter ringing in his ears.

Night was the worst. Although the chill that came creeping out of the desert after the sun sank was enough to make a man's fingers and toes tingle and ache, Mr. Death never lit a fire. He preferred the cold.

Bartholomew would fight sleep, his exhausted body twitching with the effort, but his eyes would always betray him by drifting shut, leaving him alone in the darkness.

Every time he closed his eyes, he saw blood. Welling from the blackened edges of a fresh wound. Pooling on the floor. Soaking the chaste white of his sister's gloves. But worse than the blood was the look in Esmerelda's eyes, a look he almost hadn't recognized the first time he saw it because it had been so foreign to him.

Shame.

His sister—who had glowed with pride every time he trotted home from school with a clumsily written story clutched in his plump fist; who had fussed and crowed over even his most humble efforts at badly rhymed poetry; who had held him while he wept out his disappointment, her own eyes burning with indignation, when a less talented classmate had won the annual essay contest sponsored by the *Gazette*—was ashamed of him.

One night, after he'd been cowering in the cave for over a week, his tortured imagination devised a new ending for his disjointed dreams. An ending in which it was Esmerelda who lay sprawled on the floor in a pool of blood, shot through the heart by his own hand.

Bartholomew started from sleep, his heart pounding, his shirt drenched with sweat. His lapse of consciousness had given Mr. Death the opportunity to creep a little closer. So close Bart could almost hear the rasp of his breathing in the darkness.

Bartholomew's cheeks were wet with tears. He swiped at his upper lip like the snot-nosed kid he used to be. Only this time Esmerelda wasn't there to offer him her handkerchief and gently remind him to blow.

Dropping his head into his hands, he wondered how everything could have gone so wrong so fast. When he'd created Black Bart, he'd only intended him to be a character, the immoral yet charming hero of his very first novel. Using part of the money Esmerelda had set aside for his college education, he had outfitted himself with a sharp suit of clothes and a shiny new Colt. He'd soothed the sting of his conscience by promising himself that the royalties from his first novel would double that money, perhaps even quadruple it. He would return to Esmerelda in triumph, an acclaimed author with enough money to lavish upon them both.

Garbed in his handsome new costume, he'd taken to frequenting saloons and gambling halls. He'd scripted his dialogue as he went along, then hurried back to his hotel room before dawn to carefully record his impressions on the crisp pages of his journal.

He'd soon learned that playing a role could be a heady experience. Women who wouldn't have looked twice at a plump, bashful young man studying at Boston College to be a teacher or law clerk began to lean over Black Bart's shoulder and whisper in his ear which card to play. He found the ripe musk of their perfume and the deliberate press of their breasts against his back more intoxicating than any shot of bourbon. By the time the last card was played and they took his hand to draw him up the stairs, he was already too drunk with desire to resist.

His reputation had been born there, in the darkness, between the sheets, with those velvet-soft hands ushering him into manhood. He'd swear them to secrecy, then speak in a voice still hoarse with spent passion of trains he had robbed, women he had loved, men he had killed. He would rise from their rumpled beds, buckling on his gunbelt with sure and steady hands before leaning over to give them a kiss so hot and fierce they always believed it might very well be his last. As soon as he was gone, they would seek out their sister whores. It was their hushed whispers and shivers of fearful delight that had helped him weave his own legend.

Soon men began to be drawn to him as well. Desperate men. Lazy men. Greedy men. Men like Flavil Snorton, who hoped only to be in his company when he blew open his next safe or demanded the halt of another stagecoach. Basking in their respect and adoration, Bartholomew had felt himself slowly disappearing into the skin of his creation without ever once committing an actual crime.

He was abiding quite comfortably in that skin the night Thaddeus Winstead had ambled into the Santa Fe saloon where Black Bart was holding court over a game of poker. So comfortably that he'd let Bart do all the talking while

Bartholomew Fine looked on with his mouth hanging open, mute with shock at his character's audacity.

Sadly enough, Black Bart, with his shiny guns that had never been fired and his slick veneer of sophistication, had been naive enough to believe in honor among thieves. He'd never dreamed that Winstead would use him, then betray him. After all those months of gleefully pretending to be a fugitive from the law, Bartholomew suddenly found himself trapped in the role he had created.

He'd suspected Eulalie was nothing but an ambush from the beginning, but the worshipful glint in the eyes of his men had driven him to take the bait. He'd even deluded himself into believing he could outwit Winstead now that he knew the rules of engagement. Until he'd charged into that bank and come face to face with Mr. Death.

Bartholomew shuddered.

If the creature lurking outside the cave tipped back his hat, Bartholomew knew it was that face he would see. Grim, resolute, ruthless enough to make Black Bart look like nothing more than some city cartoonist's ineptly drawn caricature of a gunslinger. If Mr. Death chose to deepen their acquaintance, Bartholomew would be forced to gaze into the smoke green eyes of the man he had murdered in cold blood. Only this time, William Darling wouldn't demand the surrender of his freedom, but his soul.

Bartholomew groped for the whiskey bottle nestled between his legs. It was his last bottle and less than half of it remained. The amber liquid glimmered like fool's gold in the moonlight, brighter even than the bags and bars of treasury gold that lined the back wall of the cave. Fool's gold indeed. Only he was the fool.

Tomorrow he would be forced to battle his demons with his senses undulled by liquor.

But not yet. Not tonight.

Bringing the bottle to his lips, he drained it in one long, thirsty gulp.

"I'm sorry, Esme," he whispered as the bitter heat scorched its way down his throat and settled in the pit of his belly. "I only wanted to make you proud."

Without bothering to wipe away the tears trickling down his cheeks or the whiskey dribbling down his chin, he slumped to his side and into a mercifully dreamless stupor.

Bartholomew woke to the glorious warmth of sunshine streaming across his face. He slowly pried open his eyes, squinting against the incandescent brilliance.

The mouth of the cave was empty. Mr. Death was gone.

He scrambled to a sitting position, hardly able to believe his good fortune. A disbelieving bark of laughter escaped his lungs.

Then died as he heard the shuffle of boots behind him. Right behind him. He clenched his teeth against a shudder of terror so keen he could actually feel the hair on his scalp begin to lift.

It seemed Mr. Death had come to call while he'd been sleeping.

Bartholomew reached for his gun, remembering too late that he'd flung the hateful thing away after fleeing the bank. Too physically and emotionally exhausted to elude his destiny any longer, he slowly turned to find himself gazing at four pairs of dusty boots.

He blinked in a vain attempt to clear his vision. He'd heard of drunks seeing double, but he'd never heard of one seeing quadruple. He was still trying to puzzle it out when a massive hand swooped down, seized him by the collar, and lifted him clear off the ground, bringing him eye to eye with a golden-haired giant.

"Howdy, son," the giant boomed, an amiable grin breaking through his sandy beard. His three companions watched with polite indifference as the giant shook him this way and that, like some gargantuan mastiff worrying a bone. "We hate to disturb your nap, but I do believe you just might be the miserable little sonofabitch who shot my baby brother."

The giant's grasp on his collar was decidedly mortal, as was the stale blast of his cigar-tainted breath. His face was curiously familiar, but lacked the ruthless cast of Mr. Death's.

Bartholomew went limp in the man's grip, so relieved he would have gladly confessed to shooting Lincoln himself.

Until he saw the braided noose swinging from the man's other hand.

CHAPTER TWENTY-ONE

Esmerelda Fine's accounts always balanced. If she came up even a penny off, short or over, she would spend half the night poring over the books by candlelight until the tidy little numbers inscribed in their neatly drawn columns began to blur before her aching eyes. She used the same meticulous care in her cooking, refusing to even consider substituting a dash of this for a pinch of that. When a piece of music was set in front of her, she played note for note what was written on the page, ignoring the yearning of her hands to ripple and soar in a flight of fancy.

Yet suddenly two and two equaled eleven, her dash of salt had been replaced by a bucket of sugar, and her heart was playing all the wrong notes, arranging them in a melody too compelling to resist.

With a fitful sigh, Esmerelda rolled herself out of her

quilt and sat up. She cast the loft a long-suffering look, surprised her heart's song wasn't being drowned out by the rumble of Zoe's snoring. The sound was enough to make the walls quake and the rafters tremble. How odd, she thought, that she had never once heard it when Billy had been so desperately ill.

Flickering moonbeams sifted through the open door, beckoning her into the night. Perhaps if she escaped the stifling heat of the house for a little while, she might be able to clear her head of the cotton batting that had filled it since sharing breakfast with Billy. Leaving the quilt in a dejected puddle, she padded across the floor and slipped onto the porch.

A puff of wind too forceful to be called a breeze stroked her brow and plucked at her unbound hair. The rising wind was scented by a hint of rain, faint enough to be nothing more than another unfulfilled promise. Clouds came billowing in from the west, casting a mighty shadow across the vast sweep of land.

Esmerelda wrapped an arm around one of the porch posts, searching the night with restless eyes. She had hoped to find peace out here, but the reckless abandon of the wind stirred something deep within her—something wild and dangerous that had been fettered for too long.

It made her want to take her mother's violin out of its case and saw madly at the strings. It made her want to laugh because she, Esmerelda Fine, a woman who had always prided herself on her stern practicality, had been foolish enough to fall in love with a man who was not only a gunslinger, but an avowed bachelor. It made her want to burst into tears.

She might have given in to that last urge if her sensitive nostrils hadn't detected a whiff of smoke. She whirled around, clapping a hand over her galloping heart.

"You do delight in sneaking up on me, don't you?" she accused.

Billy stepped out of the shadows of the yard, a lit cigar clamped in the corner of his mouth. "Since I was here first, it could be argued that you snuck up on me."

Painfully aware that Billy, shirtless and barefoot in the faltering moonlight, just might be more than she could bear at the moment, Esmerelda dropped her scowl to his cigar. "You really shouldn't be smoking right now. Where did you get that?"

"Ma's private stash." His mouth curved into a rueful grin. "I knew there'd be hell to pay if I made off with her pipe tobacco or her snuff." He flicked the glowing stub into the darkness before arching one tawny eyebrow at her. "There. You satisfied?"

Having recently learned that she never would be, Esmerelda snapped, "Nor should you be out here without a shirt. What if you catch a chill?"

The downward flick of his gaze warned her that she'd succeeded in doing nothing but drawing attention to her own attire. Or lack of it. The wind licked hungrily at her nightgown, cupping the threadbare muslin to her breasts. Her first instinct was to fold her arms protectively over her chest, but the challenging glint in Billy's eyes kept her standing straight and proud, her hands clenched into fists at her sides.

"Not much danger of that, now, is there?" he said softly. He took a step toward her, his grin softening into a quizzical half smile. "You keep nagging me, honey, I just might think you care."

His words struck a raw nerve. "Then you'd be sorely mistaken. I just don't want you lolling about in bed when you could be out looking for my brother. I hired a tracker, not some glory-seeking gunslinger."

She expected him to snap right back at her and would have felt better if he had, but he simply nodded. "You're absolutely right, Miss Fine. A man in my weakened condition shouldn't be partaking of tobacco or the night air."

He started for the porch. Esmerelda was still gaping with surprise at his amiable surrender when he hesitated and began to sway. She scrambled down the rotting steps to grab him. Stricken with guilt at her shrewish behavior, she searched his features for any hint of returning pallor.

As quick as that, in a move more graceful than any waltz, Billy reversed their positions, wrapping his arms around her.

Thrown off balance by the return of his wiry strength, she glared up at him. "You, sir, are a rascal."

"And you, ma'am, are entirely too gullible."

"Your mother—" she protested, squirming frantically.

"Works like an ox and sleeps like the dead."

As if to underscore his words, a blissful snore came floating out of the darkened house.

Billy's stern frown was softened by the hint of a dimple in his cheek. "I warned you back at the bank that I might have to arrest you. And as I recall, you promised to surrender yourself into my custody."

His teasing words took all the fight out of her.

Horrified to realize she might yet burst into tears, Esmerelda turned her face away and whispered, "Don't trifle with me. It's too unkind."

Billy's grip gentled. He cupped her chin in his palm, coaxing her into meeting his gaze. His eyes were as sober as her own. "Ah, but trifling with you, Duchess, would be such a pleasure." As if to prove his words, he lowered his head to graze her temple, inhaling deeply. "Did I ever tell you what my favorite kind of pie is?"

As he brought his lips to bear against the downy softness

of her cheek, languor melted through Esmerelda's bones in a sensation so delicious that she no longer struggled to escape, but simply to stay on her feet.

"Ummmm . . . apple?" she ventured, swallowing hard.

He shook his head. His mouth followed the curve of her cheekbone down and around to the tingling shell of her ear. "Not blueberry either. Oh, I like apple and blueberry just fine, but the one kind of pie I never could resist was . . ." Catching her earlobe between his teeth, he whispered, "peach."

She gasped as his heated breath sent a ribbon of anticipation curling deep into her womb.

"Whenever Ma baked a peach pie, I'd swipe it off the windowsill as soon as she set it out to cool. I knew she'd have cut me a piece if I'd have asked real nice, but nothing whets a man's appetite more than forbidden"—his lips just barely grazed the corner of her mouth, tantalizing a dreamy sigh from her parted lips—"fruit."

By the time Billy's mouth covered hers, Esmerelda was nearly dizzy with anticipation. So dizzy that she didn't stop to think of the consequences when she parted her lips for him, offering up a delicacy moist and luscious enough to tempt the sweet tooth of any man.

As Billy sank his tongue into her, his growl didn't come from his stomach, but his throat. The primal sound was tinged with raw hunger. When Esmerelda had first wandered onto the porch, stealing a few kisses from a pretty girl in the moonlight had seemed a harmless enough pursuit. But he'd forgotten just how dangerous Esmerelda could be. Beneath her prickly exterior lay the vulnerable innocence of a woman, tender and sweet and ripe for the plucking.

His fierce desire to do just that only served to remind him that he was still a Darling at heart. He'd never learned how to court a woman who couldn't be bought.

For a brief moment, he almost regretted that she hadn't been Fine's woman instead of his sister. Everything would have been so much more simple between them. She would know what he wanted and he would know what she needed and he wouldn't be standing there in the weeds, rigid with desire and giving her a kiss he had no business giving a virgin.

He was so distracted by the unspoken promises of her mouth that he barely felt the first raindrops strike his back. Rain was a rare and marvelous thing in New Mexico, but not nearly as rare or marvelous as the yielding softness of Esmerelda in his arms.

A sharp clap of thunder heralded the arrival of a genuine downpour. They clung to each other as the rain washed over them, neither wanting to be the first to break away. But when Billy felt a violent shiver wrack Esmerelda's delicate frame, he drew back, gently chafing her shoulders.

"Come out to the barn with me," he blurted out.

At least she didn't slap him right off. She simply blinked up at him, her eyes dark with uncertainty. She couldn't know how delicious she looked with that worn-out old nightgown plastered to her breasts and her lips still glistening from his kiss. Billy barely resisted the urge to drop to his knees and beg.

"I swear on my pa's grave that I won't compromise you," he vowed, brushing a raindrop from her silky lashes. "I just want to hold you . . . touch you."

Esmerelda's breath caught in a tremulous sigh. She could hardly believe she was actually pondering Billy's bold proposal. But there was something so tender in his touch, so earnest in his eyes. It tempted her to trust him with both her virtue and her heart. Tempted her to believe that William Darling was a man of his word.

It was that hope, however foolish, that prompted her shy nod.

As if afraid she would change her mind, Billy wasted no time in scooping her up in his arms. She curled both arms around his neck and buried her face against his breastbone, taking care not to disturb his bandage. He covered the distance between house and barn in long, urgent strides. As he shoved open the door with his foot, the animals within greeted them with curious whickers and a plaintive lowing. Leaving the barn door half-open to beckon in the brilliant flashes of lightning and gusts of wind, he deposited Esmerelda on a bed of clean hay.

He followed her down, cupping her face between his hands with fierce tenderness. Rain beat like a sonata against the tin roof, indistinguishable from the painful stammer of Esmerelda's heartbeat.

"If you don't want me to," he whispered hoarsely. "I swear I won't lay a finger on you."

"Well, maybe . . ." Esmerelda swallowed hard, wondering just what manner of wanton spirit had possessed her. ". . . just one?"

A thoughtful grin spread across his face before he reached up to tip an imaginary hat. "Very well, ma'am. I aim to oblige."

Oblige her Billy did, using a single fingertip to gently trace the arch of her brow, the flare of her cheekbones, the delicate bridge of her nose, until she had no more pride left than Sadie rolling to her back to beg for a belly scratch. Esmerelda had always lavished hugs and fond caresses on Bartholomew, but since he'd grown too big for such embarrassing displays, there had been no one to hug or caress her. She hadn't realized how starved for affection she was until that very moment.

Her hunger sharpened as Billy used the calloused pad

of his finger to explore the softness of her lips. After a moment of such delicious torment, they instinctively parted and closed around his finger, drawing him into her mouth. He let out a tortured groan of his own.

He laved her tingling lips with honey from her own kiss until they were primed for more of his kisses—a hot, wet feast for the senses that left Esmerelda so sated with delight she barely felt that same sly finger loosening the sodden ties at the throat of her nightgown.

The caress of his breath against her naked shoulder gave her a start of panic. She struggled to sit up. "Billy!"

"Mmmm?" he murmured, stroking the sensitive skin over her fluted collarbone.

Even as she pushed at him, Esmerelda knew she wasn't playing fair. After all, she was the one who had set the rules of this game, a game at which Billy was already proving himself to be a master. A game she was no longer sure she wanted to win.

Fisting her hands in his damp hair, she forced him to meet her gaze. "You won't cheat, will you?"

"I make it a habit never to cheat at cards."

"We're not playing cards," she reminded him.

His wink was pure devilment. "Then you'll just have to take your chances, won't you?"

Esmerelda despised games of chance, but something told her that if she didn't take a chance on this man tonight, she might very well regret it for the rest of her staid, lonely life. She'd long ago resigned herself to spending her life without a man, but spending this one night without Billy seemed intolerable.

So she sank back on that sweet-smelling bed of hay and surrendered herself into his custody. He hooked his finger in the bodice of her gown and tenderly peeled the wet fabric from her skin.

When a flicker of lightning limned her naked breasts in quicksilver, she might have cringed with embarrassment if he hadn't breathed a reverent sigh into her ear. "Peaches, angel. The prettiest ones I've ever seen."

Indeed, the breasts she had always considered so woefully inadequate seemed to swell and ripen beneath his touch. He kissed her softly on the mouth while that deft, wise finger of his traced ever-narrowing circles around the tender globes. He resisted the greedy thrust of her nipples for so long that when his finger finally brushed one of the aching buds, as if by chance, Esmerelda cried out at the raw wonder of it.

He captured her cry with his lips, flicking first one distended nipple, then the other. Tremors of pleasure cascaded through her, forcing her to clamp her legs together against a rush of yearning. It was almost as if he'd touched her somewhere else—somewhere dark, lush, and forbidden.

Esmerelda had struggled not to feel for thirteen years, but beneath Billy's skillful coaxing, her dormant senses came alive with a vengeance. She could smell the sharp musk of his own desire, taste the mellow hint of tobacco on his tongue, hear every nuance of his husky drawl as he murmured that it sure would be nice if she'd let him put his mouth everywhere she was letting him put his finger.

Esmerelda didn't really grasp the shocking implications of that proposal until she felt his finger slowly inching up beneath her gown. Even through the modest cotton of her drawers, it felt like a live fuse winding its way between her trembling thighs toward the narrow slit in the fabric. The explosion was inevitable. The instant his fingertip brushed that soft thatch of hair, her legs simply fell apart, yielding all to his touch.

She must have whimpered. She must have moaned.

"Shhhh, sweetheart," he murmured, "I can't hurt you with just one finger, can I?"

It wasn't pain Esmerelda was worried about, but pleasure. A pleasure so thick and sweet it seemed to dribble through her veins like wild honey, melting her resistance to his will. Billy might not mean to hurt her, but he was breaking her heart with nothing more than the tender probing of his fingertip.

She gasped into his mouth as he fondled her passion-engorged flesh, the grace of his gunslinger's hands serving them both well. He sought the taut bud nestled within her silky folds, stroking and rubbing until she was panting with delight. Only then did he dip his long, blunt finger into the nectar welling from her throbbing core.

"Peaches and cream," he groaned against her lips, making her shudder with primal longing.

To Esmerelda's dismay, she discovered that Billy was a man of his word. Although she arched her back, desperately trying to press herself into his palm, he prolonged her delicious torment by using only his calloused fingertip to tease her into a frenzy of ecstasy.

"Please," she choked out, burying her burning face in the crook of his throat. "I'm throwing myself on the mercy of the court."

"No mercy," he breathed into her ear before deliberately splintering her into a thousand glittering shards.

Esmerelda cried out her astonishment as all the pleasure she'd denied herself for the past thirteen years seemed to swell through her body in one devastating surge that left her limp and trembling in its wake.

She lay steeped in a haze of wonder until the ragged rasp of Billy's breathing coaxed her eyes open. He was no longer holding her, but sat a few inches away with his elbows propped on his knees and one of those long-boned wrists of his gripped in his other hand. His knuckles were stark white.

The rain had stopped and a shaft of moonlight pierced the musty gloom, illuminating the raw beauty of his profile. A muscle beat beneath the taut skin of his jaw. Esmerelda glanced down, seeing herself as he must see her—a wanton stranger with her breasts bared to the kiss of the moonlight, her nightgown twisted around her waist, her legs sprawled apart in reckless invitation. Shame flooded her as she realized just how generous he'd been and how selfish he'd allowed her to be.

She scrambled to a sitting position, jerking her bodice up and her gowntail down. "Oh, Lord, Billy, I'm so sorry. I didn't mean to—"

"Hush," he said harshly, still not looking at her. "You don't owe me anything. Especially not an apology."

He looked so rigid that she was afraid he might shatter if she dared to touch him. But she dared anyway, running her fingertips over the day's growth of golden bristle that shadowed his jaw.

He caught her wrist with the grace of a striking rattler, then turned her hand to press a rough kiss to her palm. Before she could recover from her breathless shock, he swept her up in his arms and started for the barn door.

"Where are you taking me?" she blurted out, struggling to clutch her bodice to her breasts and cling to his neck at the same time.

Billy's eyes narrowed in a mean-eyed squint that sent a primitive shiver rippling down Esmerelda's spine. "To bed."

Billy spent the longest night of his life watching Esmerelda sleep in his bed without him.

As the rosy blush of dawn crept across her cheeks, he sat in the old rocker with his bare feet propped on the edge of the straw mattress. Somewhere outside, a lone rooster warbled a plaintive how-do-you-do. A board directly over his head let out a mighty creak, warning him that Zoe was already awake and stirring.

Esmerelda looked so beautiful lying there on the narrow bedstead he'd slept in as a boy, with her hair spilled across the quilt his ma had stitched, that Billy had to rock backward every now and then just to catch his breath. Having her there was like having one of his more vivid boyhood fantasies fulfilled. He could still remember lying on that bed alone, gazing out his window at the Missouri moon and dreaming of a girl just like her. The kind of girl a Darling could only dream of having.

But he was no longer a boy. And Esmerelda was a woman grown. He wanted her badly. It wasn't right and it wasn't fair, but he wanted her anyway. The only thing that stopped him from taking her was knowing that if he went back on his word now, he would be no better than Jasper or Bart Fine or any of the other meanspirited sons-of-bitches who believed they could steal what they wanted without ever once having to pay a price.

There had been a moment last night, when Esmerelda had lain vulnerable and trembling in his arms, her naked breasts still flushed from her first taste of bliss, when he would have paid any price to climb between those milky thighs of hers—even his soul. Billy dropped his head into his hands, wondering if he'd ever again taste anything as sweet as the rain on Esmerelda's skin.

At first he thought the rumble of distant thunder was only the taunt of his memory. But that was before the first gunshot rang out, shattering the morning calm.

CHAPTER TWENTY-TWO

♥

"Winstead!" Billy hissed before springing out of the rocker and scrambling for the open window.

That first shot was followed by a torrent of hoofbeats and a gleeful barrage of gunfire. Billy pressed his back to the wall and stole a cautious peek out the window, half expecting to be gunned down by a spray of bullets.

When he saw who was making the racket and why, he almost wished he had been. He groaned aloud before biting off one of his more descriptive oaths. He nearly jumped out of his skin when it was greeted by a scandalized gasp.

"Why, William Darling!" Esmerelda cried, sitting bolt upright in the bed. "I know that chair isn't very comfortable and you tend to be grumpy in the morning, but you ought to be ashamed of yourself for using that kind of gutter language in front of a lady."

Billy reached behind him and snatched the burlap curtains together, wishing he'd thought to slam the window when he had the chance. At least he no longer had to worry about a stray bullet striking either of them. "Oh, I am, honey. Deeply ashamed. Now, you just go right back to sleep and I'll get Ma to wash out my mouth with some of her strongest lye soap."

Esmerelda yawned, the tumble of her hair making her look deliciously rumpled. Billy suffered a sharp pang of regret. He should have crawled into that bed with her when he'd had the chance. If she got a gander at what was outside that window, he might never get another one.

"What's that dreadful noise?" she asked, knuckling her eyes.

"It's probably just Ma shooting her some breakfast. You know Ma. When she gets a hankering for chicken gizzards, there's no dissuading her."

Esmerelda lowered her hands. "Your mother shoots chickens?"

For once in his life, Billy's glib tongue failed him. He strode toward the bed. "There's really no need for you to rise this early. Why don't you let me tuck you back in?"

He jerked the quilt out from under her and threw it over her head, hoping it would muffle the worst of the din. It barely succeeded in muffling her outraged protests. She finally managed to bat it away, but before she could do more than sputter in indignation, the gunfire ceased and a male voice boomed like cannonshot, making them both jump.

"Hey, little brother! You alive in there?"

Billy winced at that familiar bellow. A bellow even Esmerelda couldn't fail to recognize. He closed his eyes briefly and cleared his throat before calling out, "Yeah, Virg, I'm alive."

"Well, come join the party, then," his oldest brother roared in an invitation too jovial to resist. "There's a young feller out here who'd like to have a word with you. Turns out he's mighty sorry for shootin' you up like he did. He'd like to make peace with both you and his Maker before we string him up from this here oak."

Esmerelda went pale, then white. Their gazes locked for a frantic moment before she went bounding out of the bed and Billy went bounding over it, both racing for the gunbelt draped over the doorknob. Despite his well-honed reflexes, Esmerelda got there first.

She wrapped her fingers around the butt of the pistol. He wrapped his fingers around hers. They wrestled over the weapon, neither willing to be the first to let go.

"If you put another bullet in me," he muttered through clenched teeth, desperately trying to steer the barrel of the weapon away from all four of their bare feet, "I'm not going to be quite so inclined to overlook it."

"Then let go!" she demanded, straining against his relentless grip.

He did.

Esmerelda was so surprised, she stumbled against the wardrobe and nearly fell. From her triumphant look, Billy knew that she'd failed to take one thing into account. He still stood between her and the door.

He asserted his squatter's claim by leaning against it and folding his arms over his chest. "I can take the gun from you by force, but I'd rather you give it to me."

"They're going to hang him," she wailed softly. "They're going to hang my baby brother."

"No, they're not." He held out his hand. It was as steady as it had ever been without a gun in it. "For once in your life, woman, you're going to have to trust somebody besides yourself."

Although Esmerelda's face was still ashen, her eyes glittered with pride. A pride she had clung to without complaint or compromise ever since her parents had left a lonely, frightened twelve-year-old to fend for herself and her little brother. Billy held his breath. If she relaxed her white-knuckled grip on the gun, she would be offering him a gift even more precious than the generous liberties she'd allowed him in the barn.

When she lifted the pistol, pointing the barrel square at his chest, disappointment stabbed him. Then she turned the weapon and gently laid it, butt-first, into his palm. Ignoring the gun, he cupped her nape in his other hand and drew her to him for a kiss.

"You'll never regret it," he murmured into her hair. "I swear it."

After Billy had snatched up his gunbelt and gone, Esmerelda slumped against the wardrobe, unable to determine if she was more dazed by his promise or his kiss. Both had been brief, fierce, and unbearably sweet.

She might have lingered there all morning if Virgil's roar hadn't rattled the windowpanes, startling her back to sanity. "I hate to start the party without you, son, but this tenderfoot's fancy necktie ain't gonna hold forever."

"Bartholomew," Esmerelda whispered, besieged by a fresh wave of horror.

She threw open the door and raced into the parlor, forgetting about her revealing attire. She skidded to a halt, shocked to discover Zoe Darling perched on a cane-backed rocker by the hearth, rocking and puffing on her pipe as if a lynching wasn't about to occur practically in her own front yard. Sadie slept on the rag rug at her feet, blissfully snoring.

Esmerelda dropped to her knees beside the chair and

gazed up into the woman's stoic face. "Ma?" The word came easily to her tongue for the first time. "You need to fetch your shotgun. It really won't do to send Billy out there all alone. In case you haven't noticed, your sons have a tendency to be . . ." reckless? bloodthirsty? as vicious as a pack of rabid coyotes? "um . . . high-spirited."

"The boy's old enough to fight his own battles." Zoe took another laconic puff off the pipe, refusing to meet Esmerelda's eyes. "He proved that fourteen years ago when he up and ran off."

"But he almost died only a few days ago. He still hasn't regained his full strength."

Zoe cut her eyes toward Esmerelda, taking in her disheveled hair, rumpled nightgown, and bare feet. Her mouth twisted in a wry smile. "Looks to me like he has."

Esmerelda blushed to the roots of her hair. She climbed stiffly to her feet. "Very well, Mrs. Darling. But since you've decided to harden your heart against a thirteen-year-old boy who ran off to avenge his father's death, you might want to know that he didn't do it for himself. He did it for you. Because they made you cry."

Zoe's chin might have quivered just the tiniest bit, but Esmerelda wasn't inclined to comfort her. Straightening her shoulders as if they were draped with a duchess's ermine-trimmed mantle instead of an old, faded nightgown, she marched across the room and slammed her way out the door.

When Esmerelda caught her first glimpse of Bartholomew, her bravado deserted her. She had to wrap one arm around a porch post to keep from staggering to her knees.

He sat astride a dun gelding at the crest of the hill, his hands bound behind his back and a noose draped around his neck. The other end of the rope had already been knotted over a jagged branch of the dead oak so that every time the horse shifted this way or that, it pulled his neck taut. It wasn't the vivid bruises on her brother's face but the defeated slope of his shoulders and the utter lack of hope in his expression that frightened Esmerelda more than anything.

Sam and Enos watched the proceedings from the back of the same wagon Billy had rented from the livery in Calamity, while Jasper gripped the reins of Bartholomew's horse in his gloved hand. Even from that distance, there was no mistaking the nasty gleam in his eye.

Billy was already striding toward Virgil, who stood with hands on hips and feet planted wide, like some jolly giant appointed to greet the Lilliputians.

"It's good to see you back on your feet, little brother," he boomed. "Since I've elected myself president of this here hemp committee, I'd like to say a few words before we commence with the—"

"Cut him down, Virg," Billy commanded.

Virgil's face fell. He cupped a hand around his ear. "Say again. I don't think I heard you right."

Billy raised the pistol and kept walking. "I said cut him down."

Enos and Sam exchanged a perplexed glance. Virgil took a step backward, his nervous gaze flicking to the weapon in his brother's hand. "Hell, Billy, I loaned you that iron. You ain't gonna shoot me with my own gun, are you?"

Billy stopped, cocking the pistol. "Only if I have to."

Virgil gazed into his brother's steely eyes for a long minute before flaring his nostrils in a snort of disgust. "Cut him down, Jasper."

"Like hell I will."

Billy swung the pistol toward Jasper.

A lazy grin spread over Jasper's face. Esmerelda was struck anew by what a handsome man he might have been had his soul not been so ugly. "You ain't gonna shoot me, are you, little brother? Cause if you shoot me, I just might drop these reins. And if I drop these reins, Mr. Fine-and-Dandy here is goin' on the last ride he'll ever take."

"Don't!" Esmerelda hoarsely cried.

Although she'd vowed to trust Billy, she couldn't seem to stop herself. She plunged down from the porch and went racing toward her brother. She might have made it if Billy hadn't shot out an arm, caught her around the waist, and gathered her against him. She could feel his heart beating strong and steady against her back.

"Be still, sweetheart," he murmured in her ear, his voice as smooth as oiled leather. "You don't want to spook the horse, do you?"

"N-n-no," she replied, her teeth chattering with helpless fury.

He lifted his head to look Jasper straight in the eye. "This isn't your quarrel," he said mildly. "I'm the one the boy shot."

"We're blood kin," Jasper replied. "You wrong one of us, you wrong us all. Then you pay the price."

Virgil, Sam, and Enos nodded their agreement.

Billy gave Bartholomew a thorough once-over. "Looks to me like this boy's already done enough paying. Those wouldn't be your fist prints on his face, now, would they, Jasper? I always said you could whip any man as long as he had his hands tied behind his back."

"Why, you rotten little—" Jasper started for him, but his death grip on the reins brought him up short.

The horse pranced sideways, straining Bartholomew's neck to an impossible angle; Bartholomew didn't make a sound, but Esmerelda whimpered aloud.

"Whoa, there," Billy crooned, as much to Jasper and Esmerelda as to the jittery horse. "I only meant to suggest that since the boy's insult to my person turned out to be nothing more than a flesh wound, hanging might be a mite harsh."

Remembering how valiantly Billy had fought for his life only a few days before, Esmerelda's heart welled with tenderness.

"What would you rather do?" Jasper asked, sneering with contempt. "Whip out that shiny little badge of yours and arrest him?"

Billy cocked his head to one side as if he was genuinely pondering the situation. "Considering that there's been no real harm done, I might be willing to accept a sincere apology." He turned to Enos and Sam, appealing first to his less bloodthirsty siblings. "How about it, boys? If the lady's brother says he's sorry, would you vote to cut him down?"

Billy gave her a sharp squeeze. Esmerelda responded to his cue by batting her eyelashes in Enos and Sam's direction. "I'd be eternally in your debt."

Sam scratched his head. "Huh?"

"She'd be much obliged," Billy translated.

The two men exchanged a glance, then Enos shyly nodded. "She does play a m-m-mighty purty fiddle."

"Virg?" Billy asked.

Virgil tore off his hat and slapped it against his thigh. "Aw, what the hell. Though I think it's a dadburned shame to ruin a perfectly good lynchin'."

"Jasper?"

Although he refused to meet his brother's eyes, Jasper's shoulders twitched in a sullen shrug that would have to be answer enough.

Billy's attention shifted to Bartholomew. Esmerelda didn't have to see Billy's eyes to know they'd narrowed in unspoken warning. She held her breath as her brother straightened his head the best he could, swallowing against the strangling tension of the rope. He glanced briefly at Billy, then defiantly shifted his gaze to Esmerelda.

"I never meant to hurt you," he said. "I'm so sorry."

As Esmerelda gazed into his tear-glazed eyes, she knew he truly was. Perhaps for the first time in his life. A sob caught in her throat as her heart surged with love and pride. She had her brother back. The one who'd slipped his little hand into hers each Sunday afternoon when they went to put flowers on their parents' graves. The one who'd written startlingly eloquent poems about his mama playing her violin with the other angels in heaven. The one who had wrapped his chubby arms around her waist whenever he sensed she was tired or lonely or afraid.

She didn't understand the reason for the terrible resignation in those eyes until Jasper hooted. "You're sorry, all right! A sorrier sonofabitch I never saw." Before any of them could react, he let go of the reins, smacked the horse on the rump, and shouted, "Yee-haw!"

Esmerelda screamed. Flinging her aside, Billy dropped to one knee and fired six times in rapid succession, cocking the hammer and squeezing the trigger so fast his hand was nothing more than a blur.

He might have severed the rope. He might have saved Bartholomew's life. But he didn't have to. For at that precise moment, a mighty shotgun blast struck the oak, shattering the rotten wood and sending the branch and Bartholomew sprawling to the ground in a cloud of dust.

CHAPTER
TWENTY-THREE

Esmerelda's ears were still ringing when Zoe Darling came swaggering down from the porch with Sadie marching along behind her. The flared muzzle of her shotgun was still smoking, as was the pipe clamped between her teeth.

Her long strides carried her right past where Billy still knelt in the dirt; past Virgil, who looked as if he was quaking in his boots; and past Jasper, who paled as if he'd seen a ghost.

She didn't stop until she reached Bartholomew. He blinked up in astonishment at the massive Amazon towering over him, shotgun in hand.

"You all right, son?" she asked.

He slowly sat up, massaging the angry rope burns that had seared his throat. "I think so," he rasped. He had to swallow several times, his bruised Adam's apple bobbing in his throat, before he could squeak out, "Th-th-thank you, ma'am, for saving my life."

Esmerelda beamed with pride. At least he hadn't forgotten his manners.

Zoe gave him a kindly smile. "Consider it my pleasure. I never did care much for public lynchins'. Especially in my own front yard."

As she swung around, her smile darkened to a thunderous scowl. She took a long draw on the pipe, sending smoke roiling from her nostrils. Jasper flinched. Virgil began to tiptoe toward his horse. Esmerelda groped for Billy's hand.

But the first blast of Zoe's wrath was directed at the two men huddled together on the seat of the wagon. "Git down from there this instant, you yellow-bellied curs."

Enos and Sam exchanged a fearful glance, then scrambled down from the wagon as if afraid their mother just might empty that second barrel into their hides.

She shook a finger in their sallow faces. "I ought to tan your sorry behinds for bein' a party to mischief such as this."

"But, Ma," they whined in unison. "Virgil made us do it."

"And you!" She turned on Virgil, freezing him just as he was reaching for the bridle of his horse. "You ought to be ashamed of yourself! Why, you're the oldest! Just what kind of example have you been settin' for these poor, feeble-minded children?"

Virgil ducked his head and kicked at the dirt like a chastened six-year-old. "I'm sorry, Ma. I'll do better next time." He shot her a hopeful look from beneath his sandy brows. "Honest, I will!"

Esmerelda shook her head, utterly bemused. Who would have thought one cranky old woman could reduce the infamous Darling gang to sniveling shame?

Seemingly satisfied with Virgil's promise, Zoe strode over to Jasper. He stared straight ahead, as sulky and defiant as ever. Until his mother reached up and smacked his hat clean off his head.

"You know better than to leave your hat on in your ma's presence. Didn't I teach you better manners than that?"

"Yeah, I reckon you did," he drawled.

"It's 'Yes, *ma'am*,'" she corrected sternly.

"Yes, ma'am," he meekly echoed, his bottom lip starting to quiver.

Esmerelda might have felt sorry for him if he hadn't just tried to murder her brother in cold blood.

Zoe settled her shotgun in the crook of her arm and surveyed the lot of them. It was apparent from their hang-dog expressions that they were just waiting for her to order them off her land.

She shook her head in exasperation. "It looks like you haven't had a decent bath or meal between the four of you in fourteen years. Git inside and I'll boil you some water and rustle you up some grub."

Their faces brightened, making them look less like vicious outlaws and more like prodigal sons, glad to be home after a long stint of wallowing with the pigs.

"Don't you sass me none, either. I can still lick every one of you if I have to, and don't think I cain't." As they filed past with Zoe herding them along like some ill-tempered sheepdog, Esmerelda realized that Billy had not been included in the invitation.

He was already climbing to his feet and holstering his pistol, his face unreadable. Esmerelda might have thrown herself into his arms then and there if a hoarse cough hadn't reminded her that she had a prodigal of her own to welcome home.

She scrambled over to Bartholomew, dropping to her

knees beside him. He gave her a look of such abject shame that she couldn't resist opening her arms to him. Instead of ducking out of her embrace as he had so many times in the recent past, he wrapped his arms around her waist and buried his face in her bosom, his shoulders heaving with emotion.

While Esmerelda was stroking Bartholomew's hair and crooning words of comfort, Billy turned his head to squint at the horizon. The man was her brother, for God's sake. There was no need for him to feel such an ugly stab of jealousy. But Esmerelda's gentle murmur and the nagging cadence of his ma's voice telling Virgil to take off those filthy boots of his before he tracked up her clean dirt floor made him feel as if he were the only man alive on that windswept plateau.

To escape the sting of the wind, Billy moseyed on over to the buckboard and peered into the back. He whistled beneath his breath as he got his first clear look at its cargo.

Bart must have sensed his sardonic glance. Hastily extracting himself from his sister's arms, he scrambled to his feet, giving his nose a surreptitious swipe. He and Billy eyed each other warily.

Bart finally nodded toward the bandage wrapped around Billy's shoulder. "I really am sorry about that. I never shot anyone before." A faint shudder raked him. "It's not an experience I would care to repeat."

Billy simply nodded. "I'll live." He jerked a thumb toward the back of the wagon. "But you might not, if we don't figure out what to do with this."

"The treasury gold?" Bart stole a nervous glance at the house before lowering his voice to a stage whisper. "I think your brothers are planning to keep it for themselves."

Billy shook his head. "I'm afraid that just won't do."

Bart brightened. "You think *I* should keep it?"

Billy rolled his eyes and shook his head again. Esmerelda climbed to her feet, her nightgown whipping in the wind. Billy wished he was wearing a shirt he could take off and wrap around her.

She gave the wagon a despairing look. "Oh, Bartholomew, what *were* you thinking?"

Billy noted that this time Bart didn't stammer an excuse or hang his head. He met his sister's gaze dead-on. "I was thinking what a pitiful excuse for a man I'd been. I was thinking about how I let you sacrifice everything for me, including your own childhood. I was thinking that even if I went to college like you wanted me to, it would be years before I could afford to buy you the things you deserved." He caught her by the shoulders. "Don't you know that it drove me half-wild with shame to see you wearing Mama's mended dresses while you taught those spoiled little merchant's daughters in their Worth gowns and diamond pinkie rings?"

Tears glistened in Esmerelda's eyes. "But I never wanted Worth gowns and diamond pinkie rings! All I ever wanted was children of my own and a decent man to love."

Billy flinched. Her words cut to the bone. *Decent* wasn't a word he'd ever heard used to describe a Darling. *Decent* was some store clerk or lawyer coming home from the office every day with his leather satchel tucked beneath his arm. *Decent* was Esmerelda greeting her husband at the door with a tender kiss, her apron smelling of freshbaked peach pie. *Decent* was a batch of laughing, brown-eyed children gathered around a piano while Esmerelda sang shrill Christmas carols. The image made him feel funny—sad and mean all at the same time.

Half afraid of just what else he might hear, Billy gruffly interrupted. "What's done is done. There's no point in arguing about it. I can drop off the gold at the bank in

Eulalie for safekeeping on my way back to Calamity. I'll telegraph the marshal in Albuquerque and let him know it's there. He's a good man. He'll see to it that Winstead doesn't prey on any more tenderfoots like young Brat here."

Their own quarrel forgotten, brother and sister both swung toward him and said in unison, "Bart!"

He simply shrugged.

"Isn't that wonderful?" Esmerelda exclaimed. "Mr. Dar"—she slanted him a shy glance, plainly deciding that the delicious intimacies they'd shared at least entitled her to call him by his Christian name—"Billy will return the gold and you'll be free to return home."

Bart stiffened. "I'm afraid I won't be returning to Boston."

"Why, of course you will! It's where you belong."

Billy cleared his throat. This was the moment he'd been dreading. "Your brother's right. He can't go back. At least not yet. I can look after myself and you, but until Winstead and his men are behind bars, he won't be safe."

Bartholomew clasped his sister's shoulders again, more gently this time. "You can't keep me in short pants forever, Esme. It's time for me to make my own way in the world."

"But what about Boston College? Mama and Papa always dreamed you'd attend university and become a journalist like Papa."

"Mama and Papa are dead," he said softly. "I have my own dreams now. I don't want to spend my life writing editorials and obituaries for people to read over their morning coffee. I want to write stories that come from my own imagination. I want to make people laugh and cry. I want to make them dream."

"But where will you go?"

He looked toward the far horizon, the twinkle in

his eye sharpening to a dreamer's glint. "I always thought South America would be a lovely place to write my first novel." He chuckled dryly. "I've certainly had ample inspiration in the past few months."

Billy reached into the pocket of his trousers and drew out a wad of money. Instead of peeling off a few bills, he handed Bart the entire thing. "Winstead paid me this to kill you. It seems only fitting that you should use it to start a new life."

"I'm in your debt, sir," Bart replied, offering him his hand. "I won't forget it."

As they shook hands, man-to-man for the first time, Esmerelda stood blinking in bewilderment, as if everything was happening too fast for her to comprehend. Billy felt a twinge of pity. He knew exactly how it felt to be the one left standing outside when the door slammed.

Hoping to earn her some time to get used to the idea of losing her brother a second time, he nodded toward the house. "I'm sure Ma would be glad to fix you something to eat before you go. She seems to have taken quite a shine to you."

Shooting the house another fearful glance, Bart reached up to massage his throat. "I believe I'll just be on my way. I've got a long trip ahead of me. I can stop for supplies at the next town." He turned to Esmerelda, drawing her limp body in for a swift, hard hug. She hung like a rag doll in his embrace. "I'll write you, Esme, just as soon as I get settled."

It wasn't until he was striding toward the dun gelding that stood grazing on a sparse patch of grama grass halfway down the hill that she snapped out of her daze.

"Bartholomew Fine, you get back here this instant!"

He paused for a nearly imperceptible second, then resumed walking.

"Don't you turn your back on me while I'm talking. I

won't tolerate such impertinence!" Her voice broke on a quavering note.

Her brother was already throwing one leg over the saddle and turning the horse south.

Esmerelda caught Billy's arm in an imploring grip, tears spilling down her cheeks. "I just found him. I can't lose him again! Please, Billy, you have to stop him!"

He caught her shoulders in a grip as fierce as her own. "I'd shoot him in the leg if I believed you both wouldn't hate me and each other for it later."

"I don't want you to shoot him. I just want you to talk some sense into the boy!"

He deliberately gentled both his grip and his voice. "He's not a boy any longer, Esmerelda. He's a man."

Sobbing with frustration, she wrenched herself out of his grasp and went tearing down the hill. Bart had already kicked the horse into a canter. Soon he would be nothing but a puff of dust on the horizon.

Esmerelda must have realized it, too, for halfway down the hill, she stumbled to her knees, her shoulders crumpling in defeat.

Although Billy ached to go to her, he'd had plenty of practice biding his time. He leaned against the buckboard until the sun began to climb in the crisp blue sky. Until even the puff of dust had been scattered by the wind.

Only then did he start down the hillside. The brittle grasses crackled beneath his bare feet, warning Esmerelda of his approach.

She sat with one leg drawn up to her stomach, her mouth pressed to her knee. Her tears had dried to dusty streaks on her cheeks. Billy yearned to draw her into his arms, but she looked too brittle—as if one touch might scatter her on the wind as well.

He sank down on the hillside as near as he dared, leaned

back on one elbow, and tucked a hollow blade of grass between his teeth. She surprised him by speaking first.

"Bartholomew's little heart was broken when Mama and Papa died. I tried to make it up to him, but I guess I never did."

Billy frowned, pained by her choice of words. "Hell, Esmerelda, you didn't kill them."

She turned to look him straight in the eye. "Oh, but I did."

When she returned her gaze to the empty horizon, Billy could only stare at the bleak curl of her mouth. "I once had a friend named Rebecca. I was always a little shy and I didn't make friends easily, so Becky was very precious to me. One evening, I overheard Mama and Papa whispering that she was sick. I begged them to let me go visit her. Mama turned white and Papa, who had never once raised his voice to me, shouted that I was to do no such thing and I must go to my room immediately.

"I ran up the stairs, crying. I rarely disobeyed, you see. I was a *very* good girl." She slanted him a mocking smile, giving him a glimpse of the mischievous little girl she would have liked to have been. "But this time I managed to convince myself that my parents were just being selfish and mean. I knew I could make Becky feel better if I could only see her. I made her some roses out of yellow tissue paper."

Billy knew what was coming next. He couldn't begin to number the muggy summer nights back in Missouri when he'd crept out his window, shed his drawers, and plunged butt-naked into the icy cold waters of a nearby spring.

"I waited until they were all asleep," Esmerelda continued, "then I slipped down the back staircase and out of the house, clutching my pathetic little bouquet. When I got to

Becky's house, I could tell there was something terribly wrong. Although it must have been near midnight, every lamp in the house was burning. I could see strangers milling about the parlor. Becky's mother was crying, and her father was sitting with his face buried in his hands. Before I could duck, he lifted his head and looked right at the window. He didn't look *at* me." She shivered. "He looked *through* me.

"I ran, then, as fast as I could, to the back of the house where Becky's bedroom was. I could see her through the French windows, laid out on her bed in her prettiest night-gown. An old woman I'd never seen before was napping in a chair in the corner."

Billy had to clench his hands into fists to keep from reaching for her.

"I slipped into the room and crept toward the bed. Becky was always so pink and jolly. It scared me to see her lying there so still and pale. Then I felt ashamed for being afraid. So I reached up, ever so gently, and touched her cheek. Her skin was like ice. I must have made a sound because the woman in the rocking chair came awake with a start.

"'How did you get in here?' she shouted. 'Get away from her, you wicked little girl!'

"She frightened me so badly that I dropped the flowers, jumped out the window, and ran all the way home. I threw myself into my bed without even bothering to take off my shoes and pulled the blanket over my head. It took hours for my teeth to stop chattering." Esmerelda sighed. "I found out later that Becky had died earlier that afternoon. Of cholera."

Billy lowered his head. He might have been able to stand it if Esmerelda had cried. But her eyes were as dry and barren as a desert that has survived centuries without even the hope of rain.

"I never told Mama and Papa what I'd done. Not even when they lay wracked by chills and soaked in their own sweat. Not when their lips cracked and blood trickled from the corners of their mouths. I nursed them the best I could. No one else would come near the house until the disease had run its course and they were dead." Her words were edged with all the bitterness and self-loathing that had been festering beneath her composed exterior for thirteen years. "I never suffered so much as a sniffle."

But she'd been suffering ever since, Billy thought. Suffering because a single moment of willful disobedience had left her spirit crushed like paper flowers beneath the indifferent heel of fate. She'd atoned for her sin by sacrificing her every dream and desire and becoming both mother and father to Bartholomew. Now that he was gone for good, Billy supposed, she wasn't sure who she was supposed to be.

He rolled the tube of grass between his fingers, choosing his words with deliberate care. "When I was riding with Quantrill and Anderson, we lost more men to disease than we did to Yankee bullets—dysentery, typhoid, influenza . . . cholera. Almost every one of those sicknesses was spread through contaminated food or drinking water. I don't believe you could have given your parents cholera by touching a dead girl's cheek. They most likely just drank from the same water supply as your friend."

Esmerelda's gaze was fierce, as if she wanted desperately to believe him, but wouldn't allow herself. "You might assume that, but can you prove it? Can you swear with absolute certainty that I didn't invite that monster into my parents' house?"

Billy wanted to say yes, but knew she wouldn't believe him anyway. He reached over to stroke her hair. "You were a child, sweetheart. With a child's generous heart. Even if your parents had known what you'd done, do you really think they would have blamed you or wanted you to spend the rest of your life blaming yourself?"

Shaking off his caress, Esmerelda sprang to her feet, fury glittering in her dark eyes. "If I won't accept God's forgiveness, what makes you think I'd accept yours?"

Growing more wary, Billy climbed to his feet to face her.

She stiffened, looking exactly like the woman who had marched into that saloon and pointed her derringer at his heart. "Since you sent my brother on his merry way with your blessing and Winstead's money, it seems I'll no longer be requiring either your pity or your services. You're dismissed, Mr. Darling."

Billy had thought being shot in the chest hurt, but that pain was nothing but a sting compared to this. He actually glanced down at his bandage, expecting to find it stained with fresh blood.

Snatching up the dusty skirts of her nightgown as if they were the train of a velvet robe, Esmerelda went marching up the hill toward the house. The only sound he heard through the ringing in his ears was the door slamming in his face one last time.

When Billy returned to the house later that afternoon, he found Esmerelda seated on her trunk by the front door with her gloved hands folded primly in her lap. She'd donned the rumpled traveling costume she'd worn at their very first meeting, wound her hair into a knot so tight she was darn near cross-eyed, and slapped that godawful bonnet over the whole mess. She would have looked no less approachable had she been wearing a full suit of armor.

"If you're waiting for a stagecoach," he drawled, leaning against the doorframe, "you'd best be prepared to sit a spell."

She lifted her face to him. Scrubbed free of tearstains, it

was as pale and stiff as a piece of porcelain. "I was hoping you would escort me back to Calamity so I could catch the stagecoach there." Her voice dripped honeyed scorn. "I would think it would be the very least you could do."

He gave her his nastiest smile. "Oh, I could do a lot less than that. But I won't."

He straightened to find his entire family staring at him as if he were some snarling wolf who'd wandered into their midst. Jasper was polishing his boots while Virgil and his ma sat smoking companionably by the hearth. Sam was hunched over the table, picking over the crumbs of an apple pie, and Enos, still wearing his wrinkled red drawers, was submerged up to his bony knees in a round wooden tub.

Billy swept them a look so black it raised even Jasper's eyebrows. "I'm taking that treasury gold to the bank in Eulalie and wiring its rightful owners. I won't tolerate any argument on the matter."

"You won't get any from us," Virgil said heartily, casting his mother a timid glance. "Ma taught us better than that. 'Thou shalt not steal.' Right, Ma?"

Zoe rocked and nodded, taking a particularly self-righteous puff on her pipe. Sadie blinked up at her, drooling in adoration.

Billy strode into the bedroom, emerging a few minutes later wearing his boots and the same shirt he'd arrived in. While he'd been unconscious, Esmerelda had managed to mend the bullet tear and scrub most of the bloodstains out of it. He didn't care to think about what an effort that must have taken.

She was waiting for him on the porch, having already made her farewells. His stride didn't slow until he'd almost reached the open door.

"Come, Sadie," he commanded, swinging around and patting his thigh.

The hound hesitated, shooting his mother a questioning glance.

Billy squatted and stretched out his hand. "Sadie, come!" The words came out sharper than he intended. Sadie cowered against his mother's skirts.

Billy dropped his head and raked a hand through his hair. Hell, he thought, if Sadie turned on him, too, he might just break down and cry right there in front of God and everybody.

Zoe gently nudged the dog with her toe. "Git on with you, you old mutt. One crotchety old bitch around here is enough."

Taking that as a blessing, Sadie came waddling over, giving Billy's hand an affectionate snuffle with her cold, wet nose. Billy scratched behind her ears, absurdly grateful for her loyalty.

When he straightened, his brothers were all waiting to clap him on the back and wish him well. A dripping Enos elbowed Samuel aside so he could stutter a goodbye while Virgil pressed some of his own cigars on him. Even Jasper managed a grudging handshake. Billy glanced at his mother. She looked away.

He figured he ought to be getting used to women not speaking to him. Although he had to admit it was going to be mighty nice to get back to Miss Mellie's. The women there had never minded speaking to him. And they'd made it perfectly clear they wouldn't mind doing anything else to him if he were so inclined. It was only his strict code of gallantry that had kept him from taking advantage of their hospitality while he resided under their roof. A gallantry he was rapidly beginning to reconsider.

While he saddled his mare and hitched up the mule to the buckboard, Esmerelda stood on the steps, impatiently tapping her foot. He heaved her trunk and violin case into the bed of the wagon, tempted to throw her over his shoulder and do the same with her. Ignoring his outstretched hand, she clambered stiffly onto the seat and gathered the reins in her gloved hands. Sadie bounded up beside her, her tongue lolling out in excitement.

Billy wasted no time in urging his mare into a trot. He refused to give Esmerelda the satisfaction of glancing back to see if she was following. The strident jingle of the harness told him she was. They were nearly to the bottom of the hill when he heard the door creak open behind them.

He almost fell off his horse when his ma's shout rang out. "You take care, boy, you hear? And you take care of that gal, too. The good Lord knows she cain't take care of herself. Standin' off a Darling with a shotgun! Why, that child ain't got the sense of a boll weevil. You look after her, you hear!"

Billy's throat tightened. He wanted to wheel his horse around. But he knew if he did, his mother would just go right back into the house and shut the door.

So he kept riding.

"And you look after my boy, gal! Don't go lettin' him get his fool self shot up again. And don't go breakin' his heart or you'll answer to me."

Billy turned in the saddle to give Esmerelda a long, hard look. He would have almost sworn he saw a flicker of uncertainty in her eyes.

Wheeling north, he spurred his horse into a canter, riding hard until the wind had swallowed even the echo of his mother's voice.

CHAPTER TWENTY-FOUR

♥

————————————

Billy and Esmerelda arrived in Calamity just after eleven o'clock the next night with Billy driving the wagon, Esmerelda asleep in the back, and Sadie wearing the bonnet. The stolen treasury gold had been deposited in a vault at the Eulalie First National Bank to await the arrival of Elliot Courtney and his deputies. Courtney had vowed to see Winstead brought to justice. As soon as he could find him, that is. It seemed the good marshal had up and vanished right after Black Bart's disastrous raid on the Eulalie bank. That news had Billy searching every shadow and keeping his hand poised near his pistol.

But it didn't account for the tension that had been coiling tighter in his gut with each revolution of the wagon's wheels. A tension that had nothing to do with Winstead and everything to do with the woman curled up in the bed of the wagon.

"Whoa, girl," he called out softly, drawing the mule to a halt in front of the livery stable. He noticed with a flicker of curiosity that a lamp still burned in Drew's office.

The streets of Calamity slumbered beneath an overripe peach of a moon. A faint ripple of music and laughter drifted out from the saloon. The lighted windows of Miss Mellie's beckoned him home.

Home, Billy thought, closing his eyes briefly. A place where pleasure changed hands as carelessly as money, neither bringing lasting satisfaction. His jaw hardened. Maybe that was the most a man like him could ever expect.

He swung around to study his sleeping cargo. With the rosy petals of her lips slightly parted and her gloved hands folded beneath her cheek like a pair of angel's wings, she looked so sweet, so vulnerable. . . .

Billy reached back and gave her bottom a sharp swat.

"Ow!" Esmerelda sprang up, rubbing the offended territory.

Billy suspected she would have lit into him, but good, if she hadn't been distracted by the sight of Sadie. The bags beneath the basset hound's soulful eyes made her look just like old Granny Shively on a good day.

Esmerelda pointed. "May I be so bold as to inquire why that dog is wearing my bonnet?"

Billy shrugged. "The desert nights are chilly. Her ears looked cold."

"And mine didn't?"

He swept her a calculating glance. "Not any colder than the rest of you."

Grinding out an inarticulate sound, Esmerelda scrambled over the side of the buckboard, nearly falling when it turned out her foot had also been asleep. Still muttering beneath her breath, she hopped up and down, massaging it through her boot.

Billy struck a match and lit a cigar, watching her performance with detached amusement. She tried to drag her
trunk out of the wagon, but the awkward angle made it
nearly impossible.

After it tumbled back into the bed for the third time,
she arched an eyebrow in his direction. "Would you
mind . . . ?"

"Oh, but I'm afraid I would, Duchess." He puffed out a
smoke ring that would have done his ma proud. "I've been
dismissed, you see. I no longer work for you."

She breathed a theatrical sigh. "If I'd have known you
were going to be so contrary, I'd have asked Jasper to escort
me."

Billy snorted. "He'd have had those fancy drawers of
yours around your ankles before you got out of sight of the
house."

Her startled gaze searched his face. When she didn't find
any trace of amusement there, she ducked her head back
into the wagon bed, cheeks aflame. After several false starts,
she managed to wrestle both trunk and violin case to the
ground.

Still panting with exertion, she jerked her jacket straight
and adjusted her bustle with both hands. Billy cocked an
eyebrow. It wasn't the lace collar buttoned primly to her
chin or even the unspoken challenge of the tiny row of
buttons edging her sleeves that made his loins surge
with heat.

It was those ridiculous gloves.

Billy wanted to peel them off with his teeth. To tenderly
nip the tip of each finger until she cried out for the kind
of mercy only he could provide.

It was somehow fitting that she woke him from his dangerous daydream by jerking them past her wrists, as if to
deny him even a glimpse of her creamy flesh.

She tucked the violin case under her arm and hefted the trunk by its handle, staggering slightly. "Thank you ever so much for all your assistance, Mr. Darling. I should have been utterly bereft without you." She delivered this scathing speech gazing just past him instead of at him.

Then she turned and started down the street toward the hotel, wobbling beneath the weight of the trunk.

Billy's mouth fell open.

She was actually going to do it.

She was actually going to flounce right out of his life as if she'd never laid in his arms, wracked by tremors of pleasure. As if she'd never offered up her lips for a delicious openmouthed kiss. As if she'd never marched into that saloon and taken his heart into her custody.

Billy Darling had finally met an adversary he couldn't cuss, shoot, or toss into jail. It was that realization that brought his simmering temper to a boil.

He was a Darling, after all.

Maybe it was high time he started acting like one.

He bounded out of the wagon, landing smack-dab in the middle of the street. He took a long draw off the cigar, then flicked the glowing stub into the night. His fingers instinctively flexed over his gunbelt, as if preparing for a shoot-out to the death.

"Miss Fine?" he called out.

Esmerelda stopped walking, but didn't turn around.

"Take off your gloves."

He was actually going to do it.

He was actually going to let her just walk right out of his life without swearing at her, shooting her in the back, or threatening to have her thrown into jail.

Esmerelda briefly considered dropping the trunk on her toes. But she was afraid she might break them.

"Miss Fine?"

Miss Fine. Not *honey,* or *sweetheart,* or even *Duchess.*

Despite Billy's cool tone, Esmerelda's heart surged with relief at the thought that he was going to finally beg her forgiveness for letting Bartholomew go. Perhaps once he did, she would be able to put aside her own wounded pride and tell him she was sorry for all the mean things she had said to him. He would surely forgive her once she explained that she hadn't had a lot of experience with apologizing, since she was rarely wrong.

"Take off your gloves."

Esmerelda dropped both the trunk and the violin case, narrowly missing her toes. She slowly turned, her relief fading when she saw the stranger standing in the middle of the street.

His arms weren't outstretched in welcome, but hung loosely at his sides. Despite the casual posture, the tension in his lean, graceful fingers was unmistakable. His lips were faintly pursed, as if poised to blow on the barrel of a smoking pistol.

She realized that he wasn't a stranger at all. He was the man from the Wanted poster she'd kept tucked beneath her pillow all those long, lonely weeks. She had both hated and feared him, yet he'd still managed to saunter his way into her dreams night after night—hot, feverish dreams that had made her moan in her sleep and kick away the covers.

He was Billy Darling, part legend and all man, wanted by the law and, in her most secret heart, by her as well. He'd been dangerous when she'd wanted him, but now that she loved him, he might very well prove deadly.

He hooked his thumbs in his gunbelt, his stance so nonchalant and free of threat that Esmerelda thought he just might draw his gun and shoot her. He had her in his sights

all right, but the devastating charm of his smile warned her
that he had a much more diabolical fate in mind.

"Pardon?" she croaked.

"I was only suggesting that you might wish to remove
your gloves. You can leave them on if you like." His smile
took on a wicked slant as he confided, "I have heard tell of
cowboys who *never* take off their hats."

Esmerelda drifted toward him, unable to resist the hyp-
notic allure of that smile. "I don't understand. What are you
saying?"

Billy's grin faded, leaving his jaw as stern as she'd ever
seen it. "What I am saying, Miss Fine, is that the time has
come for you and me to settle up. I'm not running a charitable institution here. We had a deal." He jerked a thumb
toward the wagon. "Sadie here was a witness to it."

Stirred by the sound of her name, Sadie let out a damning "Woof."

Esmerelda's heart was beginning to skip every other
beat. "I haven't forgotten our deal," she insisted, although, in
fact, she had. "Why, as soon as my grandfather arrives—"

"Ah, the duke!" Billy drawled. "That noble chap who's
supposed to come swooping out of the clouds in his fancy
carriage drawn by six white unicorns, toss me a handful of
diamonds and rubies, and sweep you, his beloved granddaughter, into his arms."

Esmerelda glared at him. His sarcastic description was
just a shade too close to some of her more ridiculous
girlhood fantasies. "I'm almost certain he doesn't own any
unicorns."

"Then there's only one problem." Billy took a step
toward her, but she forced herself to stand her ground, her
nose quivering like a cornered rabbit's. "I don't see him
anywhere around here. Do you?"

Stalling for time, Esmerelda looked frantically around. A cheery light flickered in the window of the sheriff's office, but the street was deserted. "Nor do I see my brother," she reminded him.

Billy shrugged. "I hired on to find him, not keep him."

She couldn't argue with that. Billy might have given Bartholomew the means and encouragement to go, but in the end, her brother had left of his own accord.

Drawing in an unsteady breath, she tilted her head to study him. He might look every inch the notorious gunslinger, but beneath that rugged exterior, he was still *her* Billy. The man who had stood off his own brothers at gunpoint to protect her. The man who had tried to convince her that she hadn't murdered her parents with a single willful act. The man who had pleasured her without a thought for his own satisfaction, then tucked her into his bed as tenderly as a child.

Flooded by a tide of belated remorse, she clutched his arm. "Oh, Billy, I said some terrible things back at the ranch. I don't blame you for being angry."

"Mr. Darling," he corrected, gently removing her hand from his sleeve. At her disbelieving look, he winked and whispered, "Until we get this matter settled, sweetheart, it might be best to keep our association formal."

Her mouth and hand were still hanging open when his face recovered its grave demeanor. "Serving in your employ, Miss Fine, has turned out to be a far more costly endeavor than I anticipated. I lost the reward Winstead promised me, and until the scalawag is apprehended, I'll have to spend every minute of every day and night looking over my shoulder. If Elliot Courtney can't convince the judge to grant me amnesty for returning the treasury gold, I may even have to hightail it to Mexico for a while. The way I see it, I at least deserve to be compensated for all my trouble." His expression softened as he reached to cup her cheek in his palm, much as he had that day in his attic room. "After all, you are a woman of your word."

Esmerelda might have forgotten their bargain, but she hadn't forgotten what a consummate poker player Billy was rumored to be. He was obviously intent on playing for high stakes, and it was in that spirit of risk that she decided to take her biggest gamble.

"You're absolutely right, *Mr.* Darling," she said softly, allowing every ounce of regard she felt for him to shine from her eyes. "I would never dream of cheating you of what is rightfully yours. Especially not when I promised you"—she twined one hand around his nape and drew him down until their breath mingled and her lips were flush against his—"payment . . . in . . . full."

In the instant before he called her bluff, she was rewarded by a brief flicker of surprise in his eyes. Then he was ravishing her mouth in a kiss so sweet, so impossibly tender, it might have been their very first. He wrapped his arms around her, lifting her clean off her feet so that all the swells and hollows of their bodies meshed in perfect accord. By the time he lowered her, Esmerelda was dizzy with delight and flushed with triumph.

Sighing in utter rapture, she rested her cheek against his chest and waited for him to murmur all those tender promises she'd been longing to hear.

He grabbed her by the hand and began to march down the street.

"Wait a minute! Where are we going?" Esmerelda had to trot to keep up with his long strides. She cast a frantic glance over her shoulder. Sadie yawned beneath the drooping brim of the bonnet before turning around three times and settling down on the buckboard seat for a nap. "My trunk! My clothes!"

"You won't be needing them tonight."

That resolute prediction sent a shivery pulse of anticipation down Esmerelda's spine. Too late, she remembered
the hazards of showing her cards too soon. Billy might not
cheat, but he never stayed in the game unless he was sure
he held the winning hand. She had little time to repent her
mistake, for without warning, the door of the brothel
loomed out of the darkness before them.

CHAPTER TWENTY-FIVE

♥

When the door of Miss Mellie's Boardinghouse for Young Ladies of Good Reputation burst open, Horace Stumpelmeyer, the town banker, sprang to his feet, dumping the corset-clad young lady he'd paid for the privilege of cuddling on his lap to the Oriental rug.

He smoothed back his thinning hair and straightened his spectacles for a better look at the interloper and the rather dazed young woman stumbling along behind him.

Without breaking his stride, Billy planted a hand on his chest and pushed him back into the chair. "Don't get up on my account, Horace."

Dorothea pounced back into the man's lap like a sleek cat, gleefully kicking her slippered feet. "Welcome home, Billy," she crooned. "It's been mighty dull around here without you."

As if to agree, a glum Dauber leaned against the mantel,

nursing a glass of whiskey. Billy plucked the glass from his hand, drained it dry, then handed it back before reaching into his pocket and flipping him a silver dollar. "Out in front of the livery stable, you'll find a mare, a mule, and a hound wearing a real ugly little hat."

"It was quite a lovely bonnet until you stomped all over it and gave it to your dog!" Esmerelda protested.

Billy ignored her. "See to it that they're tended to."

"But what about me?" she wailed.

"*I'll* tend to you," Billy promised, giving her an evil wink.

Dauber gaped at them both in openmouthed astonishment. "Well, I will be darned. Does Drew know you're—"

"Go on with you!" Billy barked. "If you already had a dollar, you'd be upstairs with one of the girls instead of down here crying in your whiskey."

Conceding to his friend's wisdom, Dauber tipped his hat to Esmerelda, then went barreling out the door. With Esmerelda still tripping along behind him, Billy started for the stairs. Caroline and Esther were just slinking down them, leading one of the Zimmerman boys by his calloused paws. The man's glazed expression and rumpled blond curls proclaimed yet another satisfied customer.

The girls blocked Billy's path, stealing a worried glance at the woman behind him. "Honey, there's something you should know before you take her up there," Caroline said.

Billy's smile was so tender it made even their jaded hearts flutter. "I'm much obliged for your concern, ladies, but there's really nothing you can tell me that I haven't already figured out for myself."

Nodding politely, he brushed past them, pausing only long enough to whisper something in Zimmerman's ear. Betrayed by his fair complexion, the man blushed violently and fumbled for the gaping fly of his overalls.

Billy and Esmerelda had almost reached the second-story landing when Miss Mellie herself emerged from the kitchen, bearing a tray of fresh whiskeys. "William!" she shouted, the cry betraying more alarm than surprise.

Billy swung around, blowing out a long-suffering sigh. "Yes, ma'am?"

When Mellie saw whose hand he was clinging to with such possessive fervor, she bobbed as if she were on the verge of curtsying. Or fainting. Her voice quivered with false cheer. "I hadn't realized that you'd returned. Won't you and your lady friend join us for a drink?"

"Why, that would be lovely! I'm parched," Esmerelda exclaimed, trotting back down three steps before Billy's implacable grip on her hand brought her up short.

"I'm afraid we'll have to decline that generous offer, Miss Mellie. My lady friend and I have reached the end of a long, difficult journey and were looking forward to a little privacy." His amiable grin darkened. He swept a mean-eyed squint across the parlor. "As a matter of fact, I just might have to shoot anyone who disturbs us before dawn."

They all stood in a frozen tableau until Billy and Esmerelda had vanished into the shadows of the second landing.

It wasn't until a door somewhere in the upper reaches of the house banged shut that Dorothea dared to let out a long, low whistle. "I've never seen that boy quite so riled. Do you think he'll beat her?"

Miss Mellie cast the rafters a glance, her broad, kindly face crinkled in a frown. "I don't care how riled he is, our Billy would never raise his hand to a woman. His ma, God bless her gentle soul, taught him better manners than that."

"From the glint in his eye," Esther said, arching an immaculately plucked eyebrow, "it ain't his hand he's lookin' to raise."

Caroline sighed wistfully. "He sure is cute when he's

mad." Her lips pursed in a jealous pout. "How come those uppity gals have all the luck?"

While Dorothea raked her long fingernails through his hair, Horace plucked one of the shot glasses off Mellie's tray, his hand betraying a faint tremble. "Don't you think we should at least alert the sheriff?"

Mellie sank down on his other knee, tossing back a whiskey of her own. "You heard him, Horace. Anyone who disturbs that boy before dawn is just begging for trouble. And Lord knows, the sheriff's already got enough trouble for one man."

Esmerelda stood with her back pressed to the door of Billy's cozy attic room while he lit an oil lamp, folded back the quilt on the bed, and drew off his boots.

He raked her with a bold gaze as his deft hands moved to unbuckle his gunbelt. "You can take off those gloves of yours any time, Miss Fine."

Her instincts told her she ought to be as afraid of him as she'd been the first time they'd faced each other in this room. But for once, Esmerelda was listening to her heart.

"I think it would be best if I left them on," she said gently. The gunbelt slipped unheeded from his hand. "Don't look so dismayed, Mr. Darling. After all, it was your suggestion that we keep our association formal."

His scowl deepened. "But, honey, I—"

She held up a silencing finger. "In keeping with the spirit of our bargain, I'm sure you'll agree it would be best if we allowed no endearments, no kisses, no caresses."

"No caresses?" The heightened color beneath his cheekbones might have been a blush in a less worldly man. "You mean you just want me to . . . ?"

In reply, Esmerelda leaned against the door and delicately averted her face, slanting him a demure look from beneath her lashes. "You may commence."

His heated gaze flicked up and down her before he patted the inviting softness of the bed. "Don't you think we'd be more comfortable over here?"

"Most certainly," she admitted with a regretful sigh. "But I fear reclining might put us on far too familiar terms for a mere business transaction."

As Billy sauntered toward her, the speculative gleam in his eyes made her wonder if she'd overplayed her hand. She wasn't sure she could stop herself from squealing in alarm if he gathered her skirt and petticoats and tossed them over her head.

But he simply leaned down, without touching her, and murmured, "Can I at least take your hair down . . . ma'am?"

Esmerelda closed her eyes and swallowed, the whiskey-scented warmth of his breath melting her resolve. "Well, I suppose removing a few hairpins wouldn't hurt. Sir," she hastened to add.

He stood with his lips a whisper away from hers while his fingers sifted through her hair—searching for, plucking out, and discarding pins until her silky mane came tumbling around their faces. Her nipples stiffened against the thin silk faille of her basque, straining toward the remembered delight of his touch. Glittering so near to her own, his heavy-lidded eyes looked very green indeed.

He splayed one hand against the door behind her, cocking his knee so that the slightest move in any direction would situate it firmly between her thighs. "I still think you ought to take off those fancy gloves. I'd hate to wrinkle them, sweetheart."

"Miss Fine," she breathlessly corrected, touching a finger to his parted lips.

He startled her by catching the fingertip of her glove between his teeth and tugging, peeling the supple kid from her smooth skin in one deft motion.

Before she could protest, he had captured her hand in his own. "No endearments, angel," he murmured, the smoky timbre of his voice sending a restless shiver through her. He stroked the inside of her wrist with his thumb, making the pulse that beat just beneath her delicate skin flutter with anticipation. "No caresses." He brought her naked palm to his mouth. "No kisses." As he touched the tip of his tongue to the center of her palm, Esmerelda closed her eyes, biting back a moan.

When she opened them, Billy's eyes had darkened with need. Esmerelda knew then that the game was done. His trump hadn't turned out to be his superior strength or even his seductive charms, but the unspoken question in his eyes. A question he was giving her every right to answer with a resounding no, even if it made him crazy.

Unable to resist his grudging gallantry, Esmerelda curled her hand around his nape and pressed her lips to his, inviting him to collect his winnings. As their tongues touched, tasted, then entwined, he groaned into her mouth, the sound nearly as intoxicating as the whiskey on his breath.

Billy cupped her face between his hands and kissed her until the roaring in her ears drowned out the voice of reason she had heeded her entire life. She could not have pinpointed the moment when her own want became need and need desperation. She only knew that suddenly she was jerking off her other glove, tugging his shirt open, raking her fingernails though the crisp coils of his chest hair. When she inadvertently grazed his bandage, it took an extraordinary act of will to drag her mouth away from his.

"Your wound?" she whispered, gasping as he lowered his mouth to her throat, tearing at the tiny buttons of her bodice with his teeth.

"I don't need a nurse," he rasped. "I need a woman. I need you."

As if to prove his words, he cupped his hands around the backs of her legs—lifting her, spreading her, pressing her to the door, pressing himself to the tender mound between her thighs. Esmerelda gasped at the shivery pulse of need spawned by his shameless demand. She might be an innocent, but she wasn't a fool. She knew what he wanted to do to her just as surely as she knew she was going to let him.

"This is wrong," she moaned, licking the smooth golden skin over his collarbone. He tasted wonderful—sweet and salty and masculine all at the same time.

"I know," he muttered, sending the last of her poor beleaguered buttons plinking to the floor.

"We're n–not even married."

"I'll marry you in the morning," he growled, sinking his teeth into her freshly bared throat.

For a timeless moment, Esmerelda forgot to blink, forgot to breathe. "Was that a proposal?" she croaked, craning her neck in a vain attempt to see his face.

"No. Hell, I don't know." Curling one muscled arm beneath her hips to hold her in place, he used his other hand to tug down her chemise, then slowly lifted his gaze from her breasts to her face, looking nearly as stunned as she did. "Yeah, I reckon it was."

"But you told me you weren't looking for a wife."

"I wasn't," he replied, bending to flick her nipple with the tip of his tongue.

She squirmed with delight as he suckled her, gently at first, then hard enough to make her womb contract with longing. Coiling her fingers in his hair, she struggled to remember the words he'd uttered her first day in Calamity. "Are you saying," she bit off between broken gasps, "that you'd marry me just so you can poke me without paying?"

"Oh, I'll pay," he said grimly. "You'll have a lifetime to see that I do."

"No!" Before those skillful lips of his could close around her other breast, sapping her of strength, Esmerelda wrenched herself from his arms and staggered halfway across the room. She clutched her bodice together as if it were the tatters of her pride.

Jasper would have followed, laughing cruelly at her pitiful attempts at resistance before he bore her back on the bed. Billy could only face her, breathing hard, his shirt hanging open and his hands resting on his lean hips.

"If that don't beat all!" he exclaimed. "After three months of living in a brothel, I thought I understood women. Then *you* had to come to Calamity!" He raked a hand through his hair, leaving it as wild as the look in his eyes. "Let me get this straight—you were going to let me take you to bed a minute ago, but now that I've offered to do right by you, you don't want me."

Esmerelda could set her chin to keep it from quivering, but she could do nothing to stop the tears from trickling down her cheeks. "Of course I want you. But I have my pride, Mr. Darling. And I could never let a man marry me simply because he wants to take me to bed."

At the sight of her tears, the last trace of anger fled Billy's face, leaving it raw with vulnerability. He took one step toward her, then when she didn't bolt, dared another. His voice deepened to a hoarse rasp. "Would you want a man to marry you because he couldn't live another day without you? Because he aches so hard every time he looks at you, he's afraid he might just up and die?" Billy stretched out his hand, brushing a single tear from her cheek as if it were a droplet of dew. "Would you want a man to marry you because he loved you?"

Rendered mute by the despairing tenderness in his eyes, Esmerelda could only nod.

Billy set his jaw, looking no less grim than he had before. "Hell, Horace is right downstairs. If that's what you want, I'll marry you now."

She frowned in confusion. "I thought Mr. Stumpelmeyer was a banker."

"He is. He's also mayor, postmaster, and justice of the peace." Looking even more determined than he had when he'd dragged her into the room, Billy grabbed her hand and started for the door. Esmerelda hung back, laughing through her tears.

When he swung around, looking utterly baffled, she shook her head and said, "You don't have to marry me tonight, Billy. Morning will come soon enough."

He scooped her up in his arms, his eyes going smoky with promise. "Oh, no, angel. Morning will come too soon."

As Billy laid her back on the bed and began to gently unhook, unlace, and undress her, Esmerelda sighed her agreement. She was stirred beyond measure when those legendary hands of his trembled against her bare flesh. Being naked in Billy's bed, in Billy's arms, was a naughty delight she couldn't have conceived of in her wildest dreams.

When she'd been old enough to dream about being in a man's bed and young enough to believe those dreams might still come true, she had envisioned some faceless husband clumsily shoving her nightgown up to her waist. She had imagined him climbing on top of her, his breathing harsh in the darkness, and quickly dispensing with the mysterious act that was to be his pleasure and her duty.

She had never imagined a man like Billy Darling straddling her naked body, his golden grace even more striking in the pool of lamplight. Her breath quickened as he shrugged out of his shirt and reached for the buttons of his trousers. Although her first instinct was to burrow beneath the quilt to smother a shriek of nervous laughter, curiosity kept her riveted. Her mouth went dry when the fabric parted to reveal that his arousal was just as long and golden as the rest of him.

She stretched out her hand, daring only to brush her fingertips across its velvety tip in a butterfly's caress.

"Find what you're looking for, Duchess?" he drawled, deliberately echoing the words he'd said to her during his bath at the ranch. Only this time his jibe was punctuated by a hoarse groan.

Esmerelda snatched her hand back, mortified by her boldness. "Am I hurting you?"

He recaptured her hand and folded her fingers firmly around him. "You're killing me."

Encouraged by his rapturous expression, she tenderly traced the length and thickness of him before giving him a wide-eyed look. "And Virgil dares to call you his *little* brother?"

Although his teeth were gritted, Billy still managed a cocky grin. "Why do you think Jasper was always so darned jealous of me?"

Sobering, Esmerelda reached up to gently cup his face between her hands. "Because you were everything fine and decent that he never tried to be."

A strange expression crossed Billy's face—half pleasure, half pain. "And you, Duchess," he said, lowering himself into her arms, "are everything I ever wanted." Kicking away his trousers, he pressed his mouth to her ear. "Remember in the barn that night, when I told you it sure would be nice if you'd let me put my mouth everywhere you let me touch you?"

How could she forget? A delicious shudder raked her, born of both memory and anticipation. But no amount of anticipation could prepare her for the tender shock of Billy's lips gliding down her body, leaving a trail of pleasure wherever they went. He cupped her buttocks in his hands and lifted her to his mouth, drinking from her forbidden sweetness like a man who'd been wandering in the desert all his life and had suddenly come upon a fresh spring bubbling out of the sand.

She whimpered a protest, moaned a denial, but her instinctive shyness melted beneath the hot, sweet flame of his tongue flickering over her. She tugged helplessly at the wheaten silk of his hair as ripples of delight fanned out from her womb to engulf her entire being. She might have been able to endure that exquisite torture if he hadn't begun to probe her throbbing core with one of those long, large-knuckled fingers of his. She cried out, pulsing to rapture against his mouth.

When Esmerelda drifted back down to earth, Billy was there, softly kissing her mouth while he laved his rigid length in the rich cream he'd coaxed from her pleasuresated body. The sensation sent delicious little aftershocks through her. So delicious that she almost didn't notice when he stopped rubbing against her and started easing his way into her.

He must have felt her stiffen. He must have heard her squeak.

Holding his body in ruthless check, he peered down into her face. She forced a smile, hoping he would mistake her agonized whimper for one of pleasure.

"What are you doing, sweetheart?" He looked even more distressed than she felt.

"I'm not crying," she blurted out, bravely trying to sniffle back a sniffle. "I know how you hate to see me cry."

"Does it hurt?" he gently asked.

She nodded, chewing on her lower lip in an effort not to burst into tears.

"Well, then you just go ahead and bawl all you want, honey, and I'll see what I can do to make it nicer for you."

As he'd proved in the past, Billy was a man of his word. Esmerelda barely had time to work up a heartfelt sob before the stabbing pain began to give way to languid pleasure.

"Better?" he murmured, burying his face in her hair.

"Oh, much," she gasped.

He took that as his cue to lengthen and deepen his rhythmic strokes, sending waves of delight shuddering through her. She'd been astonished by the pleasure he'd given her before, but there was something even more miraculous about being joined with the man she loved. She was soft where he was hard. Giving where he was driven to take. As his strokes quickened to furious thrusts that seemed to fill her to overflowing, she wrapped her arms and legs around him, clinging for dear life. When his body went rigid and he tore himself from her with one last mighty groan, the tears that came spilling from her eyes were tears of joy.

Esmerelda sat in the rocking chair, cradled on Billy's lap. He'd wrapped the quilt around them both, enfolding them in a cozy cocoon. The soothing motion of the rocker created an exquisite friction between their naked, sweat-dampened bodies.

By the waning light of the moon, Billy looked troubled, like a man who'd suddenly discovered he had something to lose.

Esmerelda longed to make him smile again. She ran her fingertips along his jaw, hoping to soften its stern set. "You always call me 'honey' or 'sweetheart' or 'angel,'" she whispered, "but you never call me 'darling.'"

He slanted her a wry look. "Maybe I was just waiting until I could call you *Mrs.* Darling."

Warmed by his unspoken promise, she gave him a tender kiss and rubbed her breasts against his chest. The coarse coils of his chest hair made her nipples throb and tingle. She moaned a faint protest when he gently resituated her on his lap, turning her so that she faced away from him. He used his big hands to drape her legs over his own splayed thighs, leaving her utterly vulnerable to his touch.

Esmerelda melted into a puddle of delight when those clever fingers of his parted the dewy petals of her body, seeking the tender bud nestled within their folds. She turned her head, blindly seeking the sustenance of his mouth. He rewarded her with a taste of his tongue, then eased her hair aside and began to scatter damp kisses on her nape and throat.

As the tender flick of his fingertip sent molten pleasure cascading through her veins, she became keenly aware of the demanding weight of his arousal pressing against the cleft of her buttocks.

The very next time the chair rocked up, then down, he slid into her, just as neat as you please.

Unprepared for the shock of being so deliciously impaled, Esmerelda nearly swooned. Groaning his own delight, Billy rocked himself deeper into her with each rhythmic rise and fall of the chair.

Not sure just how much pleasure she could endure without dying, she whimpered an entreaty, urging him to go faster. But he kept up his leisurely pace, stroking her inside and out, until she was sobbing with rapture. Dark shudders of ecstasy wracked her body and soul, leaving her limp in his arms.

Only then did he take his own pleasure. When he was done, he lifted her in his arms like a child and carried her to the bed, where they fell into an exhausted slumber, their bodies nested together like two spoons in a cupboard drawer.

When Esmerelda awoke again, Billy was already inside of her. She slipped out of one delectable dream into another, a dream where Billy kept one arm wrapped tightly around her waist, all the while gliding in and out of her in long, honeyed strokes. Esmerelda arched against him, purring with pleasure. When he could no longer contain the driving rhythm of his thrusts, he urged her over to her stomach and rode her the rest of the way home.

Morning came too soon.

Sunlight filtered through the window beneath the attic eaves, bathing the bed in warmth. Esmerelda tried to resist its gentle persuasion, longing only to rock the day away in the sweet cradle of Billy's arms. When she finally pried open her eyes, it was to discover that she was sprawled on top of him with her head pillowed on his chest and her thighs straddling his lean hips. From the devilish light in the eyes sparkling so near to hers and the persistent nudge of his body, she gathered that waking up and staying that way hadn't been a problem for him.

"Mornin', Duchess," he drawled, greeting her just as he had that long-ago morning at the hotel.

"Mornin', cowboy," she replied. She could not resist a diffident sniff. "If you're ready to hit the trail, just leave your silver dollar on the bureau on your way out."

His eyebrows shot up. "Just one dollar? By my accounting, I owe you at least three, along with a fifty-dollar gold piece for . . ." He pressed his mouth to her ear, whispering something that made her both giggle and squirm. She could hardly believe herself that the haughty Miss Esmerelda Fine from Boston had dared something so deliciously bawdy.

It seemed that loving Billy had made a hoyden of her. A hoyden who delighted in the faint whisker burn on her chin, the moist tenderness between her legs. She ran her tongue over her kiss-swollen lips before pressing them to Billy's. He cupped her rump in his hands, holding her astride the instinctive buck of his hips and making her moan with anticipation.

The inviting sound was drowned out by masculine shouting, feminine squealing, and the thunder of footsteps on the stairs.

Billy rolled her off of him, instantly alert. He listened for a second, his brow creased in a frown. Then, throwing the quilt over her, he bounded out of the bed.

"Stay here, sweetheart," he commanded, jerking on his trousers. "One of the girls must have a rowdy customer."

Before he could get them buttoned, the door flew open, leaving Billy standing behind it.

Squealing in alarm, Esmerelda snatched the quilt up to her chin. The man who stood in the doorway didn't look the least bit rowdy. He certainly didn't look capable of causing the sort of commotion they'd heard. With his double-breasted frock coat and pinstriped trousers, he looked as if he'd just come from a formal ball. He wore a gray felt top hat and clutched the brass grip of a cane in his liver-spotted hand.

It wasn't his elegant attire, but the tenderness that softened his eyes when they lit on her that made Esmerelda's throat tighten with a curious mixture of awe and apprehension.

He propped his cane against the wardrobe and drew off his hat, turning it over in his trembling hands. "I would have known you anywhere, Esmerelda. You are the very image of your mother."

He didn't have snowy white hair or a bristling mustache that would tickle her cheek when he hugged her. He was as bald as a billiard ball and his square, ruddy face was clean-shaven. But the pugnacious jut of his jaw was unmistakable.

"Grandfather?" she croaked.

He beamed at her. "Ah, my sweet child, it would make this cold and unforgiving ogre ever so happy if you would consent to call him 'Grandpapa.'"

Paralyzed with shock, Esmerelda kept a death grip on the quilt as he came limping over, folded her into his arms, and gently stroked her tousled hair just like the grandfather of her dreams.

"There, there, my darling," he murmured. "You've done the very best you could for yourself, but it's time to come home now and let Grandpapa take care of you."

As she met Billy's stricken gaze over her grandfather's shoulder, Esmerelda would have been hard-pressed to decide which one of them looked more horrified.

CHAPTER TWENTY-SIX

Her grandfather continued to murmur endearments and stroke her hair, seemingly oblivious to the stream of people who came pouring into the attic room. Sheriff McGuire staggered in first, followed by a woman Esmerelda didn't recognize, the rotund Miss Mellie, a flock of her half-dressed girls, and a handful of their gawking patrons.

Flushed with mortification, Esmerelda considered dragging the quilt over her head. Billy remained frozen behind the door, looking as if he'd like to slink out the nearest window himself.

Blood trickled from a shallow wound on Sheriff McGuire's temple. The petite, gray-haired stranger stood on tiptoe to dab it away with a lace handkerchief.

"Who is that woman?" Esmerelda whispered.

"Oh, that would be my sister. *Your* aunt Anne," her grandfather explained, favoring her with a tender smile. "She's the very soul of gentility."

"If you'll stand still for a minute, you overgrown oaf," the woman snapped. "I might be able to stop the bleeding."

McGuire sneered down his nose at her. "I wouldn't be bleeding if you hadn't coldcocked me with the butt of my own pistol."

"How else was I to get the keys to my cell?"

Esmerelda gasped. "You arrested my aunt?"

McGuire turned his sullen gaze on her. "You needn't look so shocked, lass. I did it for your own good. She and this loco brother of hers had taken it into their heads to go searching for you. I didn't arrest them. I simply provided them with accommodations during their stay in Calamity. Free of charge, I might add."

The woman snorted. "Even if you did allow us separate cells, your hospitality left much to be desired."

"If you don't like it," Drew snarled, pointing at the man cowering behind two scantily clad young women, "you can take it up with the mayor."

Esmerelda's aunt spun around, clapping a hand over her heart. "Why, Mr. Stumpelmeyer!"

The mayor, banker, postmaster, and justice of the peace of Calamity was wearing nothing but a pair of spectacles and a pair of drawers. He lifted his bony shoulders in a sheepish shrug. "I've been a widower for nigh on two months now, Miss Hastings. I have my needs."

Anne appeared to ponder the matter. "Perhaps that's why your proposal was so heartfelt."

"He proposed to you?" Esmerelda squeaked, shocked anew.

Anne lifted her chin high. "He and thirty-seven other

men in the last week alone. Quite an impressive tally for an old spinster, is it not?"

"That's why she doesn't care for me," Drew said. "I'm the only man in town with the good sense not to marry her."

Anne shot him a glare that could have cut glass.

Esmerelda felt a rush of alarm as her grandfather stiffened. "Who are all these . . . *women*?" he asked, sweeping a frosty look around the room. "I thought this was a boardinghouse for young ladies of good reputation."

One of the girls trilled a sultry giggle. "I got a reputation, all right, honey, but it ain't good."

Her grandfather rose to face her, drawing his wounded dignity around him like a mantle. "I don't understand, Esmerelda. Perhaps you'd best explain the meaning of your presence in this establishment."

She gazed helplessly up at him, hating to lose his affection so soon after finding it.

When she heard a telltale creak, she knew her faith had not been misplaced. Billy wasn't the sort of man who would abandon her to face her doom alone.

Her grandfather turned as the door slowly swung toward its frame to reveal the man standing behind it. The morning sun streaming through the window gilded his bare chest, his tousled hair, the narrow V of hair-dusted belly exposed by his unbuttoned trousers. Remembering how it felt to be rocked in the golden cradle of that magnificent body, Esmerelda felt a sweet stab of desire.

Despite the obvious difficulty he was having swallowing, Billy curved his lips into an amiable grin. "It's a pleasure to finally meet you, sir." He cut his smoky eyes toward Esmerelda. "Your granddaughter's told me so much about you."

Billy Darling had finally ended up where he always

figured he belonged—behind bars. But he'd never dreamed his accommodations would be so luxurious. The lumpy, straw-stuffed tick that used to drape the bunk in the front cell of the Calamity jail had been replaced with a fluffy feather mattress. An Oriental rug covered the most ominous of the stains on the puncheon floor. The chipped plaster ceiling boasted a coat of fresh paint. Billy eyed the corner askance, reasonably sure that when he'd left Calamity less than two weeks ago, there had been no crocheted tea cozies in the cell, no ceramic teapot for them to hug, and no tea table for the teapot to rest on.

Billy rested his elbows on the crosspiece of the door, letting his forearms dangle through the bars. "Developed a fondness for decorating while I was gone, Drew?"

Drew sat behind his desk with Miss Kitty curled up on his lap. He opened his mouth, but before he could get a word out, Esmerelda's aunt paused in her restless pacing. "I'm not surprised you noticed the changes Sheriff McGuire initiated for my comfort, Mr. Darling. I would have expected a ruffian like you to be intimately familiar with the inside of this jail."

"Oh, I wasn't a prisoner last time I was here, ma'am," Billy said, deepening his drawl just to annoy her. "I was visiting your niece."

She resumed her pacing, her sharp "harrumph" warning him that she would savor any excuse to whack him over the head with the bone-handled parasol she handled like a loaded Winchester. Billy flexed his fingers. If she strayed any closer to the bars, he just might give her one.

Correctly reading his sinister expression, Drew propped his boots up on the desk and wagged an admonishing finger at him behind Anne's back. The woman reminded Billy of Esmerelda at her most scathing, a trait he might have found endearing if he'd been on the other side of those bars.

Utter chaos had broken out after he'd stepped out from behind that door at Miss Mellie's. Esmerelda's aunt had swooned into Drew's arms. Her grandfather had rushed at him, grabbing up his cane and brandishing it like a sword. Mellie's girls had leapt to his defense, claws bared. It had taken Horace and two cowboys to subdue the old man.

Although Billy suspected the pompous old fellow would have been just as happy to start bellowing "Off with his head!" it had been Esmerelda's aunt who had come to and insisted that Drew arrest him until the extent of his villainy had been determined. Plainly wanting to avoid any more mayhem, Drew had obliged her. Billy was still haunted by the helpless glance Esmerelda had cast over her shoulder at him as her grandfather ushered her from the room, wrapped in nothing but the quilt.

His heart did an unexpected belly flop when the door of the jail swung open to admit Esmerelda and her grandfather. The old man kept his arm curved protectively around her shoulders.

Garbed in one of her aunt's claret silk walking suits, she looked sophisticated, elegant, and utterly beyond the realm of possibility for a man like him. The smudges of exhaustion beneath her eyes only added to her air of genteel fragility. As he recalled what they'd been doing last night instead of sleeping, he felt a mingled rush of guilt and desire.

Despite her docile appearance, she didn't shrink from his gaze, but met it boldly. Billy wanted to wink at her, to reassure her that nothing had changed. But suddenly there seemed to be more than just iron bars separating them. She was no longer a penniless orphan. She was the granddaughter of a duke, the heiress to a vast fortune and lavish lifestyle. He was a Darling, the youngest son of a Missouri dirt farmer.

When his expression remained impassive, a bewildered frown flickered across her face.

After settling Esmerelda in a straight-backed chair, the duke turned to glower at him. "Despite all evidence to the contrary, sir, my granddaughter insists you did not ravish her."

Moving to rest her hands on her niece's shoulders, Anne gave a ladylike snort. "Ravished. Seduced. There's little difference, is there?"

"Ah, but there is," Drew provided, coming around to sit on the edge of his desk. "As I'm sure you'd know, ma'am, if you'd ever experienced either."

Billy suspected he looked nearly as dumbfounded as Anne did. Until today, he'd never before seen Drew, with his old-world gallantry and courtly charm, deliberately bait a lady.

Anne's mouth snapped shut with an audible click. "Do spare us the particulars, won't you?"

Drew sighed. "I was simply alluding to the fact that ravishing a woman is against the law, while seducing her is not."

"Well, it should be," Anne retorted, a girlish blush staining her cheeks.

Shrugging off her aunt's possessive grip, Esmerelda jumped to her feet. "As I tried to explain to Grandfath—" The duke's face fell. *"Grandpapa,"* she amended, earning a doting smile, "Mr. Darling neither ravished nor seduced me. Our assignation was simply the result of a bargain struck between the two of us."

The duke's horrified cry nearly drowned out Anne's outraged gasp. Even Drew looked torn between shock and amusement.

Billy barely resisted the urge to groan out loud. If Esmerelda was trying to improve his standing with her family, she was failing miserably.

"A bargain?" her grandfather shouted, banging the brass tip of his cane on the floor with enough force to send Miss Kitty bolting from the room. "Just what manner of bargain did you strike with this devil?"

Esmerelda refused to let his tantrum ruffle her aplomb. "Mr. Darling has a reputation for being one of the best trackers in the Territory. When I found out he didn't kill Bartholomew, I hired him to find my brother."

The duke muttered something beneath his breath, but all Billy caught were the words "more's the pity" and "wretched boy."

Esmerelda gave him a chiding look. "Although I had no resources of my own at the time, Billy graciously agreed to help me."

"Help himself to you, you mean," the duke interjected.

"And, what, pray tell," Anne asked, shooting Billy a acerbic glance, "did you offer this knight in burnished leather in exchange for his noble services?"

"I'm afraid I spun a bit of a fable. I promised Billy that he would be richly rewarded when my loving grandfather received my letter and came rushing across the sea to my aid." For the first time since entering the jail, Esmerelda lowered her eyes. "I must confess I believed at the time that it was nothing but a shameless lie."

Billy finally understood the reason for her evasive answers and furtive glances, so uncharacteristic of the forthright woman he had grown to love.

The duke sank down heavily in the chair Esmerelda had vacated and buried his ruddy face in his hands. "Dear God, child, how can you ever forgive me?"

Esmerelda's expression softened as she knelt beside his

chair and rested her hand on his knee. "You mustn't torture yourself, Grandpapa. We all have regrets we must learn to live with."

Billy wondered if she was thinking about her parents. His own regrets were beginning to burn like acid in his throat.

While the duke wallowed in his swamp of self-pity, Anne narrowed her eyes. "Are you saying that when your grandfather failed to appear as you'd promised, this man demanded your innocence as payment for your debt?" She pounded one of her dainty fists on the desk. "Why, the scoundrel shouldn't be jailed, sheriff. He should be hanged!"

Billy decided he'd better speak up before Drew decided to oblige the lady on that count, too. Since he'd yet to say one word in his own defense, all it took was a casual clearing of his throat to command their rapt attention.

He avoided Esmerelda's eyes by addressing her aunt. "I swear to you, ma'am, that I never had any real intention of holding your niece to her word."

Anne marched over to the bars. "And I swear to you, sir, that my niece is not in the habit of indulging in such scandalous behavior without a compelling reason. The stains on your bedsheets bear proof of that."

Esmerelda came to her feet, blushing furiously.

It wasn't Esmerelda's distress or the duke's posturing that shamed Billy, but the condemnation in her aunt's eyes. He saw reflected in their cool gray depths the shadow of the man he had always feared he was. A man who, when given the chance, wouldn't hesitate to steal something if he wanted it badly enough. Even the precious innocence of the woman he loved.

Esmerelda had called him fine and decent last night, but if he'd truly been either one of those things, he would have ignored her protests and dragged her before the justice of the peace to make her his wife. He would have wooed and courted her instead of taking her in a brothel like a common whore. He could return the stolen treasury gold to the U.S. government. He could wear a badge. He could even love the finest woman in all creation. But beneath his skin, where it really mattered, he was still a Darling.

Esmerelda's lingering blush didn't stop her from holding her head high. "He's telling the truth, Aunt Anne. He wouldn't have laid a finger on me if I hadn't wanted him to." She set her chin just as she had the night she'd defied his ma, making Billy's heart surge with equal amounts of pride and despair. "If I hadn't wanted him."

Plainly hoping to avert any further confessions of such an alarming nature, the duke rose, regaining his regal bearing. "Seduced, ravished, coerced. Whatever you want to call it, the damage has been done. Our Esmerelda has been compromised. All that remains is to determine what course of action must be taken next." He rested his hands on his granddaughter's slender shoulders and peered intently into her face. "My heart's desire is for you to return to London with us to claim your rightful place within the loving bosom of your family." His patrician upper lip curled in visible distaste. "But if you want me to, my dear, I shall force the rogue to marry you."

Hope leapt in Esmerelda's eyes, impossible to miss. But it was shadowed by that same stubborn pride that had kept her from accepting his clumsy proposal last night. She faced the cell, holding her head even higher than before. "I shall leave that decision up to Mr. Darling. I would never stoop to forcing him into a marriage he didn't desire."

Billy swung around, but closing his eyes didn't block out the sight of her. He could still see the hope brightening her eyes, the smile trembling around her lips.

She was his Duchess. She deserved to live in some fancy house with servants to wait on her hand and foot. She deserved to enjoy the adoration of the family she'd yearned for ever since she'd lost her own. She deserved a whole hell of a lot better than a bounty hunter with a price on his head and bad blood in his veins.

Billy swallowed hard before forcing himself to turn around. If he was going to be man enough to break her heart, then by God, he was going to be man enough to watch it break.

Praying he'd spent enough time in Jasper's wretched company to do a tolerable imitation, he choked up a mocking grin. "That's mighty generous of you, honey. Most women don't appreciate how precious a man's freedom is to him."

A frown clouded her smooth brow. "Your freedom? I don't understand."

"Oh, don't misunderstand me, sweetheart," he said, dangling his arms through the bars. "We had a fine time last night, you and I, but that's no reason to go and do something foolish like get ourselves hitched."

Esmerelda took a step toward the bars. Her stricken expression made him feel more like a monster in a cage than a man in a cell. Her voice lowered to an agonized whisper. "Why are you doing this? You called me Mrs. Darling. You said you wanted to marry me. You said you loved me."

"Hell, angel, a man'll say a lot of things when he's trying to sweet-talk a pretty girl into his bed. Right, Drew?" He winked at his friend.

If Esmerelda had turned at that moment and caught even a glimpse of Drew's appalled expression, she would have known Billy was bluffing. But she was too busy recoiling from the bars. It was Anne who cast Drew a piercing look, Anne who put her arms around Esmerelda when her niece backed into them.

"There's one possibility we haven't considered," Anne said quietly. "What if there should be a child?"

The duke purpled. Esmerelda's hand went instinctively to her belly.

Billy hesitated, knowing his next words would forever damn him in her eyes. He sobered, no longer able to keep up even the pretense of a smile. "There won't be. I saw to that myself."

Esmerelda would never know that he'd deprived himself of savoring that last surge of rapture inside of her to keep from trapping her into marriage to a man she might not want come morning.

"Thank heaven for small favors." The duke pulled a monogrammed handkerchief from his waistcoat pocket and mopped his brow, too relieved to notice his granddaughter's alarming pallor.

Esmerelda's eyes glittered like burning coals in her ashen face. Her lips were no longer trembling with grief, but with rage. If she'd had a gun in her hand at that moment, Billy knew beyond the shadow of a doubt that he would have been a dead man.

She drew herself out of her aunt's arms and approached the bars, bringing him a whiff of peaches so sharp and so sweet it was all he could do not to cry.

A scornful smile curved her beautiful lips. "I can't begin to tell you how relieved I am, Mr. Darling. Spending a night in your bed wasn't so dreadful, but the thought of enduring a lifetime of your boorish company was simply more than I could bear."

Although her words drew blood, Billy refused to flinch. She deserved to say her piece. He owed her at least that much.

"I do hope you'll choose to remember me fondly. Perhaps someday you can travel back to Missouri and marry one of your cousins, as men of your breeding and ilk are wont to do." She turned her back on him, sweeping her skirts in a graceful arc. "Come, Grandpapa, Aunt Anne. We don't owe this man another scrap of our time or our money. He's been paid"—she cast one last bitter glance over her shoulder—"in full."

The door slammed, ringing like a gunshot in Billy's ears. He staggered around as if he'd been struck in the heart and sank to a sitting position with his back against the wall.

Drew waited a merciful interval before strolling over to the cell. "It's not too late, lad," he said softly. "I can still hang you if you want."

Billy slanted him a pained smile. "Hell, Drew, we both know hanging's too good for the likes of me."

Drew slipped his keys into the lock and turned, letting the door swing wide open. Billy didn't budge. He had nowhere left to go. He sat there with his eyes closed while Drew quietly let himself out of the jail. He sat there while Miss Kitty trotted into the cell and rubbed against his legs, meowing plaintively. He sat there until a small, white-gloved hand reached down to give his shoulder a gentle squeeze.

"Mr. Darling?"

In the instant before he opened his eyes, he had the crazy thought that Esmerelda had come back. That, despite his best efforts, she'd refused to believe the worst of him. That she was going to throw her arms around his neck and press her sweet, soft mouth to his before giving him a stern lecture about the perils of trying to protect her from herself.

But when he opened his eyes, it was Anne Hastings who stood before him.

She met his grim gaze with a candor as unflinching as her niece's. "I know what you did, sir. And I want to thank you. I promise that I'll do everything in my power to see that Esmerelda gets the home and the happiness she deserves."

Billy rose. "I'd be much obliged if you'd do that, ma'am. 'Cause if you don't, you and that highfalutin brother of yours will answer to me."

Without another word, he went striding out of the jail, leaving Anne staring after him in astonishment.

The day Billy Darling went riding out of Calamity for the last time, whores cried and dogs howled. He rode tall in the saddle as he always had, his gunbelt slung low around his hips, his Winchester in its scabbard.

The cowboys who'd spent their days playing poker with him down at the Tumbleweed Saloon whispered that it wasn't another gunslinger who finally got him, but a woman. The whores at Miss Mellie's Boardinghouse for Young Ladies of Good Reputation bawled so hard that the cowboys offered them silver dollars just to stop.

Old Granny Shively told her friend Maude that if she'd been of a mind to marry, that Darling boy would have made her a fine husband. The decent folk of Calamity pretended they were glad to be rid of such a shady character, yet more than one of them stepped out of their shops and houses to lift a hand in silent salute as he passed.

He was nothing but a shadow on the horizon when that old basset hound of his escaped from the sheriff's office and went loping down the street. When she reached the edge of town, she sank down on her grizzled haunches, threw back her head, and let out a howl that broke nearly every heart that heard it.

Later, there would be many who would swear he'd reined in his mare and stood silhouetted against the sunset for a timeless moment. Some expected him to turn back. Others were not surprised when he spurred his horse into a canter and disappeared over that hill.

They all saw Billy Darling leave Calamity that day, but not one of them saw a lace curtain high in the window of the hotel twitch, then fall still.

PART THREE

I don't want your greenback dollar.
I don't want your silver chain.
All I want is your love, darlin'.
Won't you take me back again?

I'd rather be in some dark holler,
Where the sun would never shine,
Than to see you with another,
When I know you should be mine.

American Folk Song

CHAPTER
TWENTY-SEVEN

♥

Esmerelda had everything she'd ever wanted. A grandfather who adored her. All the food her belly could hold. A home that no bank or creditor could ever take away from her.

In his quest to grant her every wish, her grandfather had even hired a genuine Pinkerton detective who'd managed to locate Bartholomew in South America. He'd also grudgingly promised to act as the boy's patron, sending him a generous allowance for each chapter of his novel he completed.

She had no cares, no debts, no obligations. She wore Worth gowns and diamond pinkie rings. She slept in her mother's bedroom with its walls hung in pale blue damask bordered by tiny rosebuds. She slept in her mother's bed with its silk sheets and coverlet of tufted satin. She powdered her face and watched her lady's maid pin up her hair in the mirror of her mother's dressing table. Her grandfather probably would have dressed her in her mother's clothes if the layers of ruffles and voluminous crinolines hadn't been twenty-five years out of fashion.

For the first time in her life, Esmerelda understood just how much her mother had sacrificed for love. For the first time, she understood why.

She drifted through the cavernous halls of Wyndham Manor like Lisbeth's ghost, losing her way so many times that she started to wonder if she ought not leave a trail of biscuit crumbs or unwind a ball of yarn wherever she went. She would wander from library to music room, pausing to flip through a book or idly run her fingers over the keys of a piano so grand it made her mother's cherished old upright seem fit only for a saloon.

Her grandfather loved to hear her play, but there seemed little point to it when there was no one to learn from her flawless fingering and rippling arpeggios. She strayed into the music room one warm October afternoon to find one of the little parlormaids dusting the ivory keys with a feather duster.

"Would you like to learn to play?" Esmerelda eagerly asked.

The child clutched her apron and bobbed a terrified curtsey, her mobcap slipping down over one eye. "Oh, no, miss, I mustn't touch anything so fine with my grubby hands."

Airily dismissing the girl's objections, Esmerelda sat her down on the bench and began to teach her the major scales. When Potter, her grandfather's cadaverous butler, strolled into the room to find the child banging cheerily on the instrument, he nearly fainted dead away.

He immediately ordered the maid back to the servants'

kitchen, leaving Esmerelda sitting at the piano, alone and forlorn.

She just didn't seem to be suited for the life of the idle rich. When she offered to help her aunt balance the household books one afternoon, Anne shooed her away, telling her she should enjoy her leisure while she could because she'd have her own household to look after soon enough.

Stung by her aunt's gentle rejection, Esmerelda grabbed her rich woolen cloak and fled the house, seeking solace from a brisk walk in the crisp autumn air. When she imagined being mistress of her own household, she didn't see an elegant sandstone mansion like Wyndham Manor with its high mansard roof and formal gardens. She saw a humble frame house with a cozy corner where a father might teach his son to read by kerosene lamp. She saw a grizzled old basset hound snoring in front of the fire and a calico cat napping in a rocking chair. She saw a towheaded little boy with a wild streak and a smile that could melt hearts at twenty paces.

Esmerelda cupped a hand over her belly, her throat tightening with bitter longing. There would be no such child for her. Billy had made sure of that. She'd spent the journey to England praying that he'd failed, even knowing it would make her a social pariah in her grandfather's world. But his effort to make sure there would be no tie left to bind them had been successful, leaving her womb as barren as her heart.

A curious commotion startled her out of her brooding. She peeped around the corner of the house to find her grandfather leading a parade of tittering servants. Her aunt trailed after them, looking even more exasperated than usual.

Her grandfather beamed at her. "Good afternoon, Esmerelda. I've brought you a gift."

The servants shuffled apart to reveal a speckled horse that barely came to Esmerelda's waist. She clapped a hand over her mouth, gasping in horrified amusement. "I'm twenty-five years old, Grandpapa. If I sit on that poor creature, I'll break its legs."

His square face crumpled like a punctured pudding. "I suppose I wasn't thinking. I just always dreamed of buying my granddaughter a pony."

Feeling guilty for dampening his childlike enthusiasm, Esmerelda stood on tiptoe to give his shiny pate a fond kiss and took the lead from his hand. "And a fine pony it is. I shall name it 'Duke' in your honor." She stroked the beast's silky little face. "He looks a bit like the pony who bucked me off his back at the county fair when I was six."

Anne, a skilled horsewoman, rolled her eyes. The bolder servants cheered and applauded as Esmerelda began to march around the cobblestone drive with the pony trotting merrily along behind her.

Her grandfather delighted in lavishing gifts upon her. She would return to her bedroom to find a parasol of the finest Chantilly lace draped over a frame of heliotrope silk or a set of tortoiseshell combs for her hair. One night, she unfolded her supper napkin only to have the silver locket that had once belonged to her mother tumble into her lap. Although somewhat embarrassed by her grandfather's extravagance, Esmerelda could not bear to disappoint him by refusing any of his offerings. She supposed it was his way of atoning for his years of neglect.

Each night after supper, they would retire to the music room, where Esmerelda was expected to give an impromptu piano recital while Anne embroidered and her grandfather enjoyed a glass of port and smoked a fat cigar. Esmerelda soon grew to dread these occasions. To her ears, all the songs seemed to be played in a minor key, and the ripe aroma of her grandfather's cigar evoked a yearning so sharp she would end up struggling to read the notes through a fog of tears.

On Christmas Eve, her grandfather all but gobbled his way through seven courses of supper, his ears pink with poorly suppressed excitement. Esmerelda barely had time to dip her spoon into her steaming fig pudding when he clapped his hands and insisted they adjourn to the music room. She and her aunt exchanged a perplexed look, but dutifully rose to follow him.

The spacious white room had been draped with evergreen boughs. Their crisp fragrance scented the air. A fire crackled on the hearth and candles glowed softly in the recessed French windows, keeping the darkness of the winter night at bay.

Propped against the gilt music stand was a violin with a bright red ribbon tied around its graceful neck. Esmerelda's hand trembled as she loosed the ribbon and stroked her fingers across its taut strings.

"A Stradivarius?" she whispered, giving her grandfather a helpless look. "For me?"

He poured himself a glass of port and lifted it, his eyes shining with pride and pleasure. "To my granddaughter, who brought music back into this house and into my heart."

He sipped his port while she took up the bow and tucked the instrument under her chin. It nestled there, responding to her tuning as if to a lover's touch.

Seduced by its flawless pitch, Esmerelda closed her eyes and drew the bow across the strings, expecting to hear the bright, brittle notes of Mozart or Vivaldi. She was as stunned as her grandfather and aunt when the plaintive strains of "Johnny Has Gone for a Soldier" filled the room.

Her melancholy touch turned the folk song into a lament, making the strings sob with a passion she had felt only in Billy's arms and would never feel again. When her eyes drifted open at the end of the piece, they were wet with tears.

Unable to bear her grandfather's shaken expression or the wry sympathy in her aunt's eyes, Esmerelda mumbled an apology and fled the room, still clutching the violin.

When Esmerelda had gone, her grandfather sank into a brocaded armchair, looking his age for the first time since bringing his granddaughter home.

Anne paced back and forth in front of the hearth, the swish of her skirts echoing her frustration. "What in God's name were you thinking, Reginald? You can't keep hoping to buy the girl happiness."

He pounded his fist on the arm of the chair. "And why not?"

"Because she has a broken heart, not a skinned knee! It won't be mended by shiny baubles or a pony or even a priceless instrument."

His temper subsided, but the calculating look that spread over his face unnerved Anne more than his despair. "You're absolutely right," he said softly. "There's only one cure for a broken heart."

He bounded up from his chair and started for his study, so agitated he forgot his cane. Anne followed, wondering what mischief he was up to now.

"Perhaps the child is simply lonely," he ventured, limping over to his mahogany desk. "After all, I have been very selfish these past few months, wanting to keep her all to myself." Sinking into his brass-studded chair, he shuffled through the thick stack of cards and crumpled sheets of stationery on his leather blotter. "Why, just look at all the invitations I've turned down on her behalf. Ah!" he exclaimed, plucking an ivory card edged in gilt from the pile. "Here's one from the earl of St. Cyr requesting a theater engagement after the first of the year." Dipping the nearest available pen into a bottle of ink, he began to scribble a reply on the back of the card. "I shall accept posthaste and you, my dear, will act as her chaperone."

"St. Cyr?" Anne echoed, torn between horror and amusement. "You can't be serious. He's twice Esmerelda's age and a notorious lech."

Reginald waved away her objections. "That's because he's been nursing a broken heart for twenty-six years. The poor fellow never married after Lisbeth abandoned him at the altar, you know. And he's been very eager to meet her daughter. I'm sure he'll find the resemblance as striking as I do."

Anne narrowed her eyes. "Are you trying to play matchmaker again, Reggie? You drove Lisbeth away with your efforts. I should hope you wouldn't make the same mistake with her daughter."

Reggie blinked up at her, looking as innocent as a bald cherub. "I simply want to introduce my granddaughter to society and find her a suitable husband. Surely you can't object to that?"

Knowing it would be useless to try, Anne left her brother to his machinations and started up the stairs. She paused outside the door of Esmerelda's chamber, her hand poised to knock. Perhaps if she'd heard broken sobs coming from inside the room, she would have dared to intrude upon her niece's privacy. But she found it impossible to shatter the fragile silence.

When she arrived at her own sitting room, she went straight to her delicate rosewood writing desk and drew forth a sheet of stationery. She sat gazing into space for a long time, nibbling thoughtfully on the feather of her quill

pen. She had accused Reggie of being a shameless matchmaker, yet the scheme she was contemplating was more
audacious than his. And more dangerous. It might even put
her own well-guarded heart in jeopardy.

Unsettled by the girlish thumping of that organ, she
took a steadying breath before dipping her pen in the ink
and committing both her salutation and her niece's fate to
paper.

Dear Sir . . .

CHAPTER TWENTY-EIGHT

♥
_____

Some called him one bad hombre. Some called him a loco gringo. But no one dared to call him by his name. It was almost as if they believed uttering it, even in a whisper, would invoke the demon sleeping in his eyes—eyes that to them appeared the steely gray of the sky at dawn without even a trace of green.

The men feared him. The whores wanted him. The men cut a broad swath around him while the whores cast him longing looks with their sultry dark eyes, their expressions smoldering with lust and resentment. They weren't accustomed to being pushed out of any man's lap, especially not when they were offering their precious wares for free.

He materialized in the Mexican cantina every day around noon, the nubby wool of his poncho swaying as he made his way to the table no one else dared claim. He would sit for hours, listening to the indolent strumming of the guitarist, a glass of whiskey dangling from his lean fingers. As darkness fell, deepening the shadows beneath the brim of his hat, he would trade the glass for a bottle.

In the beginning, men approached him. Mexican men. American men. European men. Powerful men whose meaty fingers flashed diamonds and rubies while their tongues spilled promises and lies. He sent them all away, cursing beneath their fetid breath because he could not be bought for any amount of greenbacks or pesos or gold. His gun was no longer for hire. For the first time since he was thirteen years old, it belonged to him alone.

He always sat facing the door. The men whispered that it was to guard his back. That someday a man with a bigger gun than his would come swaggering through that door and blow him away. The whores whispered that he expected death, perhaps even desired it, the way a man desires a beautiful woman he knows will prove his ruin.

One sultry Saturday night, Billy sat with his back to the wall—drinking, smoking, and dreaming, as he always did, that Esmerelda would come walking through that door just like she had in Calamity. Hell, this time he would beg her to shoot him, if only to plug the hole in his heart with lead so his blood would stop seeping out one drop at a time. It was taking him too damn long to die that way.

One of the whores, a black-haired beauty with lush red lips and a reputation for using them in ways that could make a grown man beg, sashayed through the drunken crowd. She leaned over and planted her palms on Billy's table, practically begging him to look down her loose-fitting blouse at her naked breasts. Not wanting to be impolite, he obliged her.

"There's a man at the bar," she said. "A gringo. Looking for you."

Billy didn't even bother to glance at the bar. He simply

shifted his cigar to the corner of his mouth. "Tell him I'm not here. And if I was, I wouldn't want to see him."

She nodded, having known that would be his answer. "Another bottle?" she offered, touching her fingertip to the mouth of the empty one still gripped in his hand.

He slanted her a wry glance. She knew the answer to that question, too. She was only asking it as an excuse to linger. Her fall of raven hair tickled his nose as she reached across him to take the bottle from his hand.

"The whiskey can't make you forget her," she purred, her tongue flicking out to trace his ear, "but I could." Beneath the table, her other hand began to creep up his thigh.

Billy caught it a fingers-breadth from his crotch, surveying her with dark amusement. "*Muchas gracias, señorita,* but I never draw my gun unless I plan to use it."

Tossing back her hair, she went flouncing back to the bar, her lips puckered in a full-fledged pout.

Billy went back to nursing his cigar. He could hardly blame her for her mistake. It was a common enough assumption. But he wasn't drinking to forget. The whiskey could do little more than take the edge off his longing—a longing so keen that when he rolled off his cot every morning, recoiling from the merciless blaze of sunshine, he could only drop his throbbing head into his hands and pray for darkness.

He had the rest of his life to forget. To forget the sweet generosity of Esmerelda's body opening to enfold him. To forget her fearless bravado the night she'd stood down his mother on his behalf. To forget the stricken look in her eyes when he had so callously declined to marry her.

He had the rest of his life to remember. To remember the tender smile that had softened her prim lips the day she'd thrown open that hotel room door in Eulalie. To remember the taste of her mouth and the feel of her flesh beneath his hands. To remember how she had felt in his arms and to imagine how she would feel in the arms of another man.

The whiskey bottle appeared in front of him. Billy groped for it without lifting his eyes, tossing a bill across the table. It came floating back at him through the smoky air, drifting like a leaf on the wind.

"Keep your money, lad. Tonight, I'm buying."

Startled out of his shell of indifference for the first time in months, Billy looked up to find Sheriff Andrew McGuire standing over his table.

"Good God, William, you look like hell," Drew said, sliding into the chair opposite him. Despite the heat, he looked as crisp as a newly minted two-dollar greenback in his double-breasted waistcoat, shiny knee boots, and broad-brimmed white Stetson.

Billy stroked his unshaven jaw, eyeing his friend warily. "Did you come all the way to Mexico just to insult me?"

"If you must know, I came to make you a proposition."

"Sorry, Drew. I haven't been without a woman that long."

Billy reached for the fresh bottle of whiskey only to discover that a plate of steaming food had appeared in its place—pinto beans and something with a savory aroma wrapped in a corn tortilla. Its mysterious arrival confounded him nearly as much as the startling awareness that he was hungry. Maybe even ravenous, he admitted, shoveling a spoonful of beans into his mouth.

Drew watched him eat with the amused tolerance of a king presiding over a beggar's feast, holding his tongue until the plate had been scraped clean.

Billy darted him a suspicious look. "I thought you were going to buy me a drink."

"So I was," Drew admitted, snapping his fingers in the direction of the bar.

The raven-haired whore swaggered over, smug now as she swished her hips in Billy's face and thumped an earthenware flask down on the table. Billy took a long, thirsty gulp, then spat the bulk of it on the cantina floor, shooting Drew an accusing glare. "It's water!"

"Aye, it is. If you want anything stronger, you'll have to crawl over to the bar on your belly and get it yourself."

Billy surged to his feet, despising Drew for pitying him when no other man would have dared, despising himself for deserving it. His pride was the only thing that prevented him from staggering. "Go to hell. I don't need your charity."

"Sit down, William," Drew said mildly.

"And if I don't," he snarled, "what are you going to do, sheriff? Arrest me?"

"I'm afraid I'll have to leave that unenviable task to someone else. I am no longer acting as sheriff of Calamity. I have officially resigned my post."

His precarious balance unable to withstand the blow, Billy sank back into the chair. He gestured to the tin star twinkling merrily on Drew's vest. "Then why are you still wearing your badge?"

"Because I have abdicated the job, but absconded with the title." He leaned back in his chair, twirling the silky tip of his right mustache. "As you well know, it has long been a dream of mine to leave behind the dangerous vocation of law enforcement. Hence was born the notion of"—he paused for dramatic effect, his eloquent hands painting a banner in the air over the table—"'Sheriff Andrew McGuire's Wild West Extravaganza.'"

Billy leaned across the table and sniffed his breath. "Maybe you should have switched to water a little sooner."

Drew sighed. "I should like to claim credit for the idea, but its genesis came out of a recent conversation I had with a Mr. William Cody, who was starring in a theatrical melodrama penned by Ned Buntline."

Billy was familiar with Buntline. He'd written most of the dime novels that still sat on the bookshelves in Miss Mellie's attic. Remembering how much he'd enjoyed those books, he felt a pang of regret for leaving them behind.

"According to Mr. Cody," Drew continued, "all you would need to launch such an endeavor are some horses, guns, cowboys and settlers, wild Indians—"

"You don't know any wild Indians," Billy pointed out.

"Of course I do. There's Crazy Joe Cloudminder right there in Calamity."

"Joe's a barber!"

"Then I'm sure he can wield a tomahawk just as skillfully as he can a razor." Drew leaned his elbows on the table and steepled his fingers beneath his chin, studying Billy with an intensity that made him itch to bolt. "All I lack now is a sharpshooter. Oh, say, someone who could hit a dime in midair or shoot a playing card in half at a hundred and twenty feet."

Billy shoved his chair back from the table again, lunging to his feet. "Oh, no, you don't! In case you haven't heard, I've hung up my guns for good. I'm not for hire. Not even by you." He wheeled around and started for the door, determined to walk out of the cantina while he still could.

"I've already booked our first engagement."

Drew's casual announcement stopped Billy in his tracks. His nape prickled with dread. Worse than the dread was the emotion that tripped along at its heels. He'd grown comfortable with despair, but hope might just kill him.

"Where?" he whispered.

"London."

Billy turned around and returned to the table, sliding into the chair as gingerly as if his bones were made of glass. Jesus, he needed a drink, he thought bitterly, locking his hands together to hide their trembling. He doubted he could even hold a gun without dropping it.

Forcing himself to look up and meet Drew's kind blue eyes was one of the hardest things he'd ever done. It took him three tries just to swallow. "I know why you're doing this."

Drew beamed at him. "I thought you would. A man of your discerning palate must surely appreciate the charms of my Anne."

Billy continued as if he hadn't spoken. "And I thank you most kindly for your concern, but—" He stopped, scowling in bewilderment as Drew's words sank in. "Anne? Anne Hastings? That dried-up old persimmon of a—"

"Watch your tongue, lad." Drew held up a restraining hand. "I hasten to remind you that you are speaking of my future bride. She is no persimmon, but a ripe, luscious pomegranate, trembling with eagerness to fall into my waiting hand."

Billy snorted. "The last time I saw her with you, she was trembling with rage, not eagerness."

"Despite our past differences, she's agreed to finance my little endeavor. I prefer to think of it as a sort of dowry. Although it may not have been readily apparent," Drew assured him, "we have an understanding."

"Oh, I understood perfectly. She despised you and wished you would die."

"Be that as it may," Drew admitted with an injured sniff, "I can assure you that she has been very tender toward me in our recent correspondence."

Billy responded to that revelation with stony silence. If

Drew thought he was going to beg him for any pathetic scrap of news about Esmerelda, then he was wrong. Dead wrong.

Drew sat back in his chair, eyeing him shrewdly. "Anne made brief mention of her niece in her letter. If I'm not mistaken, there was talk of a suitor. An earl, I believe."

Billy's fingers began to drum on the table, losing their tremble.

Drew leaned forward as if to impart a particularly delicious snippet of gossip. "It seems the man once courted Esmerelda's mother. Since the mother left him languishing at the altar over twenty-five years ago, he's set his sights on the daughter. You might think a fifty-year-old man would be in his dotage, but Anne assures me he's a handsome, virile fellow of quite notorious appetites, perfectly capable of satisfying his young bride and providing himself with an heir to—"

Billy lunged across the table, jerking Drew out of his chair by his flawlessly folded necktie. The guitar fell silent. The occupants of the cantina ceased their smoking, chattering, and dancing to gape in fascination. They'd never seen any sign of emotion from him more intense than a bored flicker of his eyelids.

If they were astonished by his violence, they were even more dumbfounded when, after holding the stranger's gaze for a tense eternity, he gently lowered the man back into his chair, smoothed his necktie, and drawled, "So, when do we leave?"

CHAPTER TWENTY-NINE

When Billy found out who Drew had recruited to portray the notorious outlaw gang in his Wild West Extravaganza, he almost wished he'd gone ahead and choked him to death with his own necktie right there in that cantina.

"We even got Ma's blessing, little brother," Virgil told him, grinning from ear to ear as they boarded the iron-hulled steamer in New York. "She said we cain't *be* outlaws no more, but she don't mind us playin' at it like we did when we was boys." He lowered his voice to a mere shout as he leaned down and confided, "She told us to look after you, too. Said you ain't got good sense when it comes to womenfolk."

Billy rubbed his ringing ear. "I guess Ma's right on that count. If I did, I wouldn't be about to cross an ocean to win one I was fool enough to let get away in the first place."

Billy almost forgave Drew for hiring his brothers when

he saw the beautiful female who would be sharing his cabin for the next week and a half.

Sadie greeted him with a deep-throated "Woof," her entire lower half jiggling with excitement as she bounded across the cabin.

"There's my girl!" He squatted to ruffle her gray-flecked coat, laughing and groaning as his efforts to dodge her long, sloppy tongue proved to be in vain.

Billy doubted he could expect as enthusiastic a greeting from Esmerelda, especially not after he'd led her to believe she'd been nothing more to him than a lusty tumble between the sheets. But he would do whatever he had to do to convince her otherwise, even if it took him the rest of his life.

As the voyage got under way, the other passengers tended to give them a wide berth. Billy supposed he couldn't blame them, what with Virgil's bellowing, Jasper's shameless flirting with every woman under the age of seventy-five, and Enos spending all night groaning in his bunk and all day hanging over the rail, his sallow complexion bleached to seafoam green. Drew had hired a dozen or so out-of-work cowboys, including Dauber and Seal, to portray settlers in his extravaganza. Their nightly poker games had an alarming tendency to degenerate into shouted bouts of name-calling and drunken fistfights.

Billy might even have been guilty of contributing to the other passengers' alarm by spending hours standing at the stern of the ship and firing at nickel slugs Drew tossed high into the air. He made it a point to miss one every now and then, just to put their minds at ease. They still shied away, wives clutching their husbands and mothers clutching their daughters, when Drew tried to press his freshly printed fliers into their shaking hands, urging them to come visit his exhibition while they were in London.

One morning Billy came whistling his way up one of the narrow gangways. Since it was so cold he could see every note hanging in the air on a breath of fog, he didn't think anything peculiar when a figure approached, swaddled in a topcoat and scarf. The man was muffled all the way up to his eyes, which he quickly averted when Billy accidentally bumped into him.

"Sorry, partner," Billy drawled, tipping his hat.

Still whistling, he continued up the gangway for a few more steps, then halted, caught off guard by the sudden tingling of his nape. He swung around, but the other passenger had vanished. He shook his head and rubbed away the uneasy prickle, attributing it to fancy. He was probably safer on this boat than he'd ever been in Calamity with a price on his head.

Billy emerged into the winter sunshine to find the troupe's sole wild Indian already on deck. Crazy Joe was so enamored of the Savage Red Man costume Drew had commissioned for him that he insisted on wearing it day and night, despite the frigid temperatures. He might have looked more menacing in his war paint and loincloth if he hadn't also been sporting a dapper bowler and giving Samuel a haircut.

Sam perched on a wooden barrel. He kept his hand clamped over his good ear and visibly cringed at each decisive snip of the scissors.

Recalling the time his brother had poured sorghum in his hair while he was sleeping, Billy exchanged a wink with Joe, then leaned over and whispered, "I'd hold still if I were you. He's more likely to take your scalp than your ear."

Leaving his brother squirming worse than before, Billy started for the bow of the ship. He soon passed a pallid, hollow-eyed Enos, returning from yet another visit to the rail.

Recalling the time Enos had held him down and forced him to eat a june bug, Billy jerked a thumb toward the hold. "They've got quite a fine spread down there this morning. Eggs and bacon and biscuits and flapjacks and . . ."

Shooting him a black look, Enos gripped his stomach and went stumbling back toward the rail.

Billy grinned. Virgil might complain about the boredom and Jasper about the deplorable lack of whores, but he found everything about the journey invigorating—the rhythmic chug of the ship's engine, the pitching of the boat when they hit restless seas, the icy spray striking his face when he stood at the bow as he did now.

He had to admit his jubilation might have less to do with the journey than with the woman waiting for him at the end of it. He caught his hat before a blast of icy wind could tear it away. The cold couldn't touch him, not with the thrill of the hunt warming his blood.

This time his prey wasn't some bootlegger or horse thief, but a woman's heart—sweet and stubborn and dear. The only bounty he desired was to be found in her loving arms. Billy gripped the rail and leaned forward, almost as if he could urge the steamer to chug harder and cut faster through the vast plain of sea that separated them.

Esmerelda stood in front of the cheval glass in her bedroom, admiring the stranger in the mirror. She wore a pink-coral skirt trimmed with three flounces. An overskirt of Brussels lace had been gathered in the back and tied with grosgrain ribbons. A basque corsage secured by a mother-of-pearl brooch bared the creamy slope of her shoulders. A string of pearls twined through her hair, which had been looped and coiled by her lady's maid into a tremendously flattering cascade of curls.

She wore Lisbeth's locket around her neck. The delicate

chain weighed upon her skin as if it had been forged from iron.

She was finally the beauty she'd always secretly yearned to be, but the elegant creature gazing back at her from the cheval glass bore no resemblance to the strong-willed, tart-tongued girl who had crossed half a continent to seek justice for her brother. Nor even a passing likeness to the passionate woman who had given herself freely and without regret to the man she loved—the man who had invited her to share his life as well as his bed, then betrayed her.

No longer able to stand the sight of her reflection, Esmerelda went to her dressing table and groped for a bottle of *eau de cologne*. She brought the smooth glass stopper to her throat, closing her eyes as Billy whispered, *Did I ever tell you what my favorite kind of pie is?*

Just the memory of his smoky drawl was enough to send a shiver of desire through her. Sickened by the cloying floral scent of the perfume, Esmerelda set it aside and reached for the homely brown bottle of peach extract wedged behind a fat beadwork pincushion.

She was putting a defiant dab behind each ear when a knock sounded on the door. She bit back a groan. She was growing incredibly weary of the frantic round of social engagements her grandfather had pressed upon her in the two months since Christmas. Even more grueling than the engagements were the suitable companions he'd chosen for her, all simpering young ladies of eligible age from noble families. She supposed she should be thankful they were at least old enough to be let out of the nursery without their nannies. If her grandfather truly had his way, he'd probably be pushing her around the walks of Hyde Park in a giant pram.

She'd privately christened her new acquaintances "the Belles," since they all seemed to be named Isabelle, Annabel, or in one timid creature's case, simply Belle.

Although they smiled and simpered whenever she was in their company, Esmerelda knew that they regarded her with a mixture of pity and horror, holding her up as an example of the terrible fate that could befall any one of them who failed to make a suitable match before her twentieth birthday.

She could only imagine their delighted shock if they discovered their chaste new companion had been compromised by a scoundrel like Billy Darling.

With a wicked smile still playing around her lips, she swung open the door. "So what's it to be tonight?" she asked her waiting aunt. "An opera? A supper party? A musicale hosted by one of the Belles?"

Anne brushed past her, her color higher than usual. "I believe you'll find tonight's diversion quite unique."

She gave her aunt a pleading look. "Couldn't I just feign a nasty headache and stay home in bed reading one of those deliciously wicked romantic novels? After all, I only have a few more days to rest up for the masquerade ball Grandpapa is giving in my honor."

When Anne behaved as if she hadn't spoken, Esmerelda frowned. No, she hadn't been mistaken. Her aunt, a woman without a bone of vanity in her trim, spare body, was actually craning her neck to steal a glimpse of herself in the cheval glass. As Esmerelda watched, she even dared to twine a spit curl around her little finger. The iron-gray ringlet escaped with an impertinent bounce.

Esmerelda cleared her throat.

Anne jumped, her nerves of iron crumbling to rust before her niece's amused eyes. "Come, dear," she said, plucking a mantle of braided cashmere out of the wardrobe and draping it over Esmerelda's shoulders. "The earl's carriage is already downstairs waiting for us."

"Oh, no! Not the earl again. I'd rather be boiled in

porridge than spend another moment in *his* company."
Esmerelda dragged her slippered feet like a recalcitrant
child. "Can't you tell him I have amnesia? That I forgot we
had an engagement?"

Her aunt continued to tug her toward the door. "If
you'll just come with me, my dear, I believe I can promise
you an evening you will never forget."

Esmerelda no longer had any need to feign a nasty
headache. Her head had began to pound in earnest almost
as soon as they'd entered the crowded theater on Drury
Lane. Although the electric arc lamps were a vast improvement over the smelly, smoky gas and oil lamps they'd
replaced, the mingled perfumes of the elegantly dressed
theatergoers jammed elbow to elbow into the tiered
benches made her hunger for a breath of fresh air.

Aunt Anne sat on her left while the earl pressed close on
the right, taking up most of his seat and part of hers.
Esmerelda couldn't have said which was more intolerable—
St. Cyr's fawning attentions or the inane chatter of the
Belles, who surrounded them above and below in a smothering cloud of organdy and lace. She winced as one of their
shrill giggles seemed to drive a splinter of ice into her skull.

"Care for a boiled peanut, m'dear?" the earl inquired for
the fourth time, proffering a canvas sack.

"No, thank you," she coolly replied, having watched
him spit several of the shells back into the sack after he'd
divested them of their peanuts with his sharp yellow teeth.

Her aunt had refused to tell her what manner of pro-
duction they were attending, insisting with uncharacteristic coyness that it remain a surprise. From the bales of hay
that had been scattered around the circular arena, Esmerelda gathered that it must be a circus of some sort. Spot-
ting a playbill in the gloved hands of a woman seated three

rows down, she lifted her opera glasses in an impolite attempt to read over the woman's shoulder.

Anne snatched the glasses away from her and pressed them to her own eyes. "Oh, look, isn't that the Prince of Wales coming in?"

Esmerelda squinted in the same direction. "Not unless he's taken to wearing a bustle and feathers in his hair."

Unnerved by her aunt's increasingly peculiar behavior, Esmerelda sighed and settled back on the bench. The arc lamps began to dim. The buzz of conversation dwindled to an eager murmur.

Esmerelda gasped and jumped just as high as the rest of the crowd when a stagecoach drawn by four black horses came rocking across the arena. A man in a tan shirt, trousers, hat, and red bandanna drove the team, a shotgun laid across his lap. As a near-naked Indian riding a sleek pinto thundered after him, tomahawk raised high, the Belles threw their arms around each other and let out an ear-piercing shriek.

The shotgun exploded with a mighty blast. The Indian leapt from pinto to stagecoach, wresting the reins from the driver's hands. After a brief but violent struggle, he hurled the driver to the ground and pounced upon him. The stagecoach went lurching back into the darkness as the Indian unsheathed a gleaming blade and drew it downward in a slicing motion. The driver slumped into a lifeless heap.

The savage sprang to his feet, his dazzling white teeth bared in a bloodthirsty grimace, and held up a trophy that looked suspiciously like a rat pelt. Several woman screamed, and one of the Belles groped for her smelling salts.

Before the scandalized gasps and horrified cries could die out, the driver bounded to his feet and took a bow, revealing that he'd been bald as an egg the entire time. The crowd erupted in hearty laughter and thunderous applause.

A man garbed in an elegant top hat, frock coat, and shiny black boots strode to the center of the arena with a megaphone and intoned in a cultured English accent, "Welcome to the show, ladies and gentlemen! Brought to you straight from the untamed wilderness of America— the very first Wild West Extravaganza to tour England!"

As the applause soared again, Esmerelda slowly swiveled around to glare at her aunt, rigid with fury. "If this is your idea of a jest," she hissed through clenched teeth, "you have a very sick sense of humor."

Her aunt simply stared straight ahead as if she hadn't spoken. Determined to endure no more of this nonsense, Esmerelda attempted to rise.

"Oh, do sit down! We can't see!" the Belles twittered as a chorus, all aflutter with excitement.

"Down in front!" boomed a masculine voice.

Esmerelda drove an elbow into the earl's side, attempting to nudge him out of her way, but earned nothing but a distracted grunt for her trouble. He was already mesmerized by the sight of the covered wagon that came rolling across the hay-strewn floor of the arena.

Defeated for the time being, she sank back down on the bench, sulking like a child.

The same Indian on the same pinto began to race circles around the wagon, howling a fierce war cry. The plight of the family of settlers might have been more heartrending if one of the women hadn't boasted sideburns and a sandy beard. "Her" falsetto cries for mercy as the Indian jumped on the wagon and began to tear at her homespun dress soon had the audience rolling with laugh-

ter. Plagued by a nagging sense of familiarity, Esmerelda
leaned forward, but the glare of the lights obscured the
man's facial features.

The next sketch consisted of a mock cabin, more
screaming settlers, and the same Indian leaping into one
window, then running out the back door of the cabin,
around to the front, and leaping into another, pretending
to be a different Indian. By now, the poor fellow was
clutching his side and gasping for breath.

Muttering their displeasure, several men and women
rose and began to drift toward the exits. As one of the
benches below them cleared, Esmerelda breathed a sigh of
relief. Her prayers for deliverance had been answered. She
didn't think she could bear another minute of this travesty.
The west she'd known was wilder than any of them could
imagine, she thought, remembering Billy's unbridled passion with a pang of loss and yearning.

She was already poised to make a mad dash for freedom
when some unseen stagehands unfurled a painted backdrop of a street in a western town. Esmerelda was squinting at it, thinking that it looked strangely familiar, when
the lights dimmed again. As a single spotlight brightened
the darkness, the trickle toward the exits slowed to a halt.
The mutterings ceased; the murmurs faded. Even the
Belles lapsed into an expectant silence.

A lone man stepped into the circle of light.

The sinister black of his trousers and vest was relieved
only by the startling whiteness of his shirt. The broad brim
of his hat shadowed his eyes. The ruthless beam of the arc
lamp cast a shimmering halo around him.

Esmerelda's heart began to pound even harder than her
head.

She was so riveted by the cougarlike grace of his swagger that she never even felt her aunt reach over to clutch

her icy hand. She never heard the Belles titter and whisper to one another behind their cupped hands that they would surely swoon were they to be accosted by such a handsome and virile villain. She never saw the second man appear at the opposite end of the arena, dressed all in white with an oversized tin star gleaming on his lapel.

"Throw down your gun, outlaw," he barked in a rolling Scottish burr. "I'm the law in this town and we don't take to your kind here."

"Haven't you heard, sheriff?" the man replied in a drawl as sweet and thick as sun-warmed molasses. "I never draw my gun unless I plan to use it."

Jasper, Esmerelda thought frantically. Dear God, it had to be Jasper. She dragged her hand out of her aunt's and groped blindly for the opera glasses. She lifted them to her eyes, struggling to focus through the fog of panic that had descended over her vision.

The men faced off, their hands poised over the sleek leather sheaths cradling their pistols. They both drew in one quicksilver motion. A shot rang out.

Esmerelda flinched as if she'd been hit. For a taut eternity, it was impossible to tell which man was hit. Then the man dressed all in black began to stagger. His knees buckled and he slowly crumpled to the ground, a crimson stain spreading over his heart. As he sprawled on his back, Esmerelda got her first clear look at his face.

Forgetting that the shells were blanks, forgetting that the blood was probably nothing more than strawberry syrup, forgetting that she hated Billy almost as much as she still loved him and had wished him dead a thousand times since they'd parted, Esmerelda leapt to her feet and let out a piercing scream.

CHAPTER THIRTY

Esmerelda's scream fell into a silence so suffocating she wasn't sure she would ever breathe again.

Billy slowly climbed to his feet, his gaze riveted on her as if they were the only two people in the arena. He swept his hat off the floor, dusting bits of straw from its crown, before sketching her a gallant bow.

The audience erupted in a frenzied wave of applause, hoots, and approving whistles. The men stamped their feet in unison, making the tiers of benches shudder.

Esmerelda continued to stand, frozen into place by her own mortification as she realized what an utter buffoon she'd just made of herself. She looked frantically around only to find the Belles gaping at her, their little pink mouths circles of scandalized delight. The earl appeared to be choking on a peanut, while her aunt pretended to study a playbill, her face a portrait of artless innocence.

Against her will, Esmerelda's gaze was drawn back to the man who stood in that shimmering arc of light. As she met his wary gaze, her every sense came tingling to life, just as they had in that dusty saloon a lifetime ago. Unable to bear the exquisite pain of such an awakening, she turned to the left, then to the right, driven by a single primal urge.

Escape.

Ignoring the earl's muttered "I should say!" and "Well, I never," Esmerelda shoved past him, trodding ruthlessly on his feet. Although she continued to push and elbow her way toward the aisle, no one dared complain. They were too enchanted by the drama taking place practically in their laps. When her cashmere shawl snagged on the clawed grip of a man's cane, she simply left it behind, although her bared shoulders made her feel even more exposed. The spotlight swung around to follow her, high-lighting every lurch and stumble of her agonizing journey.

She reached the aisle only to discover she had nowhere to go but down. Holding her head high, she started down the carpeted stairs, praying she wouldn't end up rolling down them in her haste.

When she finally reached the floor, her heartfelt sigh of relief drowned out the admiring gasps of the crowd. She had no way of knowing that Billy had wrested the reins of the pinto from the hapless Indian and swung himself astride until he came trotting up beside her. He looked harder and leaner than she remembered. His face was darker, his hair a brighter gold.

He slowed the horse to an amiable walk, tipping his hat as if they'd just happened to meet on a tree-shaded path. "Can I offer you a ride, ma'am?"

"I can promise you, sir," she hissed out of the corner of her mouth, "that you have absolutely nothing to offer me."

Devilish charm melted through his voice as he leaned

down and murmured, "I wouldn't be so sure of that if I were you, honey."

Terrified he might be right, she quickened her steps, thinking only to reach the gilded doors at the far end of the theater before she made an even bigger fool of herself.

He nudged the horse nearer. "I need to talk to you, Esmerelda. You have to hear me out."

"I don't care to hear anything you have to say."

"If you don't care, then why did you scream when you thought I'd been shot?"

Esmerelda didn't miss a step. "Because I was afraid I'd been deprived of the pleasure of killing you myself."

Billy responded to her retort by wheeling the pinto around and cantering back toward the center of the arena. Esmerelda hated herself for feeling a stab of regret.

Andrew McGuire's Scottish burr flooded the theater, magnified by the yawning mouth of the megaphone. "Ladies and gentlemen, allow me to introduce you to the deadliest draw and quickest shot in all the American West . . ."

Warned by the thunder of hoofbeats, the relentless jingle of spurs, Esmerelda whirled around, clapping a hand over her heart.

Billy was galloping straight for her. He leaned low over the pinto's back, determination hardening his eyes to silver.

". . . the one name that strikes terror in the hearts of innocent maidens and lawmen alike . . ."

Esmerelda's own traitorous heart skipped two beats for every one it hit. She stood paralyzed with helpless anticipation until Billy leaned sideways and swept her off the floor and into his lap with one powerful arm.

". . . Mr. Billy Darling!"

The crowd roared their approval, no doubt believing the spectacle was all part of the show. The deserters who had been filing toward the exits went scurrying back to their seats.

Esmerelda squirmed in Billy's arms. Being that near to him again, breathing in his rich tobacco-and-leather scent was a taste of both heaven and hell.

"Relax, Duchess," he murmured into her hair. "You don't have to be afraid of the horse."

"I'm not afraid of the horse! I'm—"

Afraid I still love you.

She bit her lip before she could blurt out those damning words.

"Just hang on to me, angel, and pretend the saddle is a rocking chair."

Blushing furiously, she twisted around to give him a long, hard look. He cocked an eyebrow, returning it with one of bland innocence.

The horse trotted toward the center of the arena, where Drew stood in the dazzling light of the spotlight, having ousted the Englishman who had introduced the show.

Even the eloquent sheriff seemed at a loss for words to describe Billy's scandalous abduction of her. "As you can see, um, ladies and gentlemen," he shouted through the megaphone, "the notorious gunslinger has swept this beautiful little lady off her feet." He slanted them a dubious look as Billy slid off the horse, dragging a struggling Esmerelda after him. "Proving, once again, that no woman can resist the charms of an outlaw."

"I can," Esmerelda declared, landing with a deliberate crunch on Billy's toes.

He doubled over in a bow to hide his grimace of pain, taking her captive hand with him. "You might want to play along with Drew for now," he shouted over the roar of applause. "I'd hate to ruin your reputation."

"You already have," she shouted back. "Or have you forgotten?"

He gave her a smoldering look that warned her he hadn't forgotten a single touch or kiss they'd shared during that fateful night.

As much as Esmerelda hated to admit it, he was right. She was already the laughingstock of London. Struggle or flight would only humiliate her further. When Billy drew her out of the bow, she wore a smile as dazzling as his own.

Drew tugged a handkerchief from his breast pocket and mopped his brow before returning the megaphone to his lips. "Mr. Darling has traveled all the way from the wilds of America to provide you with an exhibition of crack shooting the likes of which has never before been seen in your fair country."

The bald cowboy who had portrayed the stagecoach driver came trotting out from behind a curtain, wheeling a silver tea cart. Four men with colorful bandannas tied across their noses mounted their horses and went galloping around the arena. They distracted the impatient audience by whooping a deafening chorus of rebel yells and firing their pistols in the air.

Virgil winked at Esmerelda as he raced past, looking much more natural in his outlaw's getup than he had in a bonnet and homespun dress.

Billy shook his head. "I sure hope they remembered to replace their shells with blanks."

"If not," she murmured, "several of the English stand to inherit before this night is over."

As the tea cart drew near, Esmerelda saw that it bore a crystal cup laden with dimes, a shiny new deck of playing cards, and a sleek Colt .45. Realizing immediately that it would have to be loaded with live shells instead of blanks, she grabbed for the gun.

Billy swept it out of her reach with effortless grace, *tsk*-ing beneath his breath as he slid it into his holster. She glared at him.

No doubt fearing they were about to break into fisticuffs, Sheriff McGuire hastily lifted the megaphone. "With the lady's gracious help, Mr. Darling will now favor us all with a demonstration of his prowess."

The image that popped into Esmerelda's head was so unprecedented and so utterly ribald that she blushed to the roots of her hair.

Billy held out a single dime, his lazy grin warning her that he had read her thoughts. "If you would be so kind . . . ?"

Resisting an urge to fling the coin in his smirking face, she hurled it toward the ceiling with all of her might.

The shimmering coin flipped end over end, disappearing into the glare of the spotlights. With one smooth motion, Billy drew, cocked the hammer of his pistol with the palm of his other hand, and fired. The dime shot heavenward, propelled by the impact.

The appreciative "oohs" and "aahs" of Billy's rapt audience grew in volume each time they repeated the trick. He never once missed the impossibly elusive target, not even when he backed up to a distance of ninety feet.

Hoping to thwart him, Esmerelda grabbed an entire handful of dimes and tossed them into the air. Billy fired six shots in dizzying succession, taking down six of them before they could reach the ground.

The applause was deafening.

As he strode back to her side to take his triumphant bow, the spotlight dimmed to an unearthly glow.

Drew took advantage of the audience's breathless anticipation. "Mr. Darling's next trick requires absolute silence. I can only urge you to make no careless gesture, to speak no word that would disturb his concentration." He lowered his voice to an ominous stage whisper. "The very life of the lady may depend upon it."

Esmerelda was less than heartened by that dire prediction. Billy took up the deck of cards and held them out to her, fanning them in a gesture he could have only perfected during countless poker games. He stood so near to her that Esmerelda was mesmerized by the dark gold threads of his lashes, the wary deepening of the lines that bracketed his sensual mouth.

Drew pointed the megaphone at her ear and intoned, "As he must draw, so must she."

Willing herself not to tremble, Esmerelda reached out and chose a card. She glanced at it, then turned it for Billy to see, unable to resist a mocking smile.

"The queen of hearts!" Drew called out. The audience shifted and murmured in subdued delight.

Billy strolled behind her. Esmerelda forced herself to remain pliant while he slid one arm around her waist and positioned her like some dressmaker's dummy. She refused to give him the satisfaction of knowing that his touch could still make her pulse quicken and her mouth go dry with longing.

But she could do nothing to hide the ripple of gooseflesh that danced along her skin when he pressed his mouth to her ear and whispered, "Trust me."

"Never," she replied, staring straight ahead.

But the hand he'd arranged to hold the card aloft didn't waver, not even by a fraction of an inch. Until Drew wrapped a black silk blindfold around Billy's eyes.

"Oh, no," Esmerelda said, shaking her head violently and backing away from the both of them. "I'd rather take my chances with the knife throwers."

She backed right into Virgil's burly arms. "Don't worry, honey," he boomed in his own deafening rendition of a stage whisper. "Little Brother's been doin' this trick since he was nine years old and he ain't missed yet."

"Then *you* hold the card," she retorted, trying to force it into his hand.

He declined her invitation, choosing instead to scurry safely out of range, where Jasper, Samuel, and Enos awaited him. Esmerelda turned back only to discover that while she was preoccupied, Drew had led Billy an impressive distance away and left him there. He stood in the center of the arena with his long legs splayed, his hands poised loosely over his gunbelt.

Trust me.

As that husky entreaty echoed through her mind, Esmerelda sighed, knowing she had no choice. Billy had her in his sights just as surely as he had on that moonlit night in Calamity. She couldn't stop him from shooting at her any more than she could have stopped him from breaking her heart.

She slowly lifted the card, holding it between the very tips of her thumb and forefinger, and closed her eyes.

A shot rang out. She flinched. The crowd gasped. Daring to open only one eye, Esmerelda patted her chest, trying to determine exactly where she'd been shot.

When she failed to encounter anything more alarming than her mother's locket, she screwed up the courage to open both eyes and count how many fingers she had left.

She was still holding the card.

Her mouth dropped open. Billy Darling had missed. But Billy Darling never missed, she thought wildly, her heart surging with treacherous tenderness. He'd simply refused to risk her life for the sake of a cheap parlor trick. Or at least that's what she believed until she held the card up to the light and saw the smoking hole shot clean through the heart of the hapless queen.

The crowd went wild. The Darling gang vaulted back on their mounts and went galloping around the arena, mercifully distracting the audience.

Billy dragged off the blindfold and came striding toward her. Letting the card slip from her numb fingers, Esmerelda turned to flee, desperate to lose herself among the torrent of people who had began to pour out of their seats and stream toward the exits.

"Don't run away from me, sweetheart."

Undone by that hoarse plea from a man who never begged, Esmerelda whirled around. "I'm not your sweetheart! Or your honey. Or your angel. I'm nothing to you, Mr. Darling. You made that painfully clear on the occasion of our last parting."

He shook his head. "I didn't mean a damn word I said. I swear it. If I had, I wouldn't have traveled halfway across the world to tell you different."

"Ah, but how do I know you're not simply trying to *sweet-talk* me back into your bed? After all, I know how precious your *freedom* is to a man like you."

Billy flinched, realizing just how many times Esmerelda must have heard the echo of those cruel words.

The tears welling in her eyes began to spill down her cheeks. "After all, you'd never do anything so *foolish* as *getting yourself hitched,* despite the *fine time* we had in bed together."

Helpless to stop himself, Billy reached to brush a tear from her cheek. His thumb lingered against the creamy velvet of her skin. "I only said those terrible things to scare you off. Because I believed you were too good for the likes of me."

Esmerelda drew herself up. Her chin still quivered, but she held it high and proud. "If that's what you believed, William Darling, then you were right. I am too good for the likes of you."

She turned, sweeping away from him without a backward glance. Even after she'd melted into the crowd, the aroma of peaches still hung in the air, pungent and sweet.

Billy bent to pick up the card she had dropped. The queen stared back at him in mute reproach, a scorched hole marring her noble breast.

Drew clapped a hand on his shoulder. "Perfect shot, eh, lad?"

Billy nodded ruefully, massaging his own chest. "Right through the heart."

CHAPTER THIRTY-ONE

♥

" 'The Cowboy and the Lady,' " Esmerelda's grandfather read, a sneer curling his thin lips.

Esmerelda choked in an effort not to spew a mouthful of her morning chocolate all over the back page of his newspaper. The gesture would have dismayed him deeply, since Potter had just presented him with his beloved *Morning Post*, still warm and crisp from its obligatory ironing.

As she dabbed at her lips with her linen napkin, her grandfather lowered the paper to give her a concerned look. "Are you quite all right, dear?"

She managed a wan smile. "I'm fine, Grandpapa. The chocolate's just a little bitter this morning."

Not nearly as bitter as the look she gave her aunt down the length of the dining room table as soon as her grandfather raised the paper. She hadn't spoken to Anne since last night's debacle, choosing to ride home alone in a hansom cab rather than endure the earl's wounded sniffs and the Belles' tittering inquisition. In response to Esmerelda's glower, Anne set down her own tea, her hand shaking so hard that the cup rattled violently against the saucer.

The duke snorted. "It seems some chit made quite a spectacle of herself last night in Drury Lane. Actually allowed herself to be dragged on stage. 'The Cowboy and the Lady' indeed! No *lady* would conduct herself in such a scandalous manner. She was probably some actress or prostitute masquerading as a lady."

"Reginald!" Anne nodded in Esmerelda's direction. "You mustn't use such language in front of the child."

Esmerelda pushed her plate of kippers and eggs away, losing what little appetite she had.

Her grandfather shook his shiny head. "I can't believe anyone would plunk down good coins to see a Wild West Extravaganza. It's a disgrace what they consider entertainment these days. If they're going to glorify those American savages, they might as well bring back some decent English sports like bearbaiting and cockfights." Despite his derision, his gaze eagerly leapt to the next column. "It seems they've christened this mysterious sharpshooter 'the Darling of London.' What do you think inspired them to come up with such a preposterous—"

Esmerelda upset her china cup, sending a river of luke-warm chocolate streaming into her grandfather's lap. She jumped to her feet with a piteous cry of dismay. Anne responded to her frantic cue by rushing around the table to her brother's side. Ignoring his napkin, she snatched up the newspaper and began to mop his lap with it.

"Leave me be, woman," he snapped, shoving Anne's fluttering hands away from him. "You're only making it worse."

"Oh, Grandpapa!" Esmerelda exclaimed, struggling to

blink up some contrite tears. "How could I have been so clumsy?"

As he gazed down at the sopping mess in his lap, his ears slowly darkened from pink to red. Esmerelda wouldn't have been surprised to see smoke come pouring out of them. He'd never once lost his legendary Wyndham temper with her, but when he lifted hands covered with sticky shreds of newsprint, she fully expected him to come lunging across the table to throttle her.

He managed to swallow back his rage, although his indulgent smile lacked its usual sparkle. "Not to worry, my dear. Even the most graceful of us are sometimes prone to blunders."

He rose, took up his cane, and gingerly shuffled across the dining room. He made it all the way to the door before throwing back his head and bellowing, "Potter!"

Esmerelda and Anne nearly jumped out of their guilty skins. As the sodden thud of his cane faded, they sank back into their chairs, dizzy with relief.

"Thank you," Esmerelda said stiffly.

Her aunt took a bracing gulp of her tea. "It was the least I could do."

"The very least," Esmerelda agreed, feeling less than charitable. "We may have diverted him from the society pages with their hints and innuendos, but how long is it going to be before someone tells him exactly who that *lady* and her *cowboy* were?"

Anne waved away her concerns. "Reginald is a very influential man. His circle of acquaintances have always lived in terror of his censure. No one will dare breathe a word of scandal about his beloved granddaughter in his presence."

"Perhaps not, but I'm sure they'll be more than delighted to whisper about her behind his back at the ball next week." Esmerelda rose to pace around the table. "How could you do it, Aunt Anne? Wasn't it enough that he broke my heart once? How could you bring him here to break it again?"

Anne cast her a beseeching glance. "When I wrote Sheriff McGuire and suggested he bring Mr. Darling here, I truly believed it was for the best. You were so very unhappy."

"Well, congratulations. Now I'm miserable."

Esmerelda sank into the chair next to her aunt and buried her head in her folded arms. Anne reached over and stroked her hair. Something about that awkward touch made Esmerelda remember Zoe Darling tying a faded ribbon in her hair. Made her remember how her own mother used to divide her unruly strands into neat braids before bedtime each night.

She lifted her head, seeing her aunt's kind, stern face through a veil of tears.

"I saw the way he was looking at you last night, Esmerelda. If a man had ever looked at me that way . . ." Anne's wistful sigh melted into a rueful laugh. "Well, I certainly wouldn't still be here, playing nursemaid to my overgrown child of a brother."

"He told me he never meant any of those unkind things he said. But how can I believe him? What if he's lying?"

"What if he's not?"

Utterly at a loss for an answer, Esmerelda rose and started for the door.

"Dear?"

She turned to find her aunt's face lined with concern.

"Isabelle D'Arcy told me St. Cyr may very well be planning to declare for you at the ball."

Esmerelda straightened her shoulders, using supreme effort to turn her self-pitying sniffle into a sniff of disdain.

"Perhaps I'll accept his suit. That would show the arrogant Mr. Darling that he can't just waltz back into my life and expect me to fall into his arms."

Esmerelda shuddered as she watched the earl of St. Cyr help himself to a fistful of shrimp balls from a footman's silver tray. Catching her appalled gaze from across the ballroom, he smirked and wiggled his greasy fingers at her. He took her grimace as a smile of invitation, but before he could cross the ballroom, he was mercifully distracted by the sight of another footman bearing a freshly laden tray. Licking his bulbous lips, he took off in pursuit.

Esmerelda ducked behind a marble column and adjusted her half mask, wishing the ivory silk and feather trifle provided more of a disguise. Although the masquerade ball was being given in her honor, she felt more like the hired entertainment than the hostess. The cream of London society undoubtedly found her predicament highly diverting.

As Anne had assured her, not even the most vicious gossip among them had dared to confront the duke about his granddaughter's scandalous behavior at the Wild West Extravaganza. But that hadn't stopped them from accenting their lavish ballgowns and elegant black evening dress with mocking reminders of her folly. In lieu of velvet and silk masks, some wore colorful bandannas in the dashing style of the Darling gang. Others wore masks of gingham and calico. One solemn fellow had even managed to scrounge up an entire Union uniform.

Her grandfather might be oblivious to their sly glances and coy asides, but Esmerelda was not. Although few of them deigned to address her directly, their discreet whispers and muffled laughter vied with the tinkling strains of the musicians.

Hoping to creep from column to column until she reached the French windows leading to the terrace, Esmerelda peeked around the pillar only to discover that a man had appropriated the next column. He stood with one ankle crossed over the other and one brawny shoulder braced against the marble column. The muted glow of the gasoliers burnished his hair to gold.

Unlike some of her wittier guests, he wore formal black evening dress and a stark black mask. His flawlessly cut trousers and the graceful flare of his tailcoat only emphasized the leanness of his hips. The dazzling white of his bow tie offset the sunhoneyed hue of his skin. A fluted glass of champagne dangled from his long fingers.

As he met her frustrated gaze, he lifted his glass in a silent toast.

Esmerelda had no desire to begin a flirtation with some randy young nobleman, no matter how unnervingly handsome. She leaned the other way just as Potter appeared in the vaulted doorway. She might have been alarmed by the butler's unhealthy pallor if she hadn't already suspected he slept in a coffin. Flaring his pinched nostrils, he announced another round of guests, his consumptive croak all but inaudible.

Groaning aloud, Esmerelda ducked behind the pillar. It was too late. She'd been spotted. The Belles came trotting across the parquet floor, the pitter-patter of their dainty slippers portending her doom.

"Why, Esmerelda, is that you?" trilled the boldest of them.

"No," she replied glumly.

They surrounded her anyway, their heart-shaped faces aglow with excitement.

Annabel (or was it Isabelle?) clasped her lily-white

hands beneath her pointed chin. "How incredibly brave of you to show your face in public after being so scandalously manhandled by that rogue."

"I, for one, nearly swooned when he swept you into his arms," chirped the shy little Belle named Belle. "We were all afraid he was going to carry you off and ravish you."

They bobbed their heads in eager agreement, sending their elaborate clusters of curls bouncing. Esmerelda could do nothing to stop the flush that crept into her cheeks.

Slyly noting her heightened color, Isabelle (or was it Annabel?) crooned, "Surely even a woman of your advanced age and limited prospects would be tempted to surrender her virtue to such a dashing villain."

Esmerelda couldn't bear another second of their smug pity. Leaning down until she stood nose to nose with the impertinent little vixen, she said, "I already have."

A chorus of gasps greeted her announcement. Leaving them aghast with shock, she gathered her skirts and marched away. Thinking only to escape to her bedroom or perhaps to the darkest reaches of Africa, she veered right to avoid her grandfather, then swerved left to evade St. Cyr.

And crashed right into the arms of the stranger who had sought refuge behind the other column, nearly knocking his glass of champagne out of his hand.

"Oh, I'm terribly sorry!" She dabbed at the damp spot on his crisp shirtfront with her handkerchief. "I don't know what possessed me to be so careless, sir. Please do forgive me." Genuinely embarrassed by her clumsiness, she glanced up into the eyes framed by the narrow slits of his mask.

Gray-green eyes fringed with thick gold lashes and sparkling with devilish merriment.

"I'll forgive you, honey," he drawled, capturing her hand and pressing it flat over his heart. "But only if you'll forgive me."

CHAPTER THIRTY-TWO

Billy's heart throbbed beneath her palm, much as it had that day in the jail when she'd believed him to be some demon or phantom out to steal her soul. Only it hadn't been her soul he'd ended up stealing, but her heart. As she gazed up into his dear, familiar face, she knew he still had the power to crush it with nothing more than a careless twitch of his fingers.

His appearance shouldn't have taken her breath away, but it did. He'd proved himself capable of such a transformation once before in Eulalie. His casual elegance made all the other men in the room look like graceless buffoons.

Painfully aware of the curious stares they were attracting, she snatched her hand out of his. "You, sir, were not invited to this ball."

He lifted his shoulders in a laconic shrug. "We Darlings don't get many invites to fancy shindigs such as this.

But that never stops us from making ourselves right at home."

"Darlings?" she echoed, her horror mounting. "Darlings? Surely you didn't dare . . ." A desperate glance around the ballroom proved that indeed he had.

The entire Darling gang was in attendance, all attired in elegant black masks and formal evening dress. Jasper leaned against the mantel, looking nearly as striking as Billy. Despite his jaded sneer, the Belles had already began to bat their eyelashes in his direction. Enos lurked shyly behind a bronze bust of William the Conqueror, while Sam fidgeted nervously with his hair, trying in vain to drag a lock of it over his absent ear. Virgil was nowhere in sight, but Esmerelda could hear his voice drowning out the valiant efforts of the musicians.

She might have suspected her aunt of inviting the lot of them if she hadn't spotted Anne in the corner, arguing frantically with a man in a white mask. His flowing silver hair just brushed his shoulders, and the tips of his drooping mustache had been waxed to perfection.

Esmerelda's panic grew when she remembered the guest in the Union uniform. She sighed with relief when she glimpsed his dark blue back retreating from the room. The last thing she needed was a war on her hands.

Another war, she amended, meeting Billy's challenging gaze with one of her own. "You can make yourself at home if you like, Mr. Darling, but that doesn't make you welcome."

"I remember a time when you welcomed me, Miss Fine. Into your heart. Into your arms." He leaned down, making sure his next words would be heard only by her. "Into your bed."

Her skin prickled with desire at the husky reminder. Before she could recover her composure, her grandfather materialized out of the crowd. Esmerelda nearly panicked, but the duke gave Billy a look that was more cursory than curious. She'd forgotten that he was doing an impressive imitation of an aristocratic gentleman.

"There you are, my dear!" her grandfather exclaimed, blinking behind his brown velvet mask trimmed in owl feathers. "I've been looking everywhere for you. I was hoping we could have our guests adjourn to the music room for a brief interlude before the dancing begins."

Esmerelda's hands were trembling too violently to hold a champagne glass, much less a violin bow. "Oh, no, Grand-papa. I don't think that would be a very good idea."

"Why, I think it's a capital idea," Billy said, his drawl sharpening to a clipped English accent.

The duke looked him up and down. "I don't believe I've had the pleasure, sir."

Before Billy could point out that the pleasure had been all hers, Esmerelda grabbed her grandfather by the elbow and steered him away with such haste he nearly dropped his cane. "Nor should you right now. There will be ample time for introductions later. *After* I play."

Although her sweet smile remained fixed on her lips, she cast Billy a look promising revenge over her shoulder.

At her grandfather's urging, their guests eagerly crowded into the music room. Esmerelda supposed some of them were secretly hoping for a performance as riveting as the one she'd given on Drury Lane. The Darling gang lined the right wall. Enos, Sam, and Virgil were beaming with excitement, and even Jasper's sneer was softened by a hint of anticipation. Andrew McGuire soon joined them, followed by a scowling Anne.

Billy leaned against the mantel of Venetian marble, his arms folded across his chest and a mocking smile playing around his lips.

Esmerelda reached for the Stradivarius propped against the music stand, but some sentimental urge compelled her to choose her mother's violin instead. While she was tuning the instrument and searching her beleaguered brain for a piece to play, the man in the Union uniform slipped into the room.

Knowing her avid audience would strain to hear every word uttered by the duke of Wyndham's eccentric granddaughter, Esmerelda said softly, "Since everyone seems to be buzzing with talk of the American West tonight, I'd like to honor that fair young nation and its courageous countrymen with one of their most beloved songs."

Tucking the violin beneath her chin, she gave Billy a smile so tender it earned him several fascinated stares. Then, without further ado, she launched into a rousing rendition of "The Battle Hymn of the Republic."

Billy's grin faded. His eyes narrowed.

Jasper reached for a gun he wasn't wearing. Virgil lunged toward her, forcing Sam and Enos to jerk themselves out of their own horrified stupors to hold him back. The man in the Union uniform stood stiffly at attention until she had played the last majestic note.

Her captive audience burst into applause, making her grandfather beam with pride. Deliberately avoiding Billy's gaze, Esmerelda took a bow. When the cries of "Bravo!" and "More, more!" showed no signs of diminishing, she started for the grand piano.

Halfway there, she turned back. The applause faded to rapt silence. "Since you've been such a gracious audience, I believe I'd like to favor you with a vocal selection."

Drew winced and Billy's eyes widened in alarm. Clasping her hands demurely beneath her breasts, Esmerelda drew in a deep breath and began to sing "Dixie."

Since the first few notes were so shrill as to be unrecognizable, she made it all the way to the second verse before Virgil broke free of Sam and Enos. This time it took all four of his brothers and Drew to restrain him. Billy clamped a hand over his mouth to muffle his roar of outrage.

When Esmerelda finished, her last note hanging in the air like the sound a cat makes when someone steps on its tail, there was only appalled silence and a smattering of strained applause.

Her white-faced grandfather swallowed hard before producing a doting smile. "That was lovely, my dear, but perhaps I should go signal the musicians to begin the dancing."

His hurried departure started an exodus toward the gilded doors. Leaving Virgil to his brothers, Billy strode toward Esmerelda, looking as mean and dangerous as she'd ever seen him.

Murmuring her apologies, she shoved her way through the crush, desperate to escape him. She glanced over her shoulder to find him closing on her with Drew right at his heels.

She never thought she'd be happy to see the earl of St. Cyr, but his sudden appearance sent her into an ecstasy of relief.

She latched onto his elbow, nearly dislodging the platter of hors d'oeuvres tucked in the crook of his arm. "Why, there you are, *darling*," she sang out with deliberate malice. "I hope you don't think I've been ignoring you."

He mumbled something unintelligible, his mouth full.

Still clutching his arm, she swung around to face Billy and Drew. "You'll have to excuse me, gentlemen. I've been remiss. Please allow me to introduce you to the earl of St. Cyr—my fiancé."

St. Cyr choked on whatever he'd been trying to swallow, turning scarlet. His violent coughing caused one of the brass buttons on the waistcoat stretched taut over his enormous belly to pop off and bounce across the room.

Billy arched an incredulous eyebrow. "*That's* the earl of St. Cyr?"

Drew shrugged sheepishly. "I told you he was a man of notorious appetites."

The musicians in the next room struck up a waltz. Billy grabbed Esmerelda by the hand. "Since Earl here will have the rest of his life to enjoy the pleasure of your company," he said wryly, "I'm sure he won't mind if I borrow you for one dance."

"He might not mind, but I do," Esmerelda retorted, stumbling after him.

Her protests were in vain. Billy had already swept her into the whirling throng of dancers. The music soared in a majestic counterpart to his fleet grace. His hand rested warm and low on her back, urging her nearer to him with each dizzying twirl around the parquet floor. As Esmerelda met his bold gaze, she could almost allow herself to believe that he was her cowboy and she was his lady.

To distract herself from the sheer bliss of being in his arms again, she slanted him a suspicious look. "You dance very well for a bounty hunter, Mr. Darling."

He smiled down at her, warming her to the tips of her toes. "Every self-respecting Missouri boy knows the Tennessee waltz."

As if to prove his point, Jasper went gliding by with one of the besotted Belles in his arms.

"We're beginning to attract notice, you know," she pointed out, surprised to realize that she no longer cared.

He leaned down and murmured, "Given that you're a woman of advanced age and limited prospects, they're probably wondering if I'm going to carry you off and ravish you."

"Are you?" she dared to ask.

In answer, he waltzed her right out the French windows onto the terrace.

The music faded to a ghostly echo, poignant and sweet. Still holding her in his arms, Billy reached up and untied the ribbons of her mask, exposing her face to the moonlight. Unable to bear his tender scrutiny, Esmerelda turned her back on him.

She chafed her naked arms. The winter chill was a cruel contrast to the cozy heat of Billy's body.

He dropped his coat over her shoulders, but did her the courtesy of not touching her. "I forgave you for spilling my champagne," he said lightly. "Can't you find it in your heart to forgive me for the things I said?"

She drifted toward the terrace wall, hoping the shadows would hide the crimson staining her cheeks. "It wasn't what you said that I can't forgive. It's what you did." She softened her voice until it was barely a whisper. "Or didn't do."

"You're still mad because I turned down your grandpa's offer to marry you, aren't you?"

She whirled around, allowing all the bitterness she'd hoarded since they'd parted to spill into her voice. "Why should you have married me when you made sure there would be no need of it? And I was too stupid to realize what you were doing. God, how pathetic you must have found me!"

Billy shook his head. "I never thought you were stupid. Or pathetic. I thought you were innocent."

"So innocent I couldn't tell when a man was trifling with my affections. So innocent I believed you when you said you loved me and wanted to marry me. So innocent I didn't realize there were ways a man could enjoy a woman's *company* without risking his freedom."

"Is that what you believe?" he asked hoarsely. "That I didn't get you with child that night because I intended all along to abandon you the next morning?"

"Since that's exactly what you did, what else am I to believe?"

Billy paced the length of the terrace before jerking off his mask and running a hand through his hair. When he swung around, his face was an agonized mirror of her own. "I knew I could make you want me, honey. But I wasn't sure I could make you love me. You might have wanted to spend the night with a Darling, but spending your life with one was another proposition altogether." He spread his arms, his rumpled hair and desperate expression only making his immaculate clothes look more striking. "I can dress up in fancy clothes and talk like a gentleman, but that still doesn't make me one."

He moved toward her, shaking his head in helpless wonder. "And look at you, Duchess—a lady to the bone— so fine and sweet it takes my breath away." He reached down and gently cupped her belly in his palm, his expression both fierce and tender. "Nothing would make me prouder than to watch that beautiful body of yours swell with my child."

Billy's frank confession and intimate touch thawed the icy lump in Esmerelda's throat. A single tear went tumbling from her lashes, then another.

Without bothering to brush them away, she stroked his jaw with her fingertips. "You forgot to take one thing into account, Mr. Darling." At his questioning glance, she whispered, "I already loved you."

Her mouth melted against his in a seeking caress. He wrapped his arms around her and lifted her clear off her feet, squeezing her as if he would never let her go.

"I never wanted a gentleman," she murmured, kissing his throat, his cheek, his lips. "I wanted a man. I wanted you."

This time when Billy took her by the hand and led her deeper into the garden, Esmerelda followed without protest. They ducked into the first gazebo they found.

"Oh, excuse me," Billy muttered, rapidly backing up.

Esmerelda peeped around his shoulder only to find another couple locked in a torrid kiss. Moonlight spilled through the latticed walls, frosting their hair with silver.

"Aunt Anne!" she breathed, both scandalized and delighted.

Her aunt immediately gave Andrew McGuire's broad shoulders a halfhearted shove. "Unhand me, you knave! How dare you take such liberties!"

Billy chuckled. "Don't let us disturb you, Drew. I believe the lady's about to give you a tongue-lashing you'll never forget."

He beat a hasty retreat with Esmerelda trotting along behind him, still gaping over her shoulder. He didn't pause again until a dead branch cracked behind them.

A troubled expression crossed his face.

"What is it?" Esmerelda whispered, edging nearer to him. "Is someone following us?"

He rubbed the back of his neck. "I don't think so. It's just a feeling I've had more than once lately."

Shaking it off, he cupped her waist in his hands and set her atop a low stone wall opposite a towering evergreen hedge. The hedge provided privacy, while the wall provided the perfect excuse for Esmerelda to wrap both her arms and her legs around him.

He began to bunch up her skirt, determination glinting in his eyes.

"Why, Mr. Darling, whatever are you doing?"

"I'm going to get you with child. Then I'll demand that your grandfather make you do right by me."

Biting back a delighted grin, she said, "Surely even a scoundrel like you wouldn't sink so low!"

"I'm a Darling, Miss Fine. I'll sink as low as I have to."

With that wicked promise, he slid his hands beneath her skirt, cupped her rump through her thin silk drawers, and dragged her against him for a hot, delicious mingling of tongues.

They were still locked in that rather compromising embrace when her grandfather came charging through the hedge, clutching Samuel Darling by his one good ear.

CHAPTER THIRTY-THREE

♥
───────

Esmerelda sprang off the wall, but Billy kept his arms curved protectively around her as they turned to face her grandfather together.

The duke's cane was nowhere in sight. Two winded footmen came stumbling through the hedge after him. Their eyes bulged as they saw their master's beloved grand-daughter in a stranger's arms. "Turn around," the duke barked.

Sam tried to oblige him, but only succeeded in nearly twisting off his ear.

"Not you! Them!"

The footmen did an abrupt about-face, the old-fashioned periwigs the duke insisted they wear quivering in alarm.

"You're dismissed," he commanded.

As they ducked back through the hedge, exchanging a relieved glance, Anne came racing down the path. Her chignon was hanging half over her eyes, and the hooks of her bodice looked curiously off-kilter.

She skidded to an abrupt halt on the gravel path. "For heaven's sake, Reginald, what was all that commotion about?"

The duke gave Sam a spiteful shake before freeing his ear. "I saw this ruffian sneaking out the dining room window, so I lit out in pursuit. I caught him with *this*." He wrested the grubby sack from Sam's hand and turned it upside down.

A shimmering stream of silverware, jewelry, and candlesticks came spilling out on the grass.

"Why, Samuel Darling," Esmerelda exclaimed, "what would your ma say?"

Sam hung his head in shame.

"The other young scamp got away," her grandfather informed them.

"Enos," she whispered. Billy nodded, rolling his eyes.

He stood tall and straight in the moonlight, unmasked and exposed to her grandfather's chilly regard.

"So we meet again, Mr. Darling. I suppose it wasn't enough for you to rob my granddaughter of her precious virtue. You had to bring your kinfolk all the way to England to rob my home as well."

"It was never my intention to rob your granddaughter of anything. I loved her then and I love her now."

The duke snorted. "You loved her so well that you used her, then cast her aside like some worn-out pair of boots."

"I let her go because I thought it would be best for her, but I won't make the same mistake again. I may not be the sort of man you would have chosen for your granddaughter, but I can promise you that no man will ever love her like I do. I intend to have her, sir. With or without your blessing."

Esmerelda's heart swelled with pride. The duke went purple and began to sputter.

Billy took her by the shoulders, gazing tenderly down into her face. "I'm going to go now, sweetheart, because I don't want your grandfather to have a stroke. Tomorrow is my last night in London. If you still want to be my wife, you know where to find me."

He kissed her then, a kiss that was brief and hard and sweet. As he strode away down the path, Sam trailed after him, massaging his ear.

Although her grandfather hadn't even been out of breath when he'd come charging through that hedge, he sagged against the stone wall as if barely able to stand.

Esmerelda reached for his shoulder. "Grandpapa, please . . ."

He shrugged off her touch, refusing to look at her. "Leave me, you faithless child. You're no different from your mother."

Esmerelda stood there for a long time until Anne gently put her arm around her shoulders and led her away.

Esmerelda walked the long, lonely corridors of Wyndham Manor for the last time. She'd left her lavish carriage dresses and traveling gowns hanging in her armoire, choosing instead the simple walking suit she'd been wearing on the day she climbed down from that stagecoach in Calamity.

She carried only her old battered trunk and her mother's violin case. She regretted leaving the Stradivarius behind, not because of its worth, but because of the look on her grandfather's face when he had toasted her for

bringing music back into his home and heart. She hated
the thought of it sitting silent and forlorn in the abandoned music room.

The soles of her kid boots whispered across the marble-
tiled foyer. Although the hall should have been bustling with
maids and footmen this late in the afternoon, there wasn't a
servant in sight.

As Esmerelda faced the towering teak doors that guarded
her grandfather's smoking room, she almost envied her
mother for creeping away to join the man she loved in the
dark of night.

Taking a deep breath, she eased open one of the doors.
The thick velvet drapes were drawn, and it took her eyes a
moment to adjust to the palm-shrouded gloom. Her aunt
sat stiffly in a straight-backed chair, poking an embroidery
needle through a linen handkerchief with exacting precision. As Esmerelda rested her trunk and violin case on the
floor, Anne gave her a wan but heartening smile.

Her grandfather was huddled in front of the fire in an
iron wheelchair. Despite the suffocating warmth, a woolen
lap robe was draped across his knees. Although Esmerelda
had never known him to smoke, he wore a Persian smoking cap and brown velvet smoking jacket. His shoulders
were hunched and his hands curled loosely on his knees.
He looked small and shrunken and older than she could
have ever imagined him looking.

An open rosewood coffer rested on his lap. Tucked
within its velvet lining was a bundle of yellowing letters,
painstakingly bound in a frayed ribbon she suspected
had once belonged to her mother. It took little effort for
Esmerelda to recognize her own precise handwriting.

Tears stung her eyes as she felt the pity he must have
wanted her to feel, but she struggled to blink them back.

Pity could not make her stay. Not when Billy was waiting for her at that theater in Drury Lane.

She moved to stand in front of her grandfather, but he continued to stare into the dancing flames, his bitter gaze unfocused.

"Last night you accused me of being no different from my mother," she said. "And I suppose you were right. She was willing to sacrifice everything she held dear to be with the man she loved, including the approval of the father she adored."

She drew Lisbeth's locket over her head and pressed it into his hand. As she gently folded his liver-spotted fingers around it, she leaned down and whispered, "Mama loved you until the day she died. So will I."

Esmerelda pressed a kiss to her aunt's paper-soft cheek, retrieved her trunk and violin case, then slipped quietly from the room. Her spirits lifted and her steps quickened with anticipation as she crossed the foyer.

When her niece's footsteps had faded, Anne laid aside her embroidery and stood.

She drew in a steadying breath before facing the brother who had been the only man in her life since the day she was born. "If you want to spend the rest of your life in that wheelchair nursing your shattered ego, Reggie, then you go right ahead. But I won't be here to pamper you. I'm not content to spend my waning years collecting cobwebs in my hair and babying a boy who should have grown into a man a long time ago."

Reginald roused himself from his lethargy to give her a shrewd look. "Wyndham Manor is the only home you've ever known, woman. Where do you think you'll go?"

She lifted her chin, her eyes shining with determination.

"Wherever Sheriff Andrew McGuire goes. If he'll have me, that is."

"And what if he doesn't want a sharp-tongued, peppery old wench like you?"

She pondered that question for a moment before smiling brightly. "Then I'll just go right back to Calamity, New Mexico, and marry one of those charming young cowboys or that nice Mr. Stumpelmeyer. They have their needs, and so do I."

Feeling younger than she had in years, Anne marched from the room, slamming the door behind her. She made it halfway across the foyer before an outraged bellow shattered the funereal silence. She hesitated, then kept walking. The bellow escalated to a howling whine, shrill and savage.

Curious faces began to peep out of doorways. The mob-capped heads of two of the parlormaids emerged through the banisters on the second-floor balcony. Old Brigit even doddered out of the dining room, although she was rumored not to have left the basement kitchen in over a decade.

Anne locked her gaze on the front door and kept walking. She was not about to let one of her brother's tantrums spoil what might very well be her last chance for happiness.

The howls disintegrated to a strangled gurgle. Abrupt silence followed.

Anne stopped, a scant three paces from the door. "Damn him to hell," she muttered, meeting an underfootman's appalled gaze without a shred of remorse.

She whirled around and marched right back across the foyer. She flung open both doors at once and stormed into the smoking room, fully prepared to show her brother what a real Wyndham tantrum looked like. Her mouth fell open.

Reginald stood in front of the wheelchair, his back

straight and the ball of his cane gripped in his white-knuckled hand. His face was ruddy with good health or bad temper, or what she suspected was a combination of both.

"Don't just stand their gawking like a beached fish, woman!" he shouted, banging the brass tip of his cane on the floor. "Have the carriage brought around immediately! My granddaughter needs me!"

CHAPTER THIRTY-FOUR

♥

Esmerelda leaned forward on the cracked leather seat of the hansom cab, as if she could somehow urge the horses drawing it to plod harder through the sea of mud. She checked the gold-plated watch pinned to her bodice for the sixth time. The minute hand seemed to be racing around its ivory face at an alarming pace.

She poked her head out the window, blinking against the mist of fine rain. "Can't you go any faster, sir? I'm late for an appointment." The most important appointment of her life.

The cockney driver swiveled around on his seat, rain dripping from the brim of his stovepipe hat. "Not unless ye want to get out and push, mum. This rain's made a fine mess o' things."

Blowing out a frustrated sigh, she ducked back into the cab, narrowly missing being drenched by a filthy stream of water that shot up from beneath the wheels of a passing ale wagon drawn by a team of Clydesdales.

Darkness had already fallen over the London streets. The newly installed electric street lamps did little to relieve the gloom. At this rate, she'd be lucky to reach the theater before Billy took his final bow.

She was heartened when they finally reached the mouth of Drury Lane, but her relief was short-lived. The cab lurched to a halt, its path blocked by the ale wagon—now overturned—that had gone rocking past them only minutes before. Broken barrels littered the street, spilling their amber wealth into the overflowing gutters. Shadowy figures materialized out of the alleys to press their greedy mouths to the split seams. Freed from their shattered shafts, the Clydesdales placidly watched their driver stomp around his fallen chariot, bellowing curses that would make a sailor blush.

The carriages soon began to pile up behind them, their drivers and footmen adding their own shouts and oaths to the fray. Not wanting Billy to suffer even a moment believing she wasn't going to come, Esmerelda threw open the door of the cab and jumped into the street, wincing when her boots sank ankle-deep in the mud.

"'Ey, mum! Wot about m' fare?"

She fumbled in her reticule, finally pressing everything she had into the driver's grubby white glove in her haste to be done with him. "Please deliver my trunk and violin case to the theater as soon as the road is cleared."

"Aye, mum," he said, tipping his hat to her with a reverent grin.

Then, lifting the hem of her skirts out of the goop, she began to run as if her very life depended on it.

Andrew McGuire was in love.

He slipped into his satin waistcoat, admiring its flattering fit in the backstage mirror. He'd always had a vain streak, but he'd never before had anyone to posture and preen for but the mirror.

Now he had Anne.

Anne.

He shook his head, still finding it hard to believe that such a simple name could have the ring of music about it. The emotion that warmed his heart was nothing like the feverish infatuations he'd nursed for countless saloon girls and dance-hall singers throughout the years. Their smooth white skin and plump, petulant faces were already fading in his memory. His Anne had been aged like fine wine, and that only made her all the more delicious to him.

He shrugged into his handsome white coat. Perhaps she had been the reason for his lifelong restlessness and stubborn refusal to marry. Like old Granny Shively, he'd just been waiting for the right person to come along. It was just a damn shame it had taken her fifty-nine years to do so.

But perhaps it was the waiting that had driven him to watch his back and stay alive all those years. He'd survived two wars, twenty-five years as a Texas ranger, and thirteen years as sheriff of Calamity only to finally find someone worth living for.

He buckled on his gunbelt, then pinned the gaudy tin star to his lapel, buffing it to a dazzling shine with the sleeve of his coat. He could already hear the applause of the audience soaring in anticipation of the showdown between the outlaw and the sheriff. His and Billy's nightly shootouts had quickly become one of the highlights of the show.

He regretted that tonight was to be their last performance in London, but he'd already booked engagements in Boston and Philadelphia. A smile touched his lips. After tonight's show, he planned to ride straight over to Wyndham Manor to find out if a certain starchy spinster had ever considered honeymooning in Boston.

He reached for his pistol, prepared to load it with blank shells and slide it into his tooled leather holster. His hand encountered only empty air.

He frowned down at the table. That was peculiar. Love must be making him daft. He would have sworn he'd left it on the . . .

The butt of the pistol came crashing down on the back of his head, sending him reeling to the floor.

Esmerelda shoved her way through the throng of cowboys and settlers milling around behind the canvas backdrop of Calamity's only street, pausing only long enough to give a squirming Sadie a pat on the head. She had to step gingerly over the show's industrious Indian, who had collapsed from exhaustion as soon as he raced offstage.

Virgil was stomping around in boots, bonnet, and dress, bellowing orders at the top of his lungs when he spotted her.

"Howdy, honey," he roared, sweeping her into a rib-crunching bear hug. "I sure hope you ain't here to sing." The twinkle in his eye assured her that he'd already forgiven her for massacring "Dixie" at the ball.

"Oh, I ain't—" She shook her head to clear it. "I'm *not* here to sing. I'm here to find Billy."

Virgil shook his head. "You're too late, sweetheart." For one horrible second, Esmerelda thought he meant the worst. Then he nodded toward the curtain. "He's already out there waitin' to go on."

The audience's applause had faded to expectant silence.

Esmerelda drifted toward the curtain, drawn by the same crackling aura of anticipation that held them in thrall.

She peeped through the narrow slit cut in the canvas of the saloon's painted door. A lone circle of light had already brightened the darkness on the right side of the arena. She shuffled sideways for a better view, only to bump into the silver tea cart Billy would be using for his sharpshooting demonstration. An impish grin curved her lips. Now wouldn't Mr. Darling be oh-so-surprised when she was the one to come strolling out with the cart?

She thumbed rapidly through the cards until she found the queen of hearts and placed it on top of the deck. She would hold it between her teeth to prove her trust in him if need be.

Billy stepped into that halo of light. Her heart swelled with pride. He might play the bad man for the pleasure of the crowd, but she knew beneath that sinister exterior beat the heart of a man as fine and decent as any she could ever hope to love.

Just as before, she was too enchanted by the sight of him to notice the man in white who appeared at the opposite end of the mock street.

"Throw down your gun, outlaw. I'm the law in this town, and we don't take to your kind here."

Esmerelda whipped her head around. That clipped snarl sounded nothing like Drew's rolling burr. The wide brim of the sheriff's hat shadowed his features.

Billy hesitated, shading his eyes against the glare of the arc lamps. "Haven't you heard, sheriff?" he said warily. "I never draw my gun unless I plan to use it."

The man let out a nasty bark of laughter. "Oh, I've heard plenty about you, Darling. I've heard that you betray the men who hire you. That you spend the gold they entrust you with on your pretty little whore. That you ruin the careers of decent, law-abiding men to further your own."

A river of ice poured down Esmerelda's spine as she realized she was about to make the acquaintance of Mr. Thaddeus Winstead, U.S. marshal.

CHAPTER THIRTY-FIVE

♥
_____

Billy's fingers twitched instinctively over the butt of his pistol, making Esmerelda shiver with dread. His pistol was loaded with nothing but harmless blanks, while Winstead's could only contain live shells.

Billy took a step backward, revealing the precise moment he realized that same inescapable truth.

"Why don't you run?" Winstead taunted. "I have no compunctions about shooting a yellow-bellied traitor in the back. I licked you white-trash southern boys once and I'll do it again."

"Oh, yeah," Billy drawled. "You and what Union army?"

Esmerelda clapped a hand over her mouth, remembering the Union "soldier" at the masquerade ball. Dear God, Winstead must have been tracking Billy even then.

As Billy continued to back slowly down the street, the

crowd leaned forward in their seats, believing the unfolding drama was all part of the show.

Esmerelda looked frantically around. She couldn't just stand by and let Billy be gunned down in cold blood. Virgil and Jasper were nowhere in sight, so she snatched up the loaded Colt .45 from the tea cart. But she was no Billy Darling. Her hands were shaking so hard she doubted she could hit the side of an elephant at point-blank range.

Winstead's hands flexed over his gunbelt. Billy took another step backward, but he was utterly defenseless—a helpless target for a vengeful madman.

Esmerelda grabbed a handful of dimes in her other hand and raced into the mock street.

Billy's name tore from her throat in a raw scream as she cast the dimes heavenward like a fistful of shimmering prayers. Distracted by their glitter, Winstead took his eyes off of Billy for a heartbeat.

That was all the time Esmerelda needed. She tossed the loaded gun at Billy. He caught it, cocked it, and fired, all in one smooth motion.

It was a clean shot. Right through Winstead's thigh. He collapsed, clutching his leg and howling in pain.

The audience surged to their feet, applauding wildly and screaming for an encore. Virgil and Jasper came sprinting across the arena toward Winstead. They never had been able to tolerate anybody but them bullying their little brother.

Esmerelda never stopped running. She ran right into Billy's outstretched arms. As he swept her up in his embrace, she buried her face in his sweat-dampened throat.

"You foolish, foolish girl," he scolded, giving her a half-hearted shake even as he devoured her face with his lips. "What would you have done if he'd have fired at you?"

"Ducked?" she ventured before pressing her mouth to his for a fierce kiss.

They were still kissing when Drew came stumbling into the spotlight, gripping his head and wearing nothing but a pair of immaculately starched drawers.

"Damn, that sun is bright," he muttered, sinking to his knees.

Esmerelda was shocked to see Anne come flying past them. Her aunt sank down beside Drew and gently cradled his head to her bosom, crooning in dismay.

"Don't fret, lass," he said, blinking up at her as if she were his guardian angel. "He didn't hit me nearly as hard as you did."

Esmerelda didn't even realize that it wasn't Billy but her grandfather stroking her hair until he murmured, "What a brave girl. What a smart girl. You do an old man proud."

She turned her head to give him a look that was both hopeful and disbelieving. "I make you proud?" She nodded toward the tiers of benches, where people were beginning to point and nod and whisper behind their cupped hands as they realized they'd been witness to a genuine drama instead of a contrived one. "Even after causing such a scandal?"

Her grandfather beamed at her, his ruddy face aglow. "*Especially* after causing such a scandal."

As she pressed a kiss to his bald pate, three men detached themselves from the crowd. Two wore Stetson hats and the badges of U.S. marshals while the other rather nondescript young man sported a felt bowler.

"Elliot Courtney!" Billy exclaimed, keeping his arm looped around Esmerelda's waist. "What in the hell are you doing in London?"

"Tracking Thaddeus Winstead," Courtney admitted ruefully, "with the help of Scotland Yard."

"Well, there he is," Billy said, pointing unnecessarily to the figure writhing in the hay at the far end of the street. Virgil was in the process of applying a tourniquet to his leg. Esmerelda figured he ought to be thankful it wasn't his neck.

"Yes, we gathered that was him," the Scotland Yard detective said dryly. "It's Mr. Courtney's belief that the man may have boarded your steamer in New York under an alias."

Billy rubbed the back of his neck. "One of these days I'm going to learn to pay more attention to that feeling."

"It seems you've earned the bounty on his worthless hide yourself," Courtney said. "We've also been authorized to inform you that the judge has granted you full amnesty. You're no longer a wanted man."

"Oh, yes, he is," Esmerelda said, refusing to loosen her own possessive grip on Billy's waist.

Courtney exchanged a glance with his deputy before drawing something out of the pocket of his vest. It was another badge, just as shiny and official-looking as his. "The U.S. Treasury Department has also recommended that you be offered a job as a U.S. marshal. So what do you say, Darling? You're just the kind of man we need."

Esmerelda held her breath. She could never deny Billy his dream, not even if she needed him more than they did.

Billy glanced at Anne and Drew, who were still gazing into each other's eyes with starry-eyed devotion. "I'm afraid I'm going to have to turn down your offer, gentlemen. There's this little town in New Mexico that I hear tell has need of a sheriff. They say it's a good place to raise a family." He winked at Esmerelda. "At least if I have a passel of daughters, they'll never lack for suitors."

Esmerelda blinked back tears of joy. "If that's a proposal, Mr. Darling, then I accept."

He scowled at her. "Who said anything about marrying *you*? I got my heart set on this pretty little cousin of mine back in Missouri. She'll make me a fine wife once she turns thirteen next year."

Esmerelda's mouth flew open. She stamped her foot and pointed an accusing finger at Billy. "Grandpapa, this man compromised me! I insist that you force him to marry me. At once."

Her grandfather drew himself up to his most regal height. "You heard the girl, Darling. You can either choose your weapon and step outside in the street with me or you can marry my granddaughter." He leaned forward to confide, "And I should warn you, son, that I was a wicked shot in my day."

"Well, sir," Billy looked Esmerelda up and down, heat simmering in his eyes, "if you insist."

Esmerelda bounded back into his arms, squealing with triumph. "But I don't understand," she told him. "I thought being a U.S. marshal was your heart's desire."

He gave her a lazy smile that she felt all the way to her toes. "It was. Until the day you came marching into that saloon."

As their lips brushed and lingered, Sadie came loping out to run in circles around them, woofing merrily. A group of eager reporters from the *Times* and the *Morning Post* clustered around them as well, pads and pencils at the ready.

"Is it true," one of them shouted, "that tonight was your last night to be toasted as the 'Darling of London'?"

Before Billy could reply, Esmerelda cupped his face between her hands. Although she addressed the reporter, her tender gaze was for Billy alone. "That's right, sir. Because after tonight, he's nobody's darling but mine."

EPILOGUE

♥
———————————————————

Calamity, New Mexico, 1998

Esme Darling ventured deeper into the shadowy lair of the attic, shuddering when a low-hanging spiderweb tickled her face. She swept the beam of her standard issue Maglite across the floor, praying she hadn't just seen something scuttle out of her field of vision. She'd never much cared for prey she couldn't handcuff or read its rights.

She'd just about steadied her nerves when a strong, masculine arm snaked around her waist. She might have panicked if she hadn't sucked in an enticing whiff of aftershave along with enough breath to scream.

"Jesus, Dix, I could have shot you," she wailed, twisting around to smack the smirking detective on the upper arm. Even in her agitation, she couldn't fail to appreciate the impressive bulge of bicep encountered by her palm.

"No, you couldn't," he said, holding up the pistol he'd

confiscated from her holster prior to grabbing her. His chocolate brown eyes sparkled with mischief.

Scowling, she retrieved her gun. "I'll only forgive you for scaring me half to death if you'll teach me that move later."

He swept her into his arms for a playful kiss. "I'll teach you any move you want to know. I never could resist a woman in uniform. Especially that cotton and polyester blend they make you rookies wear." He frowned down at her. "The boys down at the precinct told me you had nerves of steel. So why are you so jumpy?"

She plucked a cobweb from his thick, dark hair. "Because I don't like attics. Or spiders. Or smart-ass detectives who sneak up on you in the dark."

"Then what are you doing up here? Isn't it bad enough that you have to pull evening shift on Thanksgiving without you ducking out of dinner before your grandpa can cut the pumpkin pie?"

She made a face. "I hate pumpkin pie. You know perfectly well the only kind of pie I'll eat is peach."

"How could I forget? The first time I saw you, you were snout-first into a fresh-baked one at the department picnic. When I reached for that last piece, I thought you were going to take off a couple of my fingers."

She brought his thumb to her lips for a teasing nip. "I still might."

"Promises, promises," he murmured.

She twined her fingers through his and led him through the cluttered maze of mislabeled boxes, outdated appliances, and abandoned toys. His height forced him to duck under some of the lower beams.

"You arrived just in time, Detective. I was about to do some sleuthing of my own. You can't inherit a name like Esmerelda Darling and not be just a little curious about your ancestors." She smiled wryly. "Especially not ancestors as colorful as mine."

"Oh, come on. According to your grandmother, every Darling since the beginning of time has been born to the badge. When Adam and Eve got kicked out of Eden, one of your ancestors was probably waiting outside to arrest them for destroying public property."

Esme snorted. "Grandma Anne is a bit of a revisionist when it comes to family history. I bet she didn't tell you this house was once a brothel or that this attic was the very room where my great-great grandmother lost her virginity to that notoriously wicked outlaw, Billy Darling."

His eyebrows shot up. "Your grandmother was a hooker?"

"Of course not. Billy Darling ended up being my grandfather. We Darlings don't have skeletons in our closet. We have gunslingers." She spun around to flutter her eyelashes at him. "I should warn you, sir, that the women in my family have always had a weakness for outlaws."

Dix immediately turned serious. "Did I ever tell you about my time in prison?"

She squinted up at him. "You're pulling my leg. Felons aren't eligible for the police academy."

"I never said I was a felon. I egged the mayor's house on Halloween when I was thirteen and spent three hours in the county lockup."

"Oooooh," she crooned, pursing her lips in an inviting pout. "You were a *very* bad boy. I may just have to take you in."

Growling beneath his breath, Dix leaned forward. Before their lips could touch, Esme whirled around and scampered deeper into the attic. She might have enjoyed the last laugh if her flashlight hadn't chosen that moment to flicker and go out.

"Dix?" she whispered on a quavering note.

"I'm right here, sweetheart," he replied, the touch of his hand on her shoulder calming her fears.

Frowning, Esme tapped the Maglite against her thigh. "That's weird. I've never had it do that before."

"Hang on just a sec."

Hunching his broad shoulders to squeeze them beneath the eaves, Dix tore one of the rotting slats off the window, letting in a golden stream of sunshine.

Crouched in the farthest reaches of the attic was a lone leather trunk. With the dust motes drifting around it in a sparkling cascade, there was something almost magical about the sight. Esme's breath caught in childlike wonder.

She sank down cross-legged on the floor in front of the trunk, so enchanted by her discovery that she forgot all about the dust and the spiders and the occasional squeak coming from the corners. Dix squatted behind her, peering over her shoulder.

As she reached to lift the lid, she was surprised to realize her hands, legendary around the precinct for their steadiness, were trembling.

A crumpled gown, carefully folded, but poorly preserved, was the first thing she saw.

"A wedding dress," she whispered, stroking the fragile fabric.

The ivory silk shattered at her touch, but the veil was still strong enough to endure being picked up and gently draped over her hair. A faint aroma, sweet and strangely familiar, drifted to her nose. The creamy lace fluttered around her face like angel wings.

Realizing how ridiculous she must look, Esmerelda snatched it off, shooting Dix a sheepish glance. "It doesn't quite match my uniform, does it?"

"Oh, I thought it looked just fine," he said softly. The sober look in his eyes made her feel shy.

Hoping to hide her blush, she delved back into the trunk. "Oh, look, here's an autobiography by my illustrious ancestor, Bartholomew Fine III. He started out writing pulp fiction and ended up winning the Pulitzer prize for fiction in 1918." She idly flipped through the yellowed pages, then tossed the book aside. "You won't find any scandals there. According to family lore, he was dull as dishwater. Never so much as cheated on his income tax."

"What's that?" Dix asked, reaching around to grab a thin volume bound in orange cloth. He held it up to the light, intoning in a mock baritone, "*William Darling, Legendary Lawman,* by Mr. Bartholomew Fine. This grandfather of yours doesn't sound like much of an outlaw to me," he scoffed with an endearing hint of male envy.

"Oh, no? Then how do you explain this?"

Esmerelda unfurled the Wanted poster with a flourish. A steely-eyed desperado squinted back at them in the mug shot from hell.

Dix recoiled, looking genuinely spooked.

"What is it?"

He shuddered. "I've seen that exact same look on your face when you've got PMS."

She rolled the poster back up and glared at him. "It's a very romantic story. He gave up his life of villainy for the love of a good woman. My great-uncle Virgil, who considers himself the official historian of the family, swore that Billy Darling was so in love with my grandmother that he took a job in a Wild West show and followed her all the way to London."

Esmerelda shuffled through a stack of quaintly illustrated handbills for Sheriff Andrew McGuire's Wild West Extravaganza that promised Noble Lawmen, Wild Horses, Dastardly Outlaws, and Savage Red Men to those bold enough to purchase tickets.

"Would you follow me all the way to London, Dix?"

"Only if you promised to use those shiny new hand-cuffs of yours on me."

"In your dreams, Detective," she retorted, throwing him a laughing glance.

"Every night, sweetheart," he promised, the smoky heat in his eyes sending a shiver of desire through her.

Esme discovered a locket's silver chain coiled beneath the crumbling handbills. She gently unlatched it to find a sepia-toned miniature of a somber-eyed little girl holding a laughing baby. Beneath the locket was another ancient photograph—this one of a woman wearing the very wedding gown Esme had found when she opened the trunk. The bride stood sideways to show off the elaborate train. An enigmatic smile played around her prim lips.

"Who's the babe?" Dix quipped, squinting over her shoulder.

"It must be my namesake," Esme murmured. "My great-great-grandma Esmerelda. She was some kind of royalty, you know—a countess or a princess or something." She stole a quick look at the dates inscribed on the back, then sighed dreamily. "Isn't it strange to think that I'm exactly the same age she was when she met the man she was destined to spend the rest of her life with?"

"Not that strange," Dix replied, awkwardly clearing his throat.

The next photograph, another wedding picture, gave them their first real glimpse of a clean-shaven Billy Darling. He was standing stiffly next to his bride, her arm tucked formally through his. He might have been dressed like Redford in *Butch Cassidy and the Sundance Kid*, but the twinkle in his eyes was pure Newman.

Dix pointed. "Who's the older couple standing beside

them? The woman with the stern jaw and the guy with the Buffalo Bill hair and Custer mustache?"

"That would be Esmerelda's Aunt Anne, and the aforementioned"—she waved a handbill in the air—"Sheriff Andrew McGuire. They were married along with Billy and Esmerelda at a double wedding held at Esmerelda's grandfather's London estate. According to Great-uncle Virgil, the wedding was quite the event of the social season, especially after Billy's brothers, the infamous Darling gang, drank a little too much champagne, rode their horses into the ballroom, and shot down the crystal chandelier."

Dix chuckled. "Sounds like a definite *drunk and disorderly* to me."

The next photograph was of Billy and Esmerelda alone. Instead of glaring balefully at the photographer, as was obviously the fashion of the day, they gazed at each other with such yearning tenderness that Esme felt a curious catch in her throat.

She sniffled. "I'm not usually so sentimental. There's just something about the way they're looking at each other. You just know they'll never argue about whose turn it is to take out the trash or cheat on each other or get divorced. And they didn't." Her voice softened, betraying a note of awe. "Great-uncle Virgil said they were married for sixty-seven years. Just think—if they hadn't gotten married and had five children, I wouldn't even be here right now."

"Neither would I," Dix murmured, brushing a tear from her cheek.

She shot him a fierce glare. "If you tell any of the guys down at the station you saw me cry, this will be your last Thanksgiving dinner at the Darling house. Come to think of it, it'll probably be your last Thanksgiving dinner anywhere."

He patted her shoulder. "You can blackmail me by threatening to tell them I always break down when Linus reads the Christmas story during *A Charlie Brown Christmas*."

Esmerelda felt a pang of regret when she realized they'd nearly reached the bottom of the trunk. A single faded photograph remained, more fragile than the rest, as if it had been lovingly handled many times throughout the years. This one was a more candid shot of Billy taken outside a window with the words *Sheriff's Office* stenciled on the glass.

A tin star was pinned to his vest and he was grinning openly, his thumbs hooked in the gunbelt draped around his lean hips. He wasn't looking directly at the camera, but at someone who stood just to the left of the photographer. From the loving heat in his eyes, Esme knew exactly who that someone was. She sighed, imagining what it must have felt like to be that woman.

"He sure was a good-looking man. I can see why my grandmother was willing to give up everything for him."

"Stop lusting after your own grandpa. You're making me jealous."

"Why, Dix, I didn't know you cared."

If she had caught the look he gave her in that moment, she would have known just how much.

But she'd gone back to gazing dreamily at the picture . . . at the lazy smile crooking Billy's lips . . . the devilish spark in his long-lashed eyes . . .

Esme recoiled, blinking frantically. Shaken, she glanced over her shoulder at Dix. "I would have almost sworn he winked at me. Did you see . . . ?"

"No, I most certainly did not," Dix said, but his face was nearly as white as hers.

Esme slowly turned the picture over, her hands beginning to tremble again. Inscribed across the back of the photograph, in a woman's elegant script, were two words. The ink might have faded, but the sentiment would surely endure forever.

Dix's strong, warm arms went around her. He rested his cheek against hers as they whispered in unison, *"My Darling."*

ABOUT THE AUTHOR

USA Today bestseller Teresa Medeiros has well over three million copies of her books in print. She was recently chosen one of the Top Ten Favorite Romance Authors by *Affaire de Coeur* magazine and won the *Romantic Times* Reviewers Choice Award for Best Historical Love and Laughter. A former Army brat and registered nurse, Teresa wrote her first novel at the age of twenty-one and has since gone on to win the hearts of critics and readers alike. Teresa currently lives in Kentucky with her husband, Michael, five cats, and one floppy-eared Doberman. Writing romance allows her to express her own heartfelt beliefs in faith, hope, and the enduring power of love to bring about a happy ending.

Teresa Medeiros

Breath of Magic
___56334-3 $5.99/$7.99 in Canada

Fairest of Them All
___56333-5 $5.99/$7.50 in Canada

Thief of Hearts
___56332-7 $5.50/$6.99 in Canada

A Whisper of Roses
___29408-3 $5.99/$7.99

Once an Angel
___29409-1 $5.99/$7.99

Heather and Velvet
___29407-5 $5.99/$7.50

Shadows and Lace
___57623-2 $5.99/$7.99

Touch of Enchantment
___57500-7 $5.99/$7.99

- -

Ask for these books at your local bookstore or use this page to order.

Please send me the books I have checked above. I am enclosing $_____ (add $2.50 to cover postage and handling). Send check or money order, no cash or C.O.D.'s, please.

Name _____

Address _____

City/State/Zip _____

Send order to: Bantam Books, Dept. FN116, 2451 S. Wolf Rd., Des Plaines, IL 60018
Allow four to six weeks for delivery.

Prices and availability subject to change without notice.   FN 116 4/98

Bestselling Historical Women's Fiction

✄ AMANDA QUICK ✄

____28354-5 SEDUCTION ...$6.50/$8.99 Canada

____28932-2 SCANDAL ....$6.50/$8.99

____28594-7 SURRENDER ....$6.50/$8.99

____29325-7 RENDEZVOUS ....$6.50/$8.99

____29315-X RECKLESS ....$6.50/$8.99

____29316-8 RAVISHED ....$6.50/$8.99

____29317-6 DANGEROUS ....$6.50/$8.99

____56506-0 DECEPTION ....$6.50/$8.99

____56153-7 DESIRE ....$6.50/$8.99

____56940-6 MISTRESS ....$6.50/$8.99

____57159-1 MYSTIQUE ....$6.50/$7.99

____57190-7 MISCHIEF ....$6.50/$8.99

____57407-8 AFFAIR ....$6.99/$8.99

✄ IRIS JOHANSEN ✄

____29871-2 LAST BRIDGE HOME ...$5.50/$7.50

____29604-3 THE GOLDEN

⠀⠀⠀⠀⠀⠀⠀BARBARIAN ....$6.99/$8.99

____29244-7 REAP THE WIND .....$5.99/$7.50

____29032-0 STORM WINDS ....$6.99/$8.99

Ask for these books at your local bookstore or use this page to order.

Please send me the books I have checked above. I am enclosing $____ (add $2.50 to cover postage and handling). Send check or money order, no cash or C.O.D.'s, please.

Name _____

Address _____

City/State/Zip _____

Send order to: Bantam Books, Dept. FN 16, 2451 S. Wolf Rd., Des Plaines, IL 60018
Allow four to six weeks for delivery.
Prices and availability subject to change without notice.⠀⠀⠀⠀⠀⠀⠀FN 16 3/98

Bestselling Historical Women's Fiction

❧ IRIS JOHANSEN ❧

____28855-5 THE WIND DANCER ...$5.99/$6.99

____29968-9 THE TIGER PRINCE ...$6.99/$8.99

____29944-1 THE MAGNIFICENT
ROGUE ....$6.99/$8.99

____29945-X BELOVED SCOUNDREL .$6.99/$8.99

____29946-8 MIDNIGHT WARRIOR ..$6.99/$8.99

____29947-6 DARK RIDER ....$6.99/$8.99

____56990-2 LION'S BRIDE ....$6.99/$8.99

____56991-0 THE UGLY DUCKLING...$5.99/$7.99

____57181-8 LONG AFTER MIDNIGHT.$6.99/$8.99

____10616-3 AND THEN YOU DIE....$22.95/$29.95

❧ TERESA MEDEIROS ❧

____29407-5 HEATHER AND VELVET .$5.99/$7.50

____29409-1 ONCE AN ANGEL .....$5.99/$7.99

____29408-3 A WHISPER OF ROSES .$5.99/$7.99

____56332-7 THIEF OF HEARTS ....$5.50/$6.99

____56333-5 FAIREST OF THEM ALL .$5.99/$7.50

____56334-3 BREATH OF MAGIC ...$5.99/$7.99

____57623-2 SHADOWS AND LACE ..$5.99/$7.99

____57500-7 TOUCH OF
ENCHANTMENT.........$5.99/$7.99

- -

Ask for these books at your local bookstore or use this page to order.

Please send me the books I have checked above. I am enclosing $____ (add $2.50 to cover postage and handling). Send check or money order, no cash or C.O.D.'s, please.

Name _____

Address _____

City/State/Zip _____

Send order to: Bantam Books, Dept. FN 16, 2451 S. Wolf Rd., Des Plaines, IL 60018
Allow four to six weeks for delivery.
Prices and availability subject to change without notice.   FN 16 3/98

THE VERY BEST IN CONTEMPORARY
WOMEN'S FICTION

SANDRA BROWN

____28951-9 Texas! Lucky $6.99/$9.99 in Canada   ____56768-3 Adam's Fall $5.99/$7.99

____28990-X Texas! Chase $6.99/$9.99   ____56045-X Temperatures Rising $6.50/$8.99

____29500-4 Texas! Sage $6.99/$9.99   ____56274-6 Fanta C $5.99/$7.99

____29085-1 22 Indigo Place $6.99/$8.99   ____56278-9 Long Time Coming $5.99/$7.99

____29783-X A Whole New Light $6.50/$8.99   ____57157-5 Heaven's Price $6.50/$8.99

____57158-3 Breakfast In Bed $5.99/$7.99 ____29751-1 Hawk O'Toole's Hostage $6.50/$8.99

____10403-9 Tidings of Great Joy $17.95/$24.95

TAMI HOAG

____29534-9 Lucky's Lady $6.50/$8.99   ____29272-2 Still Waters $6.50/$8.99

____29053-3 Magic $6.50/$8.99   ____56160-X Cry Wolf $6.50/$8.99

____56050-6 Sarah's Sin $5.99/$7.99   ____56161-8 Dark Paradise $6.50/$8.99

____56451-x Night Sins $6.50/$8.99   ____56452-8 Guilty As Sin $6.50/$8.99

____09960-4 A Thin Dark Line $22.95/$29.95

NORA ROBERTS

____10834-4 Genuine Lies $19.95/$27.95   ____27859-2 Sweet Revenge $6.50/$8.99

____28578-5 Public Secrets $6.50/$8.99   ____27283-7 Brazen Virtue $6.50/$8.99

____26461-3 Hot Ice $6.50/$8.99   ____29597-7 Carnal Innocence $6.50/$8.99

____26574-1 Sacred Sins $6.50/$8.99   ____29490-3 Divine Evil $6.50/$8.99

DEBORAH SMITH

____29107-6 Miracle $5.99/$7.99   ____29690-6 Blue Willow $5.99/$7.99

____29092-4 Follow the Sun $4.99/$5.99   ____29689-2 Silk and Stone $5.99/$6.99

____10334-2 A Place To Call Home $23.95/$29.95

Ask for these books at your local bookstore or use this page to order.

Please send me the books I have checked above. I am enclosing $____(add $2.50 to cover postage and handling). Send check or money order, no cash or C.O.D.'s, please.

Name _____

Address _____

City/State/Zip _____

Send order to: Bantam Books, Dept. FN 24, 2451 S. Wolf Rd., Des Plaines, IL 60018
Allow four to six weeks for delivery.
Prices and availability subject to change without notice.   FN 24 3/98